Reconsidering the Facts 

Emily Tudor

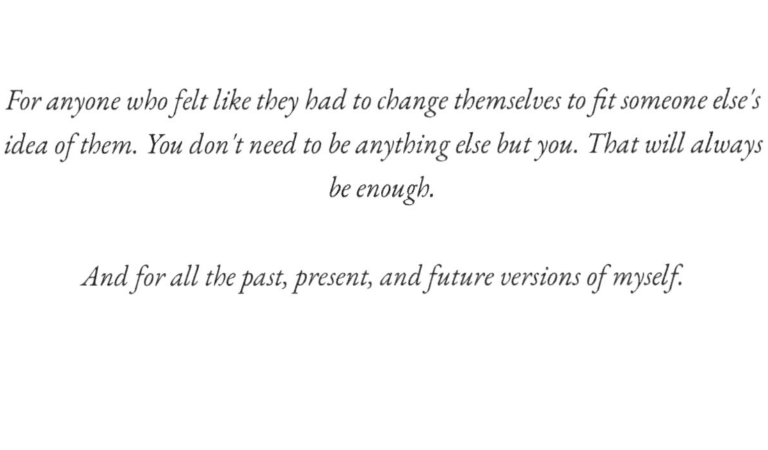

For anyone who felt like they had to change themselves to fit someone else's idea of them. You don't need to be anything else but you. That will always be enough.

And for all the past, present, and future versions of myself.

Playlist

Amsterdam - Gregory Alan Isakov
Anyway - Noah Kahan
Apple - Charli xcx
Apple Pie - Lizzy McAlpine
Best Years - 5 Seconds of Summer
Bloom - The Paper Kites
Everywhere, Everything - Noah Kahan
Fallingforyou - The 1975
Family Line - Conan Gray
Graceland Too - Phoebe Bridgers
Iris - The Goo Goo Dolls
Jackie and Wilson - Hozier
Lightning In a Bottle - Fly By Midnight
Look After You - The Fray
Lover - Taylor Swift

Mess It Up - Gracie Abrams

mirrorball - Taylor Swift

Miserable Man - David Kushner

Moonlight - Chase Atlantic

My Blood - Ellie Goulding

NDA - Billie Eilish

Remedy - Adele

Sleep on the Floor - The Lumineers

Strong - One Direction

Sweet Creature - Harry Styles

sweetener - Ariana Grande

This Side of Paradise - Coyote Theory

Yellow - Coldplay

You're On Your Own, Kid - Taylor Swift

The 30th - Billie Eilish

Content Warnings

While this story is mainly a romance, it also deals with topics such as childhood trauma, childhood abuse and neglect, suicidal thoughts, PTSD/nightmares, and panic attacks. There are also mentions of a fatal car accident off-the-page due to drunk driving.

Your mental health matters. Please proceed with caution.

"I think the saddest people always try their hardest to make people happy.
Because they know what it feels like to feel absolutely worthless and they
don't want anybody else to feel like that."

— Robin Williams

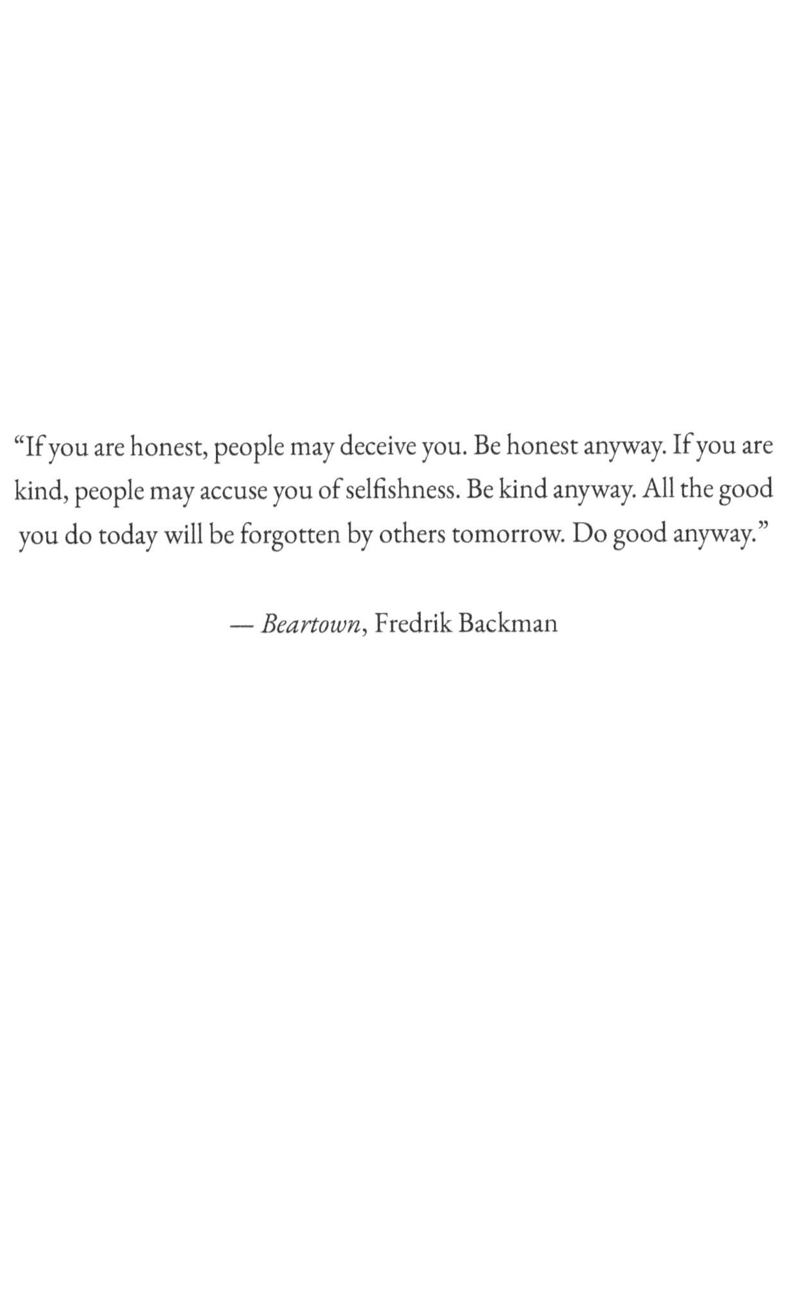

"If you are honest, people may deceive you. Be honest anyway. If you are kind, people may accuse you of selfishness. Be kind anyway. All the good you do today will be forgotten by others tomorrow. Do good anyway."

— *Beartown*, Fredrik Backman

Prologue

Friday, August 19th, 2022

I'M SITTING IN MY car at a stoplight when I look over, and someone is shaving their face—here, of all places.

Props to them because I would definitely cut myself doing that. Maybe they have an important meeting to get to and didn't have time to at home?

Or, of course, they could be a serial killer, which brings me to one of my favorite concepts. I feel that every single person has one, or a few, serial killer traits that when it turns out they're a serial killer, you look back and it all makes sense.

I don't have my own personal serial killer trait yet—Amelia says it will be revealed in time. *Maybe picking out serial killer traits is mine?*

All of my friends have them too. Everyone has at least one weird quirk that would make sense if they turned out to be serial killers.

Speaking of my friends, I've never been so excited to be going back to school. We were on summer break, and I missed them to death. It's always rough not seeing them in person over long breaks from school, but the girls did surprise me on my birthday—June 30th—by visiting. I stayed in their hotel, and we ordered room service, watched movies, and read books. It was the best birthday ever. I never like being home in between semesters. My version of home is less than ideal.

Nobody knows, though—except Amelia. When I first had a nightmare in front of her during our freshman year, she sat with me while I explained why I had them.

Everyone around me knows me as Paige, the girl who's always happy and smiling, but that happiness fades when I'm home. I make myself small when I'm there. It's easier that way, making myself so tiny nobody notices me, not that my mom would anyway. We don't talk unless we have to these days—I'm not even sure she knows what I'm studying in college.

I've never had a family. I have one solid friend I've known since I was two back home, but that's it. I often sleep at her house on break since I hate living at home. Her name is Sadie, and her family treats me better than my own.

Everything changed when I got to Grand Mountain College and found Ella and Amelia, Hads later joining our group. I felt like I could be myself with them, and they wouldn't judge me. They welcomed the real Paige with open arms and hearts. I've been alone my whole life, so knowing I have them around me still feels weird.

I've always liked the idea that family isn't just blood, but I never experienced it until I met them. I've become good at molding myself to fit others so they'll like me. I put out different versions of myself for everyone.

It's *exhausting.*

Pretending to be these different versions of yourself starts to weigh on you, but I can't help it. It's what I've always done from a young age because deep down, I want to be a good person, and I feel like I am most of the time. I don't litter. I feed birds occasionally. I try to be the best version of myself—whichever that one is.

But with my girls, I feel like the real me. I feel whole and complete. I pull up to Amelia and I's shared apartment, burst out of my car, and run to our front door. Her car's in the lot, so I know she's here. I open the front door, run to her room, bear hug her, and throw us on her bed.

She usually hates being touched, but I haven't seen her in months other than on a tiny iPad screen and those few days we spent together.

"Welcome back, P."

"It's good to be home, Ames." I shoot her a signature Paige smile and move to sit on her floor. We like to debrief about the summer every time we move back in.

"You'll never guess what I saw at a stoplight earlier."

1

Friday, August 26th, 2022

"So, DOES ANYONE HAVE any questions about restorative justice practices being used nowadays?" I ask the group. Today is the first meeting of the criminal justice club, where Oliver and I are co-chairs. We joined last semester to get extra credit but ended up staying on. When the other seniors graduated last semester, we became club co-chairs. Oliver has never said he enjoys being here, but he doesn't grunt or angrily stare anymore, which equates to not hating it. I enjoy this, though. It gets me out of my shell and out of the apartment every other Friday afternoon.

Oliver—who's sitting next to me—is 6'1" with round brown eyes. He has jet-black hair, like his sister and one of my closest friends, Hadleigh. He's got some muscles because he runs for fun all the time and likes to work out. Most people think he's a quiet, grumpy guy, but I think he's the best. I've known him since our freshman year of college. He and I got assigned to sit next to each other in Criminal Justice 101. We've had the same classes together since then, and we always pick each other as partners for projects we work on. Over the years, we've become rather close. I talk, and he listens. I say something insane, and he looks at me like I am. Most of our conversations are surface-level and not too deep, but I enjoy having someone around most of the time.

I, on the other hand, am the complete opposite of Oliver. I have long, dirty blonde hair with layers. My green eyes are my favorite part of myself since only two percent of the world has green-colored eyes. I'm around 5'6" the last time I checked, and often described as being like the sun.

The fall semester of our senior year has just started, and I adore Virginia in the autumn. It's not only my favorite season, but I love watching the leaves change and fall to the ground so I can step on them.

There are five members besides Oliver, me, and our professor, who helps chaperone the club. Jemma is an adorable little freshman. She's a bit quiet, but I always try to help her feel more comfortable. Mitchell, a sophomore-year student. He's nice but not always *present,* if that makes sense. I think he smokes a lot of weed and vibes most of the time. Eddie, a junior-year student studying psychology. He wanted to join the club to learn more about the justice system, especially with everything going on in the country. Andie is a junior-year student who likes studying cold cases as much as I do in my free time. Last, but not least, is Peggy. I think she's a freshman, but she hasn't said much yet in our meetings. She always leaves right after, so I haven't had time to get to know her.

"So, what's the entire point of this conversation we've been having?" That was Mitchell—the one who never understands what's happening. I think he may have chosen the wrong field of study. I'm about to answer him when Oliver cuts me off.

"The point is this connects to our first-semester fundraiser. Pay attention."

"Oliver, it's okay. As I said, we're meeting with the dean of students next week to discuss fundraising for our trip to the Virginia women's correctional facility next month. But that's all we have for this meeting!" I say, and Jemma claps when she gets out of her chair, making me flinch. I'm not too good around loud noises.

"Don't forget our next meeting in two weeks has been canceled. I am out of town, and you cannot meet without a faculty member present." That was Professor Craig. She has been teaching at Grand Mountain for a few years and is one of my favorite professors in the criminal justice department. She worked for the FBI until she retired and realized she wanted to teach the next generation about the law and the justice system.

"Sounds good, Professor. See you in a few weeks." That was Peggy. She puts her chair on the stack and leaves.

"Okay, if everyone could stack their chairs on top of Peggy's, that would be super helpful!" I say cheerfully as I drag my chair toward the pile. We meet in one of the auditoriums on campus, and there are no desks, so we sit on these black chairs the musical theater club uses. I throw my chair onto the pile and grab my tote bag. Ella says I show my emotions through my tote bags, and I agree. I have so many of them that the hooks in my room overflow. This one has a *Little Women* quote on it. It's one of my favorites.

Oliver throws his chair on the stack, and I flinch again, the loud noise scaring me. It just happens. It's like a reflex I can't turn off after growing up in the household I did.

"See you next week in class, Professor!" I wave to her as I leave, and she smiles at me. I'm out the door and on the sidewalk when I feel Oliver's presence next to me. I can always tell it's him because of his cologne. It has spicy undertones and some other scents I can't place.

"You know you don't have to walk me back to my apartment, Oliver. I'm sure you have better things to do with your Friday afternoon," I say, turning to face him. He's looking straight ahead, and I have to crane my neck to get a good look at his face. Yup, still has that same expression like always.

"I live in a building near yours. I'm not walking you home. I'm simply walking back to *my* home," he says, not looking at me.

"Fine, whatever helps you sleep at night. I know you care about my safety and don't want a girl like me to get kidnapped on the way back to my apartment," I say, smiling wider at him. I like this dance we do. I like to talk, and he always listens and grunts at me as if he doesn't enjoy my presence. Deep down, I think he does.

"If you ever got kidnapped, they would bring you back. Especially after hearing you talk about all those books you read." He looks over at me, smiles slightly, and then turns back. People often say he never smiles, but I find I can pull some out of him every once in a while.

"Very funny. Are you excited for our meeting, or am I going to do all of the talking like usual?" I ask him while speeding up and walking backward in front of him. He never looks me in the eye, so I always do this and force him to. I'm about to say something back to him when he grabs my arm and pulls me back on the sidewalk. A car honks at us, and I'm breathing hard. I wasn't paying attention, and that car could've hit me if Oliver hadn't pulled me back onto the sidewalk.

"Thanks," I say to him, breathing hard. I collect myself, and we look both ways before crossing the street toward our apartments.

"You should really be more careful. Hads would kill me if you got hurt in my presence."

"I know. Thank you for, you know." I motion to the road. I feel bad. Oliver has a bad history of car accidents. His high school girlfriend was killed in one, but I don't know all the details, just what Hads told us.

"Yeah, whatever." That translates to 'you're welcome' in Oliver language. We continue the rest of the walk back in silence. I steal glances at his face a couple of times, wanting to start a new conversation but knowing I might come off as being too much. He walks me to my door, and I'm unsure of what to do right now, so I throw a small wave at him.

"I'll see you in class next week?" He nods. "Bye, Oliver," I say as I open my door while he walks away. All the lights are off in my apartment, but it's still fairly bright in here since it's mid-afternoon. Amelia's probably in her room, and I don't want to disturb her, so I keep them off. I set my tote bag down and kick off my shoes, placing them gently into the shoe rack by our front door. I love Amelia and I's apartment.

Our kitchen is off to the right, with a small dining table that can seat four people. To the left is a bookshelf. Straight ahead is the living area, with a couch and a loveseat, a cute rug in the center, and a TV directly facing the couch. Hanging over the couch are a few art prints with our favorite book/movie quotes. We have a shelf above the TV that houses the Funko Pops of characters we love, such as Paul Atreides and Tony Stark. Amelia's room door is to the apartment's right, and mine is to the left.

I grab my water bottle to fill it up, along with some crackers and pepperoni. I slide down to the kitchen floor and eat. My friends think it's weird how often they find me on the floor, but it's always been a comfort thing for me. I scroll through Twitter and send some relatable tweets to Amelia, who responds to one. A few seconds later, I hear her door open, and she shuffles out.

She finds me in the kitchen with all of the lights off around me and looks down at me. "Hey, are you okay?" Amelia gets me like no other person on the planet, and I love how much she cares. On the outside, most people think she's cold and detached—which she's not—but when she loves you, she'll do anything for you. We met freshman year when we randomly got assigned to be roommates, and the rest is history. Amelia is around 5'9 with olive skin, brown curly hair, and light blue eyes.

"I'm alright. How are you?" I say, patting the ground next to me and signaling her to sit, which she does.

"I'm okay. How was your club? Did Oliver say anything this time?" she jokes with me. I shove my elbow into her side, barely. "Ow! What was that for?"

"I don't know why you all act like Oliver is Boo Radley from *To Kill A Mockingbird*. He has a personality. It's just different."

"Yeah, yeah, did he?"

"He said one sentence and it was at the end," I say flatly.

"Ha! Wow, that is surprising. Hads said over summer break, she barely saw Oliver. Which makes sense because she spent the entire summer with Grant gallivanting around their hometowns like a cute Hallmark movie."

"Oh, come on, those two are the cutest, and they deserve to be happy after everything that happened last semester," I say to her as she takes a cracker and pops it into her mouth. Last semester, Grant and Hads had this whole push-and-pull thing going on, and it ended with them confessing their love to one another in the most adorable way possible.

"I know," she says, grabbing another cracker.

"How is Hads? I haven't seen her on campus yet," I ask Amelia.

"She's good. I think she and Grant are coming over to watch this one travel documentary with me next week. I recently discovered Grant likes National Geographic, so I invited them over. It's during your meeting, but you can join us after if you want."

"That sounds good. The meeting won't take long."

"Do you want to watch a movie or something?" Amelia asks me, and I look at her straight-faced. After a few seconds, she breaks. "Fine, we can keep watching that documentary about DB Cooper." I shriek with excitement.

"Okay, let me put comfier clothes on, and you make the popcorn and grab the wine. Should we call the other girls? I miss them," I say, rising from the floor and making my way to my room.

"I asked them to come over tonight, but Ella is going out with Alissa to some club to blow off steam. Hads and Grant are having a date night with Claire and Jacks."

"Aw, that's too bad. I hope they're having fun, though," I say, changing my clothes and shoving on some fuzzy socks. Our friend Ella graduated last year, and it's been weird not having her around all the time. She's out in the real world, getting an actual job in her field. It's eerie Amelia and I will be doing the same thing next year. I shove that thought to the back of my mind because I don't feel like crying about the future. I walk back out to the living room and plop onto our couch, and a few seconds later, Amelia joins me with a blanket from her room. She covers both of us with it, and we start the documentary from the episode we left off on.

"I still don't understand how this guy just disappeared," Amelia tells me.

"Just keep watching. It's interesting how he vanished with all that money. I also liked watching the episode of Loki, where they made him DB Cooper. It was too funny."

"Tom Hiddleston can do no wrong, so I'm with you there."

We continue watching the documentary until Amelia falls asleep on me. I turn off the television and leave her on the couch while covering her with a blanket. I clean up the snacks we were eating and fall into my bed. I look at the clock—ten p.m. *At least I don't have class tomorrow.* I toss and turn for what seems like hours until I eventually end up on the floor of my room, snuggling up with a blanket and my pillow on the gray carpet next to my bed.

I've found over the years that I sleep better on the floor. I used to do this to hear my father's footsteps coming toward my room, but it stuck with me. It's a comfort thing now.

My room here at school is my safe place. It has white walls, though I wish they were lavender, my favorite color. Filling those walls are shelves with comic books, a neon light shaped like a sun, white fairy lights, and a letter board with my favorite book quote of all time on it. I have two big white shelves filled with books and cute figures on them. I have an entire hook station for my tote bags—which is overflowing. My closet has purple curtains hanging on the front of it, and my bed has lavender sheets and a comforter with sunflowers on it—my favorite flowers. My bedside table has a signed edition of my favorite book and around three other copies of it, all with different covers. It's basically a shrine at this point. The small gray rug on the floor where I currently reside is soft and fuzzy.

I sigh heavily and close my eyes, hoping to get through the night with no nightmares. Hads and Ella know I have nightmares. I admitted it to them when I was drunk at Ella's birthday last semester, but only Amelia knows why. I don't know why I'm so scared to tell Ella and Hads. My therapist says it's because I've always had to make it through life on my own. My brain worries about being emotionally open with people, making it hard to connect with others sometimes. I have to trust people so I can open up to them, but Hads and Ella are my best friends, so why don't I? Even to my brain, it doesn't make sense.

I think it's scary to tell the people who love you that you weren't okay before. It's scary to admit those things out loud because, sure, I can think them all I want, but saying them to people I love? No way. I would never admit out loud that I never saw myself making it to my 21st birthday. Never. It's scary to think about how much I used to hate being on this planet, but I'm okay now. Or, trying to be, I guess.

I feel my eyes drooping and let myself fall into it like every other night.

2

Thursday, September 1st

CLASSES HAVE ONLY BEEN going on for a few days, and I already want this semester to end. My life has been steadily declining since I came back to campus. For starters, Paige almost got run over by a car the other day, which made me feel weird for some reason. Today, we find out that one of our best professors isn't teaching anymore for undisclosed reasons.

"I think he got fired. He was always kind of sporadic." Paige leans over and whispers to me. *If he was fired, they should just say that.* We're all adults. We can handle the truth. I flip my notebook open, and a few pages rip.

"Did that notebook take your last scoop of protein powder?" Paige asks me, smiling. She's always smiling. I'll never forget the first day of freshman year when she sat next to me in our assigned seats, smiled at me, and didn't turn the other way when I glared at her. The first two years I was here were bad for me. I was still grieving everything that happened in high school senior year.

"Oliver, just relax. It's going to be fine. Just trust me for once!" Mia tells me.

"It's not you, Mi. I don't trust them! They're bad news, and I don't like when you hang out with them. They're too reckless."

"You need to learn to live a little!" She points at me and I sigh. "Stop trying to protect me from everything. I'm going and that's final. Are you coming or what?" She holds her hand out to mine, and I take a breath.

"Can't we stay in and have a movie night?" I'm pleading. I can hear it in my voice. But the knots in my stomach won't go away, and I don't trust these people. Something doesn't feel right and I don't know how to fix it. I don't know how to convince her to stay here with me. I don't think I can based only on my gut feeling, but I have to try.

"Oliver, loosen up a little. For once, don't listen to your little gut feelings. Go out and have some fun."

"Mi, something feels off. Just please don't go with them." I hear a honk from outside. They must be here already.

"Oliver, I'm going. I'll call you later, okay? In case you change your mind?" She smiles at me, and God, I wish I could move my feet toward her but something is stopping me. She walks over to me and gives me a quick kiss. "I love you, Oliver."

"I love you, too. Please be careful," I say as she smiles at me and walks out the door.

Little did I know that would be the last time I saw her smile. The last time she would talk to me, touch me, or breathe near me. She called me like she said she would, but I was too stubborn to answer. I let her last call to me go to voicemail. Minutes after Mia's call, my phone started blowing up. Her mom called me half a dozen times before I picked up and heard the seven words that would tilt my world on its axis.

"Oliver, something happened. Something happened to Mia." Her mom cries into the phone.

"Wh–What are you talking about?"

"She's gone, Oliver. Can you get to the hospital?"

"What do you mean she's gone?" My throat feels dry, and suddenly, the feeling in my gut plummets through my body.

"There's been an accident. Just please get to the hospital." I can hear sirens in the background of the call, and this feels like some sort of strange nightmare I can't wake up from. I saw her an hour ago. There's no way she's gone.

Gone. Dead.

I grab my keys and race to the hospital. Someone probably should've driven me, but nobody else was home. When I get to the hospital and into the waiting room, I see her parents. They're both crying while talking to a doctor. I go over to them and they confirm my fears. Her mom falls apart in front of me and I do my best to console her. I don't know what to do; it feels like time has stopped moving. My girlfriend—the first girl I ever loved—is dead. She was killed in a car accident. By a drunk driver. She was pronounced dead at the scene.

And I didn't answer her call.

After that, I went to therapy and talked my shit out, which helped—combined with working out. Eventually, the grief got better, but it never fully disappeared. I'm not sure if it will ever disappear; it might just fade a bit over time.

I never thought Paige and I would have any sort of relationship, so us becoming friends has been shocking. Paige has always been this fucking sunshine of a person, and I wouldn't want to block that light from her by being who I am—quiet and broody. The more time I spent with her, the more I realized I liked being in her presence, and she brought out a side of me I hadn't seen in a while. It's weird. I'm not sure how to go about it, so I tend to float around her most of the time. I also started seeing small movements she thought I overlooked.

Which I haven't.

She flinches at loud noises, and that happy mask drops from her face. Even if it's a split second, I still see it. *Fear.* She's afraid. She might look happy on the outside, but she's scared of something on the inside. I'm not sure what, but since I noticed these little things during sophomore year, I haven't stopped seeing them. She flinched the other night when a chair made a loud noise. She might not think I notice these things, but it's hard not to notice everything about her when she's always around and clouding my thoughts.

She shoves my ribs with her elbow, and I return to reality. I missed a few slides in the presentation. I grab my pencil and hurry to catch up. Paige shifts her computer over and highlights the section of the lecture I missed. I look over at her, and she smiles.

"You think Fitzpatrick got fired?" I ask her.

"Yeah, why else would he suddenly have stopped teaching? He loved to teach. You know that." Paige loves a good puzzle, and I see her eyes light up at the prospect of one to be solved. She's probably going to spend all night digging into this.

"I know, but maybe it's a medical reason or something," I whisper back to her.

She shrugs. "I guess we'll never know."

"I guarantee you'll figure it out by tomorrow."

"Oh, Oliver, you know me so well."

I turn away from her computer and smile slightly. Our class finishes after twenty minutes, and we head to our next one in the building adjacent to us. Paige and I walk side by side for a few minutes, but my neighbor Nick comes up to us when we get outside. Paige smiles at him.

"Hello, Nicholas. How's the semester treating you? Actually, how is it being neighbors with this guy?" She nudges me with her elbow, and

I sigh. She always calls him by his full name, and he never corrects her. Apparently, it's their thing.

"It's been quiet, as usual. You know Oliver. He would forget to eat if I didn't drag him out every morning." I hate these two together. It feels like I created a monster. Nick lives in the apartment down the hall from me with his roommate, Noah. Nick is brunette, around the same height as me, and he's on the baseball team here. Noah—also on the baseball team—has sandy blond hair and is two inches shorter than me. They're both nice and they both know Paige through me. I don't remember becoming acquainted with either of them, but it happened since I've lived next to them for two years. I have an on-campus apartment alone because I can't stand sharing a space with someone.

"I remember to eat breakfast most of the time," I tell them. "I cook sometimes."

"He speaks!" Nick says while high-fiving Paige.

"So, how's the baseball team looking this year?" Paige asks him. One thing I would never have guessed about Paige is how into sports she is. I never pegged her for the type, but a lot about Paige surprises me the more I get to know her.

"Pretty good. Hopefully, we can be better than last year, but I doubt it." He shrugs.

"I'm sure you guys will do great! I can't wait to watch your games in the spring. I expect many strikes from you, Nicholas!" Paige tells him, pointing at his chest. Nick's a pitcher—the best on the team, or so I've heard.

"I'll try my best, just for you, Paigey," he says to her.

I want to punch him, but I refrain. I walk faster ahead of those two as they talk about baseball and other shit. Nick's a good guy, and I know he would never hit on Paige since she isn't his type, but I can't help the weird feeling I get in my stomach whenever he shows his personality around her. Nick is a natural flirt, while Noah is introverted like me and tends not to talk much. Noah has a girl he has been in love with on campus since freshman year, but something happened, and now they don't talk anymore. I feel bad for him. He's still very hung up on her.

We get to our building and head up the stairs. Paige and I turn right, Nick goes left, and he and Paige yell goodbye to each other.

"See you later, Oliver," he says to me as he walks into his classroom and shoots me a wave. I stare back at him as Paige and I head into class. My phone buzzes as I'm about to sit down in my chair at the back of the classroom. It's from my sister.

I shove my phone back into my pocket and take a deep breath. I turn to Paige. "My sister says hi."

She smiles. "Were you just talking to her?"

"Yeah. She's with Grant."

"Ugh, I love those two."

I nod. I'm happy my sister has found someone she loves after years of keeping that side of herself hidden. I wish I could do the same, but I can't risk it. I don't think I could handle losing another person I care about. During freshman year, my mom called me and told me what had happened to my sister. Kyle cheated on her and fucked around with another girl behind her back and she was destroyed after finding out about it. So I immediately hopped on a flight home and sat with her while she cried for three days straight. Then I punched Kyle in the face and left.

Then, last semester, Grant told me what happened with her and Ryan, and I wanted to kill that kid. Grant told me he had handled it—Ryan got kicked out of school—but it still hurt that Hads didn't trust me enough to help her. I hate not being there for her when she needs me, but I had to come to terms with that, so I did. I spent the summer at the gym, lifting weights and boxing out all of the anger in my body.

It helped a bit.

The only thing that really dissolves all the anger in my body is a blonde girl whose smile lights up every fucking room she walks into. It pisses me off that she has that big of an effect on me because that means I'm starting to get close to her. But if I keep her at a distance, she can't get hurt, and our friendship will remain intact.

It's a foolproof plan.

Even if it means I'm alone for the rest of my life because I won't let anyone in.

3

Wednesday, September 7th

"I think I was rooting against this couple the entire book. They did not have a connection at all," Amelia says to the group of us. She didn't like the book club pick this month, and to be fair, it was a rough one. I think we all hated it.

"The only good thing about this book was that it ended." Ella, the oldest of the four of us, says that. She graduated earlier this year and is currently employed at a small marketing firm, and slowly climbing the ladder up to her dream job. Ella's around 5'5", with golden brown skin and reddish brown hair.

She and I formed this little book club at our college about three years ago when I was a freshman and she was a sophomore. She saw me reading a book in the library cafe she had read recently, and we talked about it for a few hours. We clicked instantly, and she thought creating a book club on campus would be fun, so she did. Amelia and I were the only ones who showed up, and a year later, Hads joined us. As our friendship has become stronger, the book club has become more of a weekly check-in. Since Ella has a full-time job, we don't talk as much as we all like, so this helps us stay in touch.

"The premise was decent but poorly executed." Hads is around 5'4" and has short black hair and brown eyes, which remind me of autumn leaves falling. She's entering her junior year, while Amelia and I are seniors.

Grand Mountain is a tiny college town in the middle of Virginia that holds our liberal arts college, creatively named Grand Mountain College—my home for almost four years. I say home because this place feels more like one than my actual home back in New York.

It's scary thinking I'll have to enter the real world soon, but I'm excited nonetheless. I hate big life changes because I've never dealt with change well. It gives me anxiety, and I hate it. It's so weird because you have this same routine for years, and now you have to upend all that and readjust.

It also makes me feel lonely. I read somewhere once that when you're going through big life changes, you often feel the most lonely. My life must be one giant change because I constantly feel alone unless I'm with the girls. They help me feel like I matter, and I'm forever grateful for them.

"I think my favorite part of this book was the arson," I say to them, and they all turn their heads my way and give me a weird look. "What?"

"That honestly doesn't surprise me," Amelia says.

"Are we condoning arson now?" Ella asks.

"Paige has always been one for threatening it," Hads says, crossing her legs.

"Thank you, Hads. Other than that, it sucked. I give it one star," I say to the group.

"Two stars. The premise was interesting, but the end and the fourth part had me ready to throw up," Amelia says.

"I can corroborate that statement. I heard her gagging while she was reading it in the living room," I say.

"One star, and Grant agrees. When I told him about the plot, he told me to donate the book. Normally, we share, but he's not even interested in this one."

I smile. Hads has been dating Grant for around five months, and they're still going strong. Those two are the cutest. I would describe Grant as a golden retriever puppy—just adorable. He's tall—over six feet—with curly brown hair, blue eyes, and an athletic-type build. I'm glad they found each other. Watching the people you care about most in the world find love is fun. It makes my heart all squishy.

"I'm going to give it a two-point-five," Ella says.

"Care to elaborate?" Hads asks her.

"I liked the premise and the female main character until the end. The relationship getting better with her dad was nice too, but that's about it." Ella is the daughter of a single dad, so I get where she is coming from. I often attach myself to characters that have similar backgrounds as me. It's any character with divorced parents who feels like they will never be good enough but try their best anyway.

That's me, Paige Yarrow. Sunshiney and happy on the outside and fearful on the inside, combined with feeling like no matter what I do, I'll never be naturally good at anything. It's a weird dichotomy, but no matter how I feel, I always try to make the best of every situation. Everything can be a learning experience in my eyes, and I have always raised myself to take something good from any situation. Even if something feels terrible, you can *always* find the good.

"All valid points. I'll combine all of this into our official book club chart. I think this is going to be the lowest overall rating ever," Hads says.

She loves charts, so naturally, she's the one who compiles all of our data together when we finish a book.

"Ella, how are you liking your new job?" Amelia asks her.

She sighs heavily.

"That rough?" I ask.

"No, it's not bad. It's just been hard juggling life at the moment. There are not enough hours in the day."

"Any coworkers you hate? Or gossip you can tell us?" Hads asks.

"Did that one guy you made cry quit yet?" Amelia asks her. This question makes sense if you know Amelia. She loves emotional warfare. Sometimes, I wake up to texts from her, and it's a sad quote from a book we've read. She stays up late, and I often go to bed earlier. I asked her once what she does at night, and she said she was trying to hack into the President's secret database where he stores the nuclear codes.

I stopped asking her questions after that.

"I didn't make him cry. I simply asked him to do something for me, and he did it wrong. Which I may or may not have loudly talked to him about."

Translation: she yelled at him in front of everyone.

"Men often find it easier to lay things out step-by-step. Their small brains can't handle more than that," Hads tells her.

"I asked him to change the water filter in the fridge, and he burst into tears! I don't even care anymore. He got fired, but it turns out he was stealing money from the company, so it's not my fault. If anything, he deserved to be yelled at!" I've never met anyone as sassy as Ella, but I wish I were. I usually let people walk all over me because I want to be liked. Last year, she taught me some tips on how to stop caring about other people's thoughts, but it's hard to undo something like that when I've been like this my entire life.

"Hads, how's your new place?" I ask her.

"We've been having issues with one of our other roommates. She doesn't do her dishes or clean up after herself. It sucks," she tells us. "Also, Jacks told me the other day that he and Claire are moving in together after college. They have a whole plan laid out, and it's adorable. Grant cried when they told him about it."

Grant and Jacks are best friends, and both play defense on the hockey team together. Jacks has been dating this girl Claire for a few more months than Hads and Grant. They all go on double dates all the time. Hads now has a four-bedroom apartment with Taylor, her old roommate, and two other girls they both don't like. Jacks is nice, and we all like him and Claire together.

"Hads, when we watched *Titanic* the other day, you were bawling your eyes out by the end. You always mock Grant, but we know he made you soft. It's cute," Ella points out.

Our little group hangs out all the time. The activities we do vary depending on the night. Sometimes, Ella forces us all to go out. Amelia usually has some weird ass activity for us to do, the last one of hers being smash therapy—which was quite fun. Hads usually picks a different museum to visit, and I usually pick a standard old movie night. Part of me feels guilty not wanting to go out and party all the time like most twenty-one-year-olds do. I don't know why I don't like partying. I prefer staying in and reading or relaxing and playing board games, rather than going out and getting drunk every night, but part of me feels like I'm wasting my twenties away.

I picked Titanic because its been my mission to make Hads cry, and I succeeded! When she didn't cry at *The Notebook* or *Good Will Hunting,* I thought it was a lost cause. Who knew *Titanic* would be the one to do it?

"First off, I didn't go soft. I still threaten Grant eighty times a day. Secondly, they could both fit on the door! The end infuriated me. That's why I was crying," Hads says to Ella.

"I agree. There was enough room," Amelia says as she high-fives Hads.

"I like the ending. It makes sense to me. Their love saved her. It was beautiful," I say, tears coming to my eyes.

"Okay, before Paige cries about Jack's death again, I'll change the subject," Amelia says.

"I wasn't going to cry." They all look at me. "Okay, fine, I was." I sulk back in my chair. I never used to be this emotional, but as I got older, all the feelings I never expressed as a child bubbled up.

"I should get going soon. I have an early meeting tomorrow with my boss," Ella says as she grabs her bag and shoves her book inside it.

"I have to go meet Grant at the rink, so I'll head out with you, Ells," Hads says, grabbing her black shoulder bag and slinging it around her.

"Can you guys fix the room back to how we found it?" Ella asks us.

"Yeah, you guys go. Paige and I have nothing important to do after this," Amelia tells them as they head to the door.

"Hey! I could have plans, you know!" I tell her.

"I thought you wanted to finish that one documentary on female serial killers tonight?" Amelia asks me.

"I forgot we were watching that!" I say, practically jumping out of my chair. I grab my tote bag that says *No Shelf Control* and put it over my shoulder. Amelia pushes the tables together, and I put the chairs back in the right spot. Ames grabs her book, and we head out of the classroom and back to our apartment.

I interlock Amelia and I's arms as we walk down the path back to our place. We see Hads and Ella in the distance and wave at each other. My phone pings a few seconds later.

Ella: Everyone text when you get home safely!

Hads: Will do! But it might be a long night for me.

Ella: Is that sexual?

Paige: Ah!

Amelia: Paige almost tripped.

Hads: Not sexual! Grant is teaching me how to skate still.

Paige: Adorbs!

Amelia: That makes me want to throw up. How cute.

Ella: I love you two together.

Hads: <3

Ella: Love you guys! See you soon!

Amelia: Xoxo! Also, Paige and I are home!

Hads: Love you, ladies!

Paige: I love you guys!

"I think it's cute they're still doing ice skating lessons," I tell Amelia.

"I think it's funny Hads is mad she hasn't mastered it yet." She giggles.

It's true. Hads is good at most things right off the bat, but ice skating is not one of them. I give major props to people who can skate. I can't even walk on flat surfaces without tripping.

"Did you get popcorn at the store the other day? I know you like to snack while we watch stuff."

"Yup. I even grabbed some chips for you," Amelia says, smiling at me.

I grab my keys and unlock the door when I hear a buzz from Amelia's phone. I check mine, and it's not the group chat. As I insert the key into the lock, her phone buzzes twice again.

"Anyone important?" I ask with a smile because I think I know who it is.

"Nope." As she speaks, it buzzes in her hand.

"You sure?" I ask again, wondering if she'll admit she likes this kid. Amelia met this guy named Henry while she was here on campus over summer break. They developed some sort of relationship Amelia has been very quiet about.

"Just unlock the door." She rolls her eyes at me.

I comply, and we head into our apartment and settle for a night of snacks and true crime documentaries.

"You get the snacks, and I'll load up the doc," I tell her.

"Sounds good to me."

A few minutes later, she comes and sits next to me on the couch, handing me a bowl of chips and my water bottle all filled up. I open the blanket for her to climb in.

"I love you," I say to her.

"I love you too, Paige. Now, let's get watching."

I press play, and we settle in.

It's good to be back.

4

????

They say you should feel guilt and remorse the first time you kill someone. As I sit across from them, I feel a sense of peace come over me, knowing this will be their last day on Earth.

Coward.

That fact alone ignites me as I grip the knife's handle in my briefcase. They keep talking about data and numbers, and I pretend to care when I know only one of us will walk out of here still breathing.

The end of the meeting is near. I stand up and shake their hand, fisting the knife with my free hand. I raise it and quickly slit their throat.

One slice is all it takes from one carotid artery to the other.

They grab their throat and sit down in their chair. *I hope the leather doesn't stain,* I think to myself.

A few seconds and they're dead.

Vengeance will come.

Step one is complete.

Onto step two.

5

Saturday, September 10th

"Worthless piece of shit."

I'm huddled in the corner of my bedroom. My father is standing in the doorway, a baseball bat in one hand and a bottle of whiskey in the other.

"I'm sorry," I whisper while my voice shakes.

I dropped a plate in the kitchen earlier. That's why he's so mad at me. It slipped out of my hands while doing the dishes. He stares at me. I know what happens next. It never makes it easier, though. He slowly steps toward me and stands above my tiny frame. I try to shrink into the wallpaper, wondering if I can melt into it and disappear from my body.

It'll be over soon, I tell myself.

He raises the bat and—

With my alarm going off, I jolt upward from my bed, covered in sweat. I reach over to my phone and stop it. I'm breathing heavily, just like every time I wake up from a nightmare. I notice five things I can see—my phone, my favorite book on my nightstand, a signed photo from my favorite actress, a book Ella lent me that I need to give back, and my tote bags. Four things I can touch—my blanket, my sweatpants, my hair, and my phone. Three things I can hear—Amelia shuffling around in the kitchen, my heavy breathing, and music from one of Amelia's playlists. Two things I can smell—a whiff of my favorite perfume from when I used it yesterday and something sweet, a candle, I think. One thing I can taste—blood. I bit my lip when I woke up.

My therapist taught me that trick to help me calm down when I feel anxious, and it helps sometimes. My therapist diagnosed me with minor PTSD from my childhood. I used to have panic attacks four to five times a week, but that has lessened throughout the years. Sometimes, I panic for no reason, and other times, I have a nightmare, which causes me to have panic attacks. I cut out caffeine to try and avoid them, but I still panic sometimes in certain situations. I shake the thought off. This isn't how I wanted to start today, but it can only go up from here. I grab my phone and open it up to my mom's contact.

Paige: Big meeting today! Thinking of you. Wish me luck!

I hop in the shower and get dressed for the day. I throw on black dress pants, a matching blazer, a fitted pink bodysuit, and black flats. Oliver and I have our meeting today to discuss fundraising for the criminal justice club, so I dress a bit nicer than normal since we need the money. With eyeliner on my waterline, I apply light makeup, filling in my eyebrows and putting mascara on. I throw some Chapstick in my tote bag with a

Pride and Prejudice quote on it, grab my meeting notes, and step into the living room.

Amelia's on the couch eating a breakfast sandwich and watching a travel documentary. I grab a granola bar, not feeling hungry because of nerves and my nightmare, and plop beside her on the couch. "Why do you look like that?"

"Like what?" I ask her, looking down at my outfit.

"Oh, you have that big meeting today. Sorry, that totally slipped my mind," she says, biting into her sandwich.

"Do I look okay?"

"You look spectacular. That's a real power fit."

"Thanks, I borrowed this blazer from Hads. My shoes are from Ella. Those two combined can help pull an outfit together," I say, looking at Amelia's phone over her shoulder. Unfortunately, she notices.

"What are you doing?" she asks as I slump back on the couch.

"What? Nothing."

"Why are you trying to look at my phone?"

"I'm not." *I am.*

"Paige."

"Amelia."

"Drop it."

"I cannot wait to meet this elusive Henry figure. He seems to be occupying a lot of your time," I say with a giggle.

"It's not a big deal."

"You giving someone besides the girls and me the time of day is a big deal."

"If I have it my way you'll never meet him, so drop it," Amelia says, turning her show back on.

"I bet twenty bucks I'll meet him by the end of the year," I say while spinning around to face her as I get off the couch.

"Fine." She stands and follows me. "I bet you twenty bucks that Oliver won't say more than three sentences at your meeting today."

"Deal. Why do you guys always say that? He talks a lot—at least around me," I say, holding my hand out. She grabs it, and we shake. "What do you have going on today?"

"Hads and Grant are coming over in a few to watch a National Geographic documentary with me."

"That sounds fun! Will you guys still be here after my meeting?" I ask them, wanting to see Grant and ask him about the upcoming hockey season. Unlike the other girls, I immensely enjoy watching hockey and a few other sports.

"Probably. Your meeting shouldn't be too drawn out, right? The documentary is kind of long," she tells me, grabbing more coffee and filling her mug.

"If it goes well, it should only take half an hour," I tell her. "I'm heading there early to prep so I'm not nervous. I'll see you later!" I say as I rush out the door.

"Three sentences, Paige! They have to be full ones too!" Amelia yells after me, and I roll my eyes and head toward the building.

"Hi. Paige Yarrow. I'm here to see the dean of students. I should have an appointment," I say to the receptionist. My voice didn't sound shaky, so I'm off to an okay start. She looks up at me and smiles, my nerves dissipating.

"Have a seat, darling. He's on a call right now that should be done in a few. Make yourself comfortable," she says while pointing to a bunch of chairs in a row, and I sit in the one closest to the door. Oliver isn't here yet and I'm starting to get anxious. I hate when people are late to things. He's usually on time for class, but what if his alarm didn't go off, or he slipped, fell, and hurt himself? I should've met him somewhere, and we should've come in together. It's too late now. I think I could do this meeting alone, but having Oliver there would calm my nerves, and it would look better if both of us were here.

Stop thinking about Oliver and look at your notes, Paige.

Right. That's why I got here early. I also have anxiety if I'm on time or late. One of my high school teachers used to drill into our heads that if we were on time, we were late. Now, that replays in my brain whenever I have to be somewhere. So, I get places early and play the waiting game most of the time. It gives me more time to read or prepare for whatever I'm doing. My ex-boyfriend used to make fun of me for wanting to get everywhere early, but luckily for him, I did what I always do with boyfriends and leave before things get serious. It's foolproof!

How ironic that the girl who wants all her friends to find love doesn't believe in it for herself.

I'm sitting for what seems like forever when the receptionist lifts her head. "You should be all set to go in now." She smiles and unlocks the door using a button behind her desk. I feel like I should wait for Oliver, but I want to get some nice small talk in before he gets here and kills the vibe. I stand before the door, take a deep breath, paste a signature Paige Yarrow smile on my face, and open the door.

They say your brain recognizes danger before the rest of your body. Your brain sends signals to your nervous system, which picks up your heart rate and blood pressure. It's weird how our minds can register it before we even notice.

I smell it before I see it.

Blood.

So much blood.

Everywhere.

The desk, the chair, the carpet, the walls, his neck, his clothes.

They also say you only know how you'll react to danger once you experience a dangerous situation. I always thought I would run away, but I'm rooted in place.

I should scream, right?

Why am I not screaming?

Can I still scream? Do I have a voice? He certainly doesn't, with his throat being cut open how it is. I should alert someone, tell someone, maybe I could help him, but who am I kidding? There's no helping him with the amount of blood all over this tiny room. Is it getting smaller? I swear it has shrunk three sizes since I've been in here. There's one window in this room, and I see the sun shining through it.

My breath hitches and I realize I can't breathe. I'm taking short and rapid breaths. How do you breathe air after seeing the dead body of your former dean of students? Is there an instruction manual for that? I'd like to see it. Spots are dotting my vision, and I think for a second I might be the one dying. I wish Oliver was here because he would know what to do. Oliver's good with split-second decisions. He would no doubt have called for help by now.

I'm still in the same spot. Frozen.

"Help," I whisper for only I to hear. I realize I can't stay in this room. I'm in here having a panic attack when someone has just died.

Died. Killed.

Murdered.

No way would he slit his own throat—I bet my life on it.

Murdered by someone on this campus, most likely. I have to get out of this room.

Get out. Get out. Get out. Get out.

I slowly shuffle my feet backward, as if the dead body in front of me is going anywhere, and run out of the room, only to fall to the floor after running into someone.

This day could *not* get worse.

6

Saturday, September 10th

I WALK INTO THE office where our meeting is, and Paige runs into me and falls on the floor. I'm about to say something when I notice she's crying and breathing heavily. Her eyes don't find mine because they shoot around like she's looking for something to latch onto. I think she's having a panic attack. What the hell happened in there? The receptionist is standing now, watching Paige and I.

I lean down to where she is and put my hand on the back of her head, forcing her to look into my eyes. She finally looks at me, and I see it register that I'm not some random person. She hasn't relaxed yet. Her whole body is trembling from how scared she is. I put her thumb over my pulse, ensuring she could feel it and hoping it would calm hers down.

Her pink shirt has black teardrop stains from her makeup, and I have no idea if what I'm doing will help, but it's worth a shot.

"Paige," I say to her.

"I didn't—I never—I thought—" She keeps trying to say something but can barely get anything out. I've never seen anyone this afraid. Her pupils are fully dilated, and I can barely see her green eyes underneath them.

"Paige, feel my pulse and breathe with me," I tell her.

"I've seen them on television and in different documentaries, but I've never—I've never seen one in person, and I don't think they look asleep. I–I–I think they look how they are, which is dead, you know? Dead people look dead. It just makes sense. Who said that in the first place, anyway? I never thought the body had that much blood. I mean, knowing all that is inside of us all the time, swimming around keeping us alive, kind of freaks me out, and next time I get a paper cut, I'm going to think about this, and it's so weird that one minute he was alive and then he died and I—"

"Paige, slow down. I can't understand you," I cut her off because, at this rate, she could pass out with how little air she is taking in. "Just take some breaths for me, please." I grab her hand, putting it on my chest so she can feel my lungs and copy. She flinches away from my hand at first but then grabs it again. I wipe a few tears away. "What happened?"

Her eyes bug out when I ask her that, and her heart rate increases again. I try to get her to stand up, but she refuses, wanting to stay on the floor, her back against a chair. The tears keep streaming down her face, and I think it might kill me if I can't get her to relax soon. I hate not being able to do anything to help her, but fuck, I'm trying.

"Paige, what happened? Please, love, just tell me." *Love?* Where the fuck did that come from? Let's call it the heat of the moment. It's a very tense situation.

"Th-The dean—He—" She's pointing at his door. I start to get up, but she pulls my arm back down. "P-Please don't leave me." The tears are still coming, and fuck, I would stay rooted in this spot if she asked me. I rub my chin and touch my mouth, unsure of what to do.

"Fuck, Paige. I'm here, but I'm going to check and make sure everything's alright. Okay? I won't leave your line of sight," I tell her, looking into those big fucking eyes of hers. She nods, and I get up, brushing my fingers around her arm as she lets me go. I take a few steps, peek into his office, and see it.

The dean—a person who has helped me in more ways than one—dead in his chair, with his throat slit.

Paige found him like this.

Holy fucking shit.

I swing my head around and look at his receptionist. "Call the police," I say to her while walking back to Paige and kneeling in front of her. The receptionist—I can't remember her name at the moment—looks terrified as well. Her hand is shaking while dialing the phone, but I disregard her. Even before myself, the only person I care about right now is on the floor having a breakdown.

She looks frozen in time. Her makeup is all over her face, and black tears drain from her eyes with no sign of stopping yet. I don't know what the fuck to do, so I do what feels right. I sit next to her, threading her hand through mine and drawing circles around her hand. I hope this will help distract her thoughts while I get her breathing under control. I feel so unprepared for this situation, and I hate it. I don't know how to help someone through a panic attack, and I wish I could do more, but for now, this has to be good enough. Her pulse is so erratic I'm afraid she'll pass out, and I'll have to take her to the hospital.

I don't do hospitals. Ever since Mia, I can't stand being in one. Too many memories of that night that I'd rather forget. I shove those feelings down because this is not about me right now. It's about Paige.

Well, and the dean, but he's dead, so he can wait.

I look over at her, and she's staring straight ahead. Her breathing isn't as erratic, but still not great. I continue drawing circles on her hand with my thumb because it seems to be helping, and she squeezes my hand. I squeeze her hand back and swear I see her mouth turn up, even if only slightly. We sit like that for a few minutes until I look over at her.

"How do you feel?"

"I-I'm okay, I think," she says, her voice sounding shattered.

"Do you need anything?" I look over at her, her eyes still straightforward.

"Don't leave my side, please." She's barely whispering, and I have the sudden urge to kiss her hand, so I do. I bring her hand up to my mouth and gently press a kiss to it. She shivers when I do that, and I feel weird. I'm usually not good at comforting people. It makes me uncomfortable to watch people cry, but with Paige, it's different. Suddenly, I wish I had gotten here first and seen it, not her.

The cops enter the room, hands on their guns and looking around at the scene. *That was quick.*

"Where's the body?" one of them asks, and I assume dispatch told them what happened.

The receptionist points to the office, and they walk by Paige and me. They come back out and speak into the mics on their shoulders, notifying dispatch they'll need backup and explaining the full context of the situation.

"Who found the deceased?" one of them asks out loud.

Paige doesn't move when he says that, so I speak for her. "She did."

"I'm going to have to ask you to come to the station with me," he says. To that, she gets all flustered. "What? Why?"

I turn to her. "Paige, it's protocol. You know this. They have to ask us some questions. You're not going to be in trouble. It's just routine."

"Okay, but you're coming with me, right?" she asks, trying to stand up.

I grab her arms and lift her onto her feet. "I have to. I'm technically a witness too."

"Right. Okay, lead the way," she says, faking a smile and walking out of the room.

"Paige, no matter how much sanitizer you use, the ink isn't going to come off. You need soap and warm water," I say to her. She has aggressively scrubbed her hands since we got fingerprinted at the station. Most stations use electronic scanning for fingerprints now, but the Grand Mountain police station is so small they haven't had the chance to update their system—hence the ink that's all over our fingers. I think she's still in shock, and honestly, I am too. It's not every day you discover a dead body. It's also not every day the dean of students at your college gets murdered on campus, but nothing about today has been normal. The police asked us typical questions, and we answered them all and were released. It took about an hour, and they dropped us back on campus, so I'm walking Paige back to her apartment.

I'm worried about her. She's been quiet and detached. I know she's in shock, and there isn't a single thing I can do to help. I can see the wheels turning in her head. She's thinking about something, but for once, I can't tell what. I don't try to make small talk as we walk. I just let her be. I try not to think about the last time I was in a life-altering situation and my breathing hitches. Fuck. I thought I was past feeling like this. The guilt overwhelms me sometimes because if I had stopped her from leaving...

Don't, Oliver.

It happened five years ago, and I know healing isn't linear or whatever, but I hate that I still think about it.

I loved her, for fucks sake.

Haven't loved anyone else since, and haven't let anyone else try.

More like won't let anyone else in for them to try...

But life goes on.

I look over at Paige, tears still falling from her eyes. We reach her doorstep, and I'm about to say something, but she opens the door and doesn't close it.

Was that an invitation? I take it as one anyway.

She goes immediately to the sink and starts scrubbing her hands. I'm still standing in the entryway to her apartment. I walk over to her to turn off the sink, but Grant blocks my path before getting to her.

Is this kid serious?

"Dude, back up, give her some space," he says to me. I take a deep breath, nod, and step back. The girls could probably help her out more than I could anyway. My sister and Amelia are standing now, probably confused about what's happening.

My sister glares daggers at me. "What did you do to Paige? She looks scared."

What did I do? Why is that her first assumption?

Amelia tries to turn the water off so Paige can stop scrubbing her hands, but Paige swats her away. She's not speaking because she's still in shock, and I can't do a single fucking thing without Grant probably punching me.

"Only took your brother three years to get on Paige's nerves. What did it this time? The grunts or the evil stares?" Amelia says, trying to lighten the mood. I send a glare in her direction. Why is everyone assuming this is my fault? Amelia shuts the water off, and Paige turns it back on. Fuck, she needs to stop or her hands are going to be redder than a tomato.

"Guys, I didn't do anything. Something happened." Paige stops when I say that. Does she not want me to bring it up? They're going to find out sooner or later. Paige is still crying, and Amelia wipes them off her face. Grant tilts his head at my sister, and she takes over his spot while he shuts their front door that's still open. Only he slams it, causing Paige to flinch.

Fuck this. I'm going over to her.

I walk by my sister, and when I reach her, I wrap Paige in my arms, and she relaxes. I'm not usually one for hugs, but Paige and I just shared an experience. I couldn't protect her from it, but maybe I can help lessen the pain of it all. Amelia whispers to my sister, and I think Grant laughs under his breath a bit, but I don't give a shit.

"Cut the bullshit and start talking you two," Grant tells us after a few seconds.

"Oliver, what happened to Paige?" my sister says to me, a bite in her tone.

I let go of Paige and walked toward my sister. "What's to say something didn't happen to me too? Why did you all assume I caused her to be like this? Do you guys think that little of me?" That came out louder than I intended, but I don't care.

"Oliver, you have one facial expression, the one you're wearing right now," Grant says. "Just tell us what happened to Paige." I'm about to speak when Paige beats me to it.

"Guys, I'm right here, and I'm fine, I swear." She's not fine, and everyone knows it. She tries to smile, but I can see right through her. She's very clearly not okay.

"P, you're not. You're shaking and crying. Something must have happened and I hate seeing you this worked up," Amelia says. "Let's sit down, and we can talk about it." What did Amelia mean? Is Paige like this a lot? *Fucking hell.*

"Amelia's right, let's relax a bit," my sister says while going over to where they stand. *Is Paige like this a lot?* My curiosity is peaked, and the way everyone's behaving right now has the wheels in my head turning.

"Oliver, can you fucking say something, please?" Grant asks, standing in front of me, and I have to look up at him. I fucking hate that he's taller than me.

"The dean of students is dead, and Paige found the body. He was murdered," I say to them, and the room goes quiet. "We just came from the police station. We had to answer questions, and they fingerprinted us." Nobody says anything. I think I could hear a pin drop in here. *Yeah, that's what I thought.*

"Do you guys need anything?" Grant asks, looking between the two of us. I look Paige in the eyes, and for the first time today, I can finally see what is going on in that head of hers.

"Paige, no." She wants to fucking solve his murder. I can see it in her eyes. They're gleaming and not just with tears. There's excitement behind her eyes, too. Is she fucking crazy? She saw his dead body two hours ago and already wants to figure out what happened.

"Why not?" she asks with a hint of challenge in her voice. This fucking girl is going to get herself in trouble. Only she would want to solve this shit like it was a real-life true crime documentary.

"It's dangerous, for one." And about a million other reasons, but I don't mention those.

"Fine," she says, finally dropping the topic.

"Okay, that was a wonderful conversation none of us had the context to. I'll call Ella, this is an emergency, and we need everyone here," Amelia says as she exits the room to grab her phone.

"The school sent out an email a few minutes ago. A shelter-in-place. Holy shit," Grant says.

"That's protocol. Plus, they probably don't want students seeing all the police on campus and causing a panic," I tell them.

"How did this happen?" my sister says, and I glare at her, silently telling her to stop talking about it.

"Excuse me," Paige says as she walks to her room, and I follow her. Her back is to me, and I softly shut her door. Her room is nice, I guess—lots of fucking books everywhere. She turns around, her phone to her ear, and jumps. "Sorry, I didn't know you were behind me." She lowers her hand and clicks off of whoever she is calling.

"Did you need to continue that?" I ask her.

"No, they didn't answer anyway. What's up?"

"What's up? Seriously?"

"What?" she says while lowering herself to the floor.

"You cannot get involved," I say, hoping she'll listen.

"I never said I was going to!"

"I can see it in your eyes! Just drop it and let the police do their jobs."

"Don't you find it a little interesting that I of all people found the body? It's like destiny or something."

I sigh heavily. "Paige, drop it. I'm serious. You don't owe him anything."

"But—"

"Paige."

Our eyes are locked in some sort of weird staring contest, and my stomach drops. She's challenging me on this, but I'm not backing down. There's no way she should put herself in the middle of all this. It could be dangerous.

She breaks eye contact first. "Fine, but you can't stop me from keeping tabs on the case!" I open her door, letting her have some time alone, when I turn back and face her again.

"Are you okay?" I whisper. I remember feeling her legs shaking while the police asked us questions, and I can't get the look off her face when she ran into me this morning. I don't think I'll ever get it out of my head. She was terrified, and you don't just get over something like this—not easily.

She looks at me and nods, saying nothing along with it.

"Are you sure?" I'm double-checking because I think she's lying and doesn't want to admit she isn't okay. I know the feeling. I pretended I was okay after Mia's death, and then one day, the dam exploded. I got angry at the world. Then I started therapy, and even though I hate talking about my feelings, it helped me get them under control. But Paige and I went through something traumatic today—her more than me—and I want to make sure she's okay.

"I'm sure." She smiles at me, still fake, but I'll leave it alone. I shut her door and return to the living room. My sister and Grant are sitting on the couch. I sit on the loveseat next to them. None of us say anything until Amelia comes back out.

"Where's Paige?" she asks.

Hads simply points to her door and Amelia tenses. "Alone?"

"Yeah, why?"

"She went through something traumatic. I don't think leaving her alone is a good idea."

"Ames, she has been surrounded by my brother and countless police today. She deserves some alone time," my sister points out, and I nod, agreeing with her.

"Oliver, is the dean really dead?" Grant asks me.

"Yeah. I saw him after Paige did. Definitely dead."

"Fuck," he says.

Their front door bursts open, and in comes Ella, looking at the four of us sitting in the living room.

"Where is she?" she asks us, and I nod over to Paige's door. "Thank you." She opens Paige's door, and a second later, she drags her out and hugs her.

"Ella, I'm fine, I promise," she says, hugging her back.

"P, can you please just sit down and explain what happened? We need to know you're okay." She points to a spot on the floor, and Paige sits down and brings her legs to her chest. The rest of us sit down around her and then she begins to explain the past few hours.

7

Saturday, September 10th

I'M SITTING ON MY living room floor, and everyone is staring at me. I don't know where to start, so I say the first things that come to mind. I tell them everything about how I found the body, ran into Oliver, had a panic attack, and felt like I was dying. I spare no details, and by the time I'm done, the girls are shocked, and Grant is almost in tears. Oliver has the same look on his face that he always does. *What's going through his head?*

I'm thankful he was there today. I was a mess—still am—but that was one of the worst panic attacks I've ever had. I enjoyed his presence even though today was so horrible—he even hugged me earlier in front of everyone. I was shocked. I've never even seen him and Hads hug before. It was comforting, though. Despite everyone calling him a statue, he gives good hugs.

"Paige, this is insane. What can I do to help? Are you hungry?" Ella asks me.

"I don't need anything right now, just you guys here with me," I say to them. Amelia rubs my shoulder, and I grab her hand and squeeze it. I look at Oliver and he's still manspreading on the loveseat with his head down. I reach over and poke one of his legs, and he lifts his head and stares at me.

"Is it weird if I want to solve this? I feel like I owe it to him after finding his body." Saying it out loud sounds crazy—I hear that now. Oliver somehow knew I was thinking about that earlier, but I haven't let the thought go. I feel like I need to *do* something. I hate sitting here feeling helpless about this entire situation.

"Paige, what the fuck?" Hads asks.

"Yes, that's weird," Ella tells me.

"Typical criminal justice major," Grant says, shaking his head.

"P, this is *not* a real-life true crime documentary," Amelia remarks with a giggle.

Oliver only sighs heavily before he speaks. "Paige, I told you to leave it alone. Let the cops handle it."

"You guys are no fun," I say, leaning back so I can stare at my ceiling.

"The past three hours are what you call fun? You need some new hobbies," Grant says.

"Paige, you need to focus on yourself right now." Ella's probably right, but I might start crying again if I focus on myself. I'm taking a page out of Amelia's book and deflecting.

"Fine. It was a dumb idea anyway," I say. "Does anyone know how to get this ink off my hands? Soap isn't working."

"I called Alissa and she said rubbing alcohol works wonders," Ella says while getting up and venturing to my closet to find it.

"I don't even want to know how she knows that," Grant says.

"Oliver, are you doing okay? This day couldn't have been easy for you either," Hads asks her brother, and he nods. She doesn't press any further and he doesn't offer anything else.

"Paige, do you want to watch a movie to make you feel better?" Amelia asks me.

"Sure, but can I shower first? I feel gross." I stand from the floor and head to my room. I love their attentiveness, but I need a shower to calm the fuck down. I've been surrounded by far too many people asking me a thousand questions today. I need a minute to gather myself. Just one minute.

"Sounds good. I'll make some snacks," Amelia says as she heads for the pantry.

"How long is everyone staying? I don't want to be a burden if you guys have plans tonight. It is a Saturday night, after all." I turn and look at my friends, and they're looking at me as if I'm crazy. "What?"

"We're staying the night," Ella says.

"All of you?"

"Not me. I have a thing with Jacks and Brendan," Grant says as he gets comfier on the couch. "But I can stay for a movie."

"Oliver?" I look over at him, and he merely stands up and walks out of my apartment. "Okay, guess there's my answer."

"He tends to do that when he needs to think," Hads tells me. "I'll check up on him tomorrow."

I can't ignore the tension in my gut. Maybe he got sick of me. It has been a long day, and he had to deal with my emotions all day, so I get it. I just find myself wishing he stayed.

"It's okay. I'm going to shower quickly, and then I'll come back."

"Here," Ella says, handing me the bottle of rubbing alcohol. "For your fingers."

"Thanks," I tell her with a smile. I walk into my room and shut my door. I turn the shower on and get in. At first, I let the water hit me, but an idea creeps into my mind. All of my greatest and most insane ideas happen in the shower it seems.

I finally get the ink off of my fingers, and after I wash my hair, the small idea I had becomes so big it's all I can think about.

"But where would I start?" I say to no one.

I could start by searching his office to see if the cops missed anything. But how would I sneak out without one of the girls noticing? I might have to wait until tomorrow, but I can't go during the day—someone will see me. Maybe I'll wait until the girls are asleep and sneak out later tonight. I know they told me to drop this, but there's no way I'm going to listen. My bones are itching to put these pieces together.

I also feel like I owe it to him—he helped Oliver and me get an internship with the district attorney's office during junior year. It usually takes a long time to get an internship there, but he pulled some strings and made it happen for both of us. He was a sort of mentor for Oliver and me, and the fact that I was the one who found him feels like fate.

I can do this, right? I know the law, and this could be training for the real thing when I graduate at the end of the year. I don't want to be a cop or detective, but having some experience under my belt can't hurt.

I am a visual learner...

I throw on sweatpants and a comfy crew neck so I can join my friends back in the living room. Right now, I'll watch one of my favorite movies and try to forget about the past few hours. Tonight, I'm going to look for evidence to solve a murder.

It's another normal Saturday as far as I'm concerned.

Sunday, September 11th

3:00 AM

IT'S AROUND THREE IN the morning, and I'm sneaking out of my room to start my investigation. I'm wearing all black—because everyone knows that's what you're supposed to wear in situations like these—while carrying a small bag with some supplies. Rubber gloves so I don't accidentally fingerprint anything. Shoe covers so I don't leave any shoe prints behind, and I have a black hat on and my hair in a bun so I don't leave any hair.

Amelia is the only one I have to worry about being awake, but she had a few too many drinks Ella made earlier and passed out on the couch. Hads and Amelia are cuddling, basically. Ella's on the air mattress, her hair sprawled everywhere. I won't be gone for too long, but I hope they don't wake up early or my plan is ruined before I've even started. I carefully open my front door, shut it softly behind me, and walk across campus.

It only takes me around ten minutes to get into the building. I was worried my swipe card wouldn't work to open the door because the school could have blocked it off, but they didn't. My next obstacle is that an officer might be posted outside of the office since this is technically an active investigation.

His *old* office. I carefully turn the corner into the waiting area—like I did this morning—and I don't see anybody.

I throw some gloves on and jiggle the handle, but it's locked. I shuffle through my bag and grab a few bobby pins and other small things to try and pick the lock. I'm crouched down and struggling for a few minutes when I hear a noise. It sounds like a door opening. Shit! I grab my stuff and figure out a place to hide when a flashlight shines on my face. I raise my hands, and my bag drops to the floor with a thump.

I'm totally busted. I'm also an idiot for thinking I could do this.

"You're stupid if you think I'm letting you do this alone."

Wait, I know that voice. "Oliver?"

8

Sunday, September 11th

3:30 AM

"How did you know I was going to be here?"

"It's the first thing I would do if I were investigating," I tell her. I had a feeling she was lying earlier when she said she would drop it, so when I left her place earlier, I took a nap and set my alarm for midnight. My parents woke me up, calling to check in since news of the death broke online. I reassured them I was okay, and we chatted for a bit before they went to sleep. Sometimes the three-hour time difference sucks, but I still love talking to them whenever possible. I sat on a bench and waited for Paige, and sure enough, when three a.m. rolled around, I saw her leaving and followed her. I felt creepy doing that, but I didn't want to scare her outside in the dark after the day we'd had.

"What are you doing here? Did you follow me?" she says, lowering her hands and grabbing her bag off the floor.

"Yes," I say while lowering my flashlight and walking past her toward the door.

"That's technically stalking. I could report you," she says and I turn around and lean against the doorframe of the office. I tilt my head at her, silently challenging her to do it. Paige has always been the best at reading my silent cues. "I'm not going to. I didn't think you would want to help me with this."

"Paige, I'm not letting you do this alone," I tell her while turning around and trying to open the door.

"It's locked."

"Thank you, Sherlock. I see that."

"Was that a joke? Wow, I should write that on my calendar." She smiles at me. "Oliver Baker's first joke ever."

"Hilarious." I crouch down and sift through my pockets. I grab my hook tool and shove it into the lock, turning it and trying to figure out which way this door unlocks.

"What are you doing?" she asks me.

"Picking the lock."

"How do you know how to pick locks? Are you a criminal on the side?"

"No. I taught myself how to do it when I was a kid."

"Why?" she asks me.

"I was bored one day." She laughs. "Why is that funny?"

"You were bored and decided to teach yourself how to pick locks? That's such a you thing to do." She crouches next to me, and I look over at her.

"Why do I feel like that wasn't a compliment?" She shrugs, and I turn back to the door. It's only a single-pin lock, so I get my hook in the right position, lift it, and the door opens.

"Good job!" she says, holding her hand up to high-five me. I sigh and high-five her back. We stand up, and I'm about to enter the room when she shoves me backward.

"What was that for?"

"Put these on." She hands me covers for my shoes, rubber gloves, and a hat. She's always thinking a few steps ahead, isn't she?

"Why do you have these if you were doing this yourself?" I ask. "And where did you get all this stuff on such short notice?" There's no way my sister and the girls would have let her leave the apartment today. *She probably has all this stuff under her bed in labeled boxes.*

"It never hurts to have extras, and I had all of it already, just in case." She smiles and waves her hand for me to go in. "Also, you're clearly an amateur at this. You're not even wearing all black." I look down at my outfit—a dark blue hoodie, jeans, and white sneakers.

"This isn't a crime show, Paige. This is real life," I say as I enter the office. She follows and stops where she stands. "Paige?" I wave my hand in front of her face, but her eyes are rooted to the chair the body was in this morning. There's a big chunk of it cut out—forensics probably took it to test it. "Are you okay?" I reach down and brush her fingers with mine, and she jolts back to the present.

"Sorry. Where should we start?" she asks, trying to pretend she's fine.

"Do you want to take a minute? We don't have to do this tonight, you know."

"Oliver, it's fine. We don't have all night or morning, I guess." She throws her bag into the hallway. "Let's do this. I'll sweep to the left. You can do the right, like how we learned in criminal investigations sophomore year."

I nod, knowing exactly what she's talking about. "What are we looking for?"

"Anything the police missed."

I start moving along the right side of this small room. His office doesn't have much to it. There are a few bookcases and some trophies, but other than his desk and two chairs on the other side, there isn't much. Sweeping it fully takes around fifteen minutes. I haven't found anything important, but I see a calendar when I reach his desk.

"Paige," I say, motioning her over. I point, and her eyes light up.

"Good find. I bet the cops took pictures of it, but why wouldn't they just take it?" she asks and I shrug. "Flip to today's date. I want to see if we can trace his movements this morning."

"Did you hear the police say how long he was dead before you arrived?"

She shakes her head at me.

"Me neither."

"He only had two meetings before ours. One of them was an hour before we showed up," she tells me. Her face scrunched as she looks at the calendar.

"What?"

"The receptionist said that he was on the phone before our meeting. So was he really on the phone or—"

"You think she had something to do with it?" I ask.

"No, she seemed surprised to find him too. It's weird. Does she not check in on him after every meeting?"

I shrug. "She's basically his assistant, but we can make a note to talk to her at some point. I think we should look at whoever met with him before us. That seems like a good starting point for our investigation."

"*Our* investigation. Mhm, yes. Detectives Paige and Oliver are officially on the case!" I chuckle at her excitement and continue to look around the room. There's black fingerprint dust all over the walls from where forensics was dusting for prints.

"Who did he meet with before us?" I ask.

"Grisham."

"Who?"

"Some marketing professor."

We continue searching for around half an hour but don't find anything of value, so we decide to call it a night. We leave the room and make sure everything's where it was before as we lock the door behind us. Paige takes a picture of the door, and we head out. She took a thousand photos of the room and all the shit that was in it. That's standard procedure for every investigation—you take pictures of anything and everything.

"I'll print these out and make a murder board."

"A what?" I ask her, a bit taken aback.

"A murder board."

"A murder board? With the red string and shit?"

She shoves my arm a bit. "No, you buffoon. Just a board with all our evidence and stuff on it."

"Isn't that the same thing?" *I'm so confused.*

"No. The one with the red string is for suspects and connecting them all together." *Of course* this girl wants to make a fucking murder board. This all seems like a fuck ton of work on top of the regular homework the two of us have to do but I can't let Paige do this alone. I feel like I have to look out for her, mostly because I'm not quite sure what we're walking into with this whole thing. The guy was murdered for fucks sake. What if he was involved in something that someone didn't want him blabbing about?

"Gotcha." We walk in silence back to her apartment. As we head toward her door, she turns around and looks at me with those big fucking green eyes.

"I can't wait to work with you, partner." She nudges my side with her elbow.

"Same...partner." I throw a smirk her way. "How have you been since earlier?"

"I'm fine." She flashes a quick smile at me—a fake one—but if she doesn't want to talk about it yet, I'm not going to force her.

"Let's keep this on the down low, so don't tell anybody, okay?"

"I know."

"Good, because I would hate having to torture you to figure out who you told." She winks, fucking *winks* at me.

I roll my eyes at her. "You could torture me anytime, and I'd tell you everything." Her cheeks turn red when I say that. "Good night, Paige."

"Good night, Oliver." She turns around and goes inside, giving me a small wave as she closes her door and locks it. I head back to my apartment, wondering what the hell I got myself into with this girl. This isn't how I imagined senior year going, but fuck it.

Can you put solving a murder that happened on your campus on a resumé?

9

Friday, September 16th

THE PAST FEW DAYS have been a whirlwind.

First, I got yelled at for deciding to conduct my investigation when the girls caught me sneaking back into the apartment. Then, Hads made Grant sit Oliver down and tell him to stop investigating, to which I received an angry face emoji text from Oliver, so now I think he's mad I dragged him into this. Which I did *not* do—he showed up willingly. The girls tried to convince me to stop, but they conceded after two hours of arguing back and forth.

It's been five days since we searched the office, and I don't know about Oliver, but I have nothing. Oliver and I have been texting about it, but we haven't had time to sit and talk about anything—at least not out of earshot from other people. We have little time to breathe between classes, meetings, homework, and the investigation. The criminal justice club has also officially disbanded as well because of what happened. Professor Craig—our club chaperone—decided it was best because of everything going on.

At least now I have more time for other things, right?

Amelia and I had some time before our afternoon classes, so we decided to head to the library. I texted Oliver earlier and asked if he wanted to meet with us to discuss where to go next, but he hasn't responded yet. We're walking to the library when I decide to bring up tomorrow's plans.

"Are you excited about your birthday tomorrow?" I ask her.

"Not really." She sighs, and I feel bad. Amelia, like myself, has never been a big fan of her birthday. We both realized we hated celebrating it when we told each other we always cried on birthdays. But I'm determined to make tomorrow her best birthday yet.

"I know you're not a big fan, so I won't get huge balloons and blast *22* by Taylor Swift to wake you up. I promise." I adjust my tote bag before it falls off my shoulder, and she looks over and smiles at me.

"Thank you. I think having you and the girls around me tomorrow will be enough. I'm excited about whatever activities you three have planned."

"Twenty-two years old is a big deal, but I don't think we went too overboard."

"Good," she says to me while pulling open the door to the library. We're heading to our usual spot when some guy walks up to us, Amelia doesn't notice him, but I do. *Where have I seen this guy before?* He's got brown hair and eyes. He's tall as fuck—I'm pretty sure he's taller than Oliver *and* Grant. He's slightly lean but he still has some muscles to him.

"Amelia? I can't say I'm surprised to see you here," he says to her. Wait a minute. I *do* know this guy. It's weird not seeing him on my laptop screen. Amelia looks up, and her face twists while I feel mine light up.

"Is this *the* Henry I've heard so much about?" I offer him my hand. "We haven't officially met. I'm Paige Yarrow, and I must say that you're much cuter than on your Instagram."

"What?" He looks at me, confused, tilting his head.

"Nothing." I smile, hoping he didn't catch that I admitted to cyber-stalking him.

"She's joking. It was a joke," Amelia says quickly, and Henry stares between us. It's a bad sign if he can't handle the two of us, imagine if Ella and Hads were here.

"What are you guys up to?" he asks.

"We were discussing Amelia's birthday plans for tomorrow, and we're going to study!" I say while looking at Amelia, who is now rivaling Oliver in glares.

"Sorry, Amelia's what?" *Oh shit.* He didn't know. Amelia remains quiet, probably not wanting to pull on that thread, so I change the subject.

"So! Henry, I hear you are studying creative writing here. What's that like?"

"Wow, did Amelia tell you all this about me? I can't see her being the talkative type." He smiles and looks at the ground. Did Amelia tell me or did I find that out myself? I guess we'll never know.

"Yes, she mentioned it over the summer, I think during the few days she visited me." I played that off pretty well, and Amelia's glare lessens.

"That's nice. You guys seem rather close."

"Paige is one of my best friends, remember?" Amelia says to him as if he should know who I am. How much has she told him about us?

"Right, the one obsessed with true crime? Or the one who likes art museums?"

"True crime! That's me," I say with a giggle. I love that being obsessed with true crime is like my brand.

"Okay, so you're the one who Amelia will get to kill me when I irritate her. Got it. I hope I'm not already on your bad side," he says, feigning a smile. He has a nice smile. Amelia really downplayed this guy.

"Not at all! Amelia, how often do you threaten this poor guy? I promise not to waterboard you or do anything Amelia said I could do."

"I don't threaten him often! I hate this conversation," Ames says while crossing her arms.

Henry leans closer to me. "At least twice a day—once in person and once over text."

"That sounds about right. So, where is home for you, Hen? Can I call you that?" I ask him, knowing some people hate nicknames.

"That's fine by me. Well, I grew up—" His sentence is interrupted by Oliver bursting through the little circle we created in the library lobby. He grabs my arm and pulls me a few feet from where Henry and Amelia stand. He leans down to my ear and whispers so they can't hear.

"We need to talk. I found something." His voice is low, and it's giving me goosebumps.

"Fine, let's go outside," I say to him while looking down at his outfit. "You choose *now* to wear all black?" He scoffs at me, and I turn back to excuse myself from the conversation I was having politely, but Oliver starts to walk away and I have no choice but to follow him.

"It was nice to meet you in person, Henry! See you, Ames!" I talk loudly and get stares from people trying to study in the library. I feel bad for yelling, but it dissipates as soon as we exit the library. We're now walking toward where a few picnic tables are outside, and neither of us has said a word.

"Who was that you were talking to?" he asks me, a hint of something in his voice.

"That was my friend Amelia. You know her, Oliver. She's friends with your sister."

"The guy, Paige." *Still with the weird tone...*

"Oh, that's Amelia's boyfriend." He stops walking and turns to me.

"Amelia has a boyfriend?" He sounds a bit shocked, and I can't help but giggle.

"Well, no. Not yet, but he's going to be her boyfriend eventually. I can feel it."

"For someone who hasn't been in a relationship the entire duration of her college life, you sure seem to love rooting for others," he says to me while sitting down at the table.

"Are you keeping track of my relationship status now, Baker?" I ask him with my arm against the table.

"Just sit down, Yarrow."

"Fine, but can you tell me why we're out here? You know we have class in an hour. Why couldn't we do this then?"

"I know, but I figured on the down low means not discussing it within earshot of our classmates. I found some interesting stuff about the dean I wanted to tell you," he says while opening up his notebook and I see a bunch of things scribbled down.

"You wrote it down? Have you heard of a shared document online? That would be much easier," I say as he passes it over to me.

"Yes, I have. Can you read it please?" I look down and start reading. There's a lot of information here, and I'm trying to digest it. After around ten minutes of reading, I look at him dumbfounded.

"His son has been missing for five years?" I wonder how he was able to continue on with his life and job knowing his son could be out there somewhere—possibly alive.

"The police think he was kidnapped. The dean was loading groceries into his car and when he looked up, his son was gone. The cops and his family looked around the surrounding areas for weeks. The case went cold after a year of searching."

"Should we start calling him by his name? It feels odd still calling him by a title, and not his name," I ask, ignoring everything he said.

"It feels even weirder calling him Erik, but you can do whatever you want. He's not around to correct you," Oliver says. "In his office the other day, some files had missing children posters. I think he was still looking into the kidnapping. It seems like his family hasn't let it go, which makes sense."

"So, you think his murder is due to his son getting kidnapped five years ago?" I ask.

"It could be connected, but I don't know how."

"Well, that's for us to figure out. We should start trying to get a meeting with the professor he saw before his death, and maybe we should dig a little deeper into his son. Those seem like two solid leads." I smile, finally happy we have something to go on.

"Sounds good," he says, still in that same Oliver facial expression. He stares at me for a beat too long, and then abruptly stands up and grabs his bag. "We have class. Let's go."

I grab my tote bag and join him in walking toward our building. "By the way, would you consider us walking to class together, or us separately walking to the same class standing side by side?" I'm making fun of him, and he shoves me over a bit. He smiles for a second but it disappears when I look over at him.

Was that a dimple I saw?

Partners in crime, the two of us.

WE WALK INTO OUR class and sit at our usual table. Oliver and I have sat next to each other since freshman year because we've had the same classes together. It's almost like an unsaid tradition between us that we sit next to or near one another.

He's also one of the only people I talk to in our major of study, and I don't care to branch out to others in our classes. I have Oliver and that's enough for me. I plop my bag down underneath the table, and Oliver does the same. I always let him have the spot closest to the wall because I know he prefers it.

Our professor comes in and gets the presentation geared up. He is a new adjunct this semester. His last name is Kennedy—like the president. He clears his throat before speaking.

"I know everyone on campus is talking about the unfortunate circumstance that happened a few days ago, but I'll be using it as an example of what not to do when conducting an investigation. I have some crime scene photos from the office. Does anyone have a problem with that?"

Wait. What did he say? Oliver elbows me, silently telling me to speak up, but I'm frozen again. Is he going to show pictures the police took of his dead body? This can't be allowed. How is this allowed? My breathing starts to pick up when I see the first slide showing the blood on the carpet and how the investigators aren't wearing shoe covers. Our professor starts talking, but my hearing has blurred and my vision is starting to go with it.

I need to get out of here before I make a scene. The police kept Oliver and I's names hidden from the record so we didn't get mobbed at school when everyone found out we were the ones to find his body. The media only said it was a student who had discovered the body. If I freak out, people might start to ask questions. I can't seem to make my legs work to be able to leave. I've never had a panic attack in class, and I have no idea what to do, so I grab my tote and speed walk out of the room.

I walk down the hallway toward the bathrooms and hope my legs can make it there before I collapse. I'm trying to go through my usual routine to regain my breathing, but my mind can't focus on anything. All I see in my head is the body, and I'm right back to where I was a week ago in his office.

I yank open the bathroom door and thank goodness nobody's in here. I try to make it to one of the two stalls, but my legs give out and I slide down to the floor. I'm counting from one to five in my head and putting all my fingers to my thumb as I do that, but nothing works. I try to reach for my water bottle but can't get enough air to take a sip. I hear the door open, and I don't even care that some random person is about to see me in this state. I just want to get out of it and be normal again. Someone leans down and looks at me. *I recognize those eyes.*

It's Oliver.

He grabs my hand and puts two of my fingers on the pulse in his neck. "Just feel my pulse, Paige. Concentrate on that," he whispers, and I suddenly feel horrible that he keeps having to see me like this. He probably hates having to help me out of these. I know it can be a lot—even I hate dealing with myself sometimes during these.

"I'm...f-fine..." I say, trying my best to concentrate on his pulse.

"Shhh. Just close your eyes and focus on my pulse." I listen and close my eyes. I hear the door open, and I feel Oliver get up and shove it closed. "Out of order."

He returns to where I'm sitting and rests my fingers on his neck. I notice how soft his skin is. I notice how comfortable I feel with him on the floor of this bathroom, right now. We sit silently for a few minutes, my fingers on his neck, and my breathing eventually returns to normal. I open my eyes, and we're face to face, staring at each other.

"Thank you. I'm sorry you have to keep helping me when I get like this," I say to him.

He rubs his chin and touches his mouth, as if annoyed. He turns his head. "You have nothing to apologize for, Paige."

"Well, I—"

"I don't mind helping you down from one of those."

"Oh. Okay. I'm sorry," I say, and he glares at me. "I'll stop apologizing."

"Are you okay?" he asks me, and I don't know how to answer that, so I shrug. "It's unfair what that professor did. Insensitive too."

"Yeah. It is." We both sit there quietly, and when I feel good enough to stand, I do.

"Where are you going?" he asks me.

"Back to class? Care to join me?"

"I told the professor you had food poisoning," he tells me.

"What? Why would you do that?"

"I figured you wouldn't want to sit through a class after a panic attack. Let's go. I'll walk you home," he says while grabbing my hand, not my arm this time, and leading me out of the bathroom.

Us holding hands feels like the most natural thing in the world, and my arm tingles at the contact. We've only touched in a joking or accidental way, but this time, it feels different.

A few seconds later, we both look down and let go of one another. I rub my hands on my leggings because they're suddenly very sweaty, and he continues walking down the hallway toward the staircase. I join his side as we walk out of the building and toward our apartments.

10

Friday, September 16th

PAIGE HAS HAD TWO panic attacks in five days, and I don't know how concerned I *should* be, but I'm pretty fucking concerned. She's not okay, but she won't admit it.

I hate to say I know how she feels because most of my life after Mia died, I blocked out everything I was feeling by running ten goddamn miles a day. Therapy eventually helped a lot more than shoving all my feelings down, but I can't help Paige until she tells me what's wrong. And I know she won't do that because she doesn't want me to worry about her.

It's too late for that to happen.

When our professor mentioned the case in class, I looked over at her and she was pale and sweaty. I followed her to the bathroom a few seconds after she left and helped her the best I could. I looked up how to help people with panic attacks on Google the other day, so I used one technique that worked well with Paige.

I must say, walking into that bathroom and seeing her falling apart on the floor cracked me open a bit. She presents herself as this happy girl when she's the complete fucking opposite on the inside. I wish she knew she didn't have to hide from me, and I wish she would stop fucking apologizing all the time. Does she know she's a real person with feelings?

I'm walking her back to her place, and it's a pretty warm day out. I can hear the birds singing and shit. I want to say something to her, but I don't know what. It's weird, I usually hate small talk and dumb conversations to fill random gaps, but I want to make small talk with Paige. I want to hear what's going on inside her head.

"Have you always had panic attacks or has our situation made them worse?" I ask her.

"I've had them since I was a kid, and certain things can trigger them. It depends on the situation, but they've been worse than normal lately." Her shoulders droop inward, and I decide to drop the subject.

"So, have you made the murder board yet?" I ask her, and her eyes light up.

"I didn't, but I have some stuff printed out and sticky notes all over my room. We haven't had many leads, so nothing is put together yet."

"Do you want help with it?" I ask, and she looks surprised.

"That depends. Are you offering?"

"Yes."

"Then yes, I would love your help. Plus, I need you to translate your writing for me. It's illegible. The day you start using a computer for notes is the day I celebrate knowing you've given up your Stone Age techniques."

"It's not the stone age. It's my preference. Like yours is smashing your fucking keyboard in every time you type." Paige's typing should come with a jump scare warning. She's the most aggressive typer I know, including my sister who types like she's running a marathon.

"I don't *smash* my keyboard. The professors talk too fast, and my hands can't keep up sometimes!" she exclaims while smiling. *I'm glad to see that back on her face.*

She unlocks her door, and I take in her apartment this time. Last time—the first time I was here—I didn't have time to look around. It looks like a normal apartment with Paige and Amelia splashed everywhere. Those two scare me sometimes. Honestly, all the girls do, including my sister. Amelia scares me the most because I can never tell what's happening in her head.

"You can set your stuff wherever. Do you want something to drink?" she asks me, setting her tote bag on the table.

"I'm okay."

"The board is in my room. We just have to put all the printouts on it. I have glue and tape too." She smiles and heads toward her door. The last time I was in Paige's room, all I saw was her. I didn't look around. I didn't fucking care about anything else but making sure she was okay. I look around now, and there are lots of books scattered everywhere on her shelves. There are a bunch of pictures of all the girls on her desk. I think my favorite part of her room is her bedside table. Four copies of what I assume is her favorite book reside on it, along with some gold rings scattered on a leaf plate and her water bottle on a coaster. It's very Paige.

"So, this is the board and all the stuff I printed out." She unfolds this trifold poster board and slams a thick stack of papers on the floor.

"Are we doing this on the floor?"

"Yes. We can spread papers on my bed and stuff if we run out of room. Plus, I like the floor. It's comfy."

"I've noticed," I say to her while flipping through some of the information she printed out. It's all stuff about the murder with different news articles that detail what the police know so far. She even has some snippets of security footage.

"How did you get these?"

"A friend," she says with a smile.

"Who? You have four friends and none of them have the skills to hack a security camera." She looks confused after I say that. I can tell in her head that she is counting the four people.

"Amelia, Hads, and Ella are only three people and you don't know Alissa, so who else are you talking about?" She smiles at me.

Seriously? "We're friends," I say to her.

"We are?" *Why did her whole face light up?*

"Yes. Do you not consider us friends?" I ask her, almost not wanting to hear her answer.

"No, *I* do. It's just nice to hear *you* admit it."

"Well, none of my other friends have ever dragged me into a murder investigation."

"Well, you decided to show up! I don't want to talk about this anymore. It was my friend Alissa. She's good with computer stuff. Take those and categorize them, please," she tells me as she sinks to the floor, grabs some tape, and starts sifting through her pile of papers. I sit down, and we organize in silence. We trade looks as we organize the piles according to different things. It's so natural for us. It takes me back to the exact moment I first felt something for Paige.

It was finals week of fall semester—our junior year. She came into class, it was a December morning, and it was freezing. Her blonde hair was stuffed into a hat, and her coat was covered in snowflakes. She had mittens on—they were black. She sat down and noticed that my hands were purple because of how cold it was, so she rubbed my hands in between hers with her mittens and warmed them up.

That small gesture by Paige made my heart flutter for the first time in a while.

She tapes all the stuff on there, and we do this for about an hour before we hear her front door open hard, and she flinches where she sits.

"Are you expecting Amelia soon?" I ask her.

"I assumed she was with Henry for the rest of the day. She doesn't have any more classes today."

"Wait here," I say to her. I reach into my pocket and take out my pocket knife.

"Where did that come from?"

"Paige, get behind me," I say and I'm about to open her door when it swings open and startles me a little. Amelia stands in the doorway and scooches back a bit when she sees me holding my pocket knife.

"What the fuck you guys?"

"Sorry," I say to her as I close my knife and put it back in my pocket.

"You two have barely started the investigation, and you're *already* paranoid?" She looks over at Paige. "This is why we told you to stay away from it."

"Amelia, it's fine. I wasn't expecting you back so soon. I thought you were with Hen."

"First of all, stop calling him that." Amelia rolls her eyes. "Second of all, why aren't you two in class?"

"Our professor pulled up crime scene photos of the dean, and I had a panic attack and left. Oliver followed me and calmed me down and we decided to make a murder board instead of going back to class," Paige tells her.

"A murd— You know what, I don't want to know. But you," she points at me, "get out. I want to spend some time with Paige," she tells me while shoving me out of Paige's room and shutting the door. I'm now standing in their living room alone. I can hear Paige and Amelia talking through the door, but I can't make out what they're saying.

"Sorry, we can continue this another day. I'll text you?" she says. "Also, don't take Amelia too seriously, she likes making fun of you."

"I bet," I say to her and she walks me out. I grab my bag from where I set it when Amelia comes out of Paige's room.

"He should start paying rent or something for how much he is over here." Amelia chuckles.

"It's only his second time here!" Paige says to her.

"For Oliver, that's like a thousand. Bye!" she says to us as she goes to sit on their couch.

"I guess I'll see you soon," I say to Paige, and she smiles at me. The next thing I know, I'm standing on the sidewalk, unable to get my legs moving toward my place. I shake the feeling of not wanting to leave and force myself to move.

11

Saturday, September 17th

I WAKE UP AT five a.m., throw my running clothes on, grab my head-phones, and head out the door for my usual run before I meet my sister for our walk. I throw my playlist on and I'm on my way—simple and easy. I never used to like running, but after the accident, my therapist suggested it to clear my head. I thought it was a bunch of bullshit until I tried it and it worked. I used to run a few miles a day, but now I try to run a few times a week. I tend to do it early in the morning because nobody bothers me and it's more peaceful with less people around.

After the accident, my family didn't know what to do with me, and I didn't know what to do with myself. Therapy helped a little but it didn't erase my pain, so I tried to channel that into other things like working out and shit. It didn't help me go back to who I was—I'm sure I can't—but it did help me realize what was most important in my life, which is my family and my well-being. So now I go running, and I focus more on myself. I have a few friends, but I make a point not to get too attached to people in the long run because it's easier than having them ripped away from me at some point.

I don't know how to put my feelings for Paige into words, but they exist and I certainly care about her. There's nothing wrong with that, right? No. We're friends, Paige said so herself yesterday.

I run about three miles before swinging by our usual meeting spot on campus. I see my sister sitting there, and I silently run up to her, taking my headphones out as I get closer.

"You're late." She looks pissed. This is going to be fun.

"I got a slow start this morning," I say to her as we start walking our regular route. We usually walk around a mile in a big circle around campus. The air around my sister feels more tense than usual, and I don't want to mention it, so I stay quiet.

"How's Paige been lately?" *And there it is.*

"Why are you asking me? You're around her more than I am," I say to her.

"Not lately. With the investigation, you spend more time with her than I do." She shoots me a look.

"Do you have something to say to me? Spit it out, Hads." That came out harsher than intended, but I hate when people skate around the true thing they want to say.

"You're not allowed to date my friends!" she yells at me.

"I never said I wanted to!" I yell back at her.

"Oliver, I'm serious. You're my brother, and they're my friends. There is a huge line and it's one you shouldn't cross or I'll make Grant deal with you."

"I would love to see him try. Plus, I'd hate to mess up pretty boy's hair." I mean that as a compliment. He has nice hair, but I'd never say that to him.

"Pretty boy? Really? That's my thing." I shrug at her, and she stares at me coldly. "Oliver, promise me you won't do anything stupid with Paige."

"I won't."

"Good."

"To be fair, I did befriend her before you."

"You're going to play that card?"

"Yes."

"You're ridiculous." She shakes her head at me.

"Yup," I agree, and we continue walking silently for about five minutes. There has been a question at the back of my mind ever since the blowup at Paige's apartment after she found the body. "Do you know anything about Paige's past? That one sentence Amelia said at their apartment that day stuck with me."

She looks over at me, her gaze softening. "It stuck with me too, but Paige has never talked about it. She mentioned briefly once last semester that her home life was never great and how she felt left behind as a kid, but that's it. I think Amelia knows more having been Paige's roommate all this time. I assume Paige will come to Ella and me when she's ready to talk about it. I never want to push about these things."

That makes sense. Hads was never one to force people to open up. She's the type of friend who's there for someone when they need her. I've always admired her for that—I was never good at comforting people. "Gotcha."

"Why did you want to know?" she asks me.

"I was just wondering."

"Are you sure?"

"Yes, Hads, drop it. I heard you earlier—no dating your friends."

"Good. Now, are you ready to open up to me or what?" she asks me this almost every time we hang out.

"Not a chance," I tell her.

"Well, it was worth a shot." We walk a bit more and talk about Grant and a bunch of other random shit to fill the time up. When we get back to the bench, she sits down, and I join her in watching the sunrise.

"How are you doing with therapy? I realize I've been so wrapped up in my own shit I forgot to check in on you. Has everything been okay?" I ask her. My sister has been going to therapy three times a month because of what happened last semester and in high school.

"It's been good, actually. I never thought talking through my feelings could help, but it has. Grant and Ella take me to my appointments, and I appreciate their comfort." She smiles when she says his name. Way back when they were figuring things out, I overheard him stand up for my sister when he was talking to that asshole Ryan. I confronted Grant about it, and we talked. I knew he was a good guy as soon as I heard what he was saying about Hads. I like to think I'm the reason he got his shit together, but I would never tell my sister that. She would get mad at me. After that, I went to The Hidden Bear—a bar near campus—and sat there. I've never told my sister any of this because I'm unsure of how to explain to her why I go to a bar once a year when I don't drink alcohol.

"I'm glad, Hads. You deserve to be happy," I tell her.

"You do too." She stops herself from saying more.

"Just not with your friends, yeah, I know," I say to her.

She smiles at me, and her phone starts ringing. "It's Grant. We're going on a coffee date with Ella before celebrating Amelia's birthday. Do you want to join us?"

"No. I'm staying away from coffee for a while. I don't like the taste anymore," I tell her.

"Wow, first alcohol and now coffee."

"Yeah, well…" I trail off, not finishing my sentence.

"I know. I'll see you soon?"

"Sounds good," I say to her. I watch my sister walk back to her place, and I don't get up quite yet. I continue watching the sunrise over the horizon. I hate the fact that I lied to my sister, but if she knew how I really felt, I would be fucked.

I want to know everything about Paige. I want to make her laugh and smile so hard that her cheeks hurt.

That's just friendship, though. *Right?*

A FEW HOURS LATER, I find myself migrating down the stairs of my building and knocking on Grant's door. I don't know why I'm down here, but there has been a question itching in the back of my mind. Grant seems like the best person to answer it, so here I am.

"Good afternoon, old sport. How can I help you?"

"Can I come in?" I ask. I know my sister isn't here because she's off gallivanting around some apple orchard with the girls. From what I've seen online, it looks like they're having fun, so I know I have a few hours before they get back. Honestly, I'll only need ten minutes for this conversation, but you never know with pretty boy over here. Grant is a fucking chatterbox.

"Uh, sure."

"Why do you sound so surprised?"

"Well, I know we bonded a lot over the summer but something about your face is screaming serious conversation, and I feel like I should mark this on my calendar."

"It's not so monumental," I say as I stand in the middle of his apartment. It's the same layout as mine, but more decorative. You can tell my sister helped with some of it because I see charts everywhere.

"You coming to me for anything is monumental," he says while sitting on his couch. "So, how can I be of assistance? Do you need a pep talk? A nice book quote to get your spirits up? How about a pro and con list for whatever dilemma you're going through." The guy smirks at me, and I can tell he's enjoying this. But damn, my sister really did a number on him, it's kind of cute, I guess.

"None of that. I just had a question." I rub my hand down my face because I'm so fucking nervous to ask him this right now. *What is wrong with me?*

"You came all the way down here because you had a question for me?" He puts his hand to his chest. "Oliver, I'm touched, truly."

"I regret not just texting you about this."

"Well, it's too late to back out now." He motions to the seat beside him on the couch. "Have a seat, bro."

I sigh heavily before succumbing to his offer and firmly planting myself as far as I can from him on the couch. I don't exactly know how to start this, so I blurt it out. "How did you know you had feelings for my sister?" He doesn't immediately answer, which is odd considering Grant *always* has something to say. I look over at him and his face is blank. *Did I catch him off guard?*

"Why are you asking? Is this some sort of trick question? Are you going to punch me after I tell you? If that's the case, I'm keeping my mouth shut."

"No, Grant. I'm genuinely asking."

"Well, right when I ran into her, I felt something. It's pretty typical of me to fall fast and hard, but I knew I couldn't do that—Hads was too guarded. I had to take it slow, and I *wanted* to take it slow with her because as soon as I saw her, she felt different than my past relationships."

"Oh, so contrary to popular belief you didn't fall madly in love with my sister one random afternoon." I'm deflecting from my actual feelings by making fun of him, but he's making sense. I always thought love wasn't gradual—it never was like that with Mia. I saw her in the hallway at school and my chest practically exploded. But maybe love can be slow, maybe it can be quiet and sneak up on you when you least expect it.

"No, Ol. I didn't. I fell in love with Hads over the small things. Like the way she looks at flashcards like they're the greatest things ever created. The way she charts out every fucking thing because she wants all of her stuff to be organized. The way she always slips some sort of note into my bookbag at random times because she wants me to know that she's thinking of me. Or she wants me to know that it's okay to fail, as long as I get back up. I fell in love with Hads over every small thing she does, because those are the things I miss most when she's not around. Sure the big stuff, like the milestones and the trips, are great, but it's the little things that make me fall deeper every day." Wow. That was surprisingly profound. *I never knew the kid had it in him.*

"Now that I've poured my heart out to you on a random Saturday afternoon, I get a question now." He smiles over at me. "Why did you want to know?" There's some sort of gleam in his eyes, and part of me doesn't want to say anything. But I know he'll badger me about this, so I'm going to be vague as hell. Even I don't quite know how to go about these feelings I'm having, and adding Grant into the mix would be a giant mistake.

"Just curious," I say as I try to get up, but he pulls my arm back down and I'm back where I started.

"You don't get curious. Is Oliver Baker having romantic feelings for someone, or have pigs finally started to fly?"

"No pigs yet, you'll have to wait a few hundred years." I smirk at him, and try to get up again—the motherfucker stiff-arms me.

"Oliver, I didn't realize you had it in you to fall in love with someone. Is it that barista from back home that was flirting with you all summer?"

"What? No! What the— She was not *flirting* with me." *Is he serious?*

"She totally was. Hads and I had a bet going to see how long it would take you to say more than a few words to her. It was hilarious. Didn't you wonder why we were always laughing when we got coffee at that place?"

"Good God, it's *not* her. It's nobody, okay? It was just a question. Now, pretend I was never here." I stand up again and this time he lets me, but as I make my way to the door, something Grant says stops me in my tracks.

"It's Paige, isn't it?"

I don't turn around to face him before I speak again. "No. It's not." I pull his front door open and I get the hell out of there as fast as I can.

It's only when I'm back at my apartment that I feel bad about lying to him. Grant and I got closer over the summer, and as much as I detest him sometimes, he's been a good friend to me and a great boyfriend to my sister. But until I figure my own shit out, nobody else can know about it.

What Grant told me earlier hasn't left my mind, but all I know is that I've found myself in a situation that I haven't been in for a while.

I have feelings for someone and I don't know what the fuck to do about it.

12

Saturday, September 17th

Today was the most fun I have ever had. We celebrated Amelia's birthday, and it was beautiful. All the girls went to brunch before we went to an orchard and picked apples. It was my first time doing something like this and it was super fun. Then we came back to campus and gave Ames her gifts. She *almost* cried, and I ended up shedding some tears because Hads got us all matching necklaces and I could finally stop holding onto that secret. I'm the *worst* at keeping secrets—I tend to blab—but I kept this one!

The necklaces say GM4L—which stands for Grand Mountain For Life. I've never had friendships where matching jewelry is a thing, but now I do, which is exactly why I cried earlier.

The four of us ate dinner together and Amelia forced us all to watch a National Geographic documentary after we ate. We chatted for a bit after, played some board games, and had some drinks before we called it a night. Overall, today is one of those days I'm going to remember forever. These moments with the four of us are always so special to me, and I love having good days like this since I haven't had many growing up.

Since they left, I've been staring at my ceiling trying to sleep, but not trying *that* hard because I don't want to have another nightmare. They've been happening a lot more lately and I feel horrible because Amelia had to calm me down the other night from how badly I was screaming.

So, I'm staring at my ceiling. I don't have anything to do tomorrow, so I could technically stay up all night, but I'm exhausted. I need to sleep, but I can't—not when I relive certain things I wish I could forget.

I could text Amelia and see if she's awake, but she might be talking to Henry and I don't want to interrupt them. *Maybe Ella's awake?* No, she has work tomorrow. Hads always falls asleep early, so she's out. I could text Oliver, but I don't think he would want to talk to me this late. I pick up my phone anyway.

Paige: Hi!

No, delete that's too aggressive for how late it is.

Paige: Hey, are you awake?

I decide to send that one. I also text Ella just in case, but if neither of them answers me, I think I'll take some Melatonin and—

My phone buzzes.

Oliver: Yeah.

Oliver: Can't sleep?

Paige: I don't know if I know how to anymore.

Oliver: Do you want to meet me somewhere?

Paige: Are you trying to kidnap me? I'm smart enough not to go to a secondary location. Everyone knows that's how they get you!

Oliver:

Paige: I was trying to be funny.

Oliver: Kidnapping is not funny.

Paige: You're right.

Oliver: Meet me outside of the criminal justice building.

Paige: Why?

Oliver: Paige.

Paige: I'm on my way.

I hop out of bed and look down at what I'm wearing—black sweatpants and a loose-fitting yellow t-shirt. I grab a fuzzy jacket and throw a bra before I shove my phone into one of my pockets. I slowly open my door and tiptoe through the living room as quietly as I can before I ruin it by tripping over something on our front porch.

So much for trying to be quiet. How did something as simple as flowers in a vase make so much noise? But also, why are there flowers on the porch so late at night?

I grab them—spray roses—and bring them to our kitchen table. The card has Amelia's name on it, and I start to laugh. I absolutely know who sent these. Wanting to see Amelia's face when she sees them, I knock on her door three times. She opens it and stares at me.

"Why are you awake?"

"Were you asleep at a normal time for once?" I ask her, still smiling.

"Yes. It was a long, emotional day. I needed sleep, and why does your face look like that?"

I shrug.

"Paige...please tell me you didn't get a singing telegram or something. It's not even my birthday anymore."

"There's something for you in the kitchen," I say with a laugh.

"Please tell me you didn't build a bomb because you were bored."

"Why do you assume a bomb? I only looked it up that one time because I was curious!" It's a lot easier than I thought, but I would never *build* one. I was simply curious about it.

"I never know with you."

"That tracks," I say. I move out of the way so she can slip past me. She's wearing her new pajama set Hads got her for her birthday, and it looks super comfortable. The silk brushes against my arm as Ames moves past me and heads for the table. As soon as she sees what's on the counter, her eyes widen in surprise.

"Are these from you?" she asks me.

"No." I have to hold down another laugh. This is *too* good.

"Paige, stop looking at me like that."

"This is my normal face," I say to her.

"No, it's your making a big deal out of nothing face."

"These are from Henry, aren't they? I think him sending you *flowers* on your birthday is very telling behavior. Maybe we should dive—" She slaps my arm.

"How did you find these if they were on the porch? Were *you* leaving the apartment?"

I'm totally busted. "No, I was just going for a walk," I lie.

"A walk?"

"Yes," I say.

"At midnight?" I know she doesn't believe my bullshit.

"Yes." We're silent for a few seconds as we stare each other down. One of us has to break first, and it's always me. "Fine. I was going to meet Oliver somewhere. I couldn't sleep, so I texted him."

"Oliver? Huh, interesting." Is she reversing this around to me? She's the one who got flowers sent from her boyfriend, that's not her boyfriend!

"Stop deflecting! You're the one with the flowers!"

"It's interesting how much time you two are spending together lately..."

"We're solving a murder, Amelia!"

"It's just an observation, Paige!"

I cross my arms at her. "I don't appreciate your tone."

Now she's laughing at me. "Okay, I'll stop insinuating things if you stop pushing me about Henry." She holds out her hand for me to shake and I let it hang there.

"The situations are entirely different. I don't see how that's fair."

"It sounds fair to me."

"Fine!" I reach out and shake her hand. I should put a keystroke logger on her phone to see what she types to Henry. I need a warrant for that, so

I can't legally do that. I might have to get creative in the future if I want to find out what's going on between them.

"Good. Well, enjoy your walk," she teases and I shoot her a look. "You're not scary, Paige." She starts going over to the coffee maker and turns it on.

"You're not going back to bed?"

"I'm already awake. I might as well stay up now."

"That doesn't make sense."

"It does to me," she says while grabbing a mug.

"That's all that matters, I guess. I'll see you later," I say as I walk to the front door.

"Tell Oliver that Hads and I say hi!"

I take a deep breath and close the door behind me. Criminal justice building, here I come.

It takes me around six minutes to walk to the building, and I don't see Oliver anywhere. I'm starting to get nervous. I'm not a massive fan of the dark, and being alone isn't helping. *Maybe this wasn't the best idea.* I should've just gone to sleep and risked a nightmare rather than distract myself. My brain is all over the place, right now. I need to stop second-guessing all my friendships. I have a hard time believing I'm worth it sometimes—being called worthless for most of your childhood will do that to you. I'm too in my head to notice the door opening, and Oliver grabs my arm and pulls me inside. All the lights are off, and it looks creepy in here.

"Why do you keep doing that?" I ask him.

"It's fun." He smiles.

"I assumed your only version of fun was glaring at annoying people." His mouth slightly turns up.

"Good one. Let's go." He grabs my arm again, slightly lower than the first time, and walks me to the staircase. "Can you handle a few flights of stairs?"

"I'm not going to take offense to that, but yes, I can." We head up the stairs, and he leads me all the way to the roof. Oh God, he's not going to push me off, is he?

"No, Paige, I'm not going to push you off the roof. What the fuck?"

I may have said that last part out loud. "Sorry."

"Paige."

"Right. Nothing to apologize for. Got it. Sor—I'll shut up now," I say as he opens the door onto the roof. It looks like, well, a roof. It's got a bunch of metal boxes, which I'm assuming are heating and cooling systems, but other than that it's boring. He leads me over to one corner of it, and I notice a blanket and a folding chair with a cooler and some snacks. "What's all this?"

"I brought it," he says.

"Why?"

"I always bring it when I come here at night."

"How often do you come up here?" I ask him.

"A few times a week."

"Is there a reason?" I ask as I sit down on the blanket across from him. We're surprisingly close right now, and I feel weird. The air seems different up here. Maybe it's the lack of oxygen from being up so high?

"I come up here when I need to clear my head and don't want to go running."

"Oh. That's nice. It's a good view." I look over at him, but he's already looking at me.

"Yeah, it is." He's still looking at me and my stomach drops. *Change the subject, Paige.*

"Were you up here when I texted you?"

"I was." He turns his head, no longer looking at me.

"Oh, so you couldn't sleep tonight either?" I ask him.

"I didn't bring you up here to discuss *my* sleeping habits." He looks at me again, silently saying he wants me to explain why I texted him. Reading Oliver is fairly easy for me—I can usually tell what he's saying even when he's not talking.

"I just couldn't sleep," I say to him.

"Any reason behind that?" he asks, opening a bag of popcorn and handing it to me. I don't want to tell him every detail about my nightmares being memories from my past and how sometimes I don't sleep for days to avoid them, so I stay on the surface.

"I haven't been sleeping well lately. I'm not sure why."

"Is it because of the investigation?" It's a valid question. I've never thought about it from that angle before.

"I'm not sure," I say to him. "I talked to my therapist about finding a dead body, and it helped to get that off my shoulders a bit."

"Paige, we can stop you know," he tells me. Does he want to stop investigating this? *I knew he didn't want to do this with me.*

"Oliver, if you want to tap out of this, you can. I'm going to see this through." It comes out sharper than I wanted, but Oliver doesn't seem fazed.

"I don't want to, but we can stop if it's too much for you. We aren't that far into it yet." I put some popcorn into my mouth to avoid how weird I feel about this—being here with Oliver on the roof. It's unraveling me a bit. It's making me want to be vulnerable with him, but I can't.

"It's not too much. I want to keep going and see this all the way through," I say, lowering my head and looking into my lap.

"Paige, you don't have to prove yourself to anyone else."

"I'm trying to prove it to myself," I say a bit louder. I don't quite know where that came from. It slipped out before I could stop it.

"Why?" he asks in the same tone.

"Because I need to prove to myself that I can do this. That I'm worth *something* other than just existing."

"Paige, you don't need to do that. You're enough just by being you. No unofficial investigation will make you believe that about yourself. You just have to know that, okay?" He reaches over and puts his hand where mine rests on the blanket. It's sweet, but he pulls away after a few seconds. I look over at him and he's staring forward, not saying another word. I suddenly want to change the subject. It's too deep for how late at night it is and I don't want to get into this right now.

"Hads always called you grumpy when I first met her." He looks over at me and raises his brow. "I knew you first, but when I met Hads, she always told stories about her grumpy older brother who she loved so much. It was sweet, but then she told me it was you, and I was surprised."

"You were surprised?"

"I was."

"Care to elaborate on that? Most people describe me as such." The way he's looking at me is making me nervous, but I continue.

"Well, I guess you can be a bit prickly sometimes but isn't everyone to some extent?"

"Not you," he tells me.

"Even I have bad days, but I would describe you more as grumpy-adjacent. Or..." I trail off and think about my words. In my time around Oliver, I've always found him to be misunderstood by everyone else, and I think it's time he knows that. "You remind me of the moon."

"The moon? You mean the planetary mass that orbits the Earth?" He's laughing a bit.

"Yes, and stop laughing. I'm serious," I say while smacking his arm.

"Okay, fine. Explain then."

"Everyone goes through phases of life—like the moon—but the moon is misunderstood by most, like you. It has its dark side, but when it's up in the sky and shining like it is, people want to take pictures of it and look at it. It's always around during the day, but people only want to look at it at night when it's glowing. It's stupid, but it reminds me of you. You put up this front all day, but with the people you care about you have this other beautiful, light side."

"A *light* side?" He quirks his eyebrow at me. "I doubt that."

"No, Oliver, I'm serious. Look at how you treat Hads. She told me when Kyle broke her heart, you flew home to comfort her for three days. If that doesn't prove that you have that side to yourself then I don't know what will. The beauty of the moon is unreachable from all the way down here on Earth. That's what makes space and its beauty so special."

"Is that what you think? I'm unreachable?" His voice is a low whisper. I thought I imagined him saying that.

"That's all you got from what I said?" I say while looking up at him. "Look at it," I say, pointing to where it sits in the sky. "The moon glows using light from the sun. It's like they chase each other in the sky from night to day, only to just miss one another every time."

"Well, if I'm the moon, would that make you the sun?" he asks me, and I freeze up a bit.

"I'm not the sun," I say, awkwardly giggling to avoid the weird feeling that won't leave my stomach. I turn to look at him, and once again, he's already looking at me.

"You are to me." It's like he's looking into my soul right now. My heart is beating so fast I think it might explode.

"No, I'm not," I whisper. "Maybe on the outside I am—it's how I present myself to the world." I pause, unsure of if I want to pour my feelings out right now on this roof. *What is it about late nights and good company that get your guard down so much?* "On the inside, I feel like a thunderstorm. I show the world this happy version of myself because I'm faking it until I eventually make it to that happy person inside and out. So yeah, I might seem like the sun to you and everyone else, but to me, I'll always be a girl who's scared to show people who I really am."

"You don't have to pretend around me, Paige. You can be whoever you want to be on this roof. I sure as hell am no ray of sunshine. The only thing I seem to be good at is being cold and miserable."

"You're not miserable. You're the moon, remember?" He smirks over at me and there's that dimple I saw the other day. *How am I noticing that after four years?* He only has one, but the glimpse I saw of it makes me want to make him smile more so I can see it again.

"And you're the sun." I start to open my mouth to respond but he cuts me off before I can. "Paige, you might be covered by some clouds lately—especially with everything going on—but that doesn't mean you can't come out from behind them and shine again. If I know you, the *real* you, then you'll be okay. That shine will come back, it might just take some time."

"What if I don't know how to get it back? What if I don't know if I ever had it in the first place?" Sometimes when I think too hard, I wonder if I ever had it at all. I was sad as a kid, and I always had one goal—to stay alive. I even struggled with that sometimes, so I faked a smile for most of my life until it became second nature.

"Thunderstorms pass, Paige. The sun always comes back out." We sit and stare at each other for what seems like hours, but in reality it was only a few seconds. What is it about him that makes time feel so fast? "I told my sister I didn't care about you yesterday."

The quick change of our conversation is going to give me whiplash. "Oh. That's nice." I shove down the emotions that are bubbling up.

"I lied," he tells me while touching his mouth and chin again. *Is he nervous?*

"What?" I whisper, feeling nervous all of a sudden. He scooches closer to me.

"I lied to my sister," he says, his voice sounding deeper than before.

"Why?"

"Because the way I might feel about you terrifies me. I don't know if I'm ready for those feelings again." His breathing got heavier, as has mine, and my hands are sweaty. *Am I imagining this conversation?* He touches his face again, and I change the subject.

"Why do you always do that?"

"Do what?"

"Touch your face, your chin like you did. You do that a lot when you're around me." I only recently started noticing it, but it's been happening a lot lately.

"I didn't think you noticed that." He shoots a small smile at me.

"I notice a lot about you. You're not hard to read."

"Likewise." He stands up when he says that. He goes to lean against the roof's ledge, and I follow him.

"So, you lied to your sister because you care about me as a friend. I didn't know I was a big topic of conversation with you and Hads."

"You aren't usually, but yesterday she yelled at me."

"Why?" I ask.

"She told me that I'm not allowed to date you."

"What? Why would she say that?" I ask him, curious.

"I think she's just cautious of us spending time together."

"Well, I did meet you before her. But I get it," I say, slightly upset at this new piece of information.

"That's what I said too." He lights up when he says that, and that split second was one of the best things I've ever seen. We're both leaning against the top of the roof, looking over our tiny campus. Our hands hang at our sides, and I have the urge to grab his, so I do. Our fingers dance where they meet, but when he grabs my hand, he pulls me closer to him. I can feel his breath on my face.

"Tell me to stop."

"Stop what?" I whisper.

"Tell me to stop what I'm about to do."

"Well, that depends on what you're going to do, Ol." That was the first time I'd called him that. It felt normal to say as if I had used it a million times before.

"I was going to kiss you, and every time you see me touch my mouth it's because I'm nervous. *You* make me nervous because I'm feeling things again and it's unraveling me. But I don't wanna feel like that anymore, or maybe just for right now. I want to do what feels right, and this feels right. So tell me to stop, or I'm going to kiss you," he says while putting his hand on the back of my neck. I don't say anything, and then he smashes his lips into mine. I practically melt into him. He's emitting so much warmth that I feel like I have a fever. His lips are soft, and the way he's touching my face is sending sparks and electricity down my entire body. I've never kissed someone and felt like this before. My heart is racing and I know I'm going to be as confused as he is after this, but I don't care.

He pulls away and looks at me. "Was that okay?"

I nod, speechless and unsure of what to say.

"Can I kiss you again?"

"Please," I say, practically standing on my tiptoes to reach his mouth sooner. He meets me halfway, and I think about all those weird feelings I had in the past. *Were those feelings for Oliver?* I don't know what to make of those, but the harder he kisses me, the harder I'm finding it to care. It's nice not to think for once. He slips his tongue into my mouth, and it's then I realize I'm kissing one of my best friend's brothers right now. And I'm liking it. I tense up a bit, and he stops.

"Are you okay?" He searches my face. "Did I do something wrong?"

"No! No, that was perfect. I just realized you're Hadleigh's brother."

"You're just now realizing that?"

"No, I..." I trail off. "This is so complicated."

"This definitely makes things more complicated but I don't regret doing that."

"I don't either," I say to him.

It feels like we both just admitted something, yet neither of us wants to dive any deeper into it. We're still standing close to one another, him looking at me with those big brown eyes that are full of some emotion I can't place. I'm sure my eyes look the same, but my head has never been more confused.

Yet neither of us says a thing. We're simply two people on a rooftop, existing only in this moment. We face each other for a few more minutes, silently taking in every unspoken thing from the past hour.

I stifle a yawn before I break the thick blanket of silence that covers us. "Walk me back to my place?"

"I was going to anyway," he says as he gathers the snacks and puts them in his bag.

"Okay." We go down the stairs, and I look at the time—one in the morning. It didn't feel like we were up there for that long. We walk back to my place in silence, and I hug him when we reach my door. "Thank you for tonight. I appreciate it."

"No problem. Text me if you can't sleep again. I don't mind sharing my spot with you." He smiles for a second, but then it drops again.

"Okay. See you soon, Ol."

"Goodnight, P," and then he turns and walks away. I open my door to find Amelia in the living room. Dammit, she's going to take one look at my face and know something is up. She turns around when she hears me, a coffee mug still in hand.

"How many of those have you had?" I ask her.

"I don't know, two or maybe four. Why do you look like you just had a bunch of coffee?" She laughs at me, and I'm going to take a page out of her book and deflect, so instead of answering her, I take my jacket off and hang it up. "Paige, what happened tonight, hmmm?"

I can still hear her giggling on the couch when I crawl into my bed, still too confused to be able to sleep.

13

Wednesday, September 21st

I KISSED PAIGE FOUR days ago and haven't stopped thinking about it.

I feel fucking stupid. I know I shouldn't have done that. I just couldn't help it. We were on that roof, and she was saying all these nice things that weren't true about me, so I kissed her.

It felt like she saw right through me on that rooftop.

Do I regret it? Not one bit. What I do regret is lying to my sister, but it's done, and I can't take it back. Everything went back to normal after the kiss, so it's not awkward, thankfully. Paige is still the same old talkative girl I've been friends with, and I still hang onto every word she says.

Neither of us has brought up the kiss. Well, kisses. I think we both decided it's better to pretend like it never happened. It's easier that way in the long run, but I can't stop fucking thinking about it, which sucks because I'm trying to be productive.

I'm in my apartment with Nick and Noah doing homework. I didn't invite them over, but they waltzed into my apartment and sat down.

My apartment is a bit plain. I don't decorate—never have—but I have the typical furniture because it's really all I need. I have the same layout as Paige's apartment—all the on-campus apartments have the same layout—so it's an open floor plan. The only difference is that I have one bedroom instead of two.

The only decorations I have are some movie posters on the walls, and I enjoy the nostalgia of seeing my favorite movies from my childhood. It's plain and perfect for me.

Nick is majoring in Business and Noah is majoring in Psychology. I don't know what either of those entails, but they have a similar workload to mine. Both of them are typing on their computers while I scroll through an article on mine.

"So Oliver, how has Paige been lately?" Nick asks me while shutting his laptop.

"Why?" I ask him.

"Why what?"

"Why the fuck are you asking me about her?"

"It was just a question, dude. You guys seem to be spending a lot of time together lately." He raises his eyebrows, and I shoot a glare at him.

"Yeah, we have the same classes, idiot."

"It seems like you two have become closer lately..." Noah says. *What's up with these two?*

"Yeah, don't think we didn't notice all the whispering and glances between you two. It's like you guys have a secret language or something," Nick tells me.

"What's going on with you two?"

"It was an observation," Noah says, continuing to type.

"So, you wouldn't mind if I asked Paige on a date? She's cute and her bubbly personality is contagious." I shoot a glare his way, but I know he's baiting me into snapping at him. He likes to think he's slick, but I can tell what he's doing. I'm not going to dignify that question with a response. "So, if I texted her right now and asked her, you would be fine with that?" He's reaching for his phone, still baiting me.

"Nick, what are you doing?" Noah asks. "You've never feigned interest in this girl before. Why all of a sudden are you doing this?"

"Noah, shush. Oliver, anything to add?" Nick asks me.

He's trying to get under my skin. But if he starts typing I'm going to smash his phone with my fist.

But of course, I say nothing.

Noah looks between us, and Nick stares at me while I glare at him. He starts typing on his phone, so I reach over and grab it out of his hands. I set it down on my coffee table and continue with my assignment.

"I knew it," Nick says.

"Knew what? What the fuck just happened?" Noah asks.

"Oliver totally likes Paige."

"What? Oliver doesn't even like us," Noah says.

"Not true. I tolerate you guys," I say to them.

"How sweet." Nick smirks at me. "I noticed it at first before all that stuff went down with the dean a few weeks ago. Oliver and Paige were walking to class when I interrupted, and I could *feel* the tension dripping off this one over here." He slaps my arm when he says that. "Then, I saw the two of them again on Monday and could see the change."

"Wow, I never knew the abominable snowman had it in him. That's cute," Noah says.

"Paige and I are working on a semester-long project, so we've been spending more time together outside of class than usual. That's all," I say, hoping they drop it. "We might have kissed over the weekend." I don't normally confide in other people besides my sister, but if I tell her this, she might stab me with one of her charts. And since these two seem to know everything, I might as well come clean.

"You *what*?" Nick says.

"Like on the lips?" Noah asks.

"What kind of fucking question is that?" I say to him.

"So what does that mean now?" Nick asks me.

"How the fuck am I supposed to know?" They both look at me like I'm nuts.

"You guys kiss and then everything stays the same. Leave it to you to fuck this up, Oliver." Nick scoffs at me when he says that. "I *knew* you didn't know how to flirt."

"I know how to flirt." *I don't even believe what just came out of my mouth.*

"Clearly you don't if you fucked up your chances with Paige," Nick says.

"Oliver, how long has it been since you practiced flirting with someone?" Noah asks me.

"You don't need to *practice* flirting. Good God, I knew I shouldn't have said anything to you two."

"Everyone needs a little practice, Oliver. Here, try flirting with me—pretend I'm Paige." Nick scoots closer to me, and I resist the urge to slap him.

"No. This is ridiculous."

"Aw, he's scared." Noah smiles at Nick.

"I'm not scared." I pause. "You know what? Fuck you guys. This was supposed to be us quietly studying, not one where you guys judge my flirting skills."

"It wouldn't hurt to sharpen up, Oliver. Especially if you like her," Nick tells me.

"And you haven't dated anyone since being here—at least not to our knowledge. You're just rusty. The more you flirt, the easier it'll be."

"Can we get back to our homework?" I ask the two of them and they hesitate for a few seconds before returning to whatever they were working on before this stupid conversation.

"I don't blame you for liking her. That girl is the sun personified. She calls me by my full name, and I don't correct her when she does, even though I hate when people do that," Nick says while opening his laptop again.

A few minutes later, my mind starts to drift back to our conversation from the other night. Paige *is* the fucking sun—at least to everyone around her—but in her eyes, she's a broken girl pasting a smile on her face every day. The thought of her doing that so her friends don't worry about her makes my body ache.

Why does she feel so broken? And how can I help her realize that she's not?

There was one thing Paige said that was true—we dance around each other and I don't know if it'll ever stop. I felt how she melted into my lips the other night—there was no question she enjoyed it as much as I did. But I think we both chose the path of least resistance—not talking about it.

Nick and Noah leave after I cook dinner for them—my family's Pho recipe—because they have practice or something. Despite me giving them a hard time, I do enjoy their company. It's nice having a few people who understand my silence and don't want to run in the other direction.

After I cleaned up, I took a shower, and now I'm sitting on my bed with a bunch of papers. I did some digging on a few professors who retired over the past five years and found some inconsistencies. I also looked into the missing son and haven't found much yet, but I plan to dig deeper tonight. I grab my phone to see if Paige has any more information since I last talked to her, and she answers right away.

Oliver: Have you found anything on his wife or the missing son yet?

Paige: Hello to you too! I haven't found anything interesting, but I'll look more after book club tonight!

Oliver: It's Wednesday, sorry. It's fine if you don't. I know book club is important.

Paige: I'm not going to sleep tonight anyway. It's fine. I'll look into it.

Oliver: Paige, you need to sleep.

Paige: Oliver, you need to sleep too.

Oliver: I'm not the one with the sleeping problems.

Paige: I don't have a sleeping problem! I just prefer not to sleep!

Oliver: -_-

Paige: Don't give me that face!

Oliver: -__-

Paige: -_______-

Paige: Two can play this game.

Oliver: Paige, go to book club and chat about whatever the fuck you talk about with my sister, do some research, and then go to bed. You told me yesterday you haven't slept in days.

Paige: It's only been two days!

Oliver: That's not normal!

Paige: Oliver, I'm fine!!!!!!

Oliver: The amount of exclamation points says otherwise.

Paige: Okay, fine, I concede. Just for you, I'll try.

Oliver: Good. Have fun at book club.

Paige: Thanks, Ol. Have fun rewatching *Twelve Angry Men* or whatever you're doing!

Oliver: I will... thanks.

Paige: <3

I smile at my phone. Last year, I told her how when I was little my dad used to show me all of his favorite movies from when he was a kid. We would watch them all the time, and it's one of my favorite memories growing up. *Twelve Angry Men* is one of my favorites he showed me. I like the premise of the movie—how a single member of the jury is skeptical about the case and it forces them all to talk it out before they jump to conclusions.

I wonder if she feels like I do when we talk—the butterflies and shit. I wonder if anything has changed for her since our kiss. *I doubt it.* I would probably just dull her shine everywhere we go. I push that thought out of my head and continue searching the web for evidence and information to go on the murder board.

Wednesday, September 21st

I PUT MY PHONE down from texting Oliver, grab my tote bag, and throw my book in it. The girls and I have book club tonight, and I can't focus this week for some reason.

I'm choosing to blame all the assignments rather than the fact that Oliver kissed me, and I've wanted to kiss him again eighty times since it happened. I feel like I'm going insane. That's my friend's brother! Hadleigh's brother! I kissed Hads' brother. My head feels like a seesaw when I try to figure out what the hell I feel about it, and on top of that, I'm trying to solve a murder with him.

How did I get here?

My thoughts get interrupted when Amelia barges into my room. "Ready to go?"

I throw my tote over my shoulder and nod. Thirty seconds later, we're out the door and on our way to our usual book club classroom.

The walk only takes a few minutes, but we're the first ones here. That's no surprise because Hads has been busy studying with Grant while tutoring on the side, and Ella has a literal job, so she isn't as close to campus anymore. Amelia and I set the chairs in a circle around the table and sat in our usual spots.

"How's Oliver been lately?" Amelia asks me, a smile on her face. I think she knows something is off because ever since I came back on Sunday, she's been asking me about him.

"That all depends on how Henry is! Any more flower deliveries that I haven't seen?"

"I'm here!" Ella says as she comes into the room, panting.

"Did you run here?" Amelia asks.

"No, but it has been a crazy day at the office." Ella sits in her usual place, and then Hads walks in. I tense up a bit, knowing what Oliver told me about their conversation the other day. I feel like she can see right through me. *Can she?* No, she can't. *Right?* Fuck. I'm not good at keeping things from my friends, and this is something huge I'm not telling them about.

But I don't want to get punched in the face when Hads finds out, so I keep quiet even if it's killing me.

"Hey, guys! Sorry, I'm late. Grant and Jacks were arguing about which hockey player was better looking and needed me to break the tie."

"I will never understand those two," Ella says to us.

"Who did you side with?" I ask.

"Grant because I have to, but Jacks' pick was better." She smiles. "Don't tell him I said that."

"Okay, this book was crazy, and I cannot wait to discuss it," Amelia says.

"No same, but I hate to admit that I liked it a little bit." Ella blushes.

"I liked the female main character, but the guy was not my favorite," Hads says.

"It was a fun time, but I was really confused about the ending," I say to them as we launch into a full discussion of this book and talk about these four guys. We chat about the book for about an hour and then comes the part of the night that I have been dreading—the debrief. I feel like I'm going to get yelled at for investigating again. I'm also afraid that if someone asks about Oliver, I'll turn into a blubbering idiot and spill everything.

"Guys. I have some exciting news!" Ella says, standing up when the book talk ceases. We all fall quiet as we wait for her to tell us. "I got an interview with that marketing company in Richmond!" We all jump up to hug her at the same time. Ella has always talked about her dream job being with this specific firm, so the fact that she got an interview is amazing.

"I'm so happy for you!" I say to her.

"This is so huge! Congrats!" Amelia says.

"I'm going to crochet you something for good luck," Hads says. She's been into crocheting lately. She made us all matching hats in different colors for the winter. Mine was lavender. I might've cried when she gave it to me.

"Thanks, but it's just an interview. It doesn't mean I'm going to get it," Ella says, looking down.

"Ella, stop downplaying this. You *will* get it," Hads says.

"Yes, but you never—" I cut her off.

"Ella, I could list a million reasons why you will get this job, but your qualifications speak for themselves. Plus, you're you. I'm convinced you can do anything."

"Paige is right. If this job doesn't work out, you should become a spy or something. I think you'd be good at it," Amelia tells her, and we all look at her. "It's always good to have a backup plan!"

"Okay, that's it for my news. How has everyone else been?" Ella asks. I look over at Amelia, and she's smiling at me already. Fuck.

"Well, Paige has been—"

"Henry sent Amelia flowers!" I yell, cutting off whatever she was about to say. Hads and Ella gasp and turn to Amelia to look for confirmation.

"He did?" Ella gasps.

"I did not see that coming," Hads says.

"Yes, he did." Amelia looks like she wants to gut me like a fish. I should lock my door tonight.

"It was so cute. I almost tripped over them on the doorstep," I say, smiling.

"Yes, she did find them. What were you doing when you found them, Paige?" Amelia asks me, knowing damn well what I was doing.

"I was about to go for a walk," I say to the room.

"What kind of flowers were they? And were they for your birthday?" Ella asks her.

Amelia explains he sent them because he never knew it was her birthday and didn't have time to get her a present. I'm amazed that Henry knew her favorite type of flower. It was such a cute gesture.

"When can we meet the mysterious Henry?" Hads asks.

"Never," Amelia says.

"I've met him! He's so much cuter than Amelia makes him out to be. Apparently, our little Amelia is a chatterbox about the three of us because he knows who we are," I tell them.

"So he knows us, but we know nothing about him?" Ella asks. "Sounds like typical Amelia."

"I'm sure Ames will tell us in time," Hads says. Amelia isn't one to talk about her feelings. She mostly runs away from them, so we all know when to change that topic of conversation.

"Paige, how's the investigation going?" Amelia asks me.

"I still think you should stop, but that's just me," Ella says.

"I think it's weird Oliver agreed to do this with you." My cheeks heat at Hads' mention of Oliver.

"It's been fine. We made a murder board the other day, but we're still digging into some areas. We're interviewing some people soon, I think? Also, Oliver didn't really agree with this. He wormed his way in because he didn't want me doing this alone," I say to them. "He's been a good partner so far. I think he's doing some digging right now." I sink into my chair a bit, suddenly feeling too on the spot. Nobody says anything for a few seconds, so I speak again. "I'm being safe, I promise. Plus, it's not like I'm the one in danger, right?"

"Just be safe, okay?" Ella tells me.

"Oh, I bet Paige and Oliver are being *really* safe," Amelia says, and I smack her.

"What does that mean?" Hads asks her.

"She was joking," I tell her while shooting a look at Ames.

"I was not joking. Oliver almost stabbed me the other day when I came home!" Amelia says.

"He what?" Hads asks.

"Since when does Oliver carry a knife?" Ella's barely holding a laugh in.

"Amelia, you entered the apartment weirdly! It's your fault you slammed the door and made a bunch of weird noises that scared me!" I say to her.

"I had my headphones on, plus it's my home! I can enter however I want to." She crosses her arms.

"Can we go back to the knife part?" Ella asks.

"Oliver carries a pocket knife. He always has," Hads tells her.

"Oh. He seems like the type." Ella nods.

"Can we talk about something else, please? I'll update you guys as our investigation progresses, I promise," I say to them.

"Well, I don't have any updates. I'm getting better at ice skating. I did a few laps the other day without falling over!" Hads smiles at that.

"That's good!" Amelia says.

"I can't wait for us to be able to go ice skating again," Ella says, and I agree with her.

"I can ask Grant if he can set a night for us to go once everything calms down," she tells us.

"That would be fun!" I say.

"Okay, cool," Hads says. "Well, I'm heading to Grant's right now. I'll see you on Sunday, Ella?" She asks her as she leans against the door.

"Yeah, of course!" Ella says back to her. They started having Sunday coffee dates last semester, and it stuck. Amelia even crashed it once last semester. I'm not allowed to have coffee, so I usually sleep in on Sundays. Well, I try to sleep in.

"I should probably get going too. I have an interview to prepare for," Ella says, rising from her seat. She meets Hads at the door, and they walk out together.

"You ready to go, Paige?" Ames asks me and I stare at her. "Are you giving me the silent treatment?"

I nod.

"Why?" I look around to make sure that Ella and Hads aren't in hearing distance.

"Why were you saying all that stuff about Oliver and me? Are you trying to get Hads to snap her ruler in half and impale me when she finds out?" I whisper to her.

"No, I was trying to confirm that something happened between you two that night. You getting all flustered confirmed my theory."

I take a deep breath. "You're the worst."

"Yeah, but you still love me."

"I do. Love you, I mean."

"I know. Now spill," she tells me as we grab our stuff and start walking back to the apartment. I tell her that we kissed and had a moment on the roof. She laughs the entire time.

"I don't think laughing is appropriate for my situation, but I should've known," I tell her.

"I feel like I've seen this coming for a few weeks. Ever since he hugged you in our kitchen I knew something was up, at least on his end and maybe yours too."

"I don't know what to do. I liked kissing him, but Hads would kill me. Apparently, she already talked to him about how I'm off-limits, but he kissed me anyway."

"Well, the heart wants what it wants, I suppose. Maybe table it until the investigation is over," Amelia says to me.

"We haven't mentioned it since."

"Perfect. Problem solved," she tells me as she opens our door. I'm still on the porch because the problem is *not* solved since I think I have feelings for him. I don't know how to go about this. I've only had one serious boyfriend that lasted two months when I was in high school. I only dated him to do all the things you're supposed to do before college, but he ended up being an asshole. I dropped him before anything else could happen, and I never really had feelings for him anyway. This situation is entirely different because *I do* have feelings for Oliver.

"Can you teach me to shove my feelings down until they don't exist?" I ask her.

She pats the spot next to her on the couch. "No, but I will sit here and make you watch National Geographic with me in exchange for my silence about this."

I sigh and trudge over to the couch. I slump down next to her and drag the blanket over us both. "I should've known that was coming."

She smiles at me and turns it on. I lean my head on her shoulder, and she puts her head against mine.

"I love you, even though you like to extort me emotionally," I say to her.

"I love you too, even though you like to solve murders as a hobby." I take my head off her shoulder, and we look at each other for a few seconds before bursting into laughter. Our phones buzzing cuts off our laughing fit.

Ella: Is everyone home safe?

Paige: Yes! Are you?

Ella: Yup!

Hads: *one attachment*

Amelia: Hi, Grant.

Ella: You two are the cutest.

Amelia: Good luck with your interview, Ells! You're going to do great! <3

Paige: You got this! You're the baddest bitch ever!

Hads: Grant says you'll crush it, and I agree! Love you, guys!

Ella liked three messages.

We set our phones on the coffee table and get comfy on the couch. Amelia turns on the documentary, and I'm smiling to myself. Feeling thankful that I have these three people around me.

Four people. I have four people beside me now—I'm the luckiest girl in the world.

14

Saturday, September 24th

IT'S AROUND SIX IN the morning when I wake up, and I'm getting dressed for my run when my phone starts blowing up. I look down, and it's Paige.

Paige: Oliver!

Paige: Ol!

Paige: I know you're awake for your run!

Oliver: Why are you up so early?

Paige: Good morning to you, too!

Oliver: Paige, what's going on?

Paige: Click this link and read the article!

I do what she tells me to, and it's an article yesterday about a police officer who committed suicide a few towns over.

Oliver: Why did you send me this?

Paige: Do you think it's connected?

Oliver: Do you?

Paige: I don't know, but two deaths in a few weeks in the same area are suspicious.

Oliver: I doubt it's connected, but we can look into it later.

Paige: Do you want to meet at the library at nine?

Oliver: Sure.

Paige: Okay, cool. Have fun on your run!

Oliver: Thanks, Sherlock.

I grab my headphones and put them in while I leave my apartment. I send my sister a text to cancel our walk this morning. I haven't been ignoring her lately, per se, but I feel weird whenever I'm around her. I don't want her to find out Paige and I kissed, especially since my feelings don't even make sense to me yet. Maybe on my deathbed I'll tell her, but for right now, I'm keeping my mouth shut.

Oliver: No walk this morning. Meeting Paige at the library soon and need to run a few errands.

Hads: You couldn't have told me this yesterday so I could have slept in?

Oliver: Whoops.

Hads: Whatever. Is everything okay?

Oliver: Yeah, why?

Hads: Just wondering. I'm going back to bed, bye.

Oliver: Make sure to call Mom next week. It's her birthday.

Hads: I know. I talked to her yesterday with Grant.

I start my playlist and take off. I think this morning I'm going to do a longer run—I have some extra energy to get rid of. So instead of three miles, I'll do six. Plus, it might help me keep a clear head if I look into the case later. I take my usual route around campus which is about three miles, I take the loop twice, which takes me around an hour. When I get back to my place, Grant is standing in front of my door.

"Did my sister send you up here?"

He looks up at me. "Why can't me being up here equate to checking up on my friend?"

"You're dating my sister. I don't think that makes us friends."

"You were the one who sat down next to me on that bench last semester and told me how great of a guy I was, so yeah, I would call us friends."

"Fine. What do you want?" I ask him as I open my door. I try to close it on him, so he knows to leave me the fuck alone, but he stops it with his foot and continues into my space.

"No matter how much time has passed, it still seems like you just moved into this place." He looks around, his face appalled. "No wall decor, no books, nothing."

"That sounded sarcastic."

"It was. It looks like a prison cell in here. How are you?" he asks while sitting on my couch.

"Please make yourself comfortable," I say to him while grabbing water from my fridge.

"Thanks, I will. So why did you cancel on Hads this morning?" He leans back and puts his feet on my coffee table. I walk over to sit on the smaller couch in my living room, and when I pass by him, I swipe his feet onto the floor.

"I have shit to do, so I canceled. It's not something my sister needs to read into," I tell him.

"She's worried about you."

"She's always worried about me. That's not new. Why did she really send you up here?"

"I forgot you're good at interrogating and shit, so I'll cut to the chase. Hads is worried you're not taking care of yourself."

"That's all she's worried about?" I ask him. I can tell from his face he has more to say.

"Well, she also mentioned Paige, but I don't care what you do with her as long as it doesn't involve breaking her heart."

What the fuck? "Stop pretending to be protective over Paige. You don't even know her."

"Oh, I don't? Please enlighten me then on how well *you* know Paige."

I glare at him. "Grant, enough. I'm not telling you anything, especially my business."

"I hope you don't forget I was the one you came to when you were asking me about my feelings for your sister. And you don't have to say anything, but I saw the way you looked at her when you guys came back from the police station—"

"Oh yeah? How did I look at her?" I ask as I cut off his sentence.

He pauses for a moment. "Like you wanted to take away all of her pain."

I'm pissed off now. Why is he coming into my apartment and telling me all this shit at seven in the morning? Wasn't he the one who blurted out his love for my sister in a fucking parking lot? "Fuck you."

"I could say something funny right now, but you might murder me if I do, so I'll refrain." I glare at him again. "I get it, Oliver. The truth hurts sometimes."

Such a fucking pretty boy.

"If you say anything about you and my sister and whatever shit you do in your free time, I'm going to punch you," I say while getting up and heading toward my door. He follows me.

"Look, Hads wanted me to come up here and tell you not to fuck up her friendship with Paige. So don't. And if you *do* decide you have feelings for Paige, you better be in it for the long haul, or Hads will make me hurt you. I know you and I both don't want that to happen. So tread very carefully with this whole fucking investigation you two have going on. Okay?"

I open my door and wordlessly invite him to get the fuck out of my apartment.

"I'm glad we're on the same page then," he says, smiling and waltzing out of my apartment. He turns around and looks at me. "I'll tell Hads this was a nice brotherly talk, but remember what I said—" I don't give him time to answer as I shut the door and lock it, so he can't come back in.

Grant is a good guy, and his presence doesn't bother me too much, but the fact that my sister sent him up here to talk to me was annoying as fuck. I hate living in the same building as him because that gives my sister and him a chance to drop by unannounced, especially on the mornings she sleeps at his place.

I drag a hand down my face and stop on my chin. I run through the list of things I have to do before meeting Paige in two hours. I start with a shower, and then after that, I'll dig a bit deeper into what she sent me before we get to the library. I like having discussion points ready with her because it allows us to work off one another when we get to theorizing.

I suddenly feel charged again, as if I didn't just go on a six-mile run.

By the time I'm out the door, I make a mental note to stop by the library cafe and get Paige a plain bagel with butter and some coffee because knowing her, she hasn't eaten breakfast yet. Hads told me once that the girls don't let Paige have coffee, but I think it's needed because she probably hasn't slept in a few days.

I'm out my door in five minutes and heading to the library when I text Paige.

Oliver: Heading over early to grab some food. Do you want anything?

Paige: Plain bagel with butter?

Oliver: Sure. Anything else?

Paige: That's all! I'll be over soon. Ames and I are debriefing.

Oliver: ????

Paige: It's a thing we do. Don't ask.

Oliver: Okay.

Paige: See you in a few!

I walk through the library doors and head to the spot my sister and Paige normally reside in the library. I figure that's where Paige would want to sit. I set my stuff down and head to the cafe to grab some food and drinks. I've been steering away from coffee, but I'm going to get one this morning. I order Paige an iced caramel latte with extra caramel and make it decaf. I order myself a black coffee—plain and simple. Once I have everything, I go back to the table to find Paige sitting there already staring at her laptop, and spreading papers all over the table.

Seeing her there stops me in my tracks for a second, so I decide to use this moment to really take her in. Her blonde hair looks like she just rolled out of bed, it's wavy and all of her baby hairs are all over the place. That girl has a lot of hair, and it's layered and shit. She's wearing black sweatpants and a purple cropped shirt with some design. She has black vans on her feet and a tote bag next to her chair. She also never sits normally in chairs, so one leg is propped up, her chin resting on her knee, and the other is crisscrossed beneath her. Her fingers are typing at normal Paige speed and she must sense me staring because her green eyes meet mine, and she smiles at me.

My heart does the thing it always does when she looks at me like that. It skips a beat or whatever.

"It's the little things that make me fall deeper every day."

Little things such as how aggressively she types and how she can never sit normally? How she has always carries a tote bag and how I like the way her hair falls down her shoulders?

Grant was onto something—I'm falling, and I don't know what to do about it.

Is it worth it—falling in love and dealing with the possibility it could get taken away again? Am *I* worth it? The only thing I know for sure is that Paige is worth every goddamn thing I feel.

Yeah, I think to myself. Yeah, it's worth it.

I realize I look insane standing in the middle of the library staring at her, so I move my feet and head to the table. I set my coffee and blueberry muffin down and handed her the bagel and coffee.

"Thanks! How much do I owe you?"

"You don't."

"Are you sure? I have a few bucks somewhere." She starts shuffling through her bag, and I grab her hand resting on the table.

"Stop. It's just one friend buying coffee for the other, don't worry about it."

"Thanks." She smiles and takes a sip of her coffee. She makes a face after drinking it. "I never told you how I liked my coffee, but you got it exactly right."

"Like I've told you before, you're easy to read." I look away from her and pull my laptop out.

"I didn't think I was *that* easy to read. Especially knowing that I like extra caramel on my coffee."

"Paige, I can read you like a children's picture book."

"Gotcha. Well, thanks." She smiles at me again.

"It's no problem." I give her a smirk back. "So, what else have you found about this suicide?"

"Oh, right. Well, it happened out of the same jurisdiction as the dean. A former school resource officer who retired even though he was only fifty years old. His name was kept off of everything I've seen about it, so I don't know it, but apparently, a note was left at the scene. Detectives on the case think it was a cut-and-dry suicide. People who knew the victim said that he struggled with PTSD for a while after an unrelated event in his life."

"Yeah, that's about what I found too. Did you find anything that could connect this guy to our investigation?" I ask her.

"Nope. Yet another thing going cold in our investigation."

"Keep your head up, Sherlock. We still have some people to talk to about what happened on campus. We don't want this to become serial, do we?" I look at her. "That seems like more work and danger for us."

"If I'm Sherlock, does that make you Watson?" She pauses for a second. "Serial would be more fun…"

"Paige, be honest with me right now. Do you *want* the dean to have been killed by a serial killer?"

"Well, no, but wouldn't it be fun if we caught a serial killer?"

"I think dangerous is the word you're looking for. And stop using fun to describe this. People are going to think you're crazy."

"People who know me should know I *am* crazy about stuff like this."

"True. Well, since the suicide isn't connected, I'm going to cross that off the list."

"Okay. When do you have time to talk to Fitzpatrick about why he got fired?"

"Well, my schedule is tight, so maybe over a weekend? I don't think it's connected at all but it still wouldn't hurt to talk to him." I say, opening up my calendar when I feel a presence next to me. I look over, and my sister looks back at me.

"I almost forgot what you looked like since you canceled on me this morning. How were those errands you had to run?"

"Hads, lay off a bit. The man is busy solving a murder." Grant shoots me a smirk from across the table.

"They were fine, Hads. What are you doing here?" I ask.

"Grant and I came for coffee, but we took a detour when we saw Paige sitting alone." My sister turns to her friend. "Hi, Paigey, how are you?"

"I'm good! Also, Oliver has been here the whole time. I wasn't alone," she says, looking between us all.

"I know, but sometimes Oliver doesn't talk, so it *feels* like you're alone." Hads shoots me a smirk. Paige turns to Grant.

"Hi! How has everything been? I haven't seen you in a while!"

"I've been wonderful. How is my favorite amateur detective on this fine day?"

"I'm great! Oliver and I are discussing murder details," she whispers the last part, so nobody around us hears.

"Sounds like a typical day for you." He winks at Paige, and I look over at my sister who seems unfazed. *What are these two up to?*

"Yup!" Paige grabs her coffee and sips it.

"Paige, why do you have coffee?" my sister asks her.

"Oliver got it for me because I haven't slept in a few days."

"A few days? Paige, I thought it was only two? What the fu—" My sentence is cut off by my sister smacking me with that fucking ruler she always has on hand. "Hads, what the fuck!"

"Yeah, that shit hurts more than you think. I would know," Grant says, laughing.

"You know she isn't allowed to have coffee, Oliver!"

"Hads, she hasn't slept in days. I figured it was fine!" I tell her as I lower my voice.

"Wait, days? Paige, how are you alive right now?" Grant asks her, and she shrugs.

"Exactly, so put that thing away, Hads," I tell her while lowering the hand that she has the ruler in.

"Fine, but I'm texting Amelia that you let her have coffee. She's going to kill you." She whips her phone out of her jacket pocket, and I hear Paige's phone buzz a few seconds later.

"Have fun dealing with Amelia. Out of all the girls, she scares me the most," Grant tells me, and I nod in agreement.

"Amelia would love that." Paige giggles and types on her phone, a few seconds later, my sister is laughing too.

"What's so funny?" I ask them.

"Nothing!" the girls say at the same time. I look over at Grant.

"I don't ask, and neither should you."

"Look, Paige having coffee isn't the end of the world, and you girls need to stop treating her with kid gloves," I say to my sister. "You guys are acting like I'm feeding a gremlin after midnight."

"Are you comparing me to Gizmo? He's so cute!" Paige's face lights up at my comparison.

"Yes, but unlike him, you're allowed to be exposed to sunlight." I smile at her while feigning a laugh that's about to come out of my mouth.

"What the fuck are you guys talking about?" Grant asks us.

"Dude, you've never seen *Gremlins?* What's wrong with you?" I ask him with a laugh.

"Listen, I don't want to call anyone tasteless here, but you had never seen *The Great Gatsby* until I forced you to watch it with me over the summer." Grant smiles back at me.

"Whatever, I think it's weird that you guys don't let her drink coffee. It's a drink, and I got it half-caffeinated," I say to them.

"To be fair, I don't let myself have coffee either. They're just looking out for me, Ol," Paige tells me, her eyes a bit sad, and now I feel like shit. My sister side-eyes me because Paige used a nickname for me that only Hads uses, and I think she might kill me.

"Baby, do you want to grab a coffee and head back to my place?" Grant asks my sister.

"Sure. It was good to see you, Paige. Are we still on for movie night tomorrow?" Hads asks her.

"Yup! Amelia and I are going out later to get snacks and stuff, so text me what you want!" She smiles at her while getting up.

"Just remember what I said, okay?" she tells me, giving me a pat on the shoulder. I think she's silently threatening me. *When did she get so scary?*

I nod at her. Grant comes over to me and claps me on the back. He leans over to me, so the girls don't hear.

"I'm rooting for you, buddy."

"Get the fuck out of here," I say, sitting back down. As my sister and Grant leave, I hear someone yell my name.

"Oliver!" I look over, and it's Amelia speeding through the library toward us. A few people shush her, and she rolls her eyes. My sister has her phone out, probably recording this for Ella, and Paige is laughing under her breath.

"Should I be scared right now?" I ask her.

"Probably," Paige tells me, and I can't help but laugh a little out of fear.

Who the fuck are these girls, and how did I get wrapped up in this? Amelia reaches our table, and I tense up. Paige apologetically looks over at me and tries to explain to Amelia why she has coffee. Amelia seems only to be focused on me, but she takes Paige's half-empty coffee, turns to a nearby garbage can, and throws it away.

"I paid five bucks for that, you know," I say to Amelia, and she takes out a five-dollar bill and throws it at me.

"Here. Next time I find out you bought her coffee, I will throw it at you. Do you understand?" I nod at Amelia and notice she's smiling. I can't tell if she's joking or if she loves to push my buttons. I think it's the latter. "I want to hear you say you understand Oliver or is speaking two words that hard for you?"

"I understand."

"Good." Amelia looks to Paige. "Now, let's go to the store and get snacks for tomorrow."

"I thought we were going later?" she asks her.

"Well, I'm here now, so let's go."

"Okay." She grabs her stuff and touches my hand on the table, I jolt a bit, not expecting the sudden contact, but her hand stays where it is. "I'll text you? And don't worry about Amelia, she's more bark than she is bite."

"Sounds good. I'll keep that in mind for the future, but Amelia's still scary," I say back to her before she turns away from the table and heads for the girls.

I hear Hads telling Amelia she reminded her of Ella a minute ago. I think Ella is more likely to actually hit me than Amelia. I look over at my sister, and she's smiling with Amelia and Paige. They all laugh at something Paige says.

I never understood how the four of them became friends. They're all opposites, but it makes sense when I look at them right now. They're different, but all have one thing in common: they would all drop everything if one person needed help. I can't imagine having that many people around me who would do that for me.

I'm happy my sister has that, but I find myself wanting it too.

Could I have that one day? I think I could. I'd like that. I've been by myself for far too long. Hads always did tell me she wished we had another sister growing up—now she has three. I smile to myself and look at where Paige is standing. She's looking at me with a face I can't read right now. She smiles at me, and I swear it's like the sun is just coming up. I smile lightly back at her, and she turns around with the girls and leaves.

Part of me longs to run after her, and it's at this moment when I fully realize it.

I like her. I like Paige. I like being around her and I don't want to be just friends with her.

I want *more*.

I'm so fucking screwed.

15

Sunday, September 25th

I'm sitting in my closet on the floor with headphones around my neck. I have a book in my lap, pillows, and blankets all around me. I can hear his footsteps coming up the stairs. I talk to myself, hoping someone will hear me this time. Hoping someone will stop him before he remembers I'm in my room.

Two bangs on my bedroom door make me jump.

"Paige, open this fucking door right now."

I put some towels and other random things in front of my door, hoping it would stop him from coming in this time. I tried to move my dresser, but it was too heavy for a 12-year-old me. My breathing picks up as I hear him come in.

I know I can't stop him.

I've tried before.

But I'm too small. It never works.

I'm too weak.

My closet door gets ripped open and flies off its hinges. I scream, I think.

"What the fuck are you doing in here?" my father asks me.

I don't say a word. It's better that way. Sometimes I wish I was two inches tall so nobody could see me—so that he couldn't see me.

"Did you dump my shit down the sink?"

I shake my head no. He probably drank it all and forgot. He's rarely coherent when I'm over here, just like always.

"Don't lie to me, girl." He's slurring his words all over the place. I continue not saying anything. The next thing I know, he has my feet, dragging me out of my closet while I scream and cry, begging him not to hurt me. We're at the staircase now. He grabs my ankle and throws me, and I don't–

"Paige! Paige, wake up!" I feel Amelia shaking me, and my eyes open, but I don't feel awake quite yet. I can't breathe, and Amelia goes through the list of things I gave her to do when this happens. "Paige, listen to my voice. It's me, Amelia. We're at college. You're *not* at home. You're safe." She's looking right at me and hands me my water bottle. I take it, drinking a few small sips of water as my breathing starts to calm down. I hear my favorite song playing softly in the background.

"Th-Thank you," I say to her. She reaches up to my face, and I flinch, but her arm comes up to wipe the tears off my face.

"You're okay, P." She smiles at me, and I throw my arms around her and hug her. I don't know what I would do without her. We sit silently for a few minutes, and my breathing settles.

"I'm sorry you keep having to do that," I whisper to her. I always feel so small after a nightmare. I often wonder if I had done things differently as a kid, could I have stopped how my dad treated me? *I guess I'll never know.*

"Paige, like I've said before, you have nothing to apologize for. I'm just happy you're okay now."

"Me too," I say while sniffling.

"Is this why you haven't been sleeping much lately? Too many nightmares?"

"I don't know why they keep happening so much. They aren't even about finding the body. It's all stuff from my past."

"Maybe you could try taking some sleep medication?"

"Coming from you, that should be considered a joke," I say while laughing under my breath. Amelia's sleep schedule has always been weird. She likes to stay up early into the morning and can function on very little sleep.

"I know, but you need sleep. Sleep *without* nightmares." She holds my hand, silently showing me she's here.

"I'll be fine, Ames. What time are the girls coming over?" I look at her, and she stares at me for a few seconds, clearly not wanting to divert from this topic, but she answers a few seconds later.

"They should be on their way now, but P, we don't have to do this tonight. I don't think the murder documentaries are helping you right now."

"Amelia, it's fine. They bring me comfort. Do you need help setting up the snacks or anything?" I ask her.

"No, everything is in bowls right now, and the blankets are on the couch."

"Okay, good. Now, if you'll excuse me, I'm going to take a quick shower and put my pajamas on." I smile, and she gives me a small one back before leaving my room. I take a quick shower and throw my favorite pajamas on. When I head into the living room, I run straight into Ella.

"Paige, I missed you so much!" She pulls me into a hug, and I return it.

"How was the interview?" I ask her.

"It went well. I think I have a shot at getting the position." She smiles at me.

"Yay! Oh my gosh, I'm so excited for you! I know how hard you've worked for this, and seeing it all pay off is so—" I stop myself from finishing that sentence for fear of crying again, but I can't help it. I'm so proud of my friends.

"Paige, I love you so much, but please don't cry or I'll start crying too."

"I won't. Did the move go okay?"

Ella moved in with Alissa Zimmerman last weekend. She was looking for a place closer to where she works because her lease was up, and Alissa had a spare room. Those two met last year and clicked instantly. The only thing Ella doesn't like is that Alissa is related to the guy she hates most. Alissa is a Zimmerman, meaning she's related to Leo—Ella's rival from back in college.

"Yes! I'm finally unpacked, and I love living with her already," Ella tells me.

"I still wish you would have let us help you move." I lean my head on her shoulder.

"Please, you guys are busy with classes and everything. Plus, Alissa made her brother move all of my heavy shit and I got to boss him around, so it was a win."

"Oh please, I know you loved watching him carry all the heavy stuff. It probably turned you on," I joke with her.

"Paige! This documentary better be a good one. I'm talking angst and drama!" Hads burst into our apartment wearing Grant's sweatpants and probably one of his shirts because it looks four sizes too big for her.

"It's about a guy who goes on a killing spree at his workplace," I say to them.

"Oh god," Ella says.

"This is going to be fun," Amelia states.

"How does she always get us over here for this?" Hads asks us.

"You guys came to watch this with me because I went through something traumatic, and you love me," I say while plopping down on our couch.

"If I saw a dead body these true crime things would be the last thing I would watch, but you're you, and it makes sense." Amelia sits beside me and smiles while carrying a bowl of popcorn.

"Yeah, maybe that is your serial killer trait? The fact that these types of shows comfort you..." Ella says while sitting on the floor in front of the couch. Amelia moved the coffee table over a bit because we all like to sit together during movie night. Hads sits next to Ella on the floor with a bowl of her favorite chips on her lap. I click play on the remote, and it starts.

The four of us have this little dance when they watch these with me. Amelia asks me to define all the terms the detectives use. Ella likes to rate how pervy she thinks the people are, including the case experts, who are usually a bunch of old guys. Hads likes to yell at the people who missed evidence that was right in front of them. It's quite a fun time, actually.

About forty-five minutes into the documentary, Amelia throws some popcorn at me, and I laugh. I zoned out a bit but turn my attention back to the documentary and listen.

The guy on the screen continues talking, but I don't hear anything because what he said lit a light bulb in my head. I pause it and feel around the couch for my phone. Ella, Hads, and Amelia all turn and look at me.

"Paige, why did you pause it? It was getting interesting! That one guy was definitely a ten on the pervy scale!" Ella shouts at me, and I jump off the couch. I lift the cushions and frantically search underneath them.

"Where's my phone?" I say.

"Why do you need your phone so badly?" Hads asks me.

"Paige, I think you left your phone in your room," Amelia tells me, not having moved from her spot on the couch even though I tried to rip her cushion out from underneath her.

"Oh, yeah!" I run to my room and grab it off my bed while shutting the door behind me. I go to my favorites list, click the fourth number, and put my phone to my ear. I hear my bedroom door open and see the girls coming in.

"Who are you calling?" Ella asks me, and I hold up a finger while the phone rings in my ear. "Girl, I know you did not just shush me."

"Oh my god, pick up the phone!" I yell.

"Why are you yelling at me?" Oliver asks me.

"We need to look into the assistant dean of students," I tell him.

"Why?"

"Because he has the most to gain from killing him! He's in the acting position of dean of students right now, right? That wouldn't have happened if he wasn't killed! He has a motive, Oliver!" I might be a bit too excited about this.

"We probably should've guessed that was who she was calling," Amelia says behind me.

"Oliver, I swear to God if you don't remember what I said the other day, so help me!" Hads yells at him.

"Is that my sister? What's going on?" Oliver asks me.

"Yes, all of the girls are over right now, and we were watching a true crime documentary about this guy who killed his boss because he wanted more power. That got me thinking about the assistant dean of students! You're slacking a bit, Watson. You need to keep up."

"Do they have nicknames now?" Ella looks over at Hads, and she shrugs.

"I-I don't even know," Hads says as she exits my room, her sweatpants dragging behind her on the floor. Amelia starts laughing as she leaves with Hads and Ella follows a few seconds later.

"Paige, I can hear you smiling through the phone. But I'll dig into him and see what I can find," Oliver tells me.

"Great, but we need to talk to him as soon as possible! I think it could be him!" I say, feeling hopped up on adrenaline after finally having a solid lead.

"Okay. I'll schedule an appointment for Saturday the 1st. That way it's not during class hours, so we have time to do some digging. Does that sound good?" he asks me, and I hear him scratching notes on his notebook as he talks.

"Sounds perfect. Thanks, Ol!"

"You're welcome. Now get back to whatever the fuck you four do when you hang out."

"Just admit you're having fun with this, and I'll hang up," I say to him.

"Love, I promise I'm having fun. Now, finish that documentary before your big brain comes up with another lead for me to follow at nine o'clock at night." My face heats when he calls me that. It's slipped out so casually twice now, and I want to scream.

"I'll see you in class tomorrow?"

"Sounds good. Have a good night."

"You too," I say while lowering my phone from my ear and hanging up the call. I smile to myself before returning to my spot on the couch. "Shall we?" I ask, raising the remote and looking around at the three of them. They all stare back at me like I'm insane. "What?"

"What the hell was that about?" Ella asks.

"I had an idea with the investigation, and I had to let Oliver know," I say.

"Do you and my brother have nicknames?" Hads asks me, and I tense up a bit. *Is she going to yell at me?*

"It's a joke since we're partners in solving this. Sherlock and Watson, you know?" I say, but only Amelia's laughing. "Okay, it's not *that* funny. Why are you laughing so hard?"

"The fact that *he* is Watson is funny to me," Amelia says while throwing popcorn into her mouth. Everyone is silent for a few moments until we all burst out laughing. "Paige, you're literally solving a murder!" Amelia's still laughing, and I fall off the couch onto Ella's lap.

"I know." I'm laughing so hard I might start crying.

"My brother is helping her!" Hads is laughing hard as well.

"You guys, what's going on?" Ella has tears streaming down her face from laughing so hard. We all shrug and laugh some more, and by the time we're done, I'm crying real tears. Ella notices first.

"Paige, what's wrong?"

"Nothing. Absolutely nothing. It's just..." I trail off and look at the scene around me. I'm on the floor with Ella and Hads. Hads has tear stains on her shirt from laughing so hard. Ella's mascara has started running, and Amelia has a huge smile on her face. "I love you guys so much."

The three of them look at each other, climb over, and attack me with a group hug. By the end of it, we're a mess of bodies on the floor, lying on top of each other. I think about how alone I used to feel as a kid, how unwanted I felt by my parents, and now I have three people beside me who have become my best friends these past few years.

No, not best friends—family. These three have become my family.

I've always felt like I never had any real family before, but now I can say for certain that I have one. We may not be blood-related, but sometimes family isn't blood. Family is those around you who care about you, and I've never had to second guess that they cared about me.

How did I get so lucky? I wish I could reach back in time and hug my childhood self. I'd tell her it'll all be okay one day. That one day she won't feel so alone anymore.

"We love you too, Paige. Now can we please continue the documentary?" Ella asks.

"Yes, we can." I smile, and we all shuffle back to our spots before I press play. I smile as I lean over, put my head on Amelia's shoulder, and drift off to sleep. Before I'm under all the way, I hear someone talk.

"The fact that she can fall asleep to these is concerning,"

"Shh, don't wake her up. She needs to rest. Poor girl hasn't slept in days," Amelia tells them.

And then I'm out.

16

Oliver

Saturday, October 1st

9:00 AM

AFTER PAIGE CALLED ME the other night, I immediately scheduled an appointment with the assistant dean of students. I'm officially whipped over this girl.

The next day I woke up to a bunch of threatening texts from my sister. She didn't like the fact that we had nicknames or whatever. I told her to stop worrying about it—she was less than pleased.

Ever since I discovered that I like Paige, I've been confused about how to go about this. Nick and Noah might've been right. I *am* out of practice when it comes to flirting and I don't want to come on too strong here.

But if I do nothing, then we remain stagnant, which I definitely don't want.

Long story short, I'm fucked. It's been a while, and I'm rusty at this. So, I'm going to wing it and hope for the best.

"Have you ever met this guy before?" Paige asks me.

"No." We're on the way to his office since he agreed to talk. Apparently, he knows we found the body. He told me in his message he's been wanting to get in touch with us. I found it a bit odd because the police were supposed to keep our names off everything, but it makes sense why they would tell the guy who's now in charge.

We get to where his office is—the same one where the murder took place—and she freezes up. We haven't been back here since we searched the office that night, and I know it still scares her, so I grab her hand and pull her inside. She relaxes a bit when we walk up the stairs, but I don't let go of her until we get to his office. Her hand feels nice in mine.

Nobody's at the reception desk when we walk in, so the two of us stand in front of it silently.

"Should we knock or something?" Paige asks me, and I'm about to answer when the door opens, and a man steps out.

"Paige Yarrow? Oliver Baker?" he asks while pointing between the two of us.

"That's us." Paige smiles at him.

"Please come on in and make yourselves comfortable." We walk toward him and through the doorway. His office looks similar to the one where the dean was found, and I feel Paige tense up again as we enter. I guide her to one of the chairs with my hand on the small of her back, and she sits down. *Does that count as flirting?*

"I was so glad when you two reached out. I wanted to talk sooner, but as you can imagine, it's been a crazy few weeks around here."

"We get it," I say to him.

"What Oliver means is this transition must not be easy considering the circumstances," Paige tells him. She's always better at conversing than I am. I shoot her a smile and she winks back at me.

"Yes, it's been less than ideal, but that's not what I wanted to talk to you two about." My stomach drops a bit when he says that. I feel uneasy about where this conversation is going. *I wonder if Paige feels it too.* "I wanted to tell you the Health Center offers free counseling services on campus if you need it. Discovering what you did must have been life-changing, to say the least. I want to ensure that you know the college will do whatever it can to help."

"We appreciate that thank you," Paige says.

"Thanks," I say to him, still feeling uneasy in my gut.

"Of course."

"I do have one question, though," Paige says.

"I hopefully have an answer," he says back with a smile.

"Is there any update on the investigation? "

"Well, the police have not shared anything with me, but last I heard they weren't worried about it being a student committing this crime, so it's still safe here, I promise you that." He smiles.

"Well, not that safe because a man was *killed,* but I appreciate that." Paige shoots back at him, and I'm a bit stunned. *Where did that come from?*

"Listen, I completely get where you're coming from. Penelope—I mean, the dean's old receptionist was distraught when I last saw her a few days ago. She can barely string two sentences together, so like I said, counseling is available." He smiles a bit looser this time, and I wonder if Paige caught what I did.

"Well, you know she was present at the time of the discovery, so I imagine she would be," I say to him.

"Of course. Listen you two, I'll always be here if you need anything, but I have a very important call in fifteen minutes. Can you find your way out?" he asks us.

"We'll be fine. Thank you for your time!" Paige says as she jumps up from her chair, and we both walk quickly down the stairs. When we get outside, I look over at her, and I can tell the wheels in her head are turning.

"Did you catch the same thing I did?" I ask her, already knowing she did.

"He called the receptionist by her first name and then corrected himself."

"You want to search his office now, don't you?" I ask.

She looks up at me and smiles.

"Tonight, I'm guessing?"

"I mean unless you have other plans..."

"Paige, you and I both know I don't. Tonight sounds good. I'll meet you outside your door at two a.m., okay?"

"Sounds perfect," she says, and we start to walk back to our apartments. "Don't forget to wear all black. We wouldn't want to get caught, would we?"

"Did I miss the memo that all black clothes are suddenly an invisibility cloak?" I ask her.

"Oliver, it's proper attire! You should know this by now."

"Then tell me one more time, and I won't forget," I say to her, my mouth turning up.

"All. Black. Ol. Or else," she says, trying to be scary.

"I like it when you do that."

"Do what?"

"Call me by my nickname. It sounds nice coming from you." Her cheeks get red. She seems flustered. *Did I accidentally flirt? And did it work?*

"I can stop using it if you want."

"Don't," I tell her. "It sounds good when you use it."

"Okay." She looks down at the ground and smiles. "I'll see you later?"

I nod.

"Perfect." She opens her door and heads in, and for some reason, I follow her. She looks back at me. "What are you doing? I mean, you can come in, but I didn't think you wanted to hang out right now."

"I wanted to talk to Amelia for a second."

"My roommate, Amelia? Did you two become friends or something? Why do you want to talk to her?"

I think of something random to say. "I wanted to give her the five bucks back that she threw at me."

"Okay...but I don't even know if she's home. She might be out with Henry." She opens her fridge and takes out a bowl of fruit.

"Henry? The guy who isn't her boyfriend?" I ask her.

"That's right!"

"Paige? That was quick—" Amelia cuts off when she sees me standing here. "I knew I felt an ominous presence in here."

"Oliver wanted to talk to you about something," Paige tells her.

"Well, I'm glad you two finally went to a meeting where everyone left alive this time." I glare at Amelia after she says that. "Too soon?"

"Yes," Paige and I say at the same time, to which Amelia laughs.

"I'll leave you two be. Just try not to yell at each other like last time," Paige says as she heads to her room. "See you later?" I nod and as soon as she shuts her door, Amelia starts laughing.

"Man, I don't know how I didn't see it before. You've got it bad for her."

"What?" How could *she* of all people know what I feel for Paige? Maybe Paige told her about the kiss.

"Nothing. Why did you want to talk to me?"

"I wanted to get your phone number. In case of emergency," I say, and she raises her eyebrows at me.

"Do you see yourself being in many emergent situations in the future?"

"No, but when it comes to Paige having panic attacks, I assume you have a whole system to help her out of it."

"I do." She looks skeptically at me.

"Okay, so here." I shove my phone at her. "Put your number in so I can leave, and we can stop having this conversation." She takes my phone, punches her number in, and hands it back to me. "Thanks."

"No problem, Romeo!"

I shake my head and sigh before heading back to my apartment.

1:50 AM

I'm on Paige's doorstep waiting for her to come out when I hear shouting from inside. I'm about to go in and see what's going on when she comes out.

"Sorry, Amelia was awake in the living room. She stole my flashlight when I told her what we were doing."

"Always one to make things easy isn't she," I say.

"She means well." Paige smiles at me while looking me up and down. "You wore all black. My threat worked."

"I wore it just for you." She smiles after I say that. "Come on, let's go."

It takes around ten minutes to get inside and to his office. I look around before giving Paige the all-clear.

"Did you bring that tool thing you had last time to unlock the door?"

"Yeah, it's in my pocket." I turn the handle to the door, and it opens.

"That was easy." Paige smiles at me.

"You go right. I'll go left," I say to her.

"Got it, partner!" she whispers as she puts her head back down and continues taking pictures. His office somehow has less stuff in it than the other one. Besides the chairs we sat in earlier and a few half-dead plants, his desk, and a filing cabinet are the only other things in here. I start to rifle through his desk and get to a jammed drawer. I know it's not locked because there's no place for a key, so I jiggle it hoping it will come loose. Paige opens and closes the filing cabinet as quietly as she can.

"There's literally nothing here. No creepy files. No pictures. No weird manilla envelopes. Nothing!" she whispers. "It's all student information, which is boring."

I finally open the drawer, and several small papers fly out. "Woah."

"What's all this?" Paige asks me as she picks a paper up. "Oh my god! This is like something I would read in one of my books!" She smiles and shoves it in my face. I like how excited she gets when we find something we're not supposed to know about. My eyes take a second to focus, and I read what it says.

I miss how you would touch me in secret.

"That's disgusting," I say as I pick up a few more. "They all seem to be dirty love notes."

"This is *not* what I was expecting to find in here, that's for sure. Who do you think they're from? His wife?" she asks, pointing to a framed picture on his desk

I shake my head as I give her another note I found. "This one is signed, and look at the name." Her eyes go wide when she sees it.

"Penelope, the receptionist! Was he having an affair? He had a wedding ring on, but the last time we saw her, she didn't! Oh, this just got interesting."

"It seems like it. I just don't get—" A noise from down the hallway stops what I was saying. Paige and I look at each other and grab a few notes while shoving the rest back in the drawer and closing it. I look at her and nod, signaling for us to leave. We quietly shut it, and I turn off my flashlight when I hear a voice coming toward us.

"Off," I say to her, and she flicks hers off too.

"What do we do?" she asks, and I grab her hand and lead her to the stairwell on the other side of the building. "I didn't know this building had more than one stairwell."

"Well, luckily one of us researched the building beforehand." I wink at her, and she scoffs at me.

"Does that just mean you looked at the campus map?" she asks me, and I'm busted because that *was* all I did. I grunt, and she laughs at me. We get out of there, and I hold her hand as I lead her to the criminal justice building.

"Where are we going?" she asks me.

"I figured we could discuss at our roof spot," I say.

"*Our* roof spot? I was under the impression it was yours."

"Well, now it's our spot. Our little secret, okay? I know you're bad at keeping secrets, but this one is ours, so you can talk to me about it."

"Okay," she says as we climb the stairs up the roof. I look back at her and sure enough, her cheeks are red. I love being the one to do that to her. *Maybe I'm better at this than I thought.*

We open the door and head to the corner where we last sat. "I didn't plan on coming here, so there are no chairs. Sorry."

"It's okay. I prefer no chairs anyway."

We sit across from one another before I break the silence. "My sister tells me you prefer sleeping on the floor to your bed, and I never understood that."

"It's a long story," she says while looking up at the sky.

"I have time," I say to her.

"I don't want to bore you with it."

"Paige, you're not going to. No pressure to tell me, but I don't mind listening if all you need is someone to hear you." I look over at her, and her green eyes meet mine. We stay like that for a few seconds before she starts talking again.

"It's something I've always done since I was a kid. It was—" She stops for a minute, takes a deep breath, and continues. "It was easiest to hear my father's footsteps when he came to my room. It's how I knew to hide." She tells me, no longer looking at my face but off into the distance.

I let her keep going. "I was an only child, and my parents divorced when I was around eleven. Even before that, I would hear them arguing all night. Flash forward to after the divorce when I had to go to my dad's house on the weekends. It was okay at first. He would put on a movie and leave me alone like he didn't know what to do with me. Looking back now, I wish it stayed like that instead of what it eventually turned into." Tears start falling from her face, and I shuffle closer to wipe them from her face.

"Paige, it's okay. You don't have to tell me if it's too much," I say to her.

"I want to, Ol. I trust you," she tells me, and I nod at her to keep going. "I would fall asleep on the floor, and his footsteps would wake me up. They were heavy and terrifying. The floor was how I stayed safe. As I got older, he got angrier at me. I never knew why. I kept to myself as a kid, so it felt like my existence was enough to make him mad. I felt like I was constantly living on edge at his house, and I hated every second of it. I would go over, and he would drink himself into a coma most nights, often leaving me to fend for myself. But other times, he would hurt me. It started small at first, he would just hit me with the phone book or something, but he threw me down the stairs one time after he thought I'd dumped all his alcohol. I was twelve years old."

She pauses before continuing on. "After that, I would always get back to my mom's house with a new bruise or cut. He left completely when I was sixteen, and I haven't seen him since."

She stops to catch her breath, and I wrap her in my arms. It all makes fucking sense now, and I have to hold down my anger before I find him and do something I won't regret. How could a father do that to his child? How do you do that to anyone, in fact?

"Did you tell your mom?" I ask her, hoping one parent was there for her.

She shakes her head. "No. My mom basically forgot I existed after the divorce. She threw herself into work—she works for a law office, so it's constant work. I faded into the background most days. We only really talked when she needed me to do something for her. I was on my own for the most part. One day I was an innocent kid, and another day an adult chose to take that from me. It was easier on my own. At least the only person who I could disappoint was myself," she says, tears still falling, and I take my sleeve and wipe them again.

I wrap her in my arms and suddenly feel like I never want to let her go. I rest my chin on her head, and she quietly sobs into my shirt. "I think the worst part about being a kid whose parents didn't want them anymore is looking around at everyone else, and seeing all the love they have that you don't. My parents chose to get pregnant and have me, but after I was born and grew up, they realized I was too much effort and discarded me. Maybe I was too much. Maybe if I were different, they would have loved me." She's still crying into my shirt, and I have to steady my voice before speaking again.

"No, Paige. You were just a kid. You were just supposed to be a kid," I say while wrapping my arms even tighter around her. I'm on the verge of tears right now. I feel like she ripped my heart out. Her voice was so low and scared when she was talking to me. "You don't have to apologize for just existing. You deserved better."

She laughs and sniffles again. "I know, but—"

"Stop making excuses for your parents. They fucked up, not you. You weren't supposed to be an adult—they were. They were supposed to love you, not treat you like you were disposable," I say, pausing for a few seconds. "I'm sorry you had to go through that on your own. I'm sorry you were the only one there for yourself, and I'm sorry you got dealt the hand you did."

"Please don't," she mumbles into my shirt.

"Don't what?" I ask her as she looks up at me.

"Don't say that, and don't look at me like that."

"Like what?"

"Like you're ready to fight off everything that's ever hurt me."

"I would if I could," I say to her, meaning every word. "I'd build a time machine right now to undo all of it, Paige.

"It's done, Oliver. I survived it. It's my memories that haunt me now."

"Is that why you don't sleep? Nightmares?" I ask, and all the pieces start to fall into place.

She nods at me. "I'm sorry."

"You have nothing to apologize for. It's okay. Thank you for listening."

I run my hand through her hair. "Thank you for trusting me enough to tell me that."

We're silent for a few moments because I no longer know what to say. She just told me something vulnerable, and now I feel like I should share something too. I don't know what compels me to speak, but I do. I hate sharing my feelings, but it seems so easy with her.

"The night Mia died, I was supposed to be with her," I say, and her head shoots up to look at mine. "We fought that night because I worried about the friends she was going to hang out with. I didn't like them—they were reckless. They liked doing drugs and drinking but weren't safe about it. I had a bad feeling—a weird gut feeling that wouldn't go away. She didn't listen to me, we argued, and she left. I should've gone with her, but I let my pride get in the way. She called me, just before—" I pause, because besides my therapist, nobody else knows about this. "She called me while she was bleeding out in the middle of the road, and I didn't answer. I let it go to voicemail. Minutes later, I got a call that there was an accident and she was pronounced dead. After that, I kept thinking that maybe if I had been there, I could've done something. Maybe I could've saved her." I look down at Paige, and she's staring at me, her eyes filling with tears.

"Oliver, you could've died if you were in that car with her. You don't know you could've helped her. Don't blame yourself for something you couldn't have controlled." She leans back into me, and I let some of my tears fall.

"She left me a voicemail. It took me a few months to listen to it because of how guilty I felt. When I finally did, it was her apologizing about how we left things." I pause as another tear falls. "She died thinking I was mad at her for leaving. While I was trying to prove I was right, she was dying on the street. And I'll spend my life wishing I wasn't so stubborn and had just picked up the damn phone."

"Oliver, it's not your fault."

"I know, I can't help but think what if," I say to her.

"I know what that feels like," Paige says while looking up at me.

I'm silent for a few moments, just looking down at her. "My sister doesn't know." It's not a question.

"No."

"Ella? Amelia?" I ask.

"Just Amelia," she says. "I don't know what's stopped me from telling them. They're basically family. I feel guilty that I haven't told them anything about my past, and now you know before they do, but I—" She pauses. "I'm not used to having genuine people around me. I'm not used to having more than one friend. I've always relied on myself and not other people, especially when I'm struggling. It terrifies me to open up when I used to keep all my feelings to myself. I don't know how to rewire my brain to think differently."

"Can I ask you a question?" I ask her, and she nods. "Why did you choose to tell me about this?"

"I trust you. I always have. You've been one of the only constants throughout the past four years, along with the girls. I guess I feel like we both have experience with not feeling like we deserve the people around us. In a way, we're kind of similar. And I trust that after this partnership is over, you won't tell anyone."

After this partnership is over. Right. I almost forgot that after we solve this together, we'll go back to just being what we were before. Never mind the fact that I want more. Never mind that Paige has been the only positive thing around me for four years. My chest hurts when I think about not having her around all the time.

"I would never do that," I tell her.

"I know."

"How do you do it?" I ask her, and she looks at me, confused. "How are you so positive about the world after going through all that you have?"

I got angry at the world after Mia died, and I don't know if I ever fully returned from it until I was around Paige. I've definitely softened these past few weeks and I don't hate it.

"I'm not sure if I'm honest. I wasn't always like this. I went through a really dark period in high school. I only had one real friend, and I felt like I was always on the outside looking in. I felt lonely most of the time. But then, when I got here I..." She pauses. "Amelia made me a playlist the first week of freshman year. It was the first time someone ever did something for me. Then Ella sat at my table and started talking to me about the book I was reading. Then a year later, Hads joined our trio and made it a quartet. She annotated a copy of her favorite book for my birthday and gave it to me because she thought I would love it, and I did."

She stops to smile at all the memories. "Those three girls were there for me in ways they never knew. Those three are why I think the world still offers beautiful things. Hads, Ella, and Amelia are why I'll never be a scared little kid on my own again. And you too, you know. You were always around. Always there for me. I don't think you knew I noticed, but I did, Ol. I see you, just like you see me." I look at her, and I have to stop myself from kissing her because right now, here on this roof late at night, I've never seen a more beautiful person than Paige.

Does she know she has been a light for me all this time? Does she know how much she's helped me just by existing? Does she know that if I'm the moon and she's the sun, I'll chase her forever, even if I never reach her? Does she know how much she matters as a person? I should tell her. Why have I never told her that?

"That was beautiful," I say to her, suddenly not having the courage to say anything else.

"Thanks." She smiles at me and wraps her arms around me again. I lean into her embrace.

"I think you're one of the strongest people I've ever met," I tell her.

"I think you're one of the most selfless people I've ever met," she tells me.

"Do you still feel lonely sometimes?"

"Not anymore, now that I have the girls...and you."

And you. "Me?"

"Oliver, I don't know anyone else who would jump feet first into a murder investigation with me, so yes, you. I never feel lonely around you, despite other people saying you don't have feelings and prefer to speak with threatening looks."

"Who says that?"

"It doesn't matter," she says quickly, and I laugh.

"Thank you for telling me all that. I know it wasn't easy."

"Right back at you. Thank you," she says, and her eyes are blazing into mine, but I don't want to kiss her in the state we're in. We were vulnerable tonight, and that means something. I don't want anything to take away from that, no matter how much I want to kiss her again.

"So, where do we go from here with these notes and shit?" I ask, taking them out of my pocket and handing them to her. "I assume you want these for the murder board?"

"I did, so thank you. We should dig more into the assistant and see what she was up to. I can call my friend Alissa and see if she can help us. She's good at computer stuff."

"Okay, that sounds good. I'll run through her social media if you want to do his accounts?" I ask her.

"Perfect," she says while standing up. "We should probably get back, though this would be a great spot to watch the sunrise soon."

"Good idea. I don't want Amelia to murder me for keeping you out late." We head back to our apartments, not filling the silence as we go home. I walk Paige to her door, and before going in, she reaches up and gives me a quick kiss on the cheek.

"Thank you."

"For what?"

"For listening. And for always being there for me." She smiles at me. "Goodnight, Ol."

"Goodnight, Paige," I say as she enters her place. I turn around and head to mine, knowing damn well I won't sleep tonight. Knowing damn well I'm going to be thinking about her all fucking night. Tonight felt like a turning point for some reason, and I feel like there's no going back now.

I'm fucking fine with that because that conversation just cemented the fact that I'm in a deep hole with this girl, and I would gladly never climb out of it if I had the option to.

Paige deserves every good thing in the world, and I want to be the one who gives it to her.

Case closed.

17

Wednesday, October 5th

"THIS BOOK ACTUALLY CHANGED my life," I tell the girls.

"Paige and I wouldn't stop crying over a few quotes this week. This was such a great book. Instant five stars," Amelia agrees with me.

"It was a bit too real, and I kind of don't want to talk about it for fear of crying again," Ella tells us.

"How did he write about a whole community and make me feel like I did? It was so cohesive too! I recommended this series to Grant because it also talked a lot about hockey." Hads smiles at us over the knowledge that Grant has become a reader now. He and Hads often swap books when they think the other would like it.

"I immediately ordered the second one. I need to read all of his books now. I think I'm in love," I say to the girls with a smile. I love when you read a book and the author connects with your soul. This one did that for me, and now I need to read everything of his. It's so interesting how books can make you feel so seen.

That's part of what I've always loved about reading. When I didn't feel like my emotions mattered as a kid, books showed me that I wasn't alone. The girls continue to talk about the book, but my mind zones out and goes back to the roof Oliver and I were on the other night.

We had a vulnerable moment. I told him things about my past and he did the same. He wrapped me in his arms while I cried into his shirt. It was the safest I'd felt in a long time. My head has been spinning since then. Oliver and I are two people who have been broken so many times before, that neither of us thinks we're capable of being loved.

Yet I like Oliver—a lot.

More than I've liked anyone romantically before. He's one of my best friend's brothers, and I have feelings for him. That scares the crap out of me. I've always been on my own, and I don't know what to do with strong feelings like this. It makes me jittery.

"I'm excited to see where the story goes in the next two books," Ella says.

"Same, I think—" Someone knocking on the door catches Amelia off guard, and I flinch because nobody ever comes up here besides Grant.

"Henry? Wh–What are you doing here?" Ames gets up and hurries over to him, trying to shove him out of the room.

"Amelia, don't be rude! Introduce the man to us!" Ella says, and when they walk back in, Amelia looks irritated and Henry looks stiff. He pulls a chair over and sits down next to where she is, and I can *feel* the tension wading off of those two.

"Well everyone, this is Henry. Henry, this is everyone," Amelia tells us.

"Nice to meet you, Paige, Ella, and Hadleigh." He tilts his head at us as if he's trying to cement our names into his head.

"He knows our names!" Hads whispers to Ella.

"Henry, tell us about yourself," Ella says. When I look over at Hads, her eyes are bouncing between Amelia and Henry as if she was at a tennis match. I think the three of us understand how big this is, but we're trying to keep calm so Henry isn't scared of us coming on too strong.

He takes a deep breath before he speaks. "Well, I'm a senior. I study creative writing—"

"That must mean you're a reader too! I've been dying to ask you what your favorite book is." Ella elbows me because I interrupted him while he was introducing himself, but I can't help it! I'm too excited about this.

"If I had to pick one favorite, it'd be *The Picture of Dorian Gray*. I'm partial to quite a few classics, probably because of all the literature classes I've taken. I really love *The Great Gatsby*, some of Hemingway's books, and I also have quite a soft spot for Austen." He smiles at us.

"Jane Austen? " I jump up and I hear a few heavy sighs.

"Here we go..." Ella says.

"Well, congrats Henry, you've summoned a monster," Hads tells him.

"I'm not a monster! I just love Jane Austen! Okay, so what's your favorite of hers? Mine is a three-way tie between *Pride and Prejudice, Emma,* and *Persuasion*."

Henry smiles and it looks like he's becoming more comfortable. I *knew* books were the right topic of conversation. "*Emma* is my favorite. I fell in love with the story."

"Paige, calm down before you have a heart attack. Don't scare him away, we just met him," Ella tells me.

"He's clearly not scared of us if he can handle Amelia all the time," Hads says.

"What's that supposed to mean?" Amelia asks her.

"Nothing! I'm just saying, you can come off as scary and intense sometimes. My brother is *terrified* of you, and Grant was scared of you until you two bonded over National Geographic," Hads says. Oliver has told me before that Amelia scares the crap out of him, and coming from him of all people made me laugh.

"Good. They should be scared. Well, Oliver should be, not Grant. He's basically an honorary member of book club," Amelia tells her.

"But Henry, you're studying creative writing? That sounds interesting. What do you hope to do with that?" Ella asks him.

"I hope to become an author someday." He smiles at the floor when he says that.

"An author! Wouldn't it be fun if we read one of his books at book club?" I say to the room and Amelia glares at me. "What?"

"Nothing," she says to me.

"That seems like an interesting career choice. Have you started writing a book yet?" Ella asks him. She always has the important questions out of the four of us.

"I've started writing something. It's in the very first stages, but it's coming along."

"What genre is it?" Hads asks him.

"It's a fantasy and science fiction." He turns to look at Amelia and she stares back at him, her face glaring at his. "What?"

"You still won't let me read it after I've pestered you about it. It's not fair."

"Mills, I've only written like ten chapters, and some of them don't even make sense with all the notes I have on it. You can read it eventually," he tells her.

"Mills?" I whisper to Ella.

"Is that a nickname? Amelia didn't kill you for calling her that?" Ella asks him.

"Um, no she didn't. Usually, she threatens to get Paige to torture me or something." Everyone turns to look at me and I smile back at them.

"Not something to be proud of, P," Hads tells me.

"Why not? I like being the friend you guys come to when you need to torture someone. It's like my thing!" I smile.

"One investigation at a time for you, Paige. You can torture Henry later," Amelia tells me.

"What?" he asks, looking a bit shocked.

"I'm not going to hurt you, I promise." I smile at him and he tilts his head at me.

"I'm changing the subject," Ella says before we get too out of control. "Are you from around here?"

"Yeah, I'm a local. Are you guys from out of state?"

"I'm from New York. Western New York, not New York City. Everyone always asks me that," I say to him.

"Oh, that's cool. A bit of a drive." He laughs awkwardly.

"I live around half an hour away now, but I grew up in Virginia. My dad lives close to here with my little sister," Ella tells him.

"Oh, that's nice! I have a little sister too!" Henry smiles widely at us.

"Aw! How old is she? Mine's sixteen, and she's a menace, but I love her." Ella smiles.

"My sister is nine. Also a menace, but the cutest menace ever. She's one of my favorite people." He smiles proudly, and judging by the way he said it, there must be a story behind that, but I'll ask him that later. "Hads, where are you from?"

"A small town in California."

"You're a long way from home," he tells her.

"Yeah, but my brother also goes here, so it's not as lonely with him here." She smiles at the mention of Oliver, and so do I.

"Oh, that must be interesting. Who's your brother? Would I know him?"

Amelia practically bursts out of her chair with laughter, which scares us a bit. "Would you know, Oliver? That would be like you becoming acquainted with a stone gargoyle."

"It would be funny to see those two interact." Hads smiles. "But Ames, he's not that stone-like. You two just like to push each other's buttons."

"It's too easy with him." Amelia smiles.

"Wait, was that the guy who interrupted us that one day and dragged Paige away?" Henry asks, and I freeze in my seat.

"He what?" Hads asks.

"I'm sorry, he dragged you away?" Ella looks over at me, and I shrug.

"Was I not supposed to say that?" Henry asks Amelia, and she's still laughing.

"Good evening, ladies! How is—" Grant steps into the room and stops talking when he notices another male present. "Well, hello. Who is this fine specimen of a man?"

"That's Henry!" I tell him.

"No kidding! Amelia's boyfriend? It's nice to finally meet you." I look over at Henry. His face has drained of color, and Amelia looks like she could shoot lasers out of her eyes at all of us. Hads elbows him as he sits next to her. "Ow! What?"

"Shh."

"At least it wasn't the ruler," Ella tells him.

"The what?" Henry asks.

"Nothing! Grant, this is Amelia's *friend* Henry." I nod at him, silently telling him to pick up what I'm saying, and he does.

"Right! Sorry, I must be thinking of someone else," Grant says. "So, how did you two meet?"

"We met at a concert over the summer," Henry tells him and a few seconds of silence pass and before I can break it, Hads beats me to it.

"Henry was telling us about his favorite books and the story he's authoring," Hads tells him while placing her head on his shoulder.

"Wow, so is this some sort of meet and greet type event for you guys to read his book for book club?" Grant asks us.

"Not that I know of…" Henry trails off.

"Okay, are we done with this tonight? Can we leave?" Amelia asks us.

"Actually, I have a few questions I would like to ask Henry, if you don't mind?" Grant asks Amelia, and she sighs.

"Go ahead." This is going to either be really good or really bad. Grant's quite protective over us. It's cute how he cares about Hads and our group—that's why I call him an honorary member of the book club. He's the first boyfriend of our little group, and I feel like that gives him an edge over possible other boyfriends.

"So, I'm assuming you're a literature aficionado—"

"Henry mentioned earlier that he loves the book *The Great Gatsby*," I tell him. "As a fellow lover of that book, I figured that was vital information."

"Paigey, how did you know that was my question? Henry, can you please confirm for me that Nick and Gatsby were in love throughout the entire book?"

"Grant, enough with this agenda. The entire book is centered around Gatsby reaching for Daisy and being unable to attain her. You of all people should know that," Hads tells him.

"Well, I mean, yeah, that's what the book is about. But if you go a bit deeper, it's blatantly obvious to me," Grant says.

"I would agree with that. Maybe not in love, but Nick and Gatsby have a special relationship. Nick was most definitely in love with Gatsby and his lifestyle, and that love went deep, so yeah, you could say that." Henry smiles at him, and there's a few moments of silence before Grant stands up and walks toward him. Amelia and the rest of us look a bit worried before Henry stands up, and Grant pulls him in for a bro hug.

"Amelia, you might have to get a scraper to remove those two. I think Grant just fell in love," Hads tells her.

"This is adorable. I love this new bromance," I say, smiling at the room.

"I'm sorry, Amelia, I'm stealing your boyf—friend. I'm stealing your friend from you." Grant awkwardly smiles at her while she glares daggers at him. "And you." He points to Hads.

"What?"

"I was right. Nick and Gatsby are in love."

"So, you two are dating then?" Henry points between Hads and Grant.

"She's my girlfriend," Grant tells him.

"Boyfriend." Hads simply points at Grant.

"You guys are cute together," Henry states. A keen observer he is.

"Thanks. You ready, Hads?" Grant stands up and offers her his hand.

"Sounds good. We're meeting Jacks and Claire for movie night. I'll text you guys later?" Hads asks us.

"Oh, for sure. We're going to need to debrief." Ella winks at her, and Hads smiles before Grant pulls her out of the classroom.

"Bye, ladies! I hope I get graced with your presence again soon!" Grant yells back to us before he stops and turns back. "Henry, my man, I hope to see you again soon. We should chat about Gatsby at some point."

Henry smiles. "I'd be happy to."

"Wonderful! But if you dare hurt that girl…" Grant points to Amelia and then back at Henry before drawing a line across his neck slowly.

"No, you won't," Hads tells him.

"Okay, fine. I'll get Paige and Oliver to do it. I'm sure those two would have fun with it." Grant smiles and turns back around, grabbing Hads' hand.

"Seriously?" I say.

"Paige, to be fair, you are the one solving a murder right now," Ella tells me. "I have to get going too. I have work tomorrow. But Henry, it was very nice to meet you. I hope we didn't scare you off too much. It would be nice to see you around some more."

"It was great to put faces to all your names finally," Henry tells her.

"Bye, girls! I'll text you when I'm home, and I expect you to do the same!" she yells back to us.

"We will!" Amelia and I say at the same time. When Ella leaves, Amelia just stares at me. Henry looks more relaxed than when he first walked here, which is good. He can accomplish anything if he can survive the four of us together.

"That went well," I say to the two of them. "I can clean up in here if you guys have plans tonight. I don't mind."

"Are you sure, P?" Amelia asks me.

"I don't mind helping either," Henry says.

"It's fine, you two. Have fun! It won't take me long and I hear my bed calling my name from here." I smile at Amelia, hoping she'll leave and have a good night with Hen. I'm sure this interaction was stressing her out, so it would be nice for her to let loose.

"Okay, we're going to my favorite Thai place tonight, so I'll be late coming home." She looks around for her bag before noticing Henry already carrying it. "Okay, come on Hen, let's go."

Those two are going to be dating in no time. I can *feel* it.

I fix the classroom back to how it's supposed to be, but before I leave, I grab my phone and dial my mom's number. I put my phone to my ear and let it ring.

"Please pick up this time," I whisper as her voicemail rings in my ear. I sigh to myself and call a different number.

"Hey girl, what's up? Is everything okay?" my friend Sadie asks.

"Hi. Can you do something for me?" Sadie still lives back home because she goes to college one town over, so sometimes I ask her to check in on my mom. Just to ensure she's alive and only ignoring me and not dead somewhere.

"Anything for you, P."

"Can you go check on my mom? She hasn't answered my calls, and I'm getting worried."

"Of course. I'll go tomorrow morning before work."

"Thanks, Sade. Just text me what you find."

"I will. Keep your head up, Paigey."

"I'll try. I love you."

"I love you too," she says as she hangs up. I throw my phone into my tote bag and shut the light off in the classroom before leaving.

As I walk back to my apartment alone, I start thinking about the past few years. My brain sometimes enters this weird, spirally mood, and before I can get out of it, it takes over. I remember people always telling me as a kid that I was mature for my age, and right now, all I can think about is the past twenty-one years I've been on this Earth.

Why did my parents treat me like I didn't exist? Why did my father do what he did to me? Why do I feel guilty about all of this, as if I was the one who did something wrong? I sometimes think I was put on this Earth to give more love to other people than I was going to get.

How do you accept the love you think you should have while feeling like you're the most unlovable person on the planet? Not even my parents loved me, so why should anyone else? I think that's mainly why I tend to avoid relationships. I feel like all the shit that happened to me and everything that made me who I am has solidified that fact. That's why my feelings for Oliver scare me so much. How do I put all my faith into someone so willingly? How do I stop being afraid of always being alone? How do I finally trust that someone will love me and not turn out like my father?

Maybe I was put here to ensure nobody felt as bad as I felt—that may be my purpose. When I get into my apartment, I sink against the door and feel some tears drop from my face.

What the hell am I doing with my life? How did I get here?

I'm solving a murder while trying to graduate and find a job. I'm finally entering the real world, but I feel like my life has been happening eighty miles away from myself.

Doesn't anyone know I've been alone since I was a kid? I've been living in the real world. I'm in it already. Sometimes, I wish I could go back and do it all again. I want a childhood. I want what other people have. I want the holidays to hurt less every year and I want a normal family. A *happy* family.

But for now, I have to keep picking myself up off the ground and moving. Because if I don't, I'm not going to make it. Now more than ever, I want to make it to the life I want—the life I *deserve*.

Don't I deserve happiness for once, rather than pretending like I am? Would Oliver make me happy?

He already has...

I take a breath before standing up. I kick my shoes off and head for my room. My safe place. Hoping that I can drift off to sleep without any nightmares.

18

Friday, October 7th

I WALK INTO THE criminal justice building, carrying my tote on one shoulder and my water bottle in my hand. Oliver and I only have one class on Friday but today we're meeting with our professor who oversaw the criminal justice club. She reached out wanting to discuss some things about it going forward since it got disbanded for the semester.

Yesterday I had a call with my therapist back home, and she helped me talk openly about what I felt. It helped a lot and she gave me some more breathing exercises to do when I feel a panic attack coming on. I didn't mention my feelings about Oliver, but maybe in the next session, I will. We mostly focused on how I was doing after finding a dead body. And to my surprise, I feel okay considering the situation.

I walk into class and find Oliver sitting in his usual spot. When I sit down next to him, he glances at me and smiles as I grab my laptop out of my bag. We've been dancing around each other since that night on the roof. We pretend everything's fine and nothing has changed—even though everything has changed.

It's awkward, to say the least, but it's no different than what we used to do before we became partners solving a murder. In a way, it's back to normal—whatever normal is for two college seniors partnering up to investigate a homicide when they should be applying to jobs and figuring their futures out.

I haven't really put much thought into it.

"When did you start getting to places early?" I ask him, trying to break some of the tension I'm feeling.

"This girl I know once told me that if I'm on time, I'm late, so now I get places early." My stomach flutters at his comment because I'm fairly certain the girl he's talking about is me.

"Well, she sounds like a smart girl."

"The smartest, actually." He looks over at me and smiles. *Smiles.* I've never seen him smile or laugh this much, but lately, he's been doing it more and more. He has a beautiful smile. I wish he showed it more often.

"Why do you think Professor Craig wants to meet with us after all this time?" I ask him.

"I'm not sure, but it's probably about fundraising or something."

"You don't think it's..." I trail off, not wanting to finish the rest of my sentence.

"No, Paige. I don't think she would bring that up. If she does, I'll steer the conversation."

"I can talk about it without panicking. I just prefer not reliving that memory," I say to him.

"I know, but if she brings it up, I'll divert the conversation."

"Okay. Thank you," I say while putting my hand on his arm. I feel his muscles tense up beneath my touch, so I quickly take my hand off and pretend to look at something important on my laptop.

Our professor walks in a few moments later, and she immediately starts talking about the homework we had to do, so Oliver and I face the front of the room. He flips his notebook open while the PowerPoint loads. I take a deep breath and start typing my notes while she speaks. Only an hour left of this class, and then we can focus on the investigation. Wherever it's headed, I hope it doesn't get to the point where one of us gets hurt. I don't think I could live with myself if I dragged Oliver into this, and he got hurt because of me.

Fingers crossed, I guess.

AN HOUR LATER, OLIVER and I head into the elevator and down to the lobby to go to Professor Craig's office. Before anyone else can get on with us, Oliver slams the button, and the guy who wants to join us in the elevator gives Oliver the finger as the door shuts.

"That was mean! What if he's late for a date or something?" I say to him.

"Well, maybe it's not meant to be," he says. I giggle a bit as I adjust the bag on my shoulder. We're standing side by side, him on the right of me, and I'm watching the numbers go down when I hear Oliver sigh heavily. I look over at him.

"Do you have any tattoos?" I ask, and he looks down at me.

"Two."

"Really?" I say, eyes widening.

"Are you surprised?"

"A little bit," I say back to him. "Why have I never seen them?"

"You would have to get my shirt off for them to be visible to you." He smirks at me and I feel my knees get all wobbly. *Get it together, Paige.*

"Oh." I laugh, trying to diffuse the tension in this tiny ass elevator. Luckily it dings, and we head to where we need to go. Oliver knocks before entering her office in his normal, insistent manner.

"Come in," she says, barely looking up from her pile of papers.

"Hi, professor!" I say while sitting in the only chair across her desk. I look at Oliver. "Did you want to sit down? I don't mind standing."

"I'm fine. Sit down, Paige." He pulls the chair out for me and I sit. "Why are we here?"

"Always straight to the point, aren't you Oliver?" she says, looking up at us.

"I don't know why anyone would be anything but."

"Is this about the club? Are we going to be able to get together next semester?" I ask, hoping she says yes.

"That's why I wanted you two here today. Moving forward, the club no longer exists. I'm sorry to tell you this, but I found out yesterday that guy who is now acting as the dean didn't think the club was necessary after what happened."

"So, what do you need us to do?" I ask. I can't lie, I'm a little disappointed. I liked being part of a club, but I guess it's for the best. Plus, after this semester, I only have one more left. This change doesn't affect me that much, and I'm sure Oliver isn't too broken up about this.

"I need you guys to email the other members and let them know. You can still put this club on your transcript if either of you decides to go to grad school. If not, then it shouldn't be a big deal," she says, looking back down at her papers.

"Is that all then?" Oliver asks, standing off the wall he was leaning on and heading for the door.

"Oliver, come back," I say to him, not having moved. He pauses and immediately turns around and stands behind my chair. "Professor Craig, what do you know about Professor Fitzpatrick getting fired?"

"Why do you two want to know?" she asks us with a questioning look.

"Call it mild curiosity," I say.

"Well, I don't know much about it. The email sent around said it was because of suspicious circumstances. Which I thought was weird because he had just gotten tenure. I tried not to pry about it, and neither should you two. I know you liked him as a professor, and so did I, but some things aren't meant to be looked into. This is probably one of them," she says back to us.

"Why do you think we would look into this?" Oliver asks her.

"You two give off real Bonnie and Clyde vibes. You always worked well together in my classes." Oliver and I both laugh.

"Well, thank you for proctoring our club, professor. We'll see you next semester in class?"

"Sounds good. Make sure to send that email out this week!"

"She will!" Oliver tells her as he grabs my hand and drags me out of her office. "Do you think Fitzpatrick still has access to his email account?"

"Probably? He just got fired, and I think it takes a bit for the system to finalize all the paperwork."

"I'll email him asking if we can talk. I feel like suspicious circumstances could be connected, but I'm not sure why," he tells me.

"The timing of it is odd. My gut is telling me that this entire situation is all connected."

"Same," Oliver tells me. "I'll text you at some point when he answers, okay? I have to go meet Grant and give him his birthday present. Are you okay with walking back by yourself?"

"Oliver, I'm not going to get kidnapped on our college campus in broad daylight. I'll be fine. Also, I think it's adorable you got Grant a birthday present. What did you get him?"

"A framed picture of him and I surfing that my sister took while he was visiting over the summer."

"Oliver! Are you secretly sentimental? That's the cutest thing I've ever heard!" Not only is that the most adorable thing I've ever heard, but the fact that he *framed* the picture too has me feeling emotional. Those two really are becoming brothers.

"I'm totally going to tell everyone about this," I say as I head through the doors and back to my apartment, hearing him sigh heavily as he walks away.

19

Oliver

Tuesday, October 10th

IT'S TWO IN THE afternoon when my phone buzzes and I get a response from Fitzpatrick. I text Paige immediately because this investigation is becoming more chaotic by the day.

Oliver: He didn't want to meet at his house. We're going to some diner.

Paige: Does that seem weird?

Oliver: Kind of?

Paige: Do you think we're safe around him?

Oliver: I don't think he would hurt former students of his.

Paige: Yeah, but what if he hurt the dean?

Oliver: Paige, he probably wouldn't have agreed to meet if he was a murderer.

Paige: You never know...

Oliver: I'll meet you at your car in ten minutes, okay?

Paige: Sounds good. Do I need to bring anything?

Oliver: Yourself and your car keys.

I grab all the shit I need before I book it out of my place and head to where Paige parks her car.

I lean against the car while I wait for her, but it's not long before I see her walking toward me, a pep in her step like always.

"Hey! Are you ready to do some interrogating?"

"Interviewing, not interrogating," I tell her.

Paige unlocks her car, and we both climb in. I move the passenger seat so my legs can stretch out. I'm pretty sure Amelia is the one who sits here, so I make a note to move it back when I get out. We may be on decent terms, but Amelia still scares me.

Paige starts driving, and I navigate from my phone to this diner in the middle of nowhere. I can't help but feel a bit nervous. We have no reason to suspect him, but who the hell knows at this point.

"Turn left here," I say to her, and she does. "Do you always drive this slow?" My sister told me that Paige is the ultimate grandma driver. I thought she was kidding, but apparently not.

"It's called being a safe driver, Oliver." I grunt at her while music plays lightly in the background—*Fix You* by Coldplay.

"You like this song?"

She scoffs at me. "Yes. It's one of my favorites, but I can change it. We need some action music." She reaches for the knob, and I push her hand away.

"It's okay. I like this song too." It plays quietly in the background as we keep driving.

It's been a while since I've listened to it, and the lyrics are kind of hitting home. I lost a beautiful part of my life once. I lost the girl that I loved, and there's nothing I can do to change that.

But Paige is here now. She's next to me and I can do something about it. I don't want to be someone who misses out on something good because I'm scared of losing someone I love.

As Paige parks at the diner a few minutes later, the two of us hop out and stop before going inside—Fitzpatrick is already sitting down sipping a coffee. "You ready?"

Paige lifts her shoulders back. "Do you still carry that knife?" she asks me, and I nod at her. "Okay, that makes me feel better."

This place reminds me of every old diner I've seen in movies. The black and white tiled floor, the swivel chairs at the bar with slices of pie in those weird ass containers. The booths are red, and the tables match them. It's like we're in the diner from *Pulp Fiction*. Paige and I walk over to where he's sitting, and we don't say a word as we slip into the booth. Paige sets her phone face down on the table, and a waitress approaches us.

"What would you two like today?"

"I don't need anything, but thank you," I say.

"I'll just take some water, please," Paige tells the woman.

"Did you want a refill on that coffee, sir?"

Fitzpatrick nods his head and comes back a few moments later with all our stuff. I see Paige unwrapping her straw and doing something to the wrapper but I can't tell what. *Is she making a circle?*

"Let me know if you need anything else," she says as she walks away.

"Thank you!" Paige says, sipping on her water. I notice she tends to drink more when she's nervous. I squeeze her hand underneath the table, silently telling her I'm here, and she squeezes it back.

"I don't know why I agreed to this," he tells us.

"Well, that's too bad because we're here now, and you're going to tell us what happened," I tell him.

"Why do you two care so much?"

"I was the one who found the body on campus," Paige blurts out, and he looks over at her, eyes wide before he sighs heavily.

"Please tell me you two aren't playing detectives and trying to figure this out. Need I remind you, you're students?"

"Call it practice for the real world." Paige smiles at him. "Now, tell us what you know."

"What do you two know so far is what I should be asking," he says to us.

"Not much. The dean has a son who's still missing. Wilson is now the acting dean of students and seems to have some sort of secret relationship. That's all we have so far," I say to him and he looks a bit shocked.

"You guys found out about his missing son?"

"All it took was a Google search and some light snooping," Paige tells him.

"What do you know about that?" I ask him.

"I've been looking into it since it happened. Well, let me back up a bit. The dean came to me about a year after his son went missing. All the leads the police had went cold, but he was still wrapped up in it. He told me he wanted me to pick up where they had left off—to dig deeper into it. So, I agreed. He told me he would pay me under the table as I pieced everything together. I was a full-time criminal justice professor, and on the side, I was trying to find out what happened to his son. He agreed to give me tenure so I could keep working on it." He pauses to sip his coffee. "At first, I was excited. I felt like I was returning to my former detective days. Working on this case gave me a new sense of purpose."

"Not like teaching the younger generation matters, but go on," I say, and Paige softly kicks me in the leg under the table.

"Keep going. Oliver likes to interrupt, but you get used to it," she tells him.

"As time passed, I had exhausted every lead. I asked his family members, and people in the area at the time, but I had nothing. Last semester, he brought me into his office. He was ecstatic about something. I sat down, and he shoved a note in my face. Just a few days before, I told him there was nothing more I could do. The case was cold, and we had no new information for years. Now here he was, showing me this note that said someone knew what happened on it. At first, I thought he wrote it because he wanted me to keep running in circles, but he showed me camera footage of someone sliding it under his office door while he was working on something. It was clear as day—someone knew something about his son. I worked tirelessly over the summer, trying to figure out who had sent this ominous note, and when nothing came of it, he fired me on the grounds of not being able to do my job. Of course he meant the case, but to the school, it meant my teaching skills."

"The note said someone knew what had happened to his son?" I ask.

"It seemed that way, yes."

"And he fired you because you couldn't figure it out?" Paige asks.

"Yes, but it's for the best. I'm going back home to live with my brother on his farm. I always wanted a quiet life. This just gives me a reason to get it." He looks happy or at peace or whatever. *Something still feels off.*

"But you didn't retaliate and kill him for firing you?"

"Oliver, why would you ask me that? You know the answer."

He's right. I know he didn't do it. He was one of my best professors, but I needed to make sure. If he said it aloud, I could tell if he was lying.

"Just double checking," I tell him.

"Do you still have that note by chance?" Paige asks him.

"No. The dean kept it. I don't know where, but he gave me a copy, not the original." He gets up and puts a five on the table before grabbing his jacket. "So, that's my story. Is that all? I have a flight to catch."

"That's all. Thanks," I say to him.

"Have a safe flight!" Paige tells him as he walks away from us. "Did you want some pancakes, or are those too sweet for you? I feel like you have a secret sweet tooth."

"I like sweet things just fine. Though nothing is sweeter than you, Paige."

Her cheeks flush at my attempt to flirt. "I might get a waffle to go. Amelia wanted me to get her French toast when I told her we were coming here." She gets up, goes up to the counter, and orders while I stay in the booth.

This entire situation feels off. I have a feeling we're missing a big piece of the puzzle, and I hope it doesn't come back to bite us at some point.

I check my phone and answer the group text with my family that's been buzzing. They wanted to know if I was coming home for my birthday, and my sister told them I was too busy. Thankfully, she didn't say why.

Paige returns with her bag, and we head back to her car. She unlocks it, and I open her door while grabbing the bag from her hands.

"Thanks," she says with a smile.

"Just try to drive faster this time."

"No," she says while shutting the door.

I climb into the passenger seat and ask Paige if she needs directions back to campus, and she tells me no. As we start driving, her music still playing softly. Something about this doesn't feel right as I sit with the information we learned.

"I think that went well, don't you?" I ask her.

"Yeah. We got more information from him, and at least we can eliminate him as a suspect now. I just feel confused. I feel like we have so much information, but at the same time we have nothing."

"I feel the same way."

"Do you regret helping me with this yet?" she asks.

"No. I don't. We just need to be careful."

"Do you think we're in danger?"

"No, Paige. But this is a *literal* murder case, so caution is necessary." I try to think of something to change the subject. "Have you been sleeping more lately?"

"A little bit," she tells me. "I don't like sleeping right now."

"Anything I can do?"

"No. But, thanks for checking on me."

"No problem, partner," I say, and she laughs. I smile as I turn to look out the window again, but before I do, something catches my eye. "What's on your finger?"

She follows my gaze to the steering wheel. "Oh." She giggles a bit. "Another long story."

"I wanna hear it."

"Okay, don't laugh. It all started when I heard the album *Lover* by Taylor Swift. She has this song called *Paper Rings*. It's one of my favorites on that album, so sometimes, when I use a straw at a restaurant, I make a ring out of the straw wrapper and wear it. It's a little thing the girls and I do when we all go out."

"Can you play me the song? I wanna hear it."

"You want me to play it right now?" She's smiling so big right now and my heart feels like it might burst through my chest.

"Yeah, I want to hear what the hype is about."

"Okay, can you pull it up?" She hands me her phone from the cupholder. "My password is 46445."

I type it in and navigate through all her music to get to this album. I press play and we listen as we drive back to campus. It's poppy and upbeat, which is the exact opposite of what I normally listen to.

I hear Paige silently singing along to it, and she's practically dancing out of her seat while she drives. The windows are down, and I reach over and turn the music up for her. She's in the moment and I can tell why she likes this song so much.

Her hair is whipping all over the place since the windows are down and her smile takes up her entire face. Suddenly, I've never felt more grateful to be living in this moment with her.

Carefree. She looks carefree. I think if I asked her how she was doing right now, she'd say she was okay. The only difference is this time, I would actually believe her. I find myself wanting to stop time so I can freeze this moment in my memories.

After all we've been through the past few weeks, I've longed for more moments with her like this. Simple ones like singing in the car to her favorite songs and driving in the cool autumn air.

Being in Paige's presence feels like I won some sort of contest. I feel like I'm seeing the real version of her, and I want to know what I can do to make her feel like this all the time.

The song ends and she turns over to me. "You can change the music back to my slower playlist if you want."

"I'm fine with this album playing." I smile at her.

"Okay." She giggles at me. "Are you a secret fan of pop music, Oliver?"

No, but for her, I'd listen to just about anything if I could see her as carefree as I just did. "I prefer slower music, but I don't mind hopping genres."

"By the end of this investigation, I'm going to make you a pop music lover. I guarantee it."

"Is that a bet you're starting, Sherlock?"

"It sure is, Watson." She reaches one of her hands over and we shake on it. "What are we wagering?"

"How about if you win, I'll read your favorite romance book."

"Are you serious?" She's practically jumping out of her seat with excitement.

I smile at her, my wager coming into my head. "Yes. But if I win, I get to teach you how to cook."

"Oliver, I can cook. Sort of." She switches from a slower song to a more upbeat one as she drives.

"Paige, when you were on the phone with my sister over the summer, you told me you made mac and cheese."

"Well, yeah. I did. It turned out really good, and I had leftovers for days."

"Okay, how about I teach you how to cook a *full* meal—with side dishes and all that."

"Fine. But I'm definitely going to win, so you better sharpen those reading skills, Baker."

"You sound confident, Yarrow. We'll see how this ends, but I'm not going down without a fight." I smirk over at her.

"I'd expect nothing less."

20

????

With Fitzpatrick out of the picture, I have to be more careful.

I've come to appreciate the hunt—it's my favorite part. Not even seeing the life drain out of their eyes, but the *chase.*

Watching their every move when they don't even realize I'm around.

None of them are going to expect a thing, and when I watch them take their last breath, I'll smile. They'll know the secret—what happens when you die.

I hope it's nothing but agony for all of them.

Wednesday, October 12th

"Paige, what did you think of this book?" Amelia breaks me out of my running thoughts.

"I really liked it! The characters were so relatable, but for the next book, can we steer away from kids trying to solve crimes involving murderers? I felt like I was looking in a mirror, but I love this series."

"Yeah, this one might have been a bad choice. We should read something smutty!" Ella says cheerfully.

"I'm down for that. Ella send some recs in the group chat later. This is your area of expertise," Amelia says as she tries to stand up.

Hads stops her from getting up. "Ames, stay here. We all need to have a chat."

"You don't have to tell me twice." Amelia sits, dropping her bag to the side of her chair. Hads starts pacing around the room like a teacher scolding her students, and I'm scared of her. Did she find out Oliver and I kissed? Does she know I took some snacks from her apartment the last time I was there?

"Hads, what's going on?" I ask, my nerves creeping into my body.

"Sorry, P." Amelia looks sorry right now, and my heart starts beating faster. *What did she tell them?*

Ella reaches over and grabs my hand. "Don't be mad at her, but Ames told us how frequent your panic attacks have been happening lately, and we're worried about you."

"We want to make sure you're okay. You've got a lot on your plate right now," Hads says to me. "It's your senior year with a full course load, and on top of that, you saw a dead body and are actively trying to solve a murder."

"Your nightmares have been happening most days out of the week. I don't mind helping you out of them, but I don't think you're okay, and it's alright if you're not," Amelia tells me.

"I-I honestly don't know how I am. It's not even nightmares about right now, it's all memories I hate reliving," I say to them. "If they keep getting worse, I'll talk to my therapist. I promise."

"Good. That's all we ask," Hads says. "Why are they becoming more frequent? I thought that's why you stayed away from coffee?"

"Coffee is only part of it," I tell them. "They're happening more now, but I need to explain for you to understand," I say as I take a deep breath. It's time to tell them *everything*. How I used to be happy as a kid until my dad took that away from me. How he used to get drunk and hurt me. How I used to wish the pain would stop. How my mom has basically ignored me my entire life. I tell them *all* of it. By the end of it, all four of us are crying.

"Paige, I–" Ella says.

"I'm so–" Hads says through tears. Amelia is silently holding my hand.

"You guys don't have to say anything. It's okay. It's time that you all knew. I'm sorry for keeping that all in but I'm not used to relying on people and talking about this stuff. I'm trying to work on that, and I'm glad you guys know now. You're my people, you know? I feel like I should've told you sooner. I'm sorry for not saying anything before."

"Paige, why are you apologizing?" Hads asks me. She sounds just like Oliver, and I laugh a bit.

"I'm trying to learn to stop doing that," I tell her while wiping some tears off my face.

"If you ever want to talk more, I'm always here," Ella tells me.

"Thanks, Ells. I feel so guilty for not telling you guys. I try my best to stay positive about things, so I don't spiral into a bad place." I sniffle. "But you guys have helped me so much even when we just chat about the little things in life. You guys feel like home to me, and I can't thank you enough for being the friends you have been these past few years."

"Paige, there's no need to thank us. We're your family and we love you. Just because you didn't grow up with us doesn't mean shit. We want you around, and you'll never have to beg us to listen. We always will." Ella grabs me and pulls me into a hug.

"I understand why you didn't say anything, Paige. But in the future, you don't have to be scared. We love you no matter what you've been through," Hads tells me, and I start crying even more.

"We are more than what we've been through. The decisions that our parents have made don't define us." Ella saying that helps because out of the three of them, she understands it the most.

"Thank you. I promise I'm going to try to stop being so afraid of talking about this stuff," I tell them.

The four of us are a giant mess of tears and hugs in this tiny classroom where we've spent most of our Wednesdays here at Grand Mountain.

"I can't believe this room will be empty next year. This is where we all became friends. It feels like a piece of our history." Amelia and I graduate at the end of this year, which leaves only Hads on campus.

"We're continuing book club!" Ella snaps at us.

"Of course! Just not in here, sadly. There's going to be lots of changes coming at the end of the year," I say to them, not wanting to think about the future quite yet.

"I don't want to think about this right now," Hads says as another tear falls. And for a few more minutes, we pretend like the future isn't rapidly coming and that the four of us aren't going to be able to walk to one another's apartments on campus whenever we want to hang out.

Hads grabs her bag off the floor and blows us all an air kiss as she gets up. "Paige, thank you for telling us. I'm proud of you, and I love you. I'll see you guys at some point, okay?"

"Yeah, uh, I have a thing to get to. I won't be back in the apartment until late," Amelia says, trying to rush out of the room.

"Are you meeting Henry for a date, perhaps?" Ella asks.

"No. I'm actually an undercover secret agent and I have to go meet my confidant. Bye!" Amelia smiles and leaves before we can question her more.

"She is obviously going to meet Hen," I say while giggling.

"I can't wait for the day that girl falls in love," Ella says as she turns to me. "So, how are you really?"

"I'm okay, I think. I feel bad I kept this from you guys for so long." I run a hand through my hair, still feeling the guilt creeping into my bones. Guilt is the only emotion I ever seem to feel. It's always there, no matter what the situation may be, and I don't know how to rewire my brain to make that go away.

Ella grabs my hand, and I feel comforted knowing she's here. "P, it's okay to be scared of opening up. It's not an easy thing to do, and it makes sense why you didn't before. Don't beat yourself up. We're not mad at you. We're happy you're okay."

"Thanks, Ells. I can't believe Oliver knew before you guys did. I think that's why I feel like this."

"When did you tell Oliver?"

"Like a week ago, I think."

"Is there a reason you told him before us? I'm not mad, just curious."

I take a second to think about an answer. I'm not sure why I told him—it kind of slipped out. "He and I are similar, and he's seen me at my worst moments this semester and has helped me every single time. I didn't have to ask—he just jumped in and helped. I've had like three panic attacks in front of him," I tell her.

"Wow. I didn't know it was that bad, Paige. I'm sorry."

"Ella, stop. You just found out about all this. If I had told you sooner, I know you and the girls would've helped." I smile at her.

"Damn right, we would've. Going forward, if you're having a hard day, don't hesitate to call me. I want to help."

"You're on speed dial, I promise." I wrap her in a hug. "How have you been?"

"I've been alright. You know how it is." She looks away from me.

"Yeah, but I want to make sure someone asks you how you're doing. Sometimes it seems like you're the one always taking care of us, and I want to make sure you're okay too."

"Paige, I like taking care of you guys."

"I know, but we don't see you as often because you're out in the world being an adult. I want you to know that the three of us are a phone call away." I knock her on the shoulder, and she smiles at me.

"Thank you."

"It's what friends are for," I say as the two of us walk out of the building. I'm about to start talking when Oliver comes up to the both of us.

"Ella, can I steal Paige from you? It's urgent," he asks and she looks between the two of us.

"Fine. I'll see you later, Paige." She rubs her hand down my arm before she heads off to her car.

"What's up?" I ask Oliver as he looks around.

"Not here, let's go to the roof." He starts toward the building and I do the same. We're both silent until we get up to the roof. The chairs are back, along with the snacks. *Did he plan this, or was he already up here?*

"Is this some sort of secret meeting? Do we need to talk in code?" I whisper to him.

"No, but we have three different leads and nowhere for them to go."

"What are we going to do about that? Maybe we could search the office again? There has to be something we missed."

He nods his head at me. "I agree. All that shit with his son makes me feel like we did miss something. We need to do a deeper dive."

"I was thinking Alissa could help us. She seems weirdly good at all this tech shit. We might be able to ask her to get information for us," Oliver says while opening a bag of goldfish crackers up.

"I knew you were an original goldfish person," I say and he rolls his eyes at me. "I can call Alissa tomorrow."

He simply nods. "Do you want to go back to your apartment? I don't mind walking you back."

"No. I like it up here. It's so quiet and peaceful." I look over at him. "Thank you for sharing your spot with me. I get why you like being up here."

"And why do you think I like it so much?" I feel like I'm being baited, but I tell him.

"My thoughts feel quiet up here. I imagine it does the same for you." He nods and we stare at each other for a few seconds.

"You know what, Paige, I think you were the first person in a long time who truly wanted to listen to the things I had to say."

"Not possible. You and your sister talk all the time."

"We do, but not about feelings and shit like that. She comes to me for guidance sometimes but other than that I'm a closed book with her. That's how my family is—we tend not to talk about our feelings much."

"Why?" I whisper.

"In my experience, if people aren't going to listen to what you have to say, it's better not to say anything at all. So I don't talk, or I selectively choose my words." He looks over at me. "And then you came along and started to bring that wall down. So, thank you is what I'm trying to say."

"You're welcome but I shouldn't get that much credit. It took me four years to tell my closest friends about my past, so I understand not talking about things, Ol."

"My sister knows now?"

I nod. "I told them earlier. Amelia told them about how bad my nightmares have been lately. It was the right time, and I'm glad I did it. I feel lighter than I did before." It felt good to talk about it with the people I love. I don't know what I was so afraid of before, but now that they know, the weight on my shoulders has lessened a bit.

"I'm proud of you. I know it's not an easy thing to talk about," he tells me and I feel tears coming because nobody ever tells me they're proud of me. I used to wish my mom would tell me that, but again, she never cared about me growing up. "Oh, shit, I'm sorry. Did I say something wrong? Fuck. Don't cry, love, please." He reaches over and wipes some tears off my face. "Just pretend I didn't say anything, we can sit up here in silence."

"It's okay, Oliver. It just feels weird hearing that. Nobody ever tells me that. I didn't mean to cry. I'm sorry." He glares at me. "I'm *not* sorry," I tell him and he laughs. "You have a nice laugh. You should do it more often."

"I seem only to do it in front of you lately," he says.

"Does that make me funny?"

"The funniest. And to reiterate, you never have anything to apologize for," Oliver tells me. "Except for being too goddamn cute."

I turn away from him because my cheeks are definitely bright red after hearing that.

"I'm proud of you too, you know."

"Why?"

"Do I need a reason? I just am, and everyone deserves to hear that every once in a while." He looks over at me and we stare at each other for a few seconds before he breaks eye contact and turns forward. We silently sit for a while and at one point I lay back to look up at the stars, until I feel myself drifting off to sleep because being with Oliver makes me feel as safe as can be.

22

Friday, October 14th

"He carried me? The whole way?" I ask Amelia as we sit at our kitchen table eating the pizza she made for dinner.

"Yeah, he knocked on our door at one in the morning and I opened it and there he was—holding you in his arms as you slept. I was equal parts impressed and confused." Amelia and I are debriefing the past few days because when I woke up this morning with no recollection of how I got back, I freaked out and called her.

I was on my floor, covered in blankets and halfway to a panic attack, when she texted me and told me what happened, which was Oliver carrying me all the way here last night.

And the weirdest part is he didn't say a word about it in class earlier. The only thing we talked about is that Alissa is coming to my place, and we're going to do some digging into our suspects.

But how would I even start that conversation?

Hey! Thanks for carrying me off the roof and back to my apartment after I fell asleep! Oh, and by the way, do you have feelings for me because I think I like you, but I don't want to tell you because then our whole dynamic will be ruined and I'll lose someone I care about!

I'm too afraid to put myself out there, but if he brings it up, I'm not going to lie. I'm scared about this blowing up in our faces, and I don't want to think about what it would be like to lose Oliver and Hads all at once. Nope.

"How come I didn't wake up?" I ask Amelia.

"You've barely slept the past month, so once you were out, you were out. Not even a tornado would have woken you up. You knocked over the lamp with your feet and didn't even move in his arms."

"Did you put me on the floor or did I fall off my bed?" I ask her.

"He knows you, Paige. He put you down there and spread your blankets over you. I almost threw up on him when he did that. It seems like this investigation has brought you two together." She wiggles her brows at me.

"Amelia, stop. How's Henry doing? Are you guys getting stuff done on your coffee dates, while you pretend not to notice how he looks at you?" She glares at me. "Two can play at this game. You make fun of Oliver and I and I'm going to make fun of you and Henry."

"Henry and I are friends. Not everything is a love match waiting to happen." She gets up from the table and washes her plate in the sink. "What time is Alissa coming over?"

"She and Oliver should be here around seven." I look over at the clock and I have fifteen minutes before they both get here.

"Okay, well, I have to go. I'm meeting a friend to work on a project," she tells me while heading into her room.

"Does that friend's name start with an H and rhyme with friendly?"

She says nothing to that before she grabs her bag, flips me her middle finger, and leaves.

After I clean our dishes, I decide to grab my favorite book and reread some of my favorite parts. I'm halfway through my favorite quote when I hear someone knock on my door. I can tell it's Oliver because he always knocks twice, and the cadence is always the same.

"Come on in, partner!" I say as I swing the door open.

"Is Alissa here yet?"

"No, but she's on her way. I told her to come right in. Apparently, she has a lot to discuss with us," I tell him. "Make yourself comfortable." He sits at the kitchen table across from me and the tension blanketing this room feels heavy, but it could only be me feeling that.

"Did you carry me back here last night?" *That was real subtle, Paige.*

"Yeah. You were asleep, and I didn't want to wake you. Was that okay?"

"It was fine. I just—"

"I didn't mean to scare you. I know you haven't been sleeping and wanted to ensure you slept through the night for once."

"Well, thanks. I did sleep through the night, and it felt weird, but it was needed. I hope I wasn't too heavy," I joke, trying to break the tension.

"Paige, I didn't even break a sweat."

"Oh, well, thanks," I tell him.

"It's no problem." He's still staring at me when Alissa bursts through the door, effectively stopping the awkward conversation Oliver and I were having.

"Hello to my favorite sunny girl! Hi, Oliver. It's nice to officially meet you." She holds her hand out, and he shakes it.

"Thanks for agreeing to help us," he says to her.

"You guys will owe me big time when I tell you what I found." She grabs her bag and sets it on one of my chairs. Then she pulls out her big and bulky laptop.

"I asked Alissa to look into email accounts and bank statements. I wanted to see if she flagged anything for our suspects." I pause. "Oh! And she also looked into security footage from the day the murder happened."

"And babes, I saw red flags all over the place. You're going to want to sit down for this." She pushes me into a seat, and I laugh as I get comfortable. Oliver wordlessly watches as Alissa sets up for her big spiel. Alissa is one of the prettiest people I've ever seen. Her hair is long and dark with some balayage. She's shorter than me but as feisty as Ella. It's no wonder those two are such good friends—they remind me a lot of each other.

"Okay, so bank statements are something I have to jump through some more hoops to be able to look at, but I did find some weird communications in some emails. Penelope was talking back and forth with some guy. When I tried to trace his email account, I found out that it was a throwaway email. He only used it with her." She smiles. "Security footage was also a dead end because someone wiped the entire day from the system, but if you guys snoop, it's probably on the cameras, so be careful."

"What were they talking about in the email?" I ask.

"I could only see the subject lines, but all of them were weird. There was one titled 'more money,' and I thought that was odd."

"More money? Was she asking for better pay or blackmailing someone?" Oliver asks.

"Extortion!" I smile at them.

"You get excited about the weirdest things," she tells me.

"You should hear her talk about serial killers. I've never seen someone's face light up at the fact that Jack the Ripper was never caught," Oliver says to her.

I simply smile at them before Alissa continues.

"I checked her credit card statements and noticed she had a charge to the same coffee shop every Saturday. I did a deep dive of her social media accounts and learned she meets there every week for book club." Alissa smiles at me.

I hear Oliver sigh heavily across the table as my face lights up. "Oliver, do you know what this means?"

"I cannot believe we're doing this." He sighs again.

"What?" Alissa asks, confusion on her features.

"Our very first stakeout!"

Alissa shakes her head. "That's all you guys. I'll be behind the monitor away from whatever antics you've got going on."

"Of course," I tell her. We would never put any of our friends in harm's way. Apparently, just ourselves. "Thank you for all your help. Can you call us when you dive deeper into her bank accounts and emails, if you're able to get into those?"

"Of course, babes. I'll send you the address of the shop when I get home. I assume you'll be doing this stakeout soon."

"Yup, and she'll probably bring the long lens camera and a notebook to write down all the shit we see so we can add it to the murder board." Oliver looks over at me, and I tilt my head at him.

"Don't be silly. I'm bringing a book, too. Who knows how long we'll be watching?"

"You might as well bring a book for me," he says.

"You want me to bring you a romance book? To read while we're on a stakeout?" I'm only double checking because I would expect this from Grant, but Oliver? I'm shocked.

"I think fiction is more my speed."

I smirk at him. "I have just the book for you. Remind me to grab it before we leave on Saturday."

"Will do, Sherlock."

"You guys have fun with that. I've got work tomorrow, and Ella wants me back to watch *Love Island* with her tonight. We'll chat again soon, okay?"

I get up and hug her. "It's always good to see you, Alissa. Thank you for your help."

"Anything for you, Paige. You know that. See you later, Oliver!" She grabs her bag and whips out of the apartment as if she was never here in the first place.

"She really gets in and out, doesn't she?" Oliver asks me.

"That's Alissa for you." I've always admired her and Ella. They're unapologetically themselves. I wish I was more headstrong like them. I usually let people walk all over me like a doormat, and I get on my own nerves sometimes. "I made a Google doc with all of our information on it. I shared it with you, so check your inbox."

"Thanks. I'll look at it when I get back."

As Oliver starts to get up, we hear someone fumbling with the lock on my door. I look over, and it seems like someone is trying to get in but doesn't have a key. Oliver gets up from his chair and steps in front of me.

"Paige, get behind me." He grabs his knife, and I reach over and grab one from the stand. I rest it by my side as I join him.

"Do you think it could be the killer?"

"It's going to be fine. Don't panic, I'll protect you from whatever's behind the door, okay?" he tells me and I nod. Whoever is out there is still fussing with the lock. Oliver and I inch closer to the front door. "Stay behind me."

"If we're going down like this, we're going down together," I tell him.

"Paige, this isn't up for discussion. I'm not letting you get hurt. Not if I'm here. Get. Behind. Me." He looks down at me, and I nod, slowly scooching behind him again.

The door finally swings open and Amelia and Henry walk in. They look at Oliver and I with wide eyes when they see us both holding knives in our hands. The two of us let out a breath at the same time.

"What the fuck? I cannot believe this is the second time this has happened." Amelia shakes her head at us.

"Why do you keep coming into the apartment so weirdly?" I yell at her.

"Has this happened before?" Henry asks.

"Yes," Oliver says.

"No," Amelia says at the same time. Henry looks over at me.

"Tonight is only the second time it's happened, but someone needs to figure out how to work her key!" I point at Amelia.

"That may have been my fault. She laughed too hard and couldn't fit the key into the door," Henry says while tilting his head at us. I look over at Amelia, and she's blushing.

"Oh, really?" I say to her. Oliver clears his throat, and I look over at him. "Oh, right. Henry, this is Oliver. Oliver, that's Henry." The two boys shake hands.

"Nice to meet you." Henry smiles at him.

"Amelia's boyfriend, right?" he asks him, and I elbow him in the ribs.

"No. Uh, we're friends," Henry says, tilting his head in the *other* direction. I think he's nervous, but I can totally feel that he likes Ames. It's glaringly obvious to me.

"Paige, can I see you for a second?" Amelia is smiling but her tone indicates something else.

"I'll get out of your hair. I'll text you later?" She nods at him, and he starts to leave. "Nice to meet you, Oliver. And good to see you again, Paige."

"Henry, you can leave that open," Oliver says as Henry starts to close the door. "I'm heading out, too. See you tomorrow, Sherlock." He's looking at me as if he wants to say more but he doesn't as his eyes shift to the left. "Amelia." He turns around and follows Henry out of the apartment. I turn to look at my best friend, and her eyes are glued to mine.

"Did you tell Oliver that Henry was my boyfriend?" She's inching closer to me, and I can feel the words fall out of my mouth.

"It might've slipped out, but I corrected myself. Oliver isn't very keen on reading the room. You have his number! Go call him and yell at him, not me!" I throw my hands up in surrender, and back up toward my room as I laugh. "I hope your night with Henry went well, but I have to study for a test I have next week. So, we can debrief in the morning!" I grab my door handle and twist it before Amelia can get to me. I hear the pillow I saw her grab plop against the floor as I shut my door before she can hit me with it.

"Paige," is all I hear her say.

"I know you're not really mad at me, but we both need sleep. I'll make you some coffee tomorrow morning and we can discuss, okay?"

"Yeah, you're right," she says, and I laugh through the door. "What?"

"Those two meeting each other for the first time reminded me of that one spider man meme," I say.

"The pointing one?" she asks, already knowing the one I was talking about.

"Yeah."

I hear her laugh as she walks away from my door, and I smile to myself as I sit at my desk.

I'm going to miss this next year—Amelia and I living together. I'm going to soak up every minute of being with my best friend because I don't know what's next for us, but I do know that I never want the girls around me to fade away. They're my forever people, and I feel so lucky to know them.

23

Oliver

Saturday, October 15th

"So, you're telling me this bank robbery and hostage crisis are connected? What the fuck is going on in this book?" Paige handed me a book before we got in the car, and I haven't put it down since.

"Task at hand, Ol. You're supposed to be watching her." She smiles over at me. "But that book is good, right? I read it in one night!"

"One night? Like a few hours?"

"Yeah! I couldn't put it down, but you have to because we're doing important things!" Her excitement is radiating, so I use one of her loose receipts as a bookmark and place it on her dashboard.

"This stakeout better be worth it because I had to cancel another walk with my sister, and if I do that one more time, she might stab me with her favorite ruler."

"Tell Hads you'll have plenty of time for walks after we solve this case!" She reaches over to her dashboard and grabs the camera from it.

"I thought that was my job?"

"No offense, Ol. But your sister is better at taking photos than you are. I got this. Just grab the binoculars and watch."

"Yeah, because this doesn't look shady as hell. You could have at least tinted your windows," I say.

"I didn't have time!" Paige tells me, and I laugh. "You're yanking my chain right now."

"Something like that," I say while putting the binoculars up to my eyes. Penelope—the receptionist—has been sitting inside, chatting with her friends while waving some book around.

"Oh, she's getting up." Paige starts clicking her camera and the flash goes off. She drops down in her seat, trying to hide. "Did anyone see me?"

"Considering there's barely anyone on this street and we're fifty feet from the coffee place, I think you're good." I laugh as I look into the binoculars again. "She's grabbing another coffee. To go it looks like," I tell Paige as her phone starts to ring.

"Alissa! I'm putting you on speaker!" She clicks her phone and I hear Alissa's voice on the other end.

"Hi, babes! Are you still on your stakeout or whatever?" she asks.

"Yes," I say.

"But we can always make time for you!" Paige says while hitting me. "What do you got?"

"I was able to get into her bank records and I found a wire transfer for ten thousand dollars that she made to an offshore account. I couldn't trace who the other account belonged to yet, but I thought that was odd. No normal person transfers ten thousand dollars to an account like that."

I look over at Paige. "Do you think she paid someone to kill the dean?"

She shrugs her shoulders. "It's possible. That's a lot of money."

"I dug through her email and found some deleted ones to her secret lover! Lots of messages about places to meet, hotels and such, and a few flirtatious messages as well. I won't repeat them, but they rival some of the romance novels I've read before."

"Those must have been to the assistant dean of students. I guess love notes turned into emails, which led to secret meetings in crappy motels."

"How romantic," I say jokingly.

"That's all I've got. I'll keep trying to trace the other offshore account but I probably won't have any luck. Stay safe, you two! Don't let her take a stab at you!" Alissa hangs up after she says that and I see Paige roll her eyes and smile.

"She's leaving," I say and she turns around while grabbing the camera. Paige takes some pictures as she leaves and gets into her car.

"We should follow her," Paige says. "If she's going home then we'll stop but what if she's meeting her secret lover!"

"On a Saturday morning?"

"You never know!" she tells me while turning her car on.

"No. If we're doing this, I'm driving."

"Fine. Just be careful with Gus."

"Who?" I say as I open the passenger door and swing around to the driver's side. She does the same, and when we get back inside the car she answers me.

"My car!" she tells me while buckling her seatbelt.

"You named your car? Who does that?"

"Everyone!" Paige yells while I put it in drive.

"I won't hurt your car, I promise."

"Oliver, your seatbelt."

"Give me a second," I say before she reaches over, grabs the buckle, and clicks it in for me. "Thanks."

"You're welcome, Watson." I glare at her, and she smiles back at me. "Make sure to stay a few cars behind so we don't look weird."

"I know, Paige."

I follow her until she stops outside an apartment building. It takes around five to seven minutes to get there from the coffee shop we were at. She parks and heads inside. We wait a few minutes to see if something shady is going to happen, but nothing does.

"Damn, I was hoping for some big reveal." Paige seems disappointed. "Can I drive my car now? It's weird not driving in my own vehicle."

"Fine, but only because we're going back to campus." We switch seats, and Paige starts playing music again, to which I silently listen because I don't want her to win the bet we have going.

She's going to win, for sure.

We're driving for a few minutes when I notice the same car has been behind us for a few miles. We're on a road where they could pass us—especially with how slow Paige is driving—but they haven't. I shake the feeling off that we're being followed and Paige continues to drive.

"Paige, take another right," I tell her, wanting to see what the car does. "Why?"

"Just do it," I say, and she does. The car behind us does the same thing. "Take another one."

"Oliver—"

"We're being followed. Any normal person would have passed you already. Just turn right one more time, love."

"Okay." She turns and the car follows us.

"Fuck."

"What do we do?" Her breathing has increased, and she sounds panicked. My heart rate has jumped because I have no idea what to do either. I've never been in this situation before but I need to think. I grab my phone. "Oliver, I swear to God, you better not be Googling *'what to do if you're being followed'* right now!"

"I wasn't!" *I was.*

"I can tell you're lying, but this isn't the time. Call Ella," she tells me, handing me her phone from the cup holder.

"So she can yell at me?"

"She lives with Alissa. They might know what to do." I go to her favorites and click on Ella's name. It rings through her car, and she picks it up immediately.

"Paigey! How is one of my favorite girls?" Ella asks.

"I've been better," she tells her. "Is Alissa around still?"

"Alissa!" she yells, and I see Paige flinch because of how loud that came through her car. I reach over and turn the volume down. I don't need any other cars to hear what we're saying.

"Hi, babes! What's up!"

"Just a typical Saturday morning of being followed by someone in the car," Paige tells them, her voice cracking a bit.

"Alissa, can you look up a license plate for me?" I ask her.

"Yes I can. Give me two seconds." I hear her typing in the background, and I pull up Maps on Paige's car screen so she can see where we are. I'm hoping they'll split when we get back to campus, but I have no fucking clue. This entire situation is charged, and I can feel Paige's tension from where I'm sitting. I should be the one driving, not her. "Okay, hit me."

"I can only see part of it," I tell her.

"I'll take whatever you've got."

"It begins with XL. That's all I have. They're too far away and keep flashing their lights at us even though it's still light out," I tell her.

"Paige, are you okay?" Ella asks her.

"Yup. Peachy," she says, but seeing her, I can tell it's a lie. Her face is pale, and I'm afraid she's going to have another panic attack while she's driving.

"Oliver, I need more. There are thousands of license plates registered with those letters at the beginning. Can you see anything else?" Alissa asks me.

"Black car with a Virginia license plate."

"That helps. Can you see any other part of the plate?"

"It looks like it ends with a three," Paige tells her as she turns toward campus. "Should I keep driving in a square or head back?"

"Head back. They should leave when we get back to campus," I say to her. I notice the car speeding up behind us, and sweat drips down my back. What the fuck is happening to me?

"The car was going so fast that it flipped three times, throwing members of the car out in all directions. She didn't stand a chance, Oliver. She was barely breathing when she made that call to you."

"Someone else hit them while they were driving, but both cars were being reckless."

"Speed up a bit, Paige," I tell her as I try not to fall apart.

"What's going on?" Ella asks.

"The car keeps inching up on us," I say.

"Ol, you don't think—" I cut Paige off.

"No, we're going to be fine," I say as the car bumps us from behind.

"What was that noise?" Ella asks, sounding as worried as I feel.

"Oliver." Paige sounds terrified, and now I'm panicking because what do you do when someone is trying to run you off the road? The car rams us again, and Paige screams when it does. "They're going to make us spin out. Oh, God." She's breathing so heavily right now. *Fuck.*

"It's okay, just speed up a bit. Put some distance between us."

"What if we get pulled over?"

"That's not our main issue at the moment," I tell her as she accelerates. I look in the rearview and see the other car slowing down. *Maybe they were just trying to scare us?*

Mission fucking accomplished.

"I'll email you guys what I find. Stay safe, please," Alissa says.

"Paige, please text me when you get home. I love you. Be careful." Ella hangs up and only our heavy breaths fill the car.

"What if we end up in a ditch? What if they have a gun? What's to stop them from shooting us!"

"Paige, they're not going to do that. It's going to be fine," I say, not believing the words coming out of my mouth. "Plus, if it's the killer, their method was a knife, so I think a gun is out of the picture."

"That doesn't make me feel better! They could run us off the road and slit our throats!" she says while turning right at the light. I watch in the rearview as the other car continues forward.

"They're gone," I say to her. "It's okay, Paige. Just go park and turn the car off." She nods, and I pull my phone out.

Oliver: SOS.

Amelia: Are you allowed to send me that? It's only for us girls.

Oliver: How do you stop Paige's panic attacks?

Amelia: It depends. How bad does it seem?

Oliver: Bad.

Amelia: Helpful, as always. Is her face pale? Is she sweating? Can she breathe?

Oliver: Yes, yes, and sort of?

Amelia: Where are you guys?

Oliver: About to park in the lot. What should I do?

Amelia: Play her favorite song and reassure her she's safe. Make sure she drinks water. It helps her breathe better. Do that thing you always do and put her hand on your pulse.

Oliver: She told you about that?

Amelia: She tells me everything. I'll meet you guys in the parking lot.

Paige parks, and I hear her struggling to breathe. I honestly don't know how she was able to drive during that.

"Paige, I'm proud of how you handled that, but I need you to breathe for me. Please," I say to her as she turns over to me. Tears are falling from her eyes, and she's clutching her chest. Fuck. "*Paige.*" I grab her phone, go to her music app, and change it to her favorite song since Amelia said it helps.

I get out of the car, go over to the driver's side, lift her out of the seat and place her in my lap as I sit back down. I yank the seat back to give myself more room, and Paige curls into a ball on my chest. I shut the door so nobody else can hear us.

"Paige, you're okay. You're safe. Nothing bad is going to happen to you," I tell her. "I'm here, it's okay." I grab one of her hands and place it on my chest, and I feel for her pulse with her other hand. It's beating like crazy. "Take a deep breath for me, P." She tries to take one, but she's still shaking. "Good girl, just like that. Can you do another one for me?"

She breathes in and out before speaking. "We're going to die, Oliver. We're not safe."

"You're okay, Paige. We're safe now. I promise." I grab her water bottle and open it. "Drink this," I tell her and she does. Her pulse slows a little as the song ends, and I replay it. "Paige, you're at school. Nobody is going to hurt you," I tell her. I repeat all those phrases ten times before her breathing returns to normal. She snaps out of her panic-induced state and relaxes against me. I keep her hand on my heartbeat, just in case. Not because I love the feel of her against my chest or anything.

"I'm sorry. I don't know why that snuck up on me."

"It was a high-stress situation, and stop fucking apologizing," I tell her.

"I feel bad you keep doing this with me. I know it's a lot. Are you okay?" she asks me. "I'm sorry I'm always so broken around you."

"You're not broken." I pause before answering her other questions. "I'm alright, but I'm more worried about you. How do you feel?" I ask while I stroke her cheek with my hand.

"Tired and scared," she tells me. "Are you okay?"

"Why do you keep asking me that?"

"Well, we were being followed in a car and the whole thing was...I'm just making sure."

"Paige, I'm okay. I promise."

"Okay. I should text Ella we're safe, so she doesn't send a swat team to look for us." She grabs her phone and starts typing, but something makes her pause. "This is my favorite song."

"I know," I tell her.

"How did you know to play it?"

"I asked Amelia."

"Oh. Okay," she says, still sitting on my lap, so I lift her and gently place her in the passenger seat so she can be more comfortable. She keeps texting, and I can't help but look at her. Her blonde hair is a mess and her face has dried tears on it, but she's smiling to herself, and I don't think

I've ever seen a more beautiful person than when Paige smiles. It lights up everything around her. She's strong—stronger than me, for sure.

She looked surprised that I knew her favorite song, but what she didn't know is that I know her favorite color is lavender, not just purple. Her favorite horror movie is *Hereditary*. Her favorite flower is the sunflower because it faces the sun, and she thinks it's cute that even the flowers greet the sun. Her favorite season is autumn because she likes to step on the leaves and rate how crunchy they are.

She doesn't know that my favorite thing about her is everything.

She doesn't know I think about her all the time and the reason she doesn't know is because I'm too scared to tell her.

"Ella's glad we're okay," she says, knocking me out of my haze. "So, what do we do now? Where do we go from here?"

"I'm not sure. We can't be certain until Alissa gives us more information. But today's events might also mean that someone is onto us. We're starting to make someone very nervous. Why else would they have followed us?"

She simply shrugs. "Next time, I'll let you drive. Maybe you can show off some of those *Mission Impossible* driving skills instead of me driving slow and making them hit my car."

I laugh at that, and so does she. The air feels lighter when someone taps the window, and Paige flinches. I look over, and of course, it's Amelia.

"Open the fucking door!" she says while pointing to the handle, so I do. "I thought Paige was driving?"

"How'd you know I was the one driving?" Paige asks.

"Oliver texted me."

"Since when do you guys text regularly?" Paige asks, and I look at Amelia.

"You're up, Loudmouth," Amelia says to me.

"We don't, but if she sends me one more weird ass meme, I'm blocking her."

She throws me the finger before looking at Paige. "Are you okay?"

"I'm fine now," she says while climbing out of her car. I step out of the driver's seat and hand Paige her water bottle. "I'll see you in class tomorrow. We can go over the next steps when Alissa texts me back."

"Sounds good, but is your car okay? Those hits we took were no joke," I say to her.

She walks around to the back of her car and we all look at it. "It's not too bad. Just a dent on my back bumper. Easy fix."

"Paige, where the fuck did this come from?" Amelia asks her.

"I'll explain when I'm wearing comfier clothes," Paige says to her. "I'll see you soon, Watson."

"Bye, Sherlock." I watch her and Amelia walk back to their place while I shove my hand into my pocket and grab my keys. This situation Paige and I have placed ourselves in seems to get weirder by the day. I hope today's occurrence was a one-time thing, but I can't help but look over my shoulder as I walk back to my apartment. I feel like there are eyes on me, and it's creeping me out. I'm a few feet away from my building when I feel a pair of arms wrap around me, and I don't even have to guess who it is.

"Thank you for what you did for me today. It means a lot to me." I wrap my arms around her and rest my head on hers. I kiss her on the forehead.

"I promise I won't let anything happen to you," I whisper to her.

"I know," Paige says against my chest. I look down at her, hoping she'll look back up at me, but she lets go of me and runs back to her place. Hurrying off as if she was never really here in the first place.

I'm walking up my stairs when I hear a voice ahead of me.

"So, loverboy, how was the stakeout?" I turn around, and Grant is leaning against my door.

"Why are you up here?"

"Why can't I check on my friend without being berated about it?"

"You're the one who hasn't played me back in Scrabble yet." I shove him out of the way of my door and put my key in.

"I've been busy. Hads just left my place but I figured I would wait for you."

"Why?" I ask sharply.

"I care about you, obviously. You're basically my brother-in-law."

"Not even close," I say to him as I open my door. I feel him follow behind me.

"Well not yet, but maybe sometime soon." Grant smiles at me as he sits down at my kitchen table. Why is he always making himself so comfortable in my apartment? It's a Saturday, how bored can he be? Why doesn't he go shoot some hoops or whatever the fuck he does?

"Are you asking for permission to marry my sister?"

"Not right now." He smiles.

"Good, now get the fuck out. It's been a stressful morning," I say while holding my door open for him.

"Stressful? What happened?" Grant asks me and I tell him all the shit that went down this morning. Hia jaw is slack by the time I finish. "Are you guys okay? Is Paige okay? What the fuck did you guys get yourself mixed up in?"

"We don't know. But suffice it to say, it's getting a little scary."

"More like dangerous, Ol. The girls are going to freak out when they hear about this." He pauses. "Leave it to you for your only hobby to end up being a murder investigation."

"This isn't my *only* hobby!"

"Oliver, since when have you had hobbies?" He puts his feet up on my coffee table.

"I do too have fucking hobbies!" I argue. The only difference between him and I is that I don't flaunt all the shit I like to do on social media. I swear to God, I get fifty notifications a day from Grant posting stories about hockey shit, my sister, and what book he's been reading. And the worst part is, I don't know how to turn those notifications off and nobody will do it for me.

"Okay, like what? Glaring? Grunting? Running?" He smirks at me from my couch.

"Those are just things I do, Grant. I have hobbies." I slam my door and head over to stand by him.

"Why don't you list a few?"

"Why don't you get the fuck out of my apartment?"

"The only hobby I know for sure that you have is surfing and working out. That's all you did over the summer."

"I like watching old movies and I enjoy cooking." Both of those things are true. Old movies are inherently better to me than some of this new shit. It's all too much green screen and it makes my head hurt. I like to cook too. It helps me think sometimes, and I like cooking for people I love because food can connect people the same way words can.

"Why have you never cooked for me?"

"You never asked."

"So, if I did, you would?" His face lights up.

"Yes."

"Can you make me dinner sometime?" he asks immediately, like I figured he was going to.

"Come over for dinner sometime and bring my sister. I'll make whatever you want." He smiles as he looks at me. "Now can you *please* get out of my apartment?"

"Only because you asked so nicely." He smiles at me as he gets up. Before he leaves, he pats me on the shoulder. "Be careful with the investigation. Do you and Paige realize you're college students and not actual detectives?"

I can only roll my eyes.

"Tread carefully buddy, especially after being followed. I don't want to see you or Paige get hurt." He pulls me in for a hug that I don't reciprocate and he finally leaves my apartment. I sigh heavily at his absence. I do have hobbies, just not many. Ever since I was a kid and had figured out what I loved, I stuck to it. I never get bored with movies and there's always something different I can learn to cook, so why would I need anything else?

There is beauty in the constants of life. Like breathing and shit.

Fuck, Grant was right. Maybe I *do* need a life.

Amelia: Paige, care to share with the class about how you were followed earlier today.

Ella: Don't forget the fact that they hit your car!

Hads: What the hell are you guys talking about?

Amelia: Paige, tell Hads what happened.

Hads: How does everyone know about this but me?

Paige: I was on the phone with Ella when it happened, and Oliver texted Amelia about the panic attack I was having. When she came out she saw the dent in my car and I told her.

Hads: You were followed? Like…in your car? Like a car chase?

Amelia: Yes, and they tried to run her off the road.

Hads: Good God. This sounds like a scene from *John Wick*.

Ella: Is this still safe? You sounded terrified on the phone earlier, Oliver too. I'm worried this could get dangerous.

Paige: We're being safe. I promise. Today was weird. I don't know. I need to process it. Can we talk more about this at book club?

Hads: Fine. But if you get hurt, I get to punch Oliver. It's only fair.

Ella: I'd pay to see that.

Amelia: I like this course of action. It's Amelia approved.

Paige: When did we get so violent?

Ella: I think it was around the time one of us started cosplaying as a detective…

Paige: I'm going to take a nap. I'll talk to you guys later, okay?

Amelia: Okay, P.

Ella: Get some rest. Call me if you need me.

Hads: I'm going to go talk to my brother. If he was in the car when it was hit, he might need me.

Paige: Tell him I hope he's okay.

Hads liked a message.

24

Wednesday, October 19th

12:30 AM

I'm scared.

That's how I've felt since Saturday. I can't shake the feeling someone is following me, and I haven't stopped looking over my shoulder for the past two days.

I don't know what I was thinking by taking on this investigation, but I didn't expect this. That person probably knows my name. What if they know where I live? Or Oliver? What if they try to hurt us again? The scenarios keep playing in my mind, and none of them end well.

I want to back out, but something keeps pulling me back in. I know it's dangerous, but that hasn't stopped me so yet. Plus, I like hanging out with Oliver, and after the investigation is over, I don't think he would want to be around me this much.

After Saturday, I went back home and immediately scheduled an appointment with my therapist. She helped me sort through some stuff yesterday, and I feel a bit better about my anxiety and panic attacks, but the fear hasn't gone away. I don't think it ever will. I've been constantly afraid since I was young, but now with everything else going on, it feels dialed up. I've tried smiling through things and telling the girls I'm okay, but they aren't buying it. My car being bumped and almost run off the road has made them more protective than ever.

Which is nice, even if they've barely left me alone the past few days. I've never had anyone care about me as much as they do.

I sneak quietly out of my apartment and head to Oliver's apartment. We decided to search the office again and when I get to his place, he's already standing outside, dressed in all black. He looks up when he hears me walking, and I reach into my bag and throw a hat at him.

"I know you don't like hats, but we can't risk leaving anything behind."

"Thanks," he says, adjusting his small fanny pack on his shoulder.

"Is that a fanny pack?" I laugh.

"Why are you laughing?" he asks me as we start to walk to our destination.

"You don't seem like the type!"

He stares over at me. "I borrowed it from my sister."

"You know it's supposed to be worn on your stomach and not carried around your shoulder." I giggle.

"It was restricting my movement when I wore it like that."

"Okay, sure. You're the one with a six-pack. I bet it was fine."

He smirks over at me. "How'd you know I have a six-pack, Sherlock?"

"Lucky guess, Watson." *Oh my God, are we flirting?*

We reach the building a few minutes later, and I swipe us in. Oliver peeks around the corner to make sure nobody is there before he waves me ahead.

"Should we make up a code word in case we hear someone, or we're in danger?" I whisper to him.

Oliver kneels before the door handle and grabs his tools to pick the lock. "We're not in danger, and I don't think we need a code."

"Did you forget someone tried to run us off the road the other day? Secondly, a code word, like satellite or goldfish. Or maybe we could have code names!" I whisper at him. "Are you reconsidering this partnership yet?"

"No, but I am reconsidering other things," he tells me as I hear the lock click. He gets up and turns the handle, and we're good to go inside. "I thought our code names were Sherlock and Watson?"

"Oh, I guess they are. But what if one of us is in trouble?" I ask him, to which he smiles at me. "It could be useful, Oliver. I say we go with something neither of us uses that often, like Tinkerbell." I look over at him, and he looks confused. "*Peter Pan?*" He shakes his head. "You've *never* seen that movie! What's wrong with you? That movie got me through my childhood! After this is over, I'm going to force you to watch it."

"Fine. Our code word for danger can be a fairy that spreads pixie dust all over the place. That seems fitting." His voice is so monotone it makes me giggle.

"So you *have* seen it!" I point up at him.

"No, but everyone knows who fucking Tinkerbell is. Can we please start searching?"

"Okay, you go left, and I'll go right. Check everything! I won't retake pictures because we have those, but I will if we find something. Got it?" I look over at him, and he nods. I start shuffling against the wall, and I search under the trophies and shake them, just in case something falls out. I pull picture frames from the wall and open them up to see if anything is hidden behind them. There's one picture I thought had something on it, but it was just writing about some fishing trip he went on with his buddies a few years ago. I gently put it back on the wall when Oliver drops something, and it rolls by my feet.

"Be careful!" I yell at him.

"It was fucking slippery! These gloves don't have a very good grip." He tells me while adjusting them on his hands.

"Just be thankful you're wearing them because now your prints aren't on anything!" I wink at him, and he rolls his eyes. I get to the area behind his desk and look at the wall with all of his degrees on it. He went from being a principal of some school to a dean of students at this tiny small-town college, and now, that's all he'll ever be. It's so weird to think about.

He probably woke up that morning and took food out of the freezer to defrost, so it would be ready for when he got home. The day you die, there are still remnants of you living scattered everywhere. Maybe you pulled your laundry to do after the day was over. That special mug you used to love now gets used by someone in memory of you.

I wonder if my dad ever thinks about me. I wonder if he thinks about who I grew up to become. I wonder if he would be proud of me if he wasn't so wrapped up with his shit. I wonder where he is right now. Those are all questions I'll never have an answer for. One day he could die, and he won't know despite everything he did to me, I turned out okay. He'll never know *this* me. He only knows the small, terrified girl afraid of her own shadow.

I don't know if I'd ever forgive him, but I do know I'm grateful he gave me the opportunity to live. My parents might not have cared about me, but I care about myself. I care that I'm alive at this moment right now. I'm probably just a memory to them, but to my friends, I'm living with them. It's a special thing to be surrounded by people you love and know they'll be by your side forever.

Oliver snaps in front of my face and puts his hand on my shoulder. "Are you okay?" he asks me, concern etched onto his features.

"Sorry. I'm fine."

"Do you feel panicky? Sweaty?" He's searching my eyes for a sign of a panic attack.

"No." I smile at him. "I'm just thinking about death."

"That's...interesting," he says to me. "Look what I found under the desk."

"A safe? I don't remember seeing this last time. Why didn't the police take it?" I ask, and he shrugs. "Can you get into it?"

"Maybe. I would need the code." He stands up, and I hear him shuffling carefully around the few papers on the desk.

"Try the date his son went missing," I tell him. People often use things they can easily remember as passwords and codes. Alissa told me that last year when I asked her about her job. I still don't quite understand what exactly she does, but she made me change all my passwords because they were too simple. Oliver bends next to me and starts shuffling with the safe. When he gets to the final number, it clicks open.

"Why the fuck does he have one of these?" Oliver pulls a gun out of the safe.

"Woah! Put that down!" I tell him, and he rests it back in the safe. "Why would he need a gun so easily accessible to him?" My eyes are wide because none of this is making any sense. Oliver grabs a manila file folder out of the safe, and holds it up to me so I can read what it says.

From Anonymous

"What's in it?" I ask, and he flips it open, and the note Fitzpatrick told us about and other random papers fall out.

Oliver reaches into the safe and pulls out a huge band of money. "He's got about twenty thousand dollars in here." Oliver digs around to grab whatever else is in there, but he comes out empty handed. "That's all that was in there."

"This doesn't make any sense," I say as I take photos of this stuff. We're silently sifting through everything when we hear a loud bang below us.

"I think someone else is here."

"Do you think it's the cops? Or..." I trail off, thinking the killer could be a few levels below us right now.

"Put all this shit back," Oliver says as he folds one of the papers up and puts it in his pocket. "Hurry, P."

"I'm trying!" I whisper at him.

"Go faster!" he whispers back at me as he tries to get off the floor and bumps his head on the desk. "Fuck, that hurt."

"Are you okay?" I ask him as I stand up unscathed. He nods before I hear a voice coming closer to where we are. Oliver grabs my hand and quietly shuts the door, locking it behind us. "What do we do? What if it's the cops, and they have others stationed outside?"

"Give me a second." He's whipping his head around, and then he grabs my hand and starts running toward the staircase we left through the last time.

"Why are we going up?" I ask, when he stops on one of the landings and pushes me against the wall, covering my mouth with one of his hands. I widen my eyes at him, and he puts one finger to his lips and tells me to be quiet. I nod with his hand still over my mouth. I hear the door of the stairwell we're in open, and I flinch. I can hear boots walking into the stairwell. Oliver takes his free hand and rubs my head, silently saying he's here and it's okay.

Both of us are breathing heavily, and he turns his head back to look at me, but he still hasn't moved his hand from my mouth. I've never noticed how brown his eyes are, like Hadleigh's, but while hers are like autumn leaves falling, his are darker. They look like they're full of depth, and if the sun was shining on them right now, they would remind me of water running over stones in a creek. I've always believed people's eyes can tell the whole story of their lives. His look like they've been broken many times, but I can see a tiny sliver of hope in them. They look beautiful. *He* looks beautiful.

He looks down at his hand and quickly removes it, running his other one down his face, stopping on his lips, and then rubbing his chin. When the two of us hear the door shut, I can see our bodies loosen.

"Sorry. I was just—"

"It's fine," he says before laughing.

"Okay, I like hearing you laugh, but is now the time?" I ask, still feeling confused. What in the past few minutes could've caused this?

"Paige, it was a janitor." He continues laughing. "We ran scared into this stairwell because of a janitor."

Oh. Maybe Amelia was right, and the two of us are a bit too paranoid. "Oh my God…" I say as I start to laugh. He looks at me for a few seconds, and I feel myself get goosebumps. Before I can say anything else he reaches down, grabs my hand, and drags me up the steps.

"Where are we going?" I ask, and he doesn't respond until he opens the door, and we step out onto the roof of this building.

1:30 AM

"Is this your thing or something? Rooftops?" Paige asks me.

"Something like that. Though, I guess it's our thing now," I say as I drag her to the corner of the roof where we usually sit—just on top of a different building this time. "We have to make sure the janitor is gone when we leave, and I figure this is a good way to pass the time."

I release our hands and sit against the wall. I have to distance the two of us because doing what I did in that stairwell made me flustered. *Flustered*. I barely touched her, and I got all shaky. It's annoying. That happens when you don't touch another woman for four and a half years.

Being around Paige this much hasn't helped either. I'm insanely attracted to this girl, but it's more than that. I like everything about her. Her mind, her view of the world, and most importantly, her. Every *single* part of her.

"Good idea," she says, sitting across from me, leaning against part of the roof. We're silent for a few moments when I hear her start to speak and then stop.

"What, Paige?"

"I was going to ask if your head was okay?" She points to the top of my head, where I bumped it.

"It's fine. Just a little bump."

"Okay." She smiles at me. "What's your favorite color?"

"Black."

"Why?"

"It's all colors in one, and it's dark," I tell her.

"Do you have a celebrity crush?" she asks.

"No."

"Guilty pleasure?"

"Paige, what's with the twenty questions right now?" I ask.

"Well, it's a good way to pass the time, plus I want to dig deeper."

"Into what? Me?"

"Yeah. I want to know you, if you'll let me. I mean, we already shared a huge part of ourselves with each other. I want more of the little things. Any question I ask you, I'll answer, too. It's only fair." She smiles at me and I move so I'm closer to where she is.

"Okay," I tell her. Being on this roof with her always feels so easy. I wish we could stay here and exist together.

"Okay then. Guilty pleasure?"

I sigh heavily before answering because I won't live it down once I say this. Not even my sister knows this. "Sometimes, when I go for my runs, I like to listen to *5 Seconds of Summer*."

Her mouth drops open. "You? You like to listen to a boy band while you run?"

"Okay, look, as my sister grew up she always listened to them, and they have some catchy shit! It's upbeat and good for my pace!" I laugh a little as I watch her clutch her stomach from laughing so hard.

"I am telling everybody on campus." She giggles.

"What's yours then, Sherlock?" I ask her. "That *was* the deal, right?"

"Mine is definitely not as funny, but sometimes when I'm in the apartment by myself, I like to turn my music really loud and dance around my living room. It's one of my favorite things to do alone, although I got Amelia to join me once." She smiles at the memory that's in her head, and I'm thankful for that. I'm glad it was a good memory and not one that seems to haunt her in the middle of the night.

"That's cute," I say.

"Favorite holiday?"

"Lunar New Year. My family and I have a bunch of traditions we always do, and I enjoy it." I nod at her to go, knowing her favorite holiday is Halloween.

"My favorite is Halloween. Not only do I like horror movies, but it's the one day that always lets me be someone else instead of myself." Her explanation stops me in my tracks.

"You've said that to me before. Why don't you like being yourself?" I ask.

"It's not that I don't like myself. I guess it's because I don't know which version I am. I feel like I put on different faces for people, and it gets exhausting sometimes. Halloween allows me to be whatever I want, no judgment."

"Which version are you right now? Or which one do you want to be?" I ask. I don't understand why she doesn't think she's good enough as is.

"That's a pretty loaded question, isn't it?" She smiles a bit and tucks a loose piece of hair behind her ear, and part of me wishes I did that.

"You don't have to say anything, but I think whoever you are underneath what you show to people is good enough. You don't have to pretend with me, Paige. No matter which part of yourself you show me, my feelings about you won't change."

She looks over at me. "Your feelings about me?"

"Well, yeah." I suddenly feel nervous. "Just forget I said anything."

"No." I look over at her and she's staring at me.

"No?"

"I'm tired of sweeping this under the rug, Ol. I *like* you. I like being around you, and spending time with you and I don't want that to stop after we're done with what we're doing." She's rambling which means she must be as nervous as I am. "I've been alone my whole life, except for the girls, these past few weeks with you have been unforgettable. So,

Oliver, I like you. Now, care to explain your feelings about me and how they won't change?"

"I like you too, P. It made me feel like shit when I realized this would come to an end. I've been writing a list full of excuses to keep being around you after all is said and done. It's all just so complicated—between the investigation and my sister, this could get messy."

"I know, but we can't keep pretending this pull doesn't exist. It's out in the open, so what are we going to do about that? You've made me smile and laugh these past few weeks, and I want to feel like that with you all the time." She pauses. "You're right. It's complicated. But maybe after all this noise is over, we can revisit this conversation?"

"I'd like that. You also never answered my question. Which version, P?"

"I like this version best."

"Which one?" We're staring at each other on this fucking rooftop. My heart is beating so fast, and it's taking all of my strength not to grab her and kiss her.

"The one I am with you. She's the brave one."

"That's just you, Paige. You're brave. That's who you are, and it's easy to see that. You're stronger than you think, P." I reach over and grab her chin. "Don't ever forget that."

"I won't." She smiles at me, and I let go of her. "I think the coast is probably clear by now."

"Yeah, you're right." Fuck. Did confessing our feelings make things weird? I just needed Paige to know I could see right through her. And to me, she'll always be worth it. I guess now we're playing the waiting game until after all this is over.

We shuffle down the stairs, and walk back to her place. It feels like we've done this dance so many times. We investigate, we drizzle our feelings out a bit at a time, I walk her back, and we go our separate ways.

But something changed tonight. We both admitted we liked each other but agreed to wait and revisit that conversation. I know it's for the better, but after all these days of doing this dance, I find myself wishing we could be something now.

We approach her door, and she turns to me. "You don't have to be afraid of showing yourself to the world, either. The Oliver I know is one of my favorite people."

"The Paige I know is one of my favorite people too," and as she smiles, I lean forward and capture it in my mouth.

She melts against me like last time, and feelings rush into me as her soft lips kiss me back. She laughs as I back her into her front door, and even though this is only the third time we've kissed, I feel addicted.

She tastes like fresh berries.

I wrap my hand around the nape of her neck to deepen the kiss, and she lets me. My other arm is stretched out against the door. This feels good. *Too good.* I don't know how I'm supposed to walk this Earth knowing I can't kiss her all the time.

I notice her cheeks are red when I pull away. I'll never get tired of doing that to her. "I'm sorry," I say.

"Why are you sorry?"

"I should've asked before I did that," I tell her. "Did I make you uncomfortable?"

"No, uncomfortable is not the word I would use." She reaches up with two fingers and touches her lips as if she still feels mine there.

"Well, what word would you use?"

"Fleeting."

Lasting for a short time. "Next time, I'll make it longer."

"I'm holding you to that," she tells me as she reaches for her door handle. "Goodnight, Oliver."

"Goodnight, Paige." I smile at her as the door closes. When I turn to walk back to my apartment, I can't help but notice my smile hasn't left my face. When I eventually lay down in bed, it's still there. *I don't know if I've ever smiled this much.*

I would wait forever for her, and now I know she feels the same way about me.

Best day ever.

25

Wednesday, October 19th

"In my opinion, this was the perfect second chance romance," Amelia says as she paces around the classroom. "You guys know I'm a sucker for that trope, and this book gets a million stars from me." Amelia dramatically sits back in her chair.

"It made me cry so much. He waited eleven years for her!" I say as I feel more tears start to bubble up.

"This is one of the best books I've ever read," Ella says.

"I wasn't expecting the big reveal at the end, and it crushed me. I gave it to Grant after I was done, and he read it in one night. Jacks called me in the middle of the night and made me bring over a box of tissues because Grant was such a mess." She laughs, and so do we.

"That's adorable," I tell her.

"It's safe to say this was definitely a favorite of all time for us," Ella says and we all nod in agreement.

"Absolutely." Hads smiles as she smooths out her skirt. "Now, it's time for a debrief."

"I'll go first!" Ella shoots out of her chair and sits on top of the desk. "I got the job!"

"What?!" I yell as my mouth drops open.

"This calls for refreshments!" Amelia says, reaching into her bag and pulling out a bottle.

"Ella! Congrats!" Hads is the first to hug her.

I look at Amelia. "Why do you have that in your bag?"

"You never know when champagne is needed!"

"You wouldn't happen to be meeting a certain someone after this, Ames?" Ella asks as she untangles from Hads.

"Shut up. I obviously stole this from the corner store I robbed before I got here." She pulls out cups from her bag.

"We walked over here together," I say to her, confused.

"And if the police ask, that's exactly what you'll say." Amelia pours into the cups and passes them to each of us. We all raise for a toast.

"To Ella. For being the best friend the three of us could ask for and for all her hard work finally paying off. There's nobody more deserving," I say.

"To Ella!" We all say as we drink. Ella downs hers in one go.

"Damn, that's strong," Hads says.

"And bubbly," I say.

"Knock, knock!" a voice says. "I'm not interrupting anything, am I?" Grant pokes his head into the room and beams when his eyes land on Hads. He comes in and shuts the door behind him. "What are you guys celebrating, and can I join?"

"Ella got her dream job!" Hads tells him.

"The one you interviewed for a while ago?" he asks and Ella nods. I love how involved he is. He's a good guy—a good friend to all of us. "Hell yeah! Hand me a cup. This is cause for celebrating!"

Ames pours him a cup and hands it to him as he sits down.

"Guys, please put that book away. I'm still reeling from finishing it the other day." I reach over and slide my copy back into my tote bag, and the rest of the girls do the same.

"Hads told us how distraught you were after reading it." I playfully punch his arm. "And here I thought I was the most emotional one here."

"I wasn't distraught. I was devastated—still am. Those two were soul-mates."

"Agreed," Hads says as she leans her head back, and they kiss again.

"Paige, how's the investigation?" Grant asks me.

"Things are getting more complicated by the day, but we're close to figuring it out. We found shady stuff last night when we searched the office again."

"Like what?" he asks me.

"Well, Oliver found a safe underneath his desk with a—" The door flies open and cuts off what I was about to say.

"Paige, stop." Oliver walks into the classroom.

"Oliver? What are you doing here? And apologize to that door you slammed open," Hads asks him.

"I need to talk to Paige, but I forgot it was Wednesday." He looks from Hads over to me, and my stomach drops. "Can I talk to you?"

"Sure," I say while turning my chair in his direction. *God, he gets prettier every time I see him.* It's hard to be around him without wanting to kiss him again. But at least we can stop pretending we don't feel anything for each other. I'm glad we were able to clear the air, finally.

Though, nobody else knows what happened last night, so all this tension is only between us. We might be in this crowded room, but nobody knows how we truly feel about each other.

Everyone might see us as Oliver and Paige, two acquaintances turned friends turned partners in crime. Except now, we're two people who admitted to wanting to be more than friends. And after all of this is over, we'll get a chance to become something more.

When I look at him, he tenses his jaw. "Alone, preferably."

"If you sign this waiver saying you won't keep her out all night again," Amelia says while rifling through her bag, and I swear if she pulls out something for him to sign, I'll laugh.

"You guys were out all night?" Hads asks us.

"I'm sure it was purely investigative work, right?" Grant tries to help us out.

"Of course it was," I say as I all but drag Oliver into the hallway and into the classroom next door. I flip the lights on and turn around, and he's leaning against the door frame.

Fuck, why does that look so good? He's wearing a black shirt that molds to his stupid six-pack and plain gray sweatpants. "Were you out for a run? It's like eight at night, and you're wearing dark colors! That's dangerous."

"I was." He pushes off the door and slowly walks toward me. The few sips of alcohol I had is making me all giggly and I grab one of his headphone strings and put it to my ear.

"Damn, no music. It must have been a bad run." I smile at him.

"I was trying to clear my head. I don't put music on for those."

"Then why do you still wear your headphones?" I ask.

"I don't want anyone to talk to me."

"Okay, well, why did you come here? What are you thinking about tonight?"

"You, but that's not why I'm here. Have you checked your email tonight?"

I try not to think about the first word he said, so I pull my phone out and open my email. There's one from Alissa. She sent an attachment, and when I click on it, my face drops.

"The money the receptionist transferred to the offshore account was two days before the murder?" I look up at him, and he's smirking.

"Yup," Oliver says to me.

Oh my God. "Are you saying what I think you are?"

"Probably," he tells me.

"The receptionist paid someone to kill her boss? Why would she pay someone if she had the best access to him outside his office all day?" I wonder. "Plus, it doesn't make sense. Who did she pay? Did she have a partner?"

"My gut is telling me she paid her lover to kill the dean for her. I don't know why those two would want him dead, but love is one of the most common motives for murder. We should look into both angles. Who knows if this was a one man job or more. Hell, the acting dean guy could have nothing to do with this, who knows." He runs a hand down his face, feeling as unsure about this as I am.

"Money can make someone do anything, even if it's out of their comfort zone. But she definitely had something to do with this. The money trail doesn't lie."

"Agreed, Sherlock." Oliver smiles at me.

"Can I go back to celebrating my friend now, Watson?"

"Yes, I'm sorry I dragged you from it but this was important." I head back to book club and as we walk by the door, Hads calls out to her brother.

"Oliver, come join us!"

"Me? Why?" he asks.

"No, the other person named Oliver, yes, you! Join the celebration." Hads waves him over and he complies.

"What are we celebrating?" he asks.

"Ella got her dream job," I say with a smile on my face.

He looks over at her. "Congrats."

"Thanks." Ella smiles at him and takes another sip of champagne. Amelia hands Oliver a cup, and he eyeballs her.

"You didn't poison this, did you?"

"If I poisoned you, then who would I make fun of?" She smiles as he takes the cup from her.

"I thought you didn't drink, Oliver?" Hads asks, confused.

"I don't." He looks over at her.

"Wait, you don't drink?" Grant pauses, clearly thinking hard about something. "Then why were you at the Hidden Bear last year?"

"You've been to the Hidden Bear?" Hads smacks his arm and then looks over at Grant. "And you saw him there? When was this?"

"I didn't see him, Brendan did," Grant tells her. "It was the same night Ryan and I had that altercation outside of my apartment building."

"We started dating in May and you never told me this?" Hads says, her voice getting louder.

"Oh, this is going to be good." Amelia pulls out a few popcorn bags and hands them to Ella and me.

"Hads, put the damn ruler away!" Oliver yells at her. *When did she get that out?*

"He was the one who approached me! Hit him first!" Grant puts both his hands up and kneels on the ground as if he's surrendering. Hads is very clearly joking and isn't going to hit either of them, but it's funny to see how scared they both are of her.

"One of you needs to tell me what you two talked about before I split this in half so I can smack the two of you!" Hads swings the ruler between them, laughing. She definitely likes having this power over them. Amelia, Ella, and I are sitting back, watching this unfold with popcorn and champagne in our hands. I laugh as I lean my head onto Ella's shoulder.

"I'm proud of you, Ells. You did the damn thing."

"Thanks, Paigey." She leans her head on mine too, and I hear Amelia start recording on her phone. Sometimes, I worry she likes our misery too much.

"Start talking!" Hads says.

"You already know about what Ryan and I talked about, but Oliver here sat on the opposite side of the bench and introduced himself. I saw him walk into our building. He must've gone to the bar after I saw him. Brendan only told me a few weeks ago about it when he saw Oliver and I walking together."

What the hell is going on?

"Well, what did you two talk about on the bench?" She points the ruler at Oliver.

"I told him how much I hated Ryan, he agreed, and then I told him he was a good guy! That's it, Hads."

"Why were you in a bar in the first place? You don't drink! This sounds like some shady operation," Hads says to them.

"Drop it, Hads. It's none of your business." Oliver steps over and puts his cup on the table, clutching the sides of it so hard his knuckles are white. He doesn't look okay, and part of me wants to grab his hand and hold it, but I don't. Why did that get him all tense? The three of them are just messing around, right?

"Oliver, I want to make sure you're okay. You've always been against alcohol, so if you're struggling, I want to know." She stares at him, and he turns around to face her.

"I go once a year on the anniversary of Mia's death." The whole room goes silent.

"Oh," is all Hads can say.

"Now drop it," Oliver says as he leaves the room. Hads is frozen where she stands, and Grant gets up and pulls her into a hug.

"It's okay. You didn't know."

"I-I was joking around. I didn't—" Hads says into Grant's chest.

I don't think about anything, I simply grab my tote bag and run after him.

I lightly touch his arm as I catch up to him, and he looks up and sees it's me.

"What are you doing, Paige?"

"Checking on someone I care about," I tell him. "Are you okay?"

He studies my face for a second. "I am now."

"Do you want to talk about it?"

"Not much to talk about. It's just a thing I do every year. I don't even know why I order a drink. I never sip it."

"I think it's sweet," I tell him. "I sometimes sit by the pond on campus because my Dad and I used to go fishing when I was a kid. It's a way for me to remember the good parts—a way to remember who he was. It's not really the same since he's still alive, but…" I trail off, feeling like I'm overstepping.

"I think grieving someone alive is worse."

"I think you shouldn't compare your pain against mine. Everyone is allowed to hurt over things that make them hurt, no matter if someone has it worse," I say as we start walking. Our arms hang at our sides, our fingers dancing between each other until Oliver threads our hands together. "Do you still love her?"

"I think part of me always will."

"That makes sense," I say. "All of the grief and pain you feel, just think of it as all the love you never got to show them before they left. Grief and love exist together, I've learned over the years. It's brave to love something or someone." I look over at him, and he's already looking at me. I wish I could do something to help. Somehow, this doesn't feel like enough.

"Just you being here is enough help, Paige." I must have said that last part out loud.

"Sorry. I—"

"You have nothing to apologize for." I turn to look at him. "Thank you for coming after me."

"I'll always chase after you, Ol."

"Is my sister alright?" he asks.

"Grant has her. She'll be fine."

"Tell her I'll see her on Saturday at the usual time," he says to me.

"Okay. Do you want me to walk back with you?"

"No, it's okay. Go back to celebrating." He waves me off and continues forward, his hand unthreading with mine. I miss the contact. I miss feeling his hand in mine.

"You sure you'll be okay?"

"Yeah, Paige. I'll be okay. I got enough sunshine to boost my mood for the night." He smiles at me.

"Could you use some extra warmth? It's a bit chilly tonight." I smile at him.

"Absolutely." He holds his arms out and I walk into them.

Oliver gives the best hugs, and they always make me feel safe. We stay like this for a few seconds, and I think I could live in Oliver's arms forever if he would let me. "Thank you for checking on me. I'll see you in class tomorrow."

With that, he turns and walks away, leaving me standing on the pavement with butterflies in my stomach. I want to scream after him that I don't want to wait until all the noise is gone. I want to be with him now, but I stay silent like I always do.

My phone buzzes in my hand.

Amelia: Paige, where are you?

Ella: Are you okay?

> **Paige: I was checking on Oliver.**

Hads: Is he okay?

> **Paige: I think so. He told me to tell you he'll see you on Saturday at the usual time.**

Ella: Let's talk more next week.

> **Paige: Sounds good! I love you guys!**

Hads: Love you guys! Sorry if I ruined the vibe.

Amelia: You didn't, Hads. I love you guys!

Ella: Love you!

I drop my phone into my tote bag and take the long route home, wanting to be alone with the butterflies in my stomach and the longing in my chest for a guy I can't have.

26

????

THEY'RE GETTING CLOSER, BUT they'll never figure it out before I finish. Two criminal justice students aren't going to stand in the way of this.

Paige Yarrow and Oliver Baker.

I may need to scare them a bit more to show them the repercussions of sticking their nose into others' business.

I didn't expect this hitch, but I'm going to have fun with this.

They'll never see me coming.

27

Saturday, October 22nd

I GROAN WHEN MY alarm wakes me up because I barely slept last night. For some reason, I couldn't stop tossing and turning as thoughts of the past few days filtered through my mind.

The main one being that I've barely talked to Paige since she ran after me the other day. I've distanced myself from everyone, and it's made me feel like shit.

All I've done the past few nights is run so I could try and relax, but it hasn't worked.

I'm not only angry about losing my cool in front of my sister and all her friends, but I also feel weird about openly airing my past out how I did.

Part of me does feel better now that it's out in the open and I'm not hiding as much anymore, but I hate that all of them were there for my outburst—if I can even call it that.

I throw my running clothes on and I'm out the door in ten minutes. I put my headphones on and no music because my head needs to get screwed back on straight.

I have to apologize to my sister this morning, and I should text Paige and ask her what our next steps are. But for some reason, I can't do that. I feel too horrible and embarrassed about what happened the other day.

I stop to stretch my calves when I feel eyes on the back of my neck, but when I look around, I don't see anybody. The past week I've felt more on edge than normal but I thought that was my body reacting to my feelings about Paige. Now, I'm worried it's something different.

I shake that feeling off and continue on the path. Nothing weird happens, and I don't get any weird feelings until I see my sister on the bench we always meet at. She's definitely wearing Grant's clothes because it all looks two sizes too big for her.

"Are you and Carter swapping clothes? Am I going to see him wearing one of your skirts?" I ask her.

"No. I just like to take things out of his closet. Comfy clothes really are the move sometimes."

"I'm glad you've finally realized that. I've told you for years you didn't have to try so hard."

"It's not my fault I think clothes are an underappreciated art form!" she tells me as we start walking. We're silent for a few moments before she speaks again. "I'm sorry for the other day. I was joking around with the two of you, and I didn't mean to pull at something you didn't want to talk about."

"Hads, it's okay. I'm sorry too."

"Why are you sorry?"

"For storming off how I did. I just didn't want anyone to see me at that moment," I tell her.

"It's okay. I get why you left. I would've done the same thing. I walked away from Grant so many times last semester just because I didn't want to feel what I felt."

"Wow, the Baker family is stellar at showing emotions," I joke.

"Well, to be fair, Mom and Dad never helped us with that."

"Yeah, they aren't ones for embracing their emotional sides," I say.

"But we're not following in their footsteps. We both need to be more open with each other and going forward, we should both agree to open up a bit more. We're siblings, Ol. I want to know about the things that still haunt you and vice versa."

"Fine. I'll try to be more open with you when things get rough. How does that sound?"

My sister smiles at me. "Perfect, Oliver. That sounds perfect." She raises her camera and takes a few pictures of the surrounding area. She does this sometimes on our walks—takes a bunch of fucking pictures. I don't know what she does with them, but I'll admit, Virginia in October is beautiful.

The leaves are falling off the trees, and I can hear some of them crunching underneath Hads's and my feet. Paige would love this. I wonder if she's been able to do this or if she's been too busy running around with me.

"So, what have you been up to lately? I feel like we've barely had time to talk," I say before feeling that weird sensation of being watched again, so I turn around and sweep the area we're in. We just went around the pond. I see a few students up and about, but nobody's looking in our general direction.

"Oliver? Why did you stop?" Hads asks me as I continue to look around.

"No reason. I—"

"Hey! What did we just talk about? Spill."

I sigh heavily before I answer, "The past few days, I've felt like someone has been watching me, but it's probably me being paranoid."

"You feel like you're being watched, and you're still investigating? How stupid are you?"

"Hads, it's fine. Paige and I aren't uncovering some mafia plot or anything serious. It's just a standard homicide investigation. Plus, somebody watching me would gain no information since I'm one of the most boring people on the planet." She nods her head and I hate how fast she agreed with me.

"Okay. I believe you."

It takes us about fifteen more minutes to finish our route before we sit down to watch the sunrise like we always do.

"I'm glad we kept this tradition up. I thought going to the same college as you was going to be the worst decision ever, but I'm glad I chose Grand Mountain." She nudges me with her elbow.

"I'm glad you chose to come here too."

"Why? So you could punch all the guys that broke my heart like you did in high school?"

"No. I like having you around, Hads. Punching them is just a plus."

Hads jolts me again with her arm before she gets up to leave. "Are you excited about your birthday next week?"

"Not really, as far as I'm concerned, it's just another day." I look over at her, and she's got a weird look on her face. "Please tell me you're not planning some huge thing where Grant pops out of a giant cake? I hate celebrating my birthday, Hads. You know that."

"No, I haven't planned anything yet, but I promise Grant won't be jumping out of a cake."

"Thank you."

"It's actually a giant cupcake. I know you like those better than cake." I shoot her a glare. "I'm kidding, lighten up a little, Ollie. Maybe we can go out to dinner or something?"

"That's fine."

"Okay, good. I have to meet Grant. Are you staying here?"

"No. I'll walk with you," I tell her as I get up, wrap my headphones in a circle, and shove them into my pocket. We walk back to my building and talk about the most random things and I have to say, it feels good to converse with my sister and not have to worry about anything else.

We head through the doors of my building and as she goes down the hallway toward Grant's place, I head up to my place.

I walk past Nick and Noah's door and before I reach mine I shuffle back and knock on their door. I look down at my phone and realize how early it is. They might not be awake yet. As I turn to walk away, the door opens and Nick stares back at me.

"Did I wake you?"

"Yeah, Oliver. You're the only one who likes to go running at the crack of dawn."

"You used to go running with me in the mornings until you got lazy."

"That's rude." He puts his hand to his chest. "I like sleeping in like a normal person. You should try it sometime. Why did you knock? Did you want to come in?"

"No. I was wondering if you and Noah wanted to come for dinner tonight. I can find something to make." He stares back at me as if I'm speaking a different language. "What?"

"Are you dying or something?"

"No, why?"

"You invited us over for dinner."

"Yeah, and?"

"It's just not like you to be so forward, I assumed you were unwell or something."

"Do you want to come over or not?" I ask, my patience wearing thin.

"We'll be there."

"See you guys then."

And as I get into my place and shut the door behind me, I immediately take my phone out to talk to someone I've missed the past few days.

> **Oliver: Sorry for being distant the past few days.**

> **Paige: It's okay. I get it!**

> **Oliver: What's the plan going forward?**

I send that message and contemplate telling her about how someone might be watching me, but decide against it. I don't want her having a panic attack over it. The last thing I want is for her to worry about me.

My phone buzzes, and I find myself smiling down at it when I see her name pop up on my phone.

> **Paige: Do you want to meet in the library tomorrow night? The girls and I are having a study date, but Grant usually joins us, so it should be fine.**

> **Oliver: Sounds good, just text me what time.**

> **Paige: We're usually at the library around 8/8:30.**

> **Oliver: See you then.**

I put my phone down and turn my shower on. I smile to myself. Paige was right. Letting people in isn't so bad after all.

28

Sunday, October 23rd

HADS, ELLA AND I plop down at our usual table in the library while Grant trails behind us carrying Hads' bookbag. They fought about that the entire way over here before Hads conceded because Grant wanted to make sure she didn't strain her back from all the heavy textbooks.

I set my tote bag down in an empty chair to save a seat for Oliver, and everyone sits down where they usually do when we get together at the library.

"Why couldn't Amelia come? Is she with Henry tonight?" Grant asks before he turns to me. "And are they dating yet or what? Their relationship confuses me."

"Amelia is studying for a test. When I left the apartment, she had her noise canceling headphones on. And no, Henry is not her boyfriend, yet," I say, noting how I think they'll get together in the future.

"You seem pretty keen on the fact that they're going to get together." Grant smiles back at me.

"She did the same thing before you two got together," Ella tells them.

"Paige told me, and I have to say, she has wonderful taste. She also told me she almost made shirts for you guys that were on Team Grant, and I have to say, I would love one. I'm a size large." Grant pauses before he speaks again. "Should we make shirts for Henry?"

My eyes bulge. "I think we should!"

"You've created a monster," Hads whispers to him.

"What? I'm rooting for Henry!" Grant says. "Paige, we'll talk."

I nod at Grant before turning to Ella. "You're obviously not studying, so what are you working on?"

"I have some paperwork to fill out now since I was officially offered the job. I have to send them tomorrow, and I haven't even started." She pushes her laptop open and gets to work.

"Paige, what about you? Are you doing homework or investigation stuff?" Grant asks me.

"Investigation stuff, but I'm waiting for Oliver to get here," I say as I grab my laptop, and when I do, a black bookbag drops onto the chair next to me.

"Oh wow, it only takes one time for someone to say your name and you appear!" Grant tells him.

"Really, G?" he says as he hands me my tote bag and sits beside me.

"Hey, guys." He looks around to all of us. "Ella. Nice to see you again. Sorry about—"

"Oliver, no worries. I'm just glad you're okay." She smiles at him and looks back to her computer.

"I printed out some more articles about his missing son because we still haven't ruled that out yet, and I printed out what Alissa emailed me back with." I shove the papers at him and he slowly sifts through them.

I open the shared file we have and look at the suspect list. I copied over all the information that Alissa sent us. We have lots of information about these people, and I think the receptionist is number one on my suspect list. Her partner possibly being the acting dean guy. Those two are definitely guilty of some shady stuff.

I see Oliver stop reading and look around the library in my peripheral vision.

"Is something wrong?" I ask him.

"No. Uh, my neck has been bothering me." He looks back down at the papers. "I think I slept on it wrong."

"Oh, that's never fun," I say, and he nods at me. "Who's number one on your suspect list, Ol?"

"I'm thinking the receptionist, but I feel like we're missing too many pieces to connect anything together. Did Alissa find any more wire transfers?"

"Wait, Alissa? Is that why she's been pulling all-nighters?" Ella asks us, and I freeze. "I thought you asked her to run a few things for you, not to illegally dig up information for you!"

"I plead the fifth?" I say, not wanting to get yelled at.

"She's been awfully peachy lately, and I should've known she was back into hacking," she looks between Oliver and me. "I'll allow it for now, but after this little charade, Alissa is done doing illegal shit for you guys. Understood?"

"I promise!"

"Got it," Oliver says as he immerses himself back into the investigation. We're all casually doing our work and making small talk, when our phones buzz on the table.

"Amber alert notification?" Grant asks as he checks his phone. "Nope."

"It's Amelia," Hads says.

Amelia: 911

Amelia: HELnjdfosnfdjafnd

"Guys something's wrong," Ella says to the table, but I'm already grabbing my stuff and trying to get out of here.

"What's going on?" Grant asks as we all rush to grab our stuff.

"Why are you guys freaking out?" Oliver asks, standing up from his chair.

"When we made our group chat, we agreed 911 would only be used in cases of emergency—the worst of the worst—and Amelia texted us one," Hads explains and Oliver grabs all of his papers before reaching for my tote bag.

"Go. I can hold this," Oliver tells me. "Just get to Amelia. Grant and I will meet you guys there."

Ella is booking it in front of me and running out the doors. I'm not far behind her and I can hear Hads behind me.

"Where are we going?" Hads yells from behind me.

"I tracked her location! She's still at our apartment!" I yell as I run. I get ahead of Ella, and my breathing starts to get more rapid.

Please let her be okay.

I'm starting to panic but I shove that down because I need to hold it together until I get to her. It'll probably be one of those situations where she fell or something small. Amelia is fine. *She's fine.*

I turn my head and see Grant and Oliver holding all of our bags and running after us. We must look insane to everyone around us but I honestly don't care.

It takes us what feels like forever to reach my apartment, and when the three of us do, my front door is wide open.

"I'm so out of shape," Hads pants. "Should we wait for the boys?"

"Why is the door open? Did you guys get robbed?" Ella asks.

"I don't know." I pause for a moment, my heart beating out of my chest. "Fuck this. I'm going in." I say as I reach my front door. I carefully enter, feeling Hads and Ella close behind. I see a bunch of papers and pillows scattered around the apartment. It looks like it was ransacked. I scan the room until I see Amelia lying on the floor. She's not moving and I can't tell if she's breathing.

"Amelia!" I yell as I run over to where she is. "Oh my, Ames." I put two of my fingers to her neck, and I feel her pulse.

She's alive. Thank God she's alive.

I hear footsteps behind me, but my vision starts to blur as tears cloud my eyes. I don't know what I was expecting when she texted us, but it wasn't this.

"What the fuck?" I think Grant said that. I feel Hads and Ella's presence next to me as I try to figure out what to do right now.

"What do we do?"

"I-I think she's passed out but she's bleeding and she has a cut on her forehead. It looks deep and I don't know what—" The words catch in my throat, and I force myself to refocus.

"Should I call an ambulance?"

"No! She's fine. Amelia's fine. Ames! Wake up!" I shake her body a little, hoping her eyes will open, but they don't. "Amelia!"

"Paige, be careful," Hads tells me. I might've shaken her a bit too hard, but I can't think of what else to do.

"Amelia!" Ella yells as she smacks her, and I see her eyes flutter open. She blinks a few times before she gets herself recentered, and then I throw my arms around her.

"You're okay. You're okay." I pull back and look at her. "What happened?"

"Grant, get the first aid kit from underneath the sink." Hads points to where it is.

"I'm on it."

"Oliver, you know how to stitch up a cut, right? You used to do it for me as a kid," Hads asks him.

"Yeah, I can do it." He walks over and sits, leaving some space so Amelia doesn't feel crowded.

"Ames, take a few breaths and try to explain," Ella tells her while she rubs her arm up and down, trying to calm her.

"Well, I–I was studying f-for my history test about the Mongols and those guys were brutal as hell and I had m–my headphones on and I was listening to my sixties music playlist–" She takes a few staggered breaths and I watch Oliver get up and go toward my room, probably giving us some space. "It's a good playlist, you know? It's one of my favorites recently and I–" She jumps all of a sudden, and I follow her eyes to where Oliver is standing as he comes back out of my room. I turn back to Amelia and she's as pale as a ghost. All the blood has drained from her face.

"Ames, why did you just get so scared of Oliver?" I ask her and watch her breathing get rougher and tears start falling in a steady stream from her eyes. Grant puts the first aid kit down on the ground a bit loudly, and Amelia jumps back and scurries to the wall to lean against it. I hold my hand out to everyone because I don't think she can handle everyone crowding her right now. I know what it feels like to be scared out of your mind after something traumatic happened. I know it almost too well.

I look behind at our friends. "Can you guys give us a second?" I say and Oliver grabs Grant, shoving him into my room. Hads and Ella get up and follow them.

I expected more of a fight from the girls, but it's easier this way. They shut my door quietly, and I turn back to her. "Ames, it's just me now. Keep going and try to mirror my breathing, okay?"

"I–I had my headphones on and I was in between songs when I heard the door fly open and I thought it was you mimicking how I enter our apartment, but I–I turned around and–"

"What did you see?" My heart is beating fast and I can feel some tears drop from my eyes. I've never seen Amelia like this. Normally, I'm the one always falling apart in front of her, but now the roles are reversed.

"It was a person. A tall one. They were dressed in black with a ski mask on, and it looked like they had a knife because I saw something shine in the light. I reached for my phone and tried to text you guys, but I didn't know if it was sent so I tried to send another one. Then they ran at me and I–I can't remember what happened after but I thought I was going to die. I thought I was going to die and you were going to walk into the apartment and find me dead on the floor and then I felt bad because that would've been two times you've discovered a dead body in the span of two months and I—"

"Amelia, hey, you're okay. You're alive and I'm fine. We're okay," I tell her. "What can I do to help? Do you need anything? Just tell me what I can do and I'll do it." Tears are still falling from both of our faces and she looks me dead in the eyes.

"Henry. I need Henry."

"Okay. I can call him. Where's your phone?" She points to the couch and I lift it up, tapping his name and putting the phone to my ear. "Ella, can you get her some water?" I ask as I wait for him to pick up the phone.

"Hey! I thought you were studying tonight?"

"Henry, it's P–Paige." I'm stuttering a bit because all my adrenaline from the past few minutes has worn off. "Something happened. Can you get over here? Amelia needs you."

"I'm on my way. Is she okay?"

"Can you just get here, please?" I say to him while I hang up and go to Amelia. She's drinking the water Ella gave her and the rest of them come out of my room except Oliver. "He's on his way, okay? Henry will be here soon."

"Thank you."

"Do you want a blanket? Do you need anything else? Do you want us to take you to the hospital?" I ask her.

"No, no. I'll be okay. A blanket sounds nice." She's shaking so badly and I know it's from fear and not because she's cold. Hads grabs the blanket we always keep in the living room and brings it over, laying it across her body.

"Can Oliver come out and stitch your head up?" I ask her and she nods, Oliver peeking out of my room as his name is mentioned. He opens the first aid kit, grabs gauze and puts some antiseptic on it. Oliver reaches up and steadies her head while he cleans the wound out.

"What did you get hit with?" Hads asks her.

"I–I think the end of a knife," she tells us, and my heart sinks. That could have easily been the other end of it.

"Fucking hell," Ella whispers.

Oliver takes a closer look at her face. "I don't think she needs stitches. I just need to clean and bandage it. Thankfully, it's only a superficial wound."

All of us let out a collective sigh.

"I'm going to call campus police. They can check everything out and make sure it's safe for you guys to be here tonight." Grant takes his phone out and starts dialing as he closes the door behind him.

"If you two want to stay at my place tonight, I'm sure Alissa wouldn't mind," Ella offers.

"No, it's fine. I don't want to burden anyone," Amelia says as she winces from Oliver bandaging her head up.

"You should be good. Just make sure to clean it tomorrow and keep something over it so it doesn't get infected." Oliver stands up and throws all of his scraps out.

"Do you think it was a robbery? Your place got trashed. Paige, your room is a mess," Hads whispers to us.

"Who would want to rob a few students?" I ask as I feel Oliver grab my hand, pull me off the ground and into my room. I look around and my stuff is everywhere. My books are scattered, my sheets are ripped off my bed, and my desk drawer is on my floor. "What the fuck?"

"I found something."

"Oliver, this isn't the time to talk about the investigation. Amelia's hurt," I say as I try to walk past him, but he stops me before I leave.

"Paige, look." He hands me a small piece of paper from his pocket. I look skeptically at him as I unfold it, but when I see what it says, my entire body goes cold.

Stop looking for answers. You're not going to find any.
This is your only warning.

I look back up at him. "Where did you find this?"

He points to my desk. "I grabbed it before anyone else saw it."

"So, the person w-who broke in here, they were looking for me?" I whisper as I feel myself about to fall apart.

"Paige, don't do that."

"This is all my fault." I look at him, and tears cloud my vision once again. "If I were here then Amelia wouldn't be the one that's hurt."

"You don't know that. Paige, they could have hurt you!" He takes a second to collect himself. "They could've hurt you, P. I don't know what I would do if..." He trails off, not wanting to finish his thought.

"I don't care about me! Amelia's sitting on the ground barely able to string two sentences together because of what we're doing!"

"Paige, it's not your fault. There's no way we could have seen this coming," he whispers at me.

"I should've known. After that car followed us, I should have known. I should've stopped. If I stopped, then she would be okay." I sink to the floor as I feel the guilt start to bury me. The thought of a person I love getting hurt because of me is overwhelming me. *What have I done?*

"Paige, look at me. Please." He kneels to where I am and tilts my head up to look at him.

"It's my fault, Ol. It's all my fault," I say as I collapse against him. "It's all my fault," I repeat over and over again. He pulls me into his arms, and the two of us are sitting on my messy floor as I cry.

This is all my fault.

"It's not your fault, love. It's not your fault. I got you. It's okay. Amelia's okay."

"I can't keep doing this, Ol. I can't," I say as I cry into his shirt.

"I'm calling it. Okay? We're done investigating. I'm not risking anyone else's safety over this—especially yours." I nod, and he hugs me tighter. "The best thing we can do right now is be there for Amelia." He pulls my head from his chest and braces my face with both hands. "We have to go out there, and we have to pretend like everything's alright. Okay?"

I nod again at him, and he stands us both up and sets me on the ground. He takes his thumbs and wipes the tears from my eyes, and I grab my shirt and try to make it seem like I wasn't just crying my eyes out. I take a big deep breath and open my door. I'm about to speak when the front door flies open, and Henry locks eyes with me.

"Paige, where is she?"

I look at him, and I've never seen calm and chill Henry so panicked. I point to where she is against the wall, and he takes a few steps and stops as if he's frozen where he stands. Amelia is in the same position, curled with her knees up against the wall, and when she spots Henry, her body loosens a bit. That must shake Henry out of his fog, and he rushes over to her.

Everyone else moves to go outside to give them a moment, and I feel Oliver behind me in my doorway as he watches the two of them converse. I can't tell what they're saying, but Amelia already looks better now that he's here.

Oliver rests his hand on my shoulder, and it takes everything in me not to fall apart again. I wipe a loose tear from my face, and Oliver grabs my hand and walks me to the front door. He drops my hand before we walk out, leaving Henry and Amelia to converse in private.

29

Sunday, October 23rd

WHEN I REACH THE girls outside, they pull me in for a hug.

"How is she?" Ella asks.

"She looks a bit more relaxed now that Henry is here." I smile at them, a fake one, but it's all I'm capable of at the moment.

"Who would do something like this? And why? It doesn't make any sense. Was it another student?" Guilt hits me in the chest again as Hads asks a bunch of questions I can answer.

"Guys, I—" I start to say, but Oliver cuts me off.

"Campus police are here." He points to the parked car in the lot.

I hear footsteps, and when I turn around, Amelia and Henry are coming out of our apartment. Amelia's still wrapped in a blanket, and

Henry has his arm around her as she shakes. I'm glad she has him. Henry would never have put Amelia in the danger I did.

Maybe I don't deserve anyone around me. Maybe I deserve to be alone. Maybe this is the universe telling me I don't deserve a family.

Grant and Oliver go talk to the two officers while the rest of us girls huddle around Amelia. I turn into myself a little bit, still feeling wrapped up in my emotions. How could I let this happen? My best friend is now scarred for life because of me.

I feel ashamed of who I am. All my life, I've lived with guilt like it was my sister, even though I'm an only child. All my life, I've thought if I just tried a little bit harder to be perfect, my dad wouldn't have become who he did, and my mom would still care I was here. On top of those feelings, I have to live knowing I caused this. I caused Amelia pain.

If I had tried harder, this could all have been avoided.

I wish it were me. I wish I had been at the apartment and not her.

"Who are the residents of this apartment?" one of the officers asks us.

"I am, and so is she." I point to Amelia.

"Ma'am, are you alright? Do you need to go to the hospital?" he asks her, and she shakes her head.

"I'm alright. It's just a cut. N–Nothing too bad."

They nod at her. "We'll sweep your apartment, and once we deem it all clear, you can return inside. We also have other housing options for now if you'd like."

"That would be great," I say.

"Paige, it's okay. That's our home. I just need to know it's safe," Amelia tells us as she leans closer to Henry.

"I wouldn't mind you guys crashing at my place," Hads says.

"Alissa would love to see you two," Ella tells us.

"Guys, I'm okay. Just let them check it out so I can go to sleep and pretend this didn't happen," Amelia says, and the two officers walk up to our place and disappear inside our apartment.

"Do you want us to stay the night? I have to work, but I can always tell them the circumstances, and they'll understand." Ella grabs her hand and holds onto it.

"No, it's okay. Don't put your lives on hold for me." Amelia doesn't like being the center of attention a lot, so I'm sure she's doing this because she's afraid and doesn't want to show it. "Plus, Henry is staying over."

"I am?"

"You offered earlier, and now you know my answer," she whispers to him.

"I think Oliver should stay over too," Grant tells the group, and Oliver smacks him in the arm.

"Why?" Hads asks curiously.

"Well, I figure he can scare off anyone if they decide to return—" Oliver smacks Grant again. "Two is better than one, you know? I don't know Henry well, but I think Oliver being inside with them will help us all sleep better knowing both of the girls are safe."

"Oh, that's a good point, boyfriend." Hads looks to her brother. "What do you say, Ol?"

"I'd be happy to, as long as it's okay with the girls," he says while looking at us, and Ames and I nod in agreement. I know I won't be sleeping, but I always feel better when he's around.

Ella reaches for Amelia, and they hug. "I'm so glad you're okay. Whoever did this is going to pay. I'll also ask campus police if they can have a car sit in the lot tonight, just in case," Ella says, and I turn away, my emotions starting to overcome me again.

"I'll check in tomorrow. I promise," Amelia says to us.

"You and Grant should go too," Oliver tells his sister. "I'll feel better knowing you're safe with Carter than in your place with Taylor." Oliver looks over at Grant and nods his head at him before he picks up Hads, throws her over his shoulder, and carries her away.

"Grant, keep your phone on. I'll send updates!" Oliver yells at him, and Grant shoots him a thumbs up. Oliver shoves his phone at Henry. "Here."

"What?"

"Put your number in."

"Oh, right." Henry punches his number and returns it to Oliver.

Campus police come back out a few moments later. "It's all clear. If you both need anything, don't hesitate to call. There's always someone available. I also recommend filing a police report tomorrow if anything was stolen. We'll have a car parked out here all night if you need any-thing."

"Thank you," Henry tells them as they walk away, and he looks to Amelia. "Are you ready?"

"Mhm," is all she says before we head back inside.

It's a mess in here, and I immediately start cleaning up the living room. Oliver comes over to me with a white plastic bag and I watch as Amelia and Henry go into her room.

Oliver and I fix the couch cushions and all of the shit thrown every-where, and it takes about half an hour to make the living room look normal. I still feel wide awake, so I continue cleaning in my room. I hear Oliver cleaning up the kitchen when Amelia lightly knocks on my door.

"Can I come in?" she asks as she looks around my room. "Did any-thing get stolen?"

I shake my head. "A-Are you okay?"

"No." I feel my tears brimming at her answer. "But I'll be okay even-tually."

"Good. That's good," I say to her, doing a poor job of holding my tears back. "I'm sorry. Amelia, I'm so sorry. This is all my fault."

"No, Paige. It isn't."

"You don't understand—"

"I do, actually. Your room was the one ransacked, not mine. From what I can tell, nothing was stolen, so it wasn't a robbery. Whoever came in here wasn't looking for me." She walks over to where I'm standing against my bed.

"I did this to you. I could've stopped investigating, but I didn't." I look down at the floor, not wanting to meet her eyes.

"Stop blaming yourself. You didn't attack me."

"No, but my actions led to this happening, and I don't know how I'm going to live with myself—"

She cuts me off. "I'm glad I was here and not you because I wasn't the one he wanted. If you were here with me, he might've really hurt you, and *that* I couldn't live with." She pulls me into a hug, and we both fall apart simultaneously.

"Amelia, I'm so sorry. I'm sorry, I'm *so* sorry," I say to her, tears streaming down my face.

"Paigey, I'm okay. It's not your fault. Please remember that going forward." She hugs me tighter, and my emotions overtake me.

"I understand if you want to pull away from me a bit over the next few weeks," I tell her.

"You're my best friend, Paige. My sister. All I want is you by my side, forever. Okay?" I nod my head at her and hug her one more time. "I want you to say it."

"Say what?"

"That it's not your fault."

"Ames, I can't."

"Stop. Tell me. Right now."

I take a deep breath. "It wasn't my fault."

"Good. Now repeat that to yourself every time the guilt creeps up on you." I nod. "Okay, let's help Oliver clean because I don't want him breaking one of my favorite mugs with his big ass hands." I laugh a little through my tears, and we open the door to find an entirely different scenario playing out.

Oliver and Henry are standing in our kitchen playing rock, paper, scissors.

Amelia and I burst out laughing. "What are you guys doing?"

"Nothing," they say simultaneously as they continue to clean, acting like nothing just happened.

Sunday, October 23rd

I'm in the kitchen trying to figure out where the silverware drawer is, when I watch Amelia go into Paige's room and shut the door. I feel like I entered a parallel universe tonight. First, all this shit happens with Amelia, and then I find a note threatening Paige in her room. On top of all that, my sister suggested I stay the night here to keep an eye on them.

What the fuck is going on? I have no goddamn idea, and the only thing I know is that I'm glad Paige wasn't here when this happened. I hate that this happened to Amelia, obviously, but I couldn't live with myself if something happened to Paige and I wasn't here to help. If I think about it too hard, my breathing gets tough, so I try not to dwell on that.

Amelia's probably in Paige's room telling her the same thing I did earlier—that it's not her fault. I could tell Amelia knew the real reason why someone broke in, and I think everyone else knows too but nobody has said a word about it. I think all of us are focused on Amelia and making sure she's okay.

"I would be careful with those mugs. Amelia would kill you if you broke one," I hear Henry tell me. He's picking up their dining table chairs from off the floor. "So, you're staying the night too? With Paige?"

"Not with Paige. Probably on the couch or something."

"Nice," he tells me, and silence covers the room. "So, are you and Paige like together or something? Amelia tells me about you two all the time."

I tense my jaw and turn around to face him. "No. We were just working on this thing together."

"The murder investigation?" he asks, and I cinch my brows together. "Oh, sorry. Amelia told me about it one day. I thought she was kidding at first, but then she told me the whole story. Was I not supposed to say anything?"

"It's fine," I tell him as I start drying the plates I washed. I'm leaning against the sink, and he's sitting at the table, and the two of us just exist. It's awkward, to say the least. I don't know how to do these types of things—small talk—and the situation we're both in is making it even weirder. "So, are you and Amelia—"

He cuts me off. "No, no. Just friends."

"You're a pretty good friend to drop everything and speed over here for her."

He smiles and shakes his head. "I feel like you would do the same thing if Paige was in trouble."

Of course I would. But all I do is keep my hands busy and say nothing.

"I didn't mean any offense."

"None taken," I tell him.

"I just get this feeling you're that girl's protector."

I look over at Paige's door. "No." I smile a bit. "No, Paige has been protecting herself since she was a kid. She certainly doesn't need me to do it for her."

He nods his head at me. "She may not need it, but she likes you being around."

Again, I say nothing.

"It was just an observation. I'll drop it." He stands and heads over to Amelia's room, returning a few seconds later with an air mattress and blankets.

"I thought you were taking the couch?" I ask.

"I was going to. I forgot Amelia mentioned having an air mattress in her closet for when Ella and Hads sleepover. I figure I'll just take this."

"Well, neither of us is supposed to be sleeping. We're supposed to keep watch so that guy doesn't come back and murder one of us," I tell him.

"Wow, straight to murder, okay." He pauses for a moment. "How about this?" He walks over to me in the kitchen and holds his fist before him.

"What do you want? A fist bump or something?"

"No, dude. Have you ever played rock, paper, scissors? I play this with my younger sister all the time."

"Your solution to this is a children's game?" I ask him.

"Yeah, it's fun. Humor me for a few seconds." He smiles, and I don't know what to do. "I mean if you prefer fighting to the death or something, we can always do that too. You seem like a sword fighting kind of dude."

"Okay, just put your fucking fist up. Let's get this over with," I say as I hold out my hand. "Are we doing one and done or best two out of three?"

"Best two out of three seems the fairest," he says, and I nod. We play one round, and he fucking beats me.

"How did you know I was going to pick rock?" I ask him.

"Just a fair assumption. One more round."

"You're fucking cocky as hell. Let's go." We start to play, and just as we finish, we hear Paige's door open.

"What are you guys doing?" Paige asks us.

"Nothing," Henry and I say at the same time. I turn around to wipe down the counter with nothing on it, and Henry goes over to the air mattress and starts blowing it up.

"Amelia, are you ready for bed?" Henry asks her, and she doesn't answer. Instead, she walks to the front door and jiggles the knob. When it doesn't open, she unlocks it, opens it, closes it, and then locks it again. She nods to herself before she goes over to the window. I let Henry deal with her and I go over to Paige, needing to be closer to her.

"Are you okay?" I ask, noticing how red and puffy her eyes are, and she nods. I watch Amelia go to every single window and try to shove them open. Henry grabs her and forces her to sit down on the couch.

"What are you doing, Ames?"

"Nothing?"

"Amelia."

"Henry, I'm simply checking all the entrance points to my apartment. I do this every night, right Paige?" She looks to Paige for confirmation, but she shakes her head. "That's right, usually when I do this, Paige is either sleeping or out with that one on some adventure. That's why she's never seen me do my night routine."

"Ames, do you want us to go around and double-check with you?" Paige asks her, and Amelia abruptly stands.

"Yes, that would be great!" I guess we're going on an apartment tour. The four of us check every window, the front door, and even the vents to ensure none are open. I see Henry split off from the group and head toward the kitchen, and a few minutes later, he returns and hands Amelia a mug.

"Coffee, thank you! I was thinking about making some. You're a mind reader, Hen."

"You were thinking about making coffee? Amelia, it's after midnight. You're insane," I say to her.

"I think Ames needs to sleep, not stay up any later," Paige tells him.

"It's not coffee, it's ice cream. I just couldn't find a bowl, so I put it in a mug." Paige looks over at the mug and nods. Huh.

"Oh. Carry on then." She smiles at him.

"Thanks, Hen," Amelia tells him as she takes her spoon and stabs her ice cream. We finish checking everything, and when we get back into the living room, Amelia breaks off from us and goes into her room, shutting the door behind her.

"So, you two are good to stay here all night, right?" Paige asks, looking between the two of us.

"Yeah, of course. Oliver's on the couch, and I'll be on the air mattress. We can take shifts, right buddy?" Henry smacks my shoulder, and I stare over at him.

"That's Oliver language for yes." Paige smiles as he nods.

"Gotcha." I move my shoulder to shake off his hand, and it falls back down to his side.

"Thank you both. For, you know," Paige says, and I can tell she still feels guilty. It's written all over her face, and there isn't a single thing I can do about it.

"Of course," Henry says.

"Anything for you, Paige," I say and immediately regret it because her face gets all red and I can practically feel Henry beaming next to me.

"Thanks. Well, goodnight. Wake me if you guys need anything," she says as she slips into her room and out of sight. I stand there for a few moments before I hear Henry sink onto the air mattress.

"Smooth, Oliver."

"Just don't, okay?" I say to him as I move over to the couch and try to get comfortable. "I'll take the first shift. I'll wake you up at three."

"I'll set my alarm, just in case," he tells me as he gets comfortable on the mattress.

"Sounds good," I tell him as I take my knife out of my pocket, and rest it on the table.

Just in case.

I'M SCROLLING ON MY phone at around two in the morning when I flick over to my messages and create a group chat with Grant and Henry.

Oliver: All good over here.

Grant: Same here. Hads is sleeping.

Grant: Who's the other number?

Oliver: Henry. He's asleep right now. I'm on the first watch.

Grant: Got it.

Oliver: Thanks, by the way.

Grant: For????

Oliver: Keeping my sister safe.

Grant: It's an honor, Ol.

I swipe out of my messages when I hear a faint noise. I look around and notice Amelia's light still on under her door. Maybe she's just moving around because she can't sleep. I ignore it, but when I hear it happen again, I get up, grab my knife, and head to her room. I lightly knock, and she opens the door.

"What?"

"I thought you were going to sleep. Why are you moving around so much?" I ask her.

"I can't sleep, but I've barely moved. I was sitting on my bed when you knocked." She tells me as I hear the noise again. I look over at Paige's door, and Amelia tries to move past me, but I put my arm out before she can get by. "Oliver, she might be having a nightmare. I got this."

"I can do it. Just try and sleep," I tell her, but she doesn't move. "Paige would kill you and me if she saw you. Go. I got this."

She nods and I shut her door before going over to Paige's. I twist her doorknob as quietly as I can, and it opens. I thought for sure she would've locked it. I open the door and see her passed out on her floor with something in her hand. She must've been cleaning and just crashed from exhaustion.

"Stop."

"Paige?" I ask, wondering if she's awake.

"Stop, please don't." Her body twitches, and I close her door as I lean down to where she is. I brush her hair out of her face, and notice how warm she is. A few beads of sweat are on her forehead. Fuck, definitely a nightmare.

"Paige, wake up." I shake her a little bit, but she thrashes in my arms.

"Don't, *please*, don't." She's still wrapped in her nightmare as I shake her a bit harder to try and get her out of it. A few tears are streaming down her face.

"Love, please wake up."

"No, no, no, no, no."

"Paige, please." I shake her, and she finally comes too, but she jerks away. I grab her arm and pull her tight against me. "It's just me. It's Oliver."

"Oliver? W–What are you—"

"Just breathe with me, okay? Nothing else matters, just breathe." I feel her try to match my pace, and after a few minutes, she lets go and leans against her bed frame. I tense at the loss of contact, but I know she's scared. "Are you alright? That one seemed bad."

"I'm sorry you heard it. Did I say anything? I sometimes do, according to Amelia."

"Paige, I'm sick of telling you that you have nothing to apologize for." I pause. "You said a few things, but I couldn't make out what. Do you want to talk about it?"

She shakes her head.

"Okay, that's fine. I'll just go then." I start to get up when I feel her arm grab ahold of mine.

"Stay."

"What?"

"Can you stay with me tonight?" she whispers again.

I hope she knows I'd do anything for her if she asked me how she just did. "Okay."

I sit down next to her against her bed frame. She doesn't let go of my arm, and I don't move to pull away. We sit in this position for a few minutes when I feel her head lean onto my shoulder, and when I look over, she's fast asleep. I reach my other arm out to grab her blanket from on top of her bed and place it over her as she continues to sleep soundly.

I shift a little, trying to get as comfortable as I can when it hits me.

I'd sleep on the floor with this girl anytime if she asked me to.

I kiss her forehead and slowly grab her shoulders to lay her across my lap. She shuffles a bit when I do, but doesn't wake up. I move her hair from in front of her face and lean my head back against her bed, hoping I'll be able to sleep tonight.

There's not a chance I'm sleeping tonight, and not one single part of me cares.

30

Monday, October 24th

WHEN I WAKE UP, it takes me a few seconds to remember where I am. I'm on the floor, so that's pretty normal, but I feel something under my head that isn't my carpet. I shift to get more comfortable, and when I look up at the ceiling, I find Oliver staring at me.

"Good morning," he says before I get off his lap, and it takes my brain a minute to play catch up. The library study date, the break-in, Amelia, me having a nightmare and waking up from it to see Oliver, asking him to stay with me, and him agreeing. He stayed with me all night because I asked him to. He barely gave it a second thought—he just agreed.

I'm tired of waiting to be with him. I have to say something.

Fuck it. I'm carpe dieming it, or whatever.

"Morning," I say back to him as I sit with my legs against my chest. Oliver is leaning against the side of my bed.

We're both looking at each other, so many unspoken things passing between us, and after a few minutes, I finally find the words I've been searching for. "I've spent most of my life afraid. Afraid to exist, afraid to speak and say something wrong. Afraid that I would always feel unlovable. Afraid I was destined to spend the rest of my life alone."

He reaches for my hand as I pause, holding my tears back.

"Then I came here, and I met you the first day. I sat down next to you and you said nothing as I introduced myself and talked your ear off. You just sat there and listened to me. As the school year went on, I realized we had the same schedule, and you were always just... around. You would save me a seat, and I started to do the same for you as each new semester came and went. And I felt like I finally had this person around me who actually wanted to be in my presence, besides the girls." I look over at him, and I can't read his face, but I keep going.

"I don't want to wait, Oliver. I don't want to wait until it's too late. I want to be happy with you now, not in the future when we come up with more excuses to not be together." I feel more tears come out of my eyes, and I go to wipe them off my face, but Oliver takes my blanket and does it for me.

"I never saw you coming, Paige."

"What?"

"I never saw you coming. You surprised me in the best way. This—us—I never thought it was possible. I never thought someone could make me feel again. Especially after I built all my walls up and reinforced them. You broke those down and I liked it."

"Oliver." I smile at him.

He looks back at me. "Paige."

"You like me."

"And you like me, so what are we going to do about that?"

"I don't know, but one of us should figure something out." I smirk at him as he grabs my hands in his.

"Paige, would you do me the honor of making me yours? Please?"

I nod and in a split second, he presses his lips to mine.

"Did you know I remember the exact moment I felt something for you for the first time?"

"Oh, really? And when was that?"

"Junior year. It was the end of the fall semester, during finals week. You walked into class with these fuzzy ass mittens on. You noticed how pale my hands were and—"

"And I rubbed your hands to try and warm them up. I remember that." I smile at him. "Way back then? Really?"

"It was when I felt it for the first time. The butterflies, the weird feeling in my stomach," he tells me. "Paige, you were the best surprise. I tried to stay away, I did. I spent the whole summer sulking and working out because of how confused I was. I never thought I was going to be good enough for you, especially since I'm so cold. You deserve happiness, not all my shit. But the last few weeks, you've softened me a bit. I feel like I could be enough for you, as long as you know I'll always try to be."

"Oliver, do you realize what you've done for me these past few months? All you've done is look after me. Why do you have this notion in your head that you're not good enough? I've only ever felt safe with you. Believe me when I say that, please." He reaches over and pulls me onto his lap, and I giggle.

"Are we doing this? For real?"

"Hell yeah we are." I smile at him, and he doesn't say a word. Instead he grabs the back of my neck, pulls me toward him, and kisses me. When he pulls away he has the biggest smile on his face, and I bet mine matches his. I love seeing his real smile. I can't wait to pull it out more and more.

"Fucking finally. I'm gonna kiss you again."

"Okay." I smile, and he captures it in his mouth. He slips his tongue in, and I giggle because I'm kissing Oliver. I feel the happiness radiate off my body. He pulls back and wraps his arms around me. I lean into his embrace, feel his hand caressing my hair, and take a deep breath. "Can I ask one thing?"

"Anything."

"I think for now, we should keep it a secret. This can be something just for us, and not everybody else. I'm not good at this." I point between us. "I've only been in one serious relationship before and that lasted all of two months before I ran away from it, but I don't want to do that with you. I want to try. But I'm afraid of messing it up."

He nods at me. "I get it. I'm fine with keeping it on the low. As long as I have you, I'm good with that." He smiles at me, and I want to capture this moment and frame it because I've never felt so happy. I've never felt so deserving of these feelings I have for this person in front of me. He leans in to kiss me again, but I put my hand on his lips.

"Can we eat first? I'm starving."

"Yeah, love, I'll make you something." I giggle. "What?" he asks me as he stands up while I'm still in his lap, my legs wrapped against his body. He sets me down gently on the floor.

"Nothing, I just..."

"Do you not want me to call you that?"

"No! No, it's perfect," I tell him as he grabs my hand and opens my door. I look around and notice Henry is nowhere to be found, and I think I know exactly where he is. Oliver pulls a chair out for me and forces me to sit.

"I can help, Ol." I go to stand up, and he grabs my shoulder and sits me back down.

"You're not allowed. Sit and relax, Paige. Let me take care of you."

He grabs some eggs from the carton and cracks them onto the pan he just grabbed. He also reaches over and turns the coffee maker on, and as soon as our apartment starts smelling like coffee, Amelia stumbles out of her room with Henry trailing behind her.

"I smell coffee," Amelia says.

"Good morning, guys," Henry says to the two of us.

"Good morning." I look at the clock above the stove, and notice we're going to be late for class. "Shit, we have class soon."

"No we don't. The acting dean emailed me and told me we could take the week to recoup. Check your email." I open it and she's right. I have a few professors saying they'll send me the lectures I'll miss.

"Oh, that's nice." I don't need the week off but I won't say no. It gives me more time to hang out with Amelia and ensure she's okay. My phone buzzes.

Ella: Everyone better respond right now, or I'll be at campus in five minutes.

Hads: Ells, you live like twenty minutes from here.

Ella: My statement stands. Amelia, are you okay?

Amelia: All good over here. Paige and I don't have class the whole week.

Ella: Are Henry and Oliver still over?

Paige: They're probably leaving soon, but we're all eating breakfast.

Amelia: Oliver is making eggs.

Hads: My brother is cooking for you guys?

Paige: Yeah...

Ella: Damn. Maybe he does have a heart.

Hads: He likes to cook, but that caught me off guard.

Ella: Well, I'm glad everyone is okay. Alissa and I'll drop off some lasagna later. I'll text you when we're coming over. Love you all!

Amelia: Kk, sounds good!

I laugh as I hear both Oliver and Henry's phones buzz. Henry picks his up and laughs.

"What's so funny?" Amelia asks.

"Nothing, just something someone sent me caught me off guard."

I look over at Oliver, and he's smiling as he scoops the eggs onto four plates and hands them off to each of us.

"Thanks!" I tell him. I look at Amelia as she sits across from me, her eyes jumping between Oliver and me. "What?" I ask her, and she abruptly gets up and heads to my room.

"Paige, morning debrief. Now!"

"Coming!" I say as I take a bite of the eggs Oliver made. "Ooo, those are good. I'll be back in a second. Nobody eat my eggs!" I point at the two of them, and head for my room.

"What are they doing?" he asks Oliver.

"It's just a thing they do. Don't ask," he says as I shut my door behind me. Amelia is sitting on my floor, and she pats the area across from her.

"What's up?" I ask.

"You tell me. Why do you look like that?"

"Like what?"

"Your face is different. Why?"

"My face? What? Amelia, I look the same as I did yesterday!" I yell at her, but my voice breaks at the end of it.

"Okay, so you're telling me nothing happened last night to make Oliver all happy-go-lucky in our kitchen? Nobody's that happy while making eggs, Paige."

"Why don't you tell me why Henry was in your room?" I poke her arm, and she tilts her head at me.

"Why don't you tell me what happened after Oliver woke you from your nightmare last night?"

"How did you know about that?"

"He knocked on my door because he thought the noise he heard was coming from my room. And when Henry woke up at three to take the second watch, Oliver wasn't on the couch, so he clearly stayed in your room all night. Care to comment?" She smiles at me. Dammit. I'm caught. Amelia isn't letting me get out of this one.

"You can't tell anyone. Do you hear me? Not even Henry," I tell her.

"I won't say a word. Spill."

"Oliver and I talked this morning. We decided not to wait until after the investigation was over to talk about our feelings for one another, and now we're dating on the down low." I can't help the smile that bubbles up.

"On the down low? Is that the best idea?"

"I don't want to mess it up and the less people involved, the easier it is for us to find our footing. And I don't want Hads to murder me for dating her brother. There's just too many factors. It's easiest this way," I tell her and she nods at me. "Also, neither of us has had more than one serious relationship before. We're both finding our footing, for right now."

"I won't say anything."

"Your turn. What's up with you and Hen?"

She rolls her eyes at me. "Okay, stop calling him that, and nothing. We're friends."

"Did he stay with you after he woke up? Or what?"

"He might have noticed my light was on when he woke and came to check on me. That's it, though."

I see that she doesn't want me to push, and I get it. It's been a crazy few days, so I switch to a different topic. "How are you feeling?"

"Jumpy. Scared. A bit off from my usual self, but other than that, I'm fantastic."

"It'll take some time for that to disappear, but I'll be here through everything," I tell her.

"I know, Paige. Now can we eat? I need coffee before I crash." We get off the floor and head back to the kitchen, where we find Oliver and Henry silently eating. Oliver looks over at me and scrunches his eyebrows.

I smile at him and he catches what I'm silently saying before taking a bite of his toast. The four of us eat breakfast, and I ask Henry a bunch of random questions, and he answers them all despite some being extremely weird. Amelia only kicks me under the table once.

Henry and Oliver still have to go to class, and before they leave Henry goes to deflate the air mattress he barely used last night.

"Hen, it's okay. Paige and I can do that. Just go. You guys have class. Paige and I are probably going to sit around and watch movies all day."

"I'm so excited!" I say. I wasn't sure what we were going to do since I didn't want to do homework, and I am always down for a movie marathon.

"I can clean up breakfast. It's only fair." Oliver starts to clear plates from the table, and I touch his arm.

"Oliver, I got this. Go home and change before class. Weston will yell at you if you're late."

"I know, but—"

I cut him off. "Ol, I have nothing else to do today. Just let me do it."

His eyes soften as he concedes. "I'll see you later, love." He kisses the top of my head, and freezes immediately after realizing he said that out loud and the two of us got caught. I look over at Amelia and her face is pinched.

"Love? Really? Got to tell you guys, I was not expecting that term of endearment to come out of Oliver's mouth, but today seems to be full of surprises."

"Okay, besides Amelia and now Henry, nobody else knows about us," I whisper to him, and he laughs and drops his head onto my shoulder.

"I'll head out with you, Oliver." Henry turns to Amelia and they exchange some sort of silent telepathic communication before he follows Oliver out of the apartment.

I lock the door behind them, and when I return to the living room, Amelia's already on the couch and turning on the television.

"Don't," I say as I sit next to her.

"You guys are so going to get busted."

"Just turn on the movie," I say as I laugh next to her.

Despite the craziness of the past few days, I'm glad we have moments like this. One's that remind me I'm still here—still alive. When I was younger, I never thought I'd make it out of the yelling and hurt that came from my father, so the fact that I'm twenty-one, living in a new state, with friends that feel like family and now a boyfriend by my side, I feel like I have to pinch myself.

Family might be messy, but I'd rather have these people around me than be alone like I used to be.

And Oliver. I have Oliver now.

31

Wednesday, October 26th

Oliver: I'm coming over after my sister leaves your place tonight.

Paige: Okay! How's Nicholas?

Oliver: He's fine. He keeps bugging me about you. Noah too.

Paige: What about me?

Oliver: They keep telling me to ask you out.

> **Paige: Well, mission accomplished!**

Oliver: Yeah, but they don't know that.

> **Paige: How adorable you three are. Isn't it nice letting people in?**

Oliver: Yeah, go ahead and say I told you so.

> **Paige: I told you so. Human interaction is important Oliver! You literally need it to stay alive!**

Oliver: Thank you for reminding me. See you later, love.

> **Paige: See you then, xoxo.**

"Paige!" someone shouts at me.

"Sorry! What did I miss?"

"You missed your favorite part of the movie. Who are you texting?" Ella asks me as I see Amelia's face perk up.

"I wasn't texting, I was on twitter. Amelia sent me a bunch of tweets and I was responding to them. I'm sorry, I'll pay attention." I hope they bought it because I'm a horrible liar.

"I'm going to rewind so you can watch it. This time pay attention," Ella tells me and I nod.

It's Wednesday night and normally we would be having book club, but obviously with everything that's been going on, none of us felt like reading the past few days. Amelia and I haven't left our apartment since Monday, so Ella and Hads picked up some groceries for us and we made pizzas together. It's been fun—my pizza was heart-shaped, and I swear that made it taste better. Now, we're continuing Amelia and I's movie marathon.

The girls and I have been trying to make sure that after this week is over we try not to leave Amelia alone. We don't want her to get scared and we want to stay cautious in case the guy comes back. I hadn't even considered that, but when I panicked about it happening, Oliver calmed me down. He told me that since we stopped investigating, the person has no reason to threaten me again.

But I'm still scared. I asked Alissa to help me install some cameras yesterday and she walked me through the entire process over the phone. Now, Ames and I have an entire camera system hidden through our apartment.

"I don't understand this movie," Hads says to us. "What stage of the dream are we in?"

"I have no idea," Ella says, "but this movie's score is phenomenal."

"Agreed!" I say. I'm a big fan of movie soundtracks like this, and I'm absolutely in love with this composer.

"This is the third time I've seen this movie and I'm just now starting to understand it," Ames tells us as she scoops popcorn out of her bowl and eats it. I grab my emotional support water bottle and take a sip of it.

My throat has been getting dry when Hads and Ella are around. It's because I hate lying to them, but I know Oliver and I keeping our new relationship a secret is for the better.

I also haven't been keeping tabs on the investigation. I threw away my murder board, and I haven't thought of any of it since. It feels good to move on. I also don't want anyone else to get hurt—especially Oliver.

It feels good being with him, and I don't know what I'd do if I lost him when I only just got him for real. We've been texting a lot and he even called me last night after I told him I couldn't sleep. He offered to come over but I didn't want to drag him over here because I was struggling.

When I said that, he scoffed and said nothing was too much for him when it comes to me.

Then he came over and we slept on the floor together. He didn't even complain. He just came in, grabbed my pillows and comforter, climbed into our floor bed, and opened his arms for me to join him.

It was the best night of sleep I've ever had.

Hads plops back down next to Ella on our couch and we sit and watch the movie until it's over. When we're trying to decide on another movie, Ames gets up.

"I'm kind of tired. I might head to bed early before I can't sleep. Thanks for coming over, you guys. I'll text you tomorrow." As soon as her door closes, Hads and Ella turn to me.

"How has she been?" Ella asks.

"You know, she's Amelia. She spends all day pretending she's fine but according to Henry, she's still terrified."

"That makes sense. It's only been like three days. It's going to take time," Hads tells us.

"I just wish she would talk to us and not shove her feelings down like always," Ella says.

"Well, to be fair, I think she's been talking to Henry about it," I tell them.

"What's going on with those two? Do you know anything?" Hads asks me.

"The only thing I know is that they walked out of her room together on Monday. But Amelia insists the two of them were talking all night because she didn't want to sleep."

"Well, I like Henry. I think her friendship with him will be good for her," Hads tells us.

"Same, it seems like he's breaking that emotional wall of hers," Ella says while cleaning up stray bowls from the living room.

"Ells, you don't have to clean. I can do it," I tell her.

"Paige, let me help. It's been a rough week for you too."

"I wasn't the one who got hurt, but thank you." I turn to Hads. "How have you been? I miss having a class with you like last semester. It was fun."

"Yeah, I bet being stuck with my brother isn't that fun."

Not exactly how I would describe it. "Yeah, it's something."

"Speaking of Oliver, I'm trying to figure out where to take him for his birthday in a few days. Do you guys have any recommendations?"

"Oliver's birthday is in a few days?" How did I not know this? Halloween is next week, too!

"Yeah, October 30th. I'm surprised he didn't tell you. I think he knows how much you love Halloween."

"Hads, everyone knows how much Paige loves Halloween," Ella says from the kitchen.

"I know it's no secret about it being my favorite holiday, but I wasn't going to do anything this year besides watch horror movies by myself." Nobody else likes watching horror movies as much as I do, but every once in a while I get them to watch them with me. It's usually only once a year, but I'll take it. "What if we had a small party for him?"

"Oliver would hate that. He doesn't like celebrating his birthday and he also hates parties."

"I know, but it doesn't even have to be called a party, just a get-together with his close friends."

Hads stares at me. "So, just Nick and Noah?"

"Okay, *our* close friends. And we could make it a costume party!" I clap my hands together and Ella comes back into the room.

"A party and costumes? Sounds like Oliver in a nutshell." She rolls her eyes.

"Come on! Where's the spooky spirit? We can do it here and I'll take all of the blame if Oliver hates it." I look between the two of them and Hads has a contemplative look on her face.

"Oliver is going to hate this," she tells me and I hang my head, "but I'm in. Let's do it."

"Yay! I'll send out the invites tomorrow and I'll see if I can get some last minute decorations. You should take him to dinner and then make up some excuse to come here and we'll surprise him!"

"Sunday? Can I bring Alissa?" Ella asks me.

"Of course! She's always invited! I'll tell Amelia she doesn't have to dress up or anything but I'll let her know our plan tomorrow when she wakes up."

"Okay, great. Paige, your kitchen is clean and the dishes are drying. Let me know if you need anything else. I don't mind helping out, but I have to get home. I have an early day tomorrow," Ella tells us.

"I'll head out with you. I'm going to Grant's place." I hug both of them before they leave. I debate about checking in on Amelia, but I don't want to wake her up if she's sleeping, so I head into my room. Fifteen minutes of doom-scrolling later, my phone buzzes.

Oliver: We're at your front door.

Paige: Coming!

Paige: Wait, we?

I put my fuzzy slippers on and open my door, only to find Amelia coming out of her room.

"I thought you were asleep?"

"I was for like fifteen minutes. Are you throwing a party here on Sunday?"

"Yeah. For Oliver's birthday, but it's a surprise, so don't tell him. What are you doing out here? Are you going to make coffee because I have orders from Ella to unplug the machine if you try to?"

"Well—" Amelia stops when we both look at our doorstep and see Oliver and Henry standing awkwardly together. "That's why I'm awake." She tells me while pointing at Henry.

"We really have to stop meeting like this," Oliver says.

"Was that a joke?" Amelia asks him and he shrugs his shoulders.

"Hi, Paige. I ran into your boyfriend as I was walking over," Henry tells me, and I smile at the fact that he called Oliver my boyfriend. It's nice not having to hide from some people.

"Well, don't just stand there. Come in!" I tell them as I grab Oliver's arm and pull him inside. He barely moves but starts walking and doesn't stop until he gets into my room, leaving me out here with Henry and Ames.

"I don't understand you and Oliver, but I'm okay with that," Henry tells me.

"You get used to it," Amelia says. "It's like the sun started dating a rock, but it also weirdly makes sense for some reason."

"Okay, Oliver's not a rock. He's the moon," I tell them.

"What?" Amelia asks me, and I give her a small wave as I join Oliver. I shut my door behind me, and he immediately picks me up and carries me over to my bed.

"Woah! Whiplash," I tell him as I push my hair out of my face.

"Sorry. I just missed you," he tells me.

"I saw you yesterday, Ol."

"Oh, so you didn't miss me then?"

"You know I missed you." I smile, and he kisses me. "What do you want to do? I'm not tired yet."

"I brought my computer. I thought we could watch a horror movie and cuddle on the floor."

"With the lights off?" I ask.

"Yes, Paige. We can turn the lights off. It's the proper way to watch horror movies, after all." He smiles down at me. *He gets it.*

"That sounds perfect, Ol. But you know I have a television, right?"

"I know, but using my computer makes it easier for the floor." He taps my nose, grabs some pillows, and drops them down.

"I feel like I'm slowly turning you into a floor person," I tell him.

"Paige, if you're one, then I'm one, too. No questions asked." I feel some tears brewing, and I try to make it seem like I'm not about to cry, but when Oliver turns around and looks at my face, he sees right through me. "Love, what's wrong? Are you okay?" He searches my face and rubs his hands over my body for a few seconds before I start to laugh as a few tears fall.

"Nothing is wrong. Everything is perfect, and I've never been this happy before, and it's overwhelming," I say, jumping off my bed and sinking onto my floor. He follows me and grabs my hand.

"I've never felt like this before either," he says to me while reaching for his laptop and opening it, already having a horror movie queued up on his screen. I notice one of his other tabs that's open.

"Are you keeping tabs on the investigation?" I ask him.

"Yeah."

"I thought we agreed to stop because it was too dangerous?"

"I need to make sure you're safe, so I check in on it every once in a while." He looks over at me. "I promise I'm not doing anything. I'm just making sure whoever was after you doesn't come back because if something happened to you—"

"Oliver, nothing's going to happen to me—or you. I haven't even looked at anything involving it. So you can stop worrying about me."

He kisses me. "I'll never stop worrying about you, Paige. It's just how I'm wired."

"Can we start the movie?" I ask.

"Of course. Are you comfy?"

I move a bit closer to him and throw my right arm across his body. "Now I am."

He kisses my forehead. "Good." He presses play, and I suddenly feel this blanket of happiness cover my entire body as I sit on the floor with my boyfriend, watching a movie.

Best night ever.

32

Oliver

Sunday, October 30th

"Thanks for dinner," I say to my sister as we walk toward my building.

It was nice to spend some time with my sister without everyone else around, but little does she know I'm heading to Paige's place after she goes to Grant's apartment. I hate sneaking around behind her back, but Paige is most comfortable this way, and I've warmed up to the idea. Don't get me wrong, I loved spending some time with my sister on my birthday, but the real person I want to spend tonight with is currently on lockdown in her apartment.

"No problem. I captured the look on your face when they started singing to you. Priceless," she tells me as I roll my eyes. "Oh, wait. Can we stop by Paige and Amelia's place? I left one of my textbooks there yesterday."

"Do I have to come with you?" I ask, my throat feeling a bit dry. *Does she know?*

"Yes. It'll only take two seconds, and then you can return to brooding in your apartment." *I don't brood.* She shoves me to the side as we change directions and walk to their place. All the lights are off even though it's not that late.

"Hads, hurry up. Did you let them know you were coming? You can't just barge into their place."

"Yes, I did! Hush, it'll be two seconds." She opens the door and walks through it, leaving me alone on their porch. I look at my phone to see if Paige has texted me back, but I have zero notifications. When my sister doesn't return, I knock on the door.

"Hads!" She doesn't answer. "Hads!" I have a weird feeling in the pit of my stomach, so I take my pocket knife out and slowly turn the knob. The fact that the lights are off and my sister hasn't returned yet scares me. I can feel my heart rate picking up.

What if something happened again?

I slowly make my way from their entrance, and when I get into the open space with their living room and kitchen, the lights go on.

"Surprise!" they yell at me, and I stand frozen where I am. I see a flash and turn to look at my sister—her camera in her hands and pointed at me.

"Henry! We owe Paige ten bucks. I didn't think he would go for the knife," Grant tells him.

"Did I miss it?" I hear Paige yell as she returns from her room dressed as Tinkerbell and trying to fix her hair. "Dammit! I knew I should have waited. Grant, did he have his knife out?"

"Yup. Henry and I owe you," he tells her.

"Did you bet on that? What the hell is going on?" I ask the room.

"It's a surprise party, Oliver. For your birthday," Amelia tells me.

"I got that. Why are you all dressed up?"

"It's also a Halloween party," Nick tells me. *What's he doing here?*

I look over at my sister and see her dressed up as Cruella Deville, and she has a huge smile on her face. "Really?"

"Hey, this wasn't my idea," Hads tells me as she looks over at Paige. *Did she plan this entire thing?*

"Surprise?" I walk over to her, grab her hand and drag her into her room. Before I shut the door, she yells to everyone outside. "Keep the party going! It's going to be fine!"

"You planned this?" I ask, and she looks at the floor and nods. *Shit. Does she think I'm mad at her?*

"Here's what happened. Hads told me your birthday was today, and I didn't know that, so obviously I wanted to plan something. I also didn't want to make it too big because of all the shit that has been going on, and Amelia and I haven't left our apartment all week besides going on our daily walks. I just wanted to make you feel special on your birthday! It's also Halloween tomorrow, isn't it funny that your birthday is so close to my favorite holiday and now we're dating and—" I stop her spiral by kissing her, and she's surprised by the gesture, but soon enough she melts into me.

"Thank you. I've never had anyone go to so much trouble for my birthday." I pause as I pull her in for a hug. "Also, the costume. Seriously?"

She smiles, happy I remember our conversation from a few weeks ago. "Do you like it?"

"I do." I smile at her. "You look adorable, Tink."

"Grant got you a costume, if you want to wear it." She goes over to her desk and pulls out some sort of torture device.

"Paige, what the hell is that?"

"It's a hook. He thought you would want to be Captain Hook. He also suggested something from *The Godfather* but he thought this was funnier. He thinks you and Captain Hook are similar."

"And how's that?"

"Well, Grant said it's because you terrorize everyone around you, brutalize your enemies, and have no fear."

"Of course he said that." I grab the hook from her and fasten it around my hand. Hilarious. I bet Grant won't think it's funny when I stab him with it.

"But I think you're Captain Hook because of your intelligence and passion. She smiles at me, and I pull her in for another kiss. "We should probably get back to the party. We don't want your sister getting suspicious..."

She taps my nose with her finger before she heads back out into host mode. "Who needs a drink?"

I exit her room, and my sister comes over to me. "To be fair, it was her idea, but I went along with it. Just don't be too mad at her."

"I'm not. It just caught me off guard, that's all."

"Good. It's hard to be mad at her, anyway. The girl loves Halloween." She takes a sip of her drink, and Grant comes over to us.

"How are you liking your costume, Mr. Hook?" He laughs, and I look him dead in the eyes.

"Well, it looks like my sister is literally walking you like her dog, so how's your costume, pretty boy?"

"I'm proud to be wearing this right now. Everyone knows who wears the skirt in this relationship." He points to my sister, and she smiles.

"On that note, please don't talk to me for the rest of the night," I say as I stab Grant in the side and head over to Paige's couch. Amelia and Henry are sitting on it. "What are you two supposed to be?"

"I'm King Henry. Get it?" He smiles at me. He has a weird-looking hat on his head and an oversized coat that looks like it's from a museum my sister likes to visit.

"Isn't that the guy who killed all his wives? I don't know if that's someone you'd want to dress up as," I tell him. I have to say I never pegged him as a history nerd, but there's a lot about this kid I don't know.

"Well yes, but I think it's funny because we have the same name. Amelia helped me come up with it." I look over at her.

"And what are you supposed to be?"

"The devil," she tells me.

"Amelia, you—" Henry starts to say, but she holds a finger up at him, and he stops talking.

"You look the same as you always do," I tell her. I'm so fucking confused. She looks normal, but I'm worried she's going to sprout horns and banish me to hell. I wouldn't put it past her.

"No, Oliver. I am dressed up. As the devil."

"Okay, well this was very unhelpful," I say as I get up and leave yet another weird conversation. As I get over to Nick and Noah, there's a knock at the front door.

"I'll get it!" Ella says, and she disappears into their entryway.

"You guys have terrible costumes by the way," I joke with them. They're both dressed as baseball players, which is the easiest thing for them since they play baseball for the school.

"Hey! It was the best we could do on short notice," Nick tells me.

"Happy birthday, by the way." Noah hands me a present.

"Why did you get me something? I don't need anything from you two."

"Yes, we know you don't need friendship from us either, but you got it." Nick slaps me on the back, and I roll my eyes.

"You guys are my friends. I enjoy your company more than most."

"It's a Halloween miracle," Noah tells me as I see Ella walk back from the door, talking to Alissa with some random dude behind them. Ella's fuming and it looks like she's about to kill someone.

It appears she and the random dude are dressed as if they were a couple. Ella is Harley Quinn, and the other dude is the Joker. Alissa seems to be dressed as a cowgirl, and she's laughing, too. I look over at Paige from across the room, and she's about to topple over while talking to Grant. *What the fuck is so funny?*

"Paige, what's so funny?"

She only bursts out laughing. "Oh my God, she's going to kill him. Tonight's the night it finally happens."

"Who the hell is that?" I ask and they continue laughing. Before anyone can answer my question, my sister and Amelia walk over to us.

"Ella's stronger than me. I don't know why or how she hates that man," Hads says to us.

"This is hilarious. Matching costumes with the guy you hate the most on the planet? Priceless." Amelia takes a sip of her drink.

"Can we back up for a second? Who the hell—" Grant cuts me off.

"God really does have their favorites. Imagine looking like that and having an accent."

"Shut it, pretty boy. He's not even that good-looking," I say, and four heads turn to stare at me like I just announced the next space shuttle mission. "You're kidding, right?"

"Oliver, if you think he isn't that good-looking, what do you think of yourself?" my sister asks me.

"Yeah, he has a nice face," Amelia says.

"The accent is what gets me. I heard him speak, and almost fell over. He sounds like Tom Hiddleston," Paige says and I look over at her with wide eyes. She just shrugs at me.

"He's what I think I look like when drunk," Grant tells us.

"He looks like an art sculpture come to life," Hads says, and I sigh.

"Maybe I should go introduce myself," Paige says, and I drag her back as she starts to move forward.

"Not a chance. I got this." I look over at Grant. "Shall we?"

"I'm not going over there to talk to that specimen of a man. I'm going to look like Nick Carraway standing next to Gatsby. It's just no comparison."

"Are you being serious?" I grab his shoulder and drag him with me.

"Hads, please don't forget about me." Grant and I slowly approach him. Fuck. What did Paige say his name was again? He's standing at their kitchen table, looking at all the snacks they laid out. Alissa is across from him.

"Oliver! Happy birthday!" Alissa says to me when she sees me.

"I'm going to be honest, I forgot about today being your birthday. Your gift is coming in the mail soon," Grant whispers to me, and I sigh again.

"This is my brother, Leo. He graduated from Grand Mountain a year ago, like Ella." She smiles, and Leo tenses up when she mentions her name. *So the hatred feeling is mutual, it seems?*

"Nice to meet you. Though Grant, I've seen you around the bar before with the team. Nice to meet you officially, though." He holds his hand out, and I shake it, Grant does too. Did his face get red? *Is he blushing right now?*

"It's nice to see you again," Grant tells him.

"Oliver Baker. I'm Hads' brother," I tell him.

"So, you're the birthday boy, huh? How old?"

"Twenty-two," I tell him. That accent is growing on me a bit. "So, you and Ella seem to be—"

"Matching. Which I'm sure she's thrilled about. If only my sister told me what Ella was going as, this problem wouldn't be happening," he tells us while looking over my shoulder. Suddenly, a hand grazes my bicep and I don't even need to turn my head to know who it is.

"Leo, I'm glad you could make it!" Paige says as she refills her water.

"Thanks for inviting me, love." *What the fuck? Who even is this guy?* "Are you the one my sister told me was working on some sort of investigation? Alissa was cheeky about whatever you two had going on. She wouldn't tell me a thing."

"Her and Oliver, actually. I have to find Ella. Be back in a flash!" Alissa tells him as she leaves the kitchen.

"They aren't working on it anymore since the incident happened," Grant tells him. *He's still over here?*

"Incident?" Leo asks.

"So! The joker! How did you end up in that costume?" Paige asks, trying to steer the conversation.

"Well, a certain someone described me as the joker last year during our internship, so I thought it would be funny. What I didn't bet on was her showing up as Harley. I think it's hilarious, but my sister will probably tell me all the ways she threatened me tonight." He smiles. Does he enjoy the fact that Ella hates him?

"Well, it was nice to meet you..." Fuck, I forgot his name again. Liam? Lucas? Levi? Fuck. What was it?

"Leo. Zimmerman." He shakes my hand again, and I feel a bit awkward now.

"Let me know if you need anything!" Paige tells him, and he grabs her hand and kisses her knuckles.

"You're a wonderful host, Paige. I'll find you if I do."

You've got to be kidding me. I'd give anything to show all these people that Paige is off the market, but that's not a can of worms I want to open right now.

"Dude, he's stealing your girl, but I wouldn't try to fight him, so you might just have to bow out," Grant whispers at me, and I stab him with my hook again. I walk away from whatever was going on and into Ella and Alissa's silent conversation.

"Ella, can I join the Leo hate club?" I ask her.

"Absolutely! I'd be glad to have someone else with me. Alissa thinks I'm being crazy."

"It's literally a costume, Ells!"

"Yeah, and this bat is real, believe it or not!" she says, holding it up, and I lean back so as not to get whacked.

"Yes, I know. It hurt trying to stop you when you swung it at him after you opened the door," Alissa says while rubbing her arm.

"I said I didn't mean to hit you! It's not my fault his costume perfectly matches his insides. Everything's a joke to him!" Ella tells her as Leo sits down on the loveseat.

"Talking about me again? How cute. I hope it's something different than usual." He smiles, and she glares back at him.

In the time I've known Ella, I've never seen her this pissed. What's the story here?

This is *not* how I expected the rest of my night to go. Though, it's kind of entertaining.

"So, Leo, what do you do besides go to parties with your sister?" I ask him.

"Annoy me," Ella says beside me.

"Well, I went back to England for a bit, but my sister convinced me to come for a vacation because she missed me. I don't know if or when I'll move back here, but if I do, I'd love to grab a pint with you both sometime."

Damn. I hate that he's nice.

"I would be all for that," Grant says.

"At least someone would be happy to see you if you were to move back." Ella rolls her eyes, and I never used to care about other people's shit before, but I want to know the full story here.

"I'm sure you would love me being at your place all the time, Williams. Keep the light on for me, would you?"

"Bite me," Ella says.

"You know I would." He winks at her before she heads for the front door. I watch Leo follow her body out of the door, and to my surprise, he gets up and follows her out.

"Why do they hate each other?" I ask Alissa.

"Babes, I have no idea. They need to have sex to work out that frustration." *What?* Paige comes over to me.

"It's almost over, I promise. I told everyone to leave by nine." She pats my back, and I resist grabbing her hand because if my sister sees it, she'll make me leave this party with an actual hook hand. But I do want to get a picture of the two of us since we are matching.

"Oliver, we're heading out. We'll see you soon, okay?" Noah tells me.

"We can do dinner this week again. You make pretty good food." Nick winks at me, and I throw a stupid fucking smirk at him.

"Nicholas! Oliver has cooked for you?" Paige's face lights up as she looks at me.

"Better than that, he invited us over. It was a dinner to remember." He smiles at her.

"Wow, high praise. Thanks guys," I say as I get up, pat them both on the back, and head over to where my sister and Grant are.

"Grant, I don't think you embarrassed yourself in front of Leo. It's fine," my sister tells him.

"I know, but you weren't over there. Oliver, good timing. Do you think Leo likes me or did I totally blow it?"

I roll my eyes. "Why are you acting like Leo is the fucking president? It was a normal conversation."

"Technically, he can't be president since he's from England, Ol," my sister tells me.

"You know what—" I say as Leo and Ella burst back in.

"You are so infuriating!" Ella yells at him while she swings that bat around.

"Forgive me, but that's not what you said when we—" She slaps him, and we all go quiet.

"Don't." She points at him. "Don't even think about it."

"Afraid to get too flustered in front of everyone? I remember once when you were begging me to—" Ella swings the bat at him, and he catches it with one hand.

"Stop." She's practically seething, right now when she looks over at Alissa. "We're leaving."

"But we just—"

"Leaving!" Ella says as she grabs her coat and heads for the door. "Happy birthday, Oliver! Paige, I'm calling you late and you better pick up!"

"Okay!" Paige squeaks as she slumps down in her chair. I look over at her and give her a small smile. I see Leo grab his jacket before he follows his sister out.

"Nice to meet you all! Sorry about that. Ella and I tend to push each other's buttons a bit. So on my behalf, I apologize. Fun party, though! Paige, you're a wonderful host." He smiles at her, and I hear her giggle.

As those three leave, only Paige, my sister, Grant, and I are left.

"Well, that was something, wasn't it?" Grant says to us.

"I guess you could call it that," I tell him.

"Paige, did you catch all that?" my sister asks her.

"Yes! Did Leo and Ella hook up?" she asks, and my sister moves over to sit on the couch with her.

"It sounds like it," Hads says to her.

"You guys got all that from what just happened?" I ask them.

"Even I picked up on it. Huge sexual tension with those two," Grant tells me.

"Keep talking, and you'll lose your pretty boy status to Leo."

Grants face falls. "You wouldn't."

"I would. You know I would."

My sister gasps where she sits. "Wait! Ella told me last semester on one of our coffee dates that she had a regrettable hookup with someone! A male someone! What if that was who she was talking about?"

"They're so going to get together. I can feel it." Paige smiles excitedly.

"Paige, they literally just tried to kill each other," I remind her.

"Yes, but I'm good with these things. I called it with these two," she says, pointing between my sister and Grant.

"I can't argue with that logic," Grant says. "Hads, we should go. You have an early class tomorrow."

She nods at Grant before hugging Paige. "I'll text the group chat later to set up a time to debrief whatever the hell happened tonight. Do you want help cleaning up?"

"I'll help her. You guys go," I tell my sister.

"Are you sure?" she asks me while eyeing me weirdly. "It's your birthday, Ol. Isn't it kind of lame cleaning up your own birthday party?"

"It's just another day to me, Hads. And I only have two classes tomorrow, both in the afternoon. Go get some sleep."

"Let's go, girlfriend." Grant comes over to me.

"Happy birthday, bro."

"Thanks for everything, pretty boy."

After the two of them leave, I slump next to Paige on the couch, and I turn to face her, but she's already looking at me. I take my hook hand and tap her on the nose like she does to me all the time.

She simply smiles at me, and that's the best birthday present I've ever gotten.

"You don't have to keep that on, you know. The party's over."

I nod at her. "If I take it off, we're not matching anymore."

"I knew you were secretly sentimental." She smiles at me. "Did you have fun tonight?"

"The most fun I've ever had on my birthday before. Thank you for planning all this. It means a lot," I tell her as she leans into me.

"You deserve it, Ol." I feel her smile into my chest. "Where did Amelia and Henry go?"

"I saw them go into her room a little while ago."

"Amelia missed all that? Damn, she's going to be pissed. She usually loves having a front-row seat to things." She jumps off the couch and heads for Amelia's door, and when she opens it her face lights up. I rush up to her side and even what I'm seeing is shocking. It looks like Amelia is asleep on Henry's chest.

Not her boyfriend, my ass.

"What's going on here?" Paige whispers so as not to wake up Amelia.

"The party was too much for her, so we came in here and started watching a movie. Then she fell asleep and I heard a bunch of yelling. I didn't want to move because I didn't want to wake her and don't tell her I told you this because she might make you murder me, but she hasn't slept in two days," Henry blabs out, still partially dressed in his costume.

"She hasn't slept in two days?" Paige asks.

"She looks weirdly peaceful when she's asleep. It's a shame she's terrifying when she's awake," I say to them.

"She would love that you just said that," Henry tells me.

"Yeah, I bet calling her terrifying is a compliment," I say.

"Okay, well, we won't disturb you anymore. Have a good night!" Paige says as she shoves me into the living room and shuts the door. "I didn't realize she was struggling this much."

"Paige, remember what we told you."

"Right. It wasn't my fault." She pauses. "But it still feels like it is."

I sigh and wrap her in my arms. "I can clean up if you want to shower or get comfier clothes on."

"Oliver, I'm not letting you clean up your own birthday party."

"Fine. We'll do it together then," I say as I reach for a cup on her coffee table.

"I'm not going to win this one, am I?"

"Nope," I say as I go to the kitchen to grab a big plastic bag. I watch as Paige turns on some music and connects to the speaker they have in their living room. I recognize the lyrics from that day in her car a few weeks ago.

As the two of us clean up, I hear her hum the words to herself, and I find myself thinking that maybe someday in the future, Paige and I will be cleaning up after a party like this again. Maybe in the future, we'll throw our own Halloween party at our house, and the group of us will still be together and we'll all reminisce about this night twenty years from now.

I guess I can only hope about that becoming a reality, but now more than ever, I want to get to those moments with Paige by my side.

33

Saturday, November 5th

"So WAIT, YOU SWUNG that bat at him?" Amelia asks Ella.

"Can we please drop this? We went over it in enough detail on Wednesday," Ella says to us.

"I'm sorry! I ended up falling asleep, so I missed all this. I need to know everything," Amelia practically begs. I knew she was going to hate missing out on all that went down.

"Amelia, I could've cut the tension between them with Oliver's hook hand," Hads tells her, and she gasps.

"I'm going to get another coffee," Ella tells us as she gets up.

I giggle as I scroll through the news on my laptop. Sometimes, when I need a break from homework, I like to check out what's going on in the world. All of my professors say we should get into that habit because of the field of study we're in.

"You guys made her mad. You know it's a sore subject. I haven't even brought up that I think they'd be cute together because I'm worried Ella will slap me like she did Leo," I say to them.

"Well, at least they don't have to see each other anymore. I remember how bad it was last semester," Hads tells us as she continues working.

"Yeah, but she and Alissa are roommates. I bet he shows up unannounced at their place when he's over here. They seem close," Amelia says.

"They're Irish twins," Ella says as she sits back down, carrying another coffee for Amelia.

"Thanks." Amelia smiles at her. "That explains a lot."

"Irish twins? I thought they were British?" I say.

"Paige, that just means they were born less than a year apart," Hads tells me.

"Oh, that makes sense," I say, scrolling on my computer.

The four of us continue working and my computer chimes a few seconds later. It's a notification for an article that was posted a few hours ago. I set up a Google alert to notify me if certain words were used together in any articles and such. Curiously, I click the notification.

Grand Mountain Police Commissioner dead at 48.

I suddenly have a weird feeling in the pit of my stomach. It's the kind of feeling where you know something but don't want to believe it could be true. I start reading more of the article and my heart starts racing.

The commissioner of the Grand Mountain police department, Tim Nixon, was found dead in his office today. According to a source inside the department, it appears to be a homicide.

My heart drops through my chest. I keep reading, not wanting to confirm what my head already seems to know.

The department has not commented yet, but we can confirm that the manner of death was a cut throat. Similar in the manner to the friend of Nixon, the dean of Grand Mountain College, Erik Millard. No comment has been made about if these two cases are related, but from what we know, these are two separate incidents.

The office has yet to release a statement, but in the coming days, we can expect them to. The family is asking for prayers and privacy at this time.

"I have to go," I say as I shove my laptop into my tote bag. I see Amelia flinch next to me when I slam my computer shut and I look over at her. "Sorry."

"I'm fine. Are *you* okay?" she asks me.

"Yes. No, everything's fine. I just have a thing to do back at the apartment. Can someone walk Amelia back? I don't want her walking by herself."

"We'll make sure she gets back safe." Hads makes a weird face at me.

"I can, but Paige, what's—" I cut Ella off.

"I have to go! I'll text you guys later!" I say as I walk away, not looking behind me at them. I have to get to Oliver.

I pull my phone out.

> **Paige: Where are you right now? I found something weird.**

"I knew you were at the library," I hear a voice say. I look up, and it's Oliver. We seemed to have walked right past each other.

"Did you see my texts?" I'm a bit out of breath because of what I saw. I don't think I'm going to have a panic attack but I feel weird. Scared, maybe? I don't know.

"I was on my way to find you when I felt my phone buzzing, I figured it was just Grant playing me back in Scrabble."

"Okay, remind me to ask you later when you and Grant started playing Scrabble," I say before I grab his arm and drag him to a picnic table. "I have to show you something."

"I was coming to show *you* something."

"Is it the same thing?" I ask him as I open my laptop and he shoves his phone in my face, and sure enough, it's the same article. "Did we just have a cute relationship telepathy moment?"

"No."

"We definitely did. Admit it."

"Fine. We're adorable."

"I know right!" I smile at him. "What do you think this means?"

"This means that you kept tabs on the investigation when you said you weren't going to."

Busted. "I know I said I wouldn't, but I wanted to make sure—"

"Paige, I understand why you did it. The question I have to ask you is what we're going to do about it?"

"What do you mean?"

"I've never known you to stop when your mind gets hooked onto something. So, I guess what I'm asking is if you want to start the investigation up again?" He looks at me, really looks at me. I know he knows what I'm going to say, but I'm scared to say it.

How can I say I want to pick up where we left off when our investigation is the reason Amelia got knocked out in our apartment? She got hurt because I was getting too close to something that someone didn't want me to see. Not to mention, Oliver and I almost got run off of the road.

"I don't know what I would do if someone else got hurt because of me," I tell him.

"Paige, it wasn't your fault."

"I know. But that note was left on my desk, Oliver. *Mine.* It was for me. Whoever this person is knows who I am. They know how to hurt the people closest to me, including you. And if you were to get hurt, I don't think I could forgive myself—" He reaches over and grabs my hand before a tear falls from my eye.

"Paige, I'm not even worried about me. But if you want to keep investigating, I'm in it with you. We can do it, we just have to keep it quiet this time. Nobody can know. That way, nobody gets hurt. It's your decision, love. I'll follow you whichever way you want to go," he says to me as he looks into my eyes.

I love you. I think to myself. It's the first thing that crosses my mind as he says what he just did. *I love you, Oliver. I don't think I've ever felt this way about someone so wholly. I've never met anyone who cared about me this much, and it feels good. I always felt discarded by my family, but it's like you came in and swept me up and now I feel like I deserve to feel this way. But I don't want to lose this, and I'm nervous if we keep investigating that something will happen.*

I've never said those words to someone and meant it, but I know if I say them right now, I'll mean it with every fiber of my being. Obviously, I say it to the girls all the time, but that's platonic love. This thing with Oliver is different.

"I'm scared, Ol."

"But?"

"But I need to see this through. Something's up at our small college. Call it a gut feeling but I want to figure out what's going on before someone else gets hurt."

"Okay. Then we'll pick up where we left off," he tells me as he gets up.

"Where are you going?"

"The craft store to pick you up another murder board." I chuckle at him as he holds his hand out for me. I take it immediately. "What? We have to start someone. I figure we can make another one."

"Oliver?" I say as I look over at him and he looks down at me. *Say it. Say it right now, Paige. Tell him how you feel. Don't be scared and just say it.* "I should probably text the girls."

> **Paige: I have to go to the store to get a few things. Sorry I left in a rush, but it was an emergency.**

> **Amelia: Oh, so that's why you ran off so suddenly.**

> **Hads: Paige, is everything okay?**

> **Paige: Yup! Peachy!**

> **Ella: Hads, make sure Ames gets back okay. I'm sorry I left, but Alissa needed my help.**

> **Hads: Grant and I are on it, I promise.**

Amelia: Why are you guys acting like I need a babysitter? I'm fine!

Paige: Amelia, when I accidentally left you alone at home the other day, I came back and you were studying with a knife next to you! That's not normal!

Amelia: It was a simple precaution!

Ella: You guys are going to give me gray hairs thirty years too early, I swear.

Paige: I love you guys! See you later!

"Okay, I'm ready," I say as he grabs my hand and holds it all the way to my car. *Is this what love feels like?*

If it is, I never want to let it go.

Not with him, at least.

He puts my favorite romance books to shame, and I wouldn't have it any other way.

OLIVER AND I HAVE been sitting in his living room for a few hours, remaking the murder board and trying to figure out a connection between all the homicides.

We have nothing so far.

Well, not nothing. We found out they were friends. Apparently, they used to work at the same school a while back, but other than that, we have nothing.

Oliver throws a strawberry at me.

"What was that for?"

"You're not paying attention. I found something." He pats the couch next to him. "Come here."

"The floor is more comfortable. You come to me," I say as I tap the small, navy blue carpet next to me. Oliver gets up and awkwardly sits down next to me. He has a hard time sitting cross-legged and eventually gives up and just puts his legs straight out.

"Look." He shows me his laptop.

"Oliver, this doesn't make any sense. It's all redacted information."

"I know. This is all I could find, but look at the names." I do, and it's the dean and the commissioner's names on this court file.

"Is there a way you can get the original with no redactions?" I ask.

"No, the files are locked. But it's something right?"

"I wish we could ask Alissa to help, but I don't want to risk it."

"I know. I'll keep digging." He kisses my forehead and I can feel my cheeks turn red.

"I will too."

We both work in silence next to each other for around half an hour when Oliver's phone starts to ring. "Fuck."

"What?" I ask him.

"My sister's calling me. She never calls me."

"It's cute that you're scared of your sister."

"If you were related to her, you would be too. I'll be right back. I have to take this," he says as he walks into his room and closes the door.

"I'll be right here! Your ringtone being the default sound is the worst and we must handle that right away!" I look down at my computer again and an idea pops into my mind, but it doesn't make sense. I decide to look into it, anyway.

I look up articles about that police officer that committed suicide a few weeks after the dean died, but I find no connection between the two cases since one is a homicide and one is a suicide. It makes sense that I haven't found anything, but call it a gut feeling. I thought there was a thread I could have pulled, but it turned out to be nothing.

Oliver whips his door open a few seconds after I give up my search.

"One of these days, you're going to break—" I don't have time to finish my sentence because he scoops me up by my shoulders and shoves his hand over my mouth. He pushes me behind his front door, and I try to speak, but all this weird stuff makes sense when he opens his front door and speaks.

"Hads, I'm busy. What do you want?"

"Nice to see you, too. I was at Grant's place and figured I would stop by."

"Why?"

"Because I'm a good sister." I can hear her smile when she says that.

"What's the real reason?" he asks, his hand still over my mouth. My heart rate is picking up because if Hads barges in and sees me like this, our night could end *very* badly because I would for sure reveal our secret.

I'm nervous, but why is this all kind of exciting?

"Paige left the library really oddly today and I was wondering if you've talked to her lately? I'm worried about her." *Aw.* It's strange having so many people worry about me. Normally, I don't even worry about myself.

"The last time we talked was in class yesterday and she seemed fine to me," he tells her.

"Are you sure? I feel like the whole break-in really fucked with her but she's too afraid to show it. Can I come in? I feel weird standing in the hallway." She takes a step forward but he stops her.

"No! No. Sorry, I have stuff everywhere and it's not a good time." I've never seen Oliver so flustered, it's making me laugh and he has to shift his hand to keep me quiet.

"Why do you have papers all over the place? Are you sure you haven't talked to Paige?"

"I'm working on a project and it's easier for me to see all the data like this," Oliver says. "If you want I can text Paige and ask her how she is."

"Thanks. You two seem like good friends. I'm warming up to that idea, too. It's nice seeing you break out of your shell."

"I don't have a shell," he tells her.

"Yes, you do," she says and I nod along with her. I feel his hand tense up over my mouth. "Okay, well, I'll leave you to it. Sorry to bother whatever you were doing. I'll see you on Saturday!"

"Yup. Bye," he says as he pulls his hand from my mouth, slams his door, and locks it. He then walks across the room and sits down on his couch. I'm rooted in place still. I feel jittery at the concept of being caught by Hads but another part of me feels giddy. It's simultaneously terrifying and exciting sneaking around like this.

"Good friends, huh? I guess you could call us that," I say to try and break some of the tension in the room.

"Did you want me to tell her you were standing behind my door?"

"Well, no, but..." I say as I walk back to my spot on the floor.

"Isn't this what we wanted? To keep other people—especially my sister—from meddling in our relationship? I thought we were going to tell people after all the craziness died down."

"No, yeah, it is. I just—" I stop speaking when I hear him get up and sit next to me on the floor. The air feels thicker now that he's closer to me.

"Paige." How does him just saying my name make me melt? His voice is low, and I can feel the tension in the room when he asks me the next question. "Do you not want us to be a secret anymore?"

I look down. "I don't know."

"Can I tell you something?"

"Always." I look over at him.

"If it were up to me, we wouldn't have been a secret from the start."

My heart skips a beat and I start breathing heavily. "What?"

"I know relationships scare you. They scare the hell out of me, too. But when we were at my birthday party it took everything in me to not reach over and kiss you all night. I was jealous of my sister and Grant. They were able to freely hold hands all night and I couldn't do that. I don't get fucking jealous, and I never liked holding hands, but with you I do. It's fucked my head up. *You* have fucked my head up." He's looking right at me, and my stomach drops.

"I–I don't know what to say."

And instead of talking, he leans over and kisses me. I'm so surprised by it that it takes my brain a moment to catch up. When I kiss him back harder, he grabs me and pulls me onto his lap. He slips his tongue into mine and I let him, and when we pull back we're gasping for air.

"Paige, tell me to stop."

"This again?" I ask him, my head feeling light from the kiss.

"Paige," he says as his head falls to my chest.

"Oliver." I smile at him and I grab his face with both my hands. "Please don't stop," I whisper to him and that's all it takes before he lifts me up and carries me into his room. He sets me down on his bed, not breaking the kiss until he rips his shirt off of his body.

Holy fucking shit.

I knew he had a nice body because he wears those tight shirts when he runs and they practically mold to his figure, but this? Nothing could have prepared me for what was underneath.

"It looks like I finally got you shirtless," I say to him.

"Like what you see?" he asks me and I raise my eyebrows. I nod and try to conceal the fact that my mouth started watering. I'm fully looking at the tattoos he has. One of them is on his chest, it's a dragon. The other one is on his rib cage, and that one is coordinates.

"Coordinates?" I ask him. "Where do those go?"

"Vietnam. My mom took us back to where she grew up a few years ago and I loved it." Oliver *is* sentimental. He just doesn't show it. I trace the numbers with my finger and he looks down at me. "Are you sure?"

"I'm sure." His mouth is back on mine, and he's running his hands all over me, and I've never wanted someone to touch me more. He slips his tongue into my mouth and puts one hand behind the small of my back. While still kissing me, he flips our positions, and now I'm on top of him like I was in the living room.

"Smooth," I say, disconnecting from his lips for a fraction of a second before he pulls me back in.

"Mhm," he says into my mouth, and I feel that all the way to my toes. He's already hard. In the position we're in, I can feel it. I grind against him a little bit, and his head whips back.

"Really?" I say to him.

"Paige, you drive me nuts by not realizing what you do to me." He pushes his hips into me, and a moan slips out of my mouth. I haven't had sex since my last boyfriend in high school. Oliver has only had one girlfriend, and he hasn't dated since then, so I imagine it's been around the same amount of time for him.

"What is it that I do to you?"

"Don't play dumb. You can *feel* what you do to me."

I giggle and grind against him more, bracing my hands against the back of his headboard. I lean in to kiss him again, and he grabs my neck and squeezes a bit. I gasp.

"You like that, huh?" His eyes are blazing into mine. "Tell me, love. Do you like being choked?"

I open my mouth to say yes, but he squeezes my throat harder so I can't. Technically, I didn't know that until right now, but that doesn't matter. I've only ever read about it, and I won't lie when I say that it piqued my interest.

"I don't need you to answer. I can feel how wet you are through your tight fucking pants." His voice is low and deep, and I think I might explode. His hand is still on my throat, and he kisses me harder this time.

"Oliver—" I say, breathlessly getting that word out.

"I know, love." He flips me over again, and now I'm on my back. He pulls my pants with my underwear down over my legs, carefully keeping my socks on. I look at him, confused as to why he didn't just take all of it off. "Your feet are always cold."

My heart lurches, and I don't have time to react before he kneels down on his bed and hovers near my pussy. Nobody has ever done this to me before, and I flinch a bit when I feel his heavy breathing.

"Paige, what's going on?"

"Well, nobody has ever—" I stop and hope he understands what I'm trying to say. He comes back up to my face and kisses me again.

"Nobody? Not your last boyfriend?"

"I've only had one, a long time ago, and nope. He said he didn't like doing it." He looks...angry, I think?

"Didn't like doing it?" His jaw tenses.

"That's what he said, yeah."

"Then he was a fucking idiot." He kisses me and slides two fingers into me at the same time. I moan into his mouth, and he groans right back at me. "Love, you're not even touching me and you're making me crazy right now."

He's pumping his fingers in and out of me while his thumb moves up and lands right where it needs to. He draws his thumb in slow circles and curves his fingers up, hitting every spot inside of me.

"*Oliver*," I say.

"I know, Paige, I know." I'm holding onto him for dear life. My nails are scratching up his entire back, and he pulls his fingers out of me, kneels down, and I feel his tongue on me. He's going slow, and he moves up and sucks on my clit. Another moan slips out of my mouth. "That's it, scream for me. I want people to hear you getting properly worshiped for the first time."

"Oh my god, Oliver, please—" I moan again at the end of that as he continues. I can feel my orgasm building, and I have to say this is way better than just using my vibrator.

"Come on, love, come for me."

"Fuck, Oliver, right there, *please.*" He doesn't move, and I explode. He rides it out with me, continuing to run his tongue where he was. It's too much. I'm feeling things I've never felt before, and sparks are clouding my vision. I come down a few seconds later and feel him press a kiss to the top of my head.

"Tired?" he asks while laying down next to me on his bed. I nod wordlessly while dragging one of his blankets up my body. It's gray and soft and I can feel myself starting to fall asleep before my brain starts working.

"As much as I want to stay here and never get up again, I can't leave Amelia in the apartment by herself," I say as I try to move, my body so tired that it won't let me.

"One second," he says as he gets back up and goes to the living room. He sits back down on his bed and hands me my phone. "I'm going to ask Henry to stay the night at your place with her, so you can continue to be comfy here and not have to worry about Amelia. Does that sound good?" He asks me, and I look down at him. "What, Paige?"

"Nothing! I just— I mean you just— you know and you're still, and I just thought—" He leans over and kisses me, stopping the rest of my incoherent mumbling.

"It's okay."

"Are you sure? I don't mind helping with your little situation." He glares at me. "I didn't mean it like that! I swear!" I tell him, and as I start laughing, his right hand slowly creeps up my body and stops at my neck. We lock eyes as he squeezes my neck, just hard enough to stop my laughter from coming through.

"Tonight was about you, okay?" he whispers while squeezing a bit harder. "And I assure you it won't feel so little when you're begging me for it next time."

He releases his grip, and I feel more flustered than before about everything that just happened. He adjusts himself as he hands me my pants that were discarded on his floor.

"I wasn't begging..." I say to him.

"I think 'Oliver, please,' speaks for itself." He smiles over at me and raises his arm, motioning me to cuddle against him and I do. He types away on his phone and then sets it down while I open up Amelia and I's message thread.

Paige: Are you good if I stay the night at Oliver's?

Amelia: Does he sleep in a coffin?

Paige: Ames, for the last time, he is not a vampire.

Amelia: I'm just making sure! You never know!

Paige: As if vampires are just constantly around us! That's not normal!

Paige: Are you with Henry?

Amelia: Weirdly enough, he just offered to stay with me tonight.

Amelia: Did you plan this or something? He got all excited when his phone buzzed.

Paige: Oliver might have texted him the idea.

Paige: I didn't want to be worried all night that you're all by yourself. I just want to make sure you're okay, and you seem okay when Henry is around.

Amelia: I'll be good. He's going to stay. Don't read too much into this.

Paige: I won't. I love you, I'll see you tomorrow.

Amelia: I love you too. Tell Oliver that I have garlic cloves on standby!

"Okay, everything's all set." I smile over at him. I open my phone again to check on a text thread that just crossed my mind.

Paige: Mom, are you up? I'm at the police station right now.

Mom:

> **Paige:** I'm alright. I wasn't being charged or anything like that. It's been a weird few weeks.

Mom:

> **Paige:** Hello? Mom, can you please answer so I know you're okay?

Mom:

> **Paige:** Sadie came by to check on you but you weren't home. Is everything alright?

Mom:

> **Paige:** I'm scared someone might be after me, so if anything happens, I love you.

Mom:

> **Paige:** Mom, someone broke into my apartment tonight. Can you please call me back?

Mom:

> **Paige:** Can you please answer me?

All the messages I've left my mom this semester have gone unanswered. I should be worried about her but my friend from home, Sadie, said she saw her at the grocery store the other day, and she was on the phone. So, she's alive and well, just not well enough to answer her own daughter.

I would say it hurts, but at this point, I'm not surprised. Over the summer break, we barely talked due to the fact that I was working two jobs trying to save money for school and because *she* was working all day too. We barely crossed paths even though we lived in the same house. It's almost Thanksgiving, and I have to figure out if I want to go back to the house and life I don't feel thankful for.

"What's wrong?" Oliver asks me while stroking up and down my arm.

"Nothing. Just looking through some old unanswered texts between me and my mom."

"Unanswered?" he asks and I nod while I show him my phone. His face falls as he scrolls through them until I feel him wrap his arms around me. "I'm sorry."

"It's okay. I'm used to it," I tell him.

"You shouldn't be. But I'm hoping I can change that for you. I *want* to change that for you."

"Oliver, it's okay. I know you'll always answer my texts or calls if I need you." He smiles at me when I say that.

"Damn right. That you can count on, I promise." He leans in and kisses me as I rest my head on his chest, and feel myself drifting off to sleep.

34

????

I KNEW A GOOD old fashioned apartment trashing would make those kids back off. What I didn't see coming was one of them being home.

Oh well. Collateral damage.

Only one more to go in my quest for vengeance. I can see the finish line from here. After this, I won't be the only one left grieving something that could've been avoided.

That *should* have been avoided.

It's not my fault these people have succumbed to their fate. After all, I'm just the one dealing out their punishments.

Enjoy Hell, boys. I went easy on you.

I have one month to plan the perfect end for the one who set all of this in motion. He's going out with a bang.

And he'll never see it coming.

35

Thursday, November 10th

9:25 PM

MY GIRLFRIEND AND I—GRANT was right, that phrase is nice—are currently sitting in the computer lab trying to make a link chart between all of our suspects. Paige is thrilled about this. Apparently, like my sister, she also appreciates a good chart.

There's nobody else in the computer room of the criminal justice building that we inhabit, so we've spread all around the room. It's nice and quiet, except for Paige eating her chips. I look over at her, she's standing up at the board since we're projecting it off the monitor. It's easier to see all the connections between suspects and victims this way.

"I hate that there's no way to eat these quietly. Whoever made chips didn't take into account how awkward it is to eat them in a silent room." She's currently drawing lines on the board between all the people on our suspect list. Since we already had a lot of information on them from what Alissa gave us, it was pretty easy to put all this together into one big chart.

"It's fine, P. Make sure to make the lines different for the different connections everyone has. That'll make it easier for us when we print it out," I tell her.

"Got it!" She shuffles back over to the board and starts to draw. "Can you please come up here? I feel like I'm teaching you right now, and it's weird."

"I'm trying to find more information on that one police officer. Just give me like five minutes."

"Fine, but anything you find has to go on the shared document!"

The concept of sharing something as small as that with Paige makes me feel like I won a contest or something. When we had that moment on her bedroom floor that morning, I couldn't believe the things she was saying to me. It kind of killed me a bit to know how she sees me. In a good way, of course, but I wasn't expecting it. I always thought we'd just continue to spin around each other in a circle, but now that we've caught on to one another, I don't want to let go.

I copy and paste a few things onto the shared document and I see Paige highlight it and comment something. "Did you see what I added on the Google Doc?"

"Yes. Let me just add it to the chart." When she's done doing that she takes a step back and admires her work. "I think we did it."

I look over at the board and all I see is a bunch of circles and names with lines all over the place. To a normal person, it probably looks like a mess. But to Paige and I, it makes perfect sense.

"So, let's go over what we know."

"Alright well it's a lot, so bear with me. First, we have the dean—death by a slit throat. Connected to him is his son who has been missing for five years, and that could be connected to why he's dead but we don't know for sure." She stops and looks over at me to see if I'm still following.

"You're doing great, P. Keep going."

"We also have the dean's assistant, who was there when we discovered the body. She was as scared as I was, so I don't know what to think about her. However, she was also having an affair with the assistant dean of students, who has now moved up the ladder. He's also high on our suspect list because he had the most to gain from the murder."

"Which was a better job, more benefits, and more money," I add.

"Correct. He has a wife, but he was having an affair with the assistant. They would write steamy notes to each other."

"Some of those got really graphic," I say.

"Now, the dean was friends with the police commissioner. Both of them died in the same manner only a few months apart, which doesn't feel like a coincidence."

"I don't believe in those," I say. Everything happens for a reason and if someone calls it a coincidence then they probably had something to do with it happening in the first place.

"I'm aware," she reminds me. "Another random police officer was killed in between the murders—it was allegedly a suicide. According to what you found, the family suspects foul play. He was killed differently, but if the killer was smart and wanted to hide the connection, that would make sense. I just don't know how it would all connect," Paige sighs heavily.

"Fitzpatrick also fits in. He was the one who got fired when he found nothing on the missing son. He doesn't have any reason to kill anyone, but he is still involved," I say to her. I step back and take in the chart we made. The loose connections or ones we aren't sure of are dotted, bold lines mean there's a relationship, and the ones with hearts on them indicate an affair. The three people crossed off are the three victims from the surrounding area.

"I don't think the son has anything to do with this."

"Why?"

"Just a gut feeling. Something bigger seems to be at play here. Whoever this person is has killed two people in two months. It feels like we're close to the end but who knows when or if something else will happen." Nothing jumps out at me as I stare at the board. "I think we're still missing something."

"Yeah, but what?" she asks me, her face pinching. "Ol, what if we don't figure this out before Thanksgiving or mid-semester break? Does it just go cold and we have to forget about it?"

"Paige, we'll figure this out. I have faith in us," I say to her. "You're not excited to go home for break are you?"

She shakes her head. "I don't usually feel very thankful for anything around this time of year. I tend to stay off of social media. All the people on my feed and everything being thankful for their family makes me wonder why I couldn't have that."

I walk over and wrap my arms around her. She slumps against me, and her arms hold tight around me. "I wish I could bring you back to California with me, but—"

"Your sister would kill us," she reminds herself. "I'll be okay, Ol. I'll probably just go to my friend Sadie's house for the week."

"You seem to spend a lot of time there when you're home," I say as she pulls back from me.

"Well, yeah. Before I met the girls, Sadie was pretty much my only solid friend throughout my life. We met when we were two and just stuck together the rest of our lives. She's been one of the only constants in my life, her and her family. Her parents say I'm an honorary member of their family because of how much time I spend at their house. I even have my own room. They converted the guest room for me because I used to sleep on Sadie's floor."

"That was nice of them." I'm glad at least someone was looking out for Paige when her own parents weren't. The fact that Sadie's family treated her better than her own says a great deal to me about these people. I just wish she felt like she mattered to her parents. I'm not saying they never loved Paige, but she deserved to be treated better than she was.

"They're like my second family. I used to hate Thanksgiving when I had to spend it with my dad, but over the years it's been a little better."

"Besides the obvious, why else was it bad?" I want to know all about Paige and her past. I want to know all these little secrets so I can make sure in the future I make every holiday the best I can for her.

"Well, my dad's family used to play the guilt game with me. They would complain about how they didn't see me enough and to call more. The last Thanksgiving I had with them I yelled at them and said the phone worked both ways. They lived about an hour from where I did, and I was just a kid. I couldn't drive, and I was too busy worrying about trying to survive and protect myself. And they were adults. I shouldn't have to teach them how to communicate. I was fifteen when I last saw them, and I'm glad they don't exist to me anymore." She lowers her head and I lift her chin up with my fingers.

"I'm sorry you had to go through all that alone," I tell her, lightly brushing my lips against hers.

"It's okay. I survived it. Plus, it brought me to you." She smiles at me.

"How's that?"

"Well, I knew I wanted to leave New York when I went to college. I picked Virginia because it was the exact opposite of where I grew up. Mostly warm, and a small town with a quaint college. And low and behold, I met you on the first day. The rest is history," she says with a chuckle.

"I guess you're right."

"Why did you pick Grand Mountain?" she asks me.

"It had a good program, and I was running away from a lot of things back home." It's the truth, and it still surprises me how easily it comes out. "After Mia's accident, her family kept reaching out and offering comfort and stuff, but I just couldn't do it. I felt like I failed them. I felt like I failed myself by not getting in the car that night, so I ran away."

"I know you love running, but apparently the only running I do is away from my problems." She giggles before we hear a loud bang. "What was that?"

"I don't know." I walk over to the door and pull it open. I look around but I don't see anyone.

"Let's go."

"Did you see something?" Paige asks me.

"No, but it's better to be safe than sorry. Especially with what happened to Amelia." Paige shuts the computer off and grabs her tote bag. I reach out and grab her hand, pulling her out of the room. The two of us are running down the stairs and I hear Paige giggling behind me.

Never a dull moment with this girl that's for sure.

36

Wednesday, November 16th

I SMILE NERVOUSLY AT my phone wondering if I should mention the anxiety I'm feeling to Oliver tonight.

I'm second-guessing things.

This always happens. I wish I could squash it, but the anxiety won't go away. I walk out of my bedroom wanting to ask Amelia for advice, but the scene in front of me stops me in my tracks. My mouth drops because Ames is on the couch with Henry's arm around her, and she isn't doing anything to swat it away.

The energy in here feels different tonight.

Has it finally happened?

"Is this real life or am I being pranked?" I say as they turn around. Henry has a huge smile on his face, and Amelia looks like a deer in headlights.

"Paige," Amelia says to me as I sit across from them.

"Something to admit, Ames?" I smile, knowing what she's about to say.

"Well, I was hoping you wouldn't find out this way but I did eat the last croissant this morning." That's now what I was referring to, but I am kind of bummed about that.

"Oh, just tell her already." Henry pats her shoulder.

"It's not like this is national news! I don't get what the big deal is." She gets up and goes to her room.

"Are you guys dating?" I ask Henry since Amelia doesn't want to talk about it. He simply nods at me, his smile growing wider as he does.

"Ah!" I say as I hug him. "I was rooting for you the entire time!"

I pull back and he laughs at me, his face turning red.

"Ames, when did this happen?" I yell to her in her room.

"A few days ago," she whispers, a smile peeking out from her mouth.

"A few days ago? I told you about Oliver and I like an hour after it happened, and you waited days?"

She nods at me. "It's different! You and Oliver are hiding your relationship. I didn't want you throwing a whole party over this. Plus, one hour for you is equivalent to a few days for me, and you're terrible at keeping your mouth shut."

"Yeah, I guess. Are you ready for book club?" I ask.

"Yes. Henry's going to walk me over, so you can go ahead," she tells me and I know she's going to regret saying that because as soon as she says that, I turn around and sprint out of our apartment. I cannot wait to tell Hads and Ella about this.

I also can't wait to tell Oliver about this, but I'm sure he'll make a thousand jokes because him and Ames don't exactly get along. But that's just their relationship, I think. Deep down, I think they like each other, or eventually, they will.

It takes me a few minutes to reach the building—I almost trip up the stairs a few times—but thankfully, Hads and Ella are already here.

"Woah, Paige. Where's the fire?" Hads asks me.

"You look like you're going to pass out. Sit down." Ella pulls a chair over for me and I sit.

"A-Amelia," I'm panting because I just ran what feels like miles, and I'm severely out of shape.

"Amelia? Why isn't she with you? Is she alone? Paige! You're not supposed to do that!" Ella tells me and I shake my head.

"What could've caused you to run here without her?" Hads asks me.

"Amelia and Henry are dating!" I shout as I regain my breath. Ella and Hads' mouths drop open in shock.

"Wait, are you serious?" Ella asks me.

"As in like, a relationship?" Hads asks and I nod.

"Yes! She's on her way here but I wanted to give you guys these before she got here." I take a few confetti poppers out of my bag that have been in here since after Henry comforted Amelia after the break-in. I had to have them on standby in case Amelia just dropped this news at random, like I knew she would.

"Is this necessary?" Ella asks me.

"Don't worry I have my mini vacuum to clean it up." I smile at her.

"Paige!" I hear Amelia yell from the stairwell.

"We're not talking about the book tonight are we?" Hads says and I nod. There's no way this book will be discussed tonight.

When Ames walks into the classroom, we pull them and confetti falls around us. She looks pissed.

"So, you must have told them. Can we be done with the topic now?" She walks through the confetti and sits in her chair, completely disregarding the three of us.

"Let us enjoy this moment of you having feelings, Ames," Hads jokes with her.

"So, you and Henry are official. I knew you'd open up eventually. I just didn't imagine someone like Henry being able to do that," Ella says.

"We actually broke up," Amelia says deadpanned.

"What?" I ask her. "You guys were together like five minutes ago!"

"Amelia, what?" Ella asks.

"Well, that was short-lived. Why did we need confetti for this?" Hads looks at me, and I'm still rooted to the ground, confused as fuck.

"I'm obviously kidding." Amelia starts laughing and has to brace on the table because she's laughing so hard.

I walk over and sit next to her. "That wasn't funny. I thought I might've cried."

Hads and Ella join us in their usual spots.

"Can we jump back a bit? I can't believe this is real," Hads says. "We need every detail."

"Fine, yes, Henry is my boyfriend," Amelia says, in a monotone voice.

"Damn, the joke of Henry being her boyfriend isn't that funny anymore now that it's true," Ella says, and I laugh a bit. She's right. It was fun to see her reactions to that before it was true. Now that it's real, it's less fun.

"Well, I'm very happy for you. Who knew you and Hads would have boyfriends before Paige and I?" I spit the water that was in my mouth out when she says that, and I feel them all turn and look at me. Amelia is half a second away from laughter and Ella and Hads just look concerned.

"Yeah! Who would've thought?" I smile, trying to make sure that nobody can tell how much of a liar I am.

"Paige, that is so weird," Amelia says to me, a mischievous look on her face.

"I didn't mean it as a bad thing. Just a general statement as the two who hate feelings of the four of us find themselves in relationships." Ella smiles as she reaches over and grabs my hand. "Paige, you'll find a person someday who deserves you. And so will I."

"Oh, Paige's soulmate is coming soon. Very soon, I think. They might even be right around the corner!" Amelia throws her head back in laughter and I glare at her.

"Exactly! That's the spirit!" Ella says as we all hear a door bang outside of our room. I flinch because it was loud and unexpected and then in comes Grant carrying something.

"Where is he?" Grant asks and I notice he's wearing a Team Henry shirt. *Where did he get that?*

"What the hell are you wearing?" Hads asks him as stunned as I am.

"Are you guys being serious?" Amelia puts her hand to her forehead.

"Grant, I didn't even send the designs off! Where did you get that?" I ask him.

"It doesn't matter. Now, where's my new brother-in-law?" he asks.

"What?" Hads says.

"Brother-in-law?" Ella asks, confused because only Hads and Oliver are related.

"What are you carrying?" Amelia asks him.

"A cake. Paige told me to have it ready just in case." Grant smiles as he walks over and takes a seat next to Hads, placing the box on the table behind us. I look over at Amelia and based on the look she's giving me, it might be best to sleep at Oliver's tonight. I think she might kill me in my sleep. I grab my phone and text Oliver the big news.

Paige: Amelia and Henry are finally dating!

Oliver: My condolences.

Paige: Oliver! This is good news!

Oliver: Oh, right.

Paige: Can you meet me in the classroom?

Oliver: Right now? Isn't that a bit conspicuous?

Paige: It's fine, just say that Grant told you or something. He's here right now with cake!

Oliver: Why the fuck do you guys have a cake?

Oliver: Don't answer that. On my way.

"Ames, tell us everything! Spare no details. Was there a big confession? This feels like the slowest burn of all time." Grant smiles at her and she stares back at him, very clearly wanting to change the subject.

"It's not that serious, can we just talk about the book?" Amelia asks and all of us shake our heads.

"Ames, you have to give us something," Ella tells her.

"We barely know the guy, and if he wants to get inducted into this group, he has to agree to a blood oath," I tell her.

"What?" Hads says.

"Oh, not this again," Ella sighs.

"Wait, do I have to do that? We can do it right now, let's get it out of the way. Not the palms though because I need to be able to hold my stick." Grant rolls up his sleeves and I start laughing.

I slap his arm. "I'm joking! Grant, put your sleeves down, you should know how much we love you already."

He puts his hand to his chest, feigning surprise even though he knows how much we adore him.

"He asked me to be his girlfriend, and I said yes. Are you happy? Can we move on?" Amelia asks. "And if you brought that cake, can we at least eat it? It looks good."

Grant grabs the box, and I take plates and forks out of my bag so we can eat it.

"Did you bring those with you?" Ella asks me.

"They've been in my bag. Grant and I have been preparing for this for a while." Ella stares at me. "Don't judge! I wanted to celebrate!"

"How long have you two been preparing for this?" Hads asks, looking between Grant and I, but the two of us stay quiet.

"If I had more time, we all would be wearing Team Henry shirts. Now, who wants a big piece?" Grant asks as Oliver comes into the room.

"Oliver, what are you doing here?" Hads asks him.

"I heard the unfortunate news." He turns to look at Amelia. "Congrats on finding someone that tolerates you." He pats her on the shoulder and she dips away from him.

"How did word travel so fast?" Amelia asks, looking right at me because she knows how he found out.

"Grant told me as he was rushing out of his apartment with a giant box in his hands," Oliver says.

"I didn't—" Grant starts to say when Oliver cuts him off.

"Yes. You did. You probably just forgot." He glares at him and Grant seems to pick up what he's saying because he looks over at me and I widen my eyes, silently telling him not to say anything.

"Right! Sorry, I was in such a rush, it must've slipped my mind." Grant grabs another slice of cake and hands it to me and smirks. Great. Now he knows too and Hads is for sure going to kill me when she finds out that everyone knew before her. I've dug the hole even deeper, and I'm not sure how to get out of it.

"Oliver can be quite forgettable, so that makes sense. When Grant gets excited about something he tends to get tunnel vision." Hads takes a bite of her cake.

"So, what are everyone's plans for Thanksgiving Break?" Grant asks the room.

"I'm working and my family's coming over." Ella smiles. "I love my new job. It's everything I thought it was going to be."

"Good for you, Ells." Grant holds out his fist for her to bump and she does. "Oliver, I think Hads told you I'll be joining you for break. I'm sure you were ecstatic to hear that."

"Thrilled," Oliver tells him while scraping off his frosting. "Paige, do you want my frosting?" He asks me, already knowing my answer. I get up and hold my plate out to him.

"Man, you guys really did get close with the whole investigation," Hads says and I freeze up as Oliver scrapes it onto my plate. "How has it been not investigating?"

"Fine," Oliver tells her.

"A lot less stressful," I tell her. Great. Now we're lying about two things to our closest friends and family. "I'm going home, so nothing too exciting."

"Paige, you can always come to Alissa and I's apartment for the week," Ella offers to me.

"No, it's okay. I want to see my mom anyway." I weakly smile, knowing I'll probably be working the whole time. My mom hasn't made Thanksgiving dinner in years, and I'm not expecting it this year since she can't answer any of my calls or texts.

"The offer always stands, P. Even if you come back early, okay?" She leans over and I return the hug she offered.

"Thanks, Ells. Maybe after the break we can talk?" I ask, knowing she understands the most about my family troubles.

She nods. "Of course. Alissa misses you, so you'll have to come over."

"Perfect," I look over at Amelia, "are you just going home?"

"No, um, my parents are going to be on vacation in Barbados. I'm, uh, I'm going to Henry's house." She looks down at the floor.

"Seriously?" Hads asks.

"Yeah? It's not a big deal," Amelia tells us.

"It kind of is," Ella says.

"Meeting the parents is a big step," Grant tells her and Amelia is about to say something, but Oliver cuts her off.

"Like you were nervous meeting our parents? You brought them gifts and they loved you instantly."

"They did tell me I was like the son they never had." Grant smiles at him, and Oliver throws his fork at him.

"Please don't impale my boyfriend, Ol," Hads says while slightly giggling.

"Knock, knock!" Henry says as he stands in the doorway. "What's going on here?"

Grant immediately goes over to him, and pulls him into a hug. "Congrats, buddy. I knew you could do it."

"What's that?" Henry motions to his shirt.

"Oh this? Just something Paige and I whipped up." Grant smiles over at me, and I wave to Henry.

"And the cake?" Henry asks.

"We're celebrating," Ella tells him.

Henry looks at the floor. "Confetti? Something big must have happened."

"Hen, they're acting like us getting together is national news," Amelia tells him. "We should leave."

"Ames! Let him have some cake!" I yell to her.

"Henry hates cake."

"No, I don't—" Amelia pushes him out the door away from the classroom, and they leave.

"That was fun while it lasted," Grant says.

"Did we overdo it?" I ask.

"Yes," Oliver, Ella, and Hads say at the same time.

"As a matter of fact, I don't think we did enough," Grant tells me, and I laugh.

We all chat for another half an hour before Oliver gets up.

"Can you guys clean up? I have to talk to Paige about a project for a class." Oliver looks at me. "Can I walk you home?"

"Of course," I say as I dig through my tote bag and pull out my mini vacuum. "Don't worry about returning it. I'll get it whenever I see you next."

"I hope you two have fun talking about this project. Have a great night." Grant winks at the both of us.

"Why are you being so weird?" Hads slaps his shoulder.

"I'm not, Hades. But let's hurry so we can watch more of *One Tree Hill*."

"Okay, well, see you guys later," Oliver says to the room as he grabs my arm and pulls me down the stairs and into the night. Instead of walking me home, he turns the other way so we can head to our roof spot.

"Well, that was something," he says to me.

"I'm happy for Amelia. She deserves this," I say to him.

"I guess."

"I know deep down you're happy for her even though you two like to make fun of each other." I smile as he opens the door to the building for me.

When we get up to the roof, I notice a bunch of blankets and pillows in our corner. "What's all this?"

"Our first official date."

"Oliver, we've been on plenty of dates," I tell him.

"Stakeouts and car chases don't count."

"Fair point," I say to him as he leads me over, his hand on the small of my back. I settle into the blankets, and Oliver grabs a bottle of something and two glasses. "Oliver, neither of us likes to drink alcohol, so what is that?"

"Sparkling grape juice." He smiles at me as he hands me a cup. "What's on your mind, love?"

"How do you know something's on my mind?"

"You've got your nervous face on. So, tell me what's up in that beautiful brain of yours."

"I'm just afraid. Anxious."

"Afraid of what?"

I hesitate before saying something, but it tumbles out of my mouth anyway. "This. Us. It scares me."

"Are you having second thoughts?"

"No, I-I don't know. I just have this weird feeling in my stomach that won't go away. This happened with my last boyfriend, too. But instead of telling him about it, I ran. But I don't want to run from you."

"Okay, let's talk this out." He sets his cup down and grabs both of my hands in his. "What's scaring you? Is it me? Are we going too fast?"

"No, Oliver. You know I always feel safe with you. I'd tell you if it was too fast. I'm just scared."

"P, I can't help you if I don't know what you're scared of."

I feel a few tears fall from my eyes, and I hate that anytime I try to talk through my emotions, I end up crying. My therapist says it's because my feelings were never heard as a kid. But I know Oliver will hear me regardless of what I say. He's the best listener I know. "I'm just scared it's all going to crash and burn, and I'm going to end up alone again."

"No, love, that won't happen. I know me saying that isn't going to make you believe me, but I'm scared as hell, too. I'm scared that some twist of fate could take you away from me, just like Mia. I couldn't handle that happening again, not to you. But I'm not going to let my fear stand in the way of us being happy. And I know you're scared, P. I'm terrified. I have this beautiful thing with you, and I don't want to lose that." He squeezes my hands in his. "But don't you think the two of us deserve to be happy and not afraid it'll only last a little while?"

"After seeing how nice it is to have people around me that care, I don't know what I'd do if I lost that. I don't want to lose that, or you. I just can't stop myself from feeling like all of this is short lived. But I'm willing to risk it." Isn't that what love is? A risk that something might end horribly? Maybe. But love is also knowing when we're old and gray, one of us will be gone before the other. But I would love to grow old with someone and learn all of their quirks, and doing that with Oliver would make me happy. "You might need to remind me a few thousand times that it'll be okay because my mind likes to overthink everything."

"I'll tell you however many times it takes that I'm not going anywhere, P."

I smile as I take a sip and scooch over to where Oliver is. I lean my head down so I'm in his lap and his hand finds my messy hair as he brushes over it. I'm glad I told him about my feelings. I think sometimes my brain needs a reminder that not everyone in my life is going to leave me high and dry like my parents did.

"I'm going to miss you over break. It's going to be weird not seeing you for a week," he tells me.

"I'm only a phone call away, Ol. I'll probably be busy working, but I'll always make time to talk to you. The time zone thing is going to suck, but we'll make it work." I shift my head so that I can see his face.

"I know, love. I'm not worried. Just a bit upset."

"About what?"

"Well, Amelia and Henry are out in the open now, and it just has me thinking about our situation."

"I've been thinking about it too. I hate keeping this a secret. I know it was my idea, but it feels wrong now." I sit up and face him. "Should we tell people?"

"I don't even know how we would go about that."

"I don't either," I sigh.

"How about we talk about this after break? I don't want to dwell on this while I can still hold you." He shifts my head up. "Come here."

I smile at him and place my cup to the side before I sink into his embrace and feel him wrap his arms around me. He lays us both down, and we look up at the stars together. I feel him open his mouth about to say something and my stomach drops.

Is he about to tell me he loves me?

Does he know I feel the same way?

I feel him take a deep breath, but he doesn't say anything. We continue to lay tangled up in blankets for a few more minutes until I feel my eyes start to droop.

"I never imagined I could feel this happy again. Thanks to you, I know what it feels like. I don't know how you did it. I don't know how you stayed soft despite all you've been through, but I'm glad you did because without the shine you have, you wouldn't be you," I hear him whisper as he kisses my cheek, and I fall deeper into sleep while wrapped in the arms of the guy I love.

37

Sunday, November 27th

I'm about to knock on Ella's apartment door when I hear yelling. I pause for a moment, not wanting her to miss my knocking, and then I raise my fist to the door. As soon as she opens it, I can tell she's pissed off.

"Is something wrong?" She only continues to stare at me until she opens her door wider and I notice someone behind her.

It's Leo—Alissa's brother, and Ella's least favorite person on the planet.

"Should I come back?" I ask her before she pulls me into her apartment and slams the door. I take my shoes off and awkwardly follow her into the living room. Leo is sitting on the couch on his phone, and he looks up when I walk in.

"Nice to see you again," I say, trying to ease the weird tension I'm feeling.

"Paige, right?" Damn. That accent gets better every time I hear it.

"That's me." I smile. "So, why are you two sitting here by yourselves? I assumed if you were ever left alone together you would kill each other, especially after what happened on—" I look over at Ella and she's glaring daggers at me, so my sentence fades off and I'm left in the awkward silence that blankets this room.

I can feel the sexual tension coming off of these two, and that is the main reason why I believe these two could be something someday. I'm not saying they'll be a couple at any point in the future, but they could be *something*.

This is the first time I've been to Ella's new apartment and it's very different from the last one she had, but it still has notes of her style around it from what I can see.

There's a lot of notes from her last place still around, but the openness of the floor plan makes the space seem way bigger. Alissa's plants are all over the place, and Ella's coffee table books are the main centerpiece of their living room where I'm sure the two of them watch reality television. Alissa's room is off of the kitchen, and Ella's is right across the hall from the guest bedroom.

"I'm waiting for my sister to come home. I thought she'd be here already, but she got stuck at work. We're going to happy hour." Leo smiles at me and I can practically hear Ella roll her eyes. "I offered to wait in the hallway, but I love pushing this one's buttons a little too much."

"You don't push my buttons, you infuriate me beyond reason. It's different," Ella snaps at him.

"Darling, I'll be out of your hair in no time." Leo looks down at his phone and smiles to himself. I look over at Ella, and she's just watching him, her eyes all fired up. I hope Alissa gets here soon. I don't want to have to clean up Leo's body after Ella decides to kill him.

"Do you want something to drink, P?" Ella asks me.

"I'll just take some water," I say when she gets up.

"I'm good, thanks," Leo says even though she didn't ask him.

"There's a reason I didn't ask you, London Boy. I wouldn't want you bitching about my heinous tea-making skills again," Ella shoots back at him. "You literally choked and spit it out last time."

"Darling, I'm perfectly capable of working my own mouth, and if I recall, you seemed to like how it worked when—" Ella throws an apple at him from the bowl sitting on their counter. They definitely had sex at some point. "Why did you throw this at me?"

"To shut you up," she snaps at him.

"I can go wait in your room, Ells if—"

"No! It's fine. He's just being annoying because he spends too much time around people who kiss his ass all day."

"Has he been spending time around Grant?" I ask her.

"No, but after the Halloween party, I wouldn't be surprised."

"Was that the hockey player? I did like him, nice lad." Leo smiles at us and then Ella's front door opens.

"I'm here! Please tell me you didn't kill my brother!" Alissa flies into the room, panting. "I'm sorry I'm late. This prick wiped an entire computer of information, and I only had a few hours to restore it."

"No apologies needed, Liss. Both Ella and Paige were wonderful company." Leo smiles at his sister.

"Paigey! My favorite little sunshine, how have you been?" Alissa walks over and pulls me in for a hug.

"I've been good! Just trying to focus on school, you know how it is." I smile at her.

"Well, I would love to stay and chat, but my brother is getting restless. I'll be back in a few hours. Will you still be here?"

"Paige has a paper to write, so this is just a little chat to catch up," Ella tells her.

"Well, you ladies have the most fun! I'll be back for dinner, Ells. Chinese food tonight?"

"That depends, is your brother joining us?" Yikes, I almost feel bad Ella has to deal with seeing Leo all the time while he's here, but it makes me laugh when I think about it. I would never tell her that, though.

"No. He's got a date tonight," Alissa tells her.

"Oh, wow. Another woman fell into that Venus fly trap of a man. Best of luck to her." Ella smiles as Alissa leaves their apartment.

As the door closes, I turn to face Ella. "So, where should we migrate to? Living room? Dining room table?"

"I'm good with the couch." Ella swings her hand out to motion me into the living room. I make myself comfortable and take a few breaths. "You know I love hanging out with you, Paige, but I was nervous when you texted me so ominously."

"Yeah, sorry. I'm working on that. I just wanted to talk to you about a few things."

"About Thanksgiving? Was it okay for you? I know you hate going home," she says to me.

"It was okay. I didn't talk to my mom, but I went to Sadie's house and had dinner with them. It was nice compared to other years." I smile thinking about how Sadie's family has always let me join them on holidays. She's a forever friend for sure.

"That sounds nice. I remember Sadie from when we surprised you for your birthday over the summer. She seems like a sweet girl."

"She is, but that's not what I wanted to talk to you about." I take a breath before I speak. "Did you ever feel guilty for leaving home? I know when you were at school you were a lot closer to your family, so it was easier to catch up with them. Now you're a bit farther away."

"Well, I miss them all the time, but sometimes I do feel guilty about it. When I was a kid and my mom left, I basically had to raise my sister. I put my life on the back burner to be there for her and my dad. Sometimes the guilt of leaving comes back."

"Have you figured out how to get rid of that feeling?"

She furrows her brows at me. "Why? Are you thinking of leaving home after college?"

"I don't know yet. But I feel like it's the best decision for my future. I don't want to go back home after graduation and feel stuck there because I'm afraid of starting over. It's terrifying."

"Moving on from the life you had—especially yours—can be a terrifying step. Paige, you basically raised yourself. You were on your own for so much of your life. It's okay to want to leave those memories behind for something brighter. It's what you deserve."

I feel my eyes start to tear up. "I feel guilty about it. I mean, I feel like my mom still needs me, despite everything. I feel like if I leave she'll forget about me completely."

"Paige, it's tough mourning a person that's still alive. The same thing happened to me when my mom left." She takes a breath. "Having to wake up every day and know that she's out there somewhere with a whole new life, while she left me to pick up the pieces of what she destroyed is hard. It hurts like a bitch. My family still relies on me, even when I'm so far away, but the distance has helped me see things a little clearer."

"And what have you seen?"

"My life. You're allowed to live just for yourself. It's your life after all. Sometimes you have to recognize that living solely for other people and not yourself can hurt you more than anything. You have to do what's best for your future, P. Not the one your parents carved out for you. If that means leaving New York behind, then so be it."

"I don't know if I know how to do that," I admit to her. "My whole life has been focused on surviving and helping my mom make sure there's always food in the fridge. I don't know how to let myself leave when it feels like she could need me."

"Paige, when was the last time she texted you back? Or called you just to talk and check how you're doing?" Ella asks me, and it doesn't take long for the answer to become clear.

"She hasn't."

Ella shuffles over on the couch, and she's officially entered my personal space bubble, but I don't mind it. She grabs both of my hands and holds them tight. "Paige, I need you to listen to me when I say this. You don't have to apologize to anyone for doing what's best for you. I know you always walk around with your smile on, pretending everything you've been through isn't a big deal, but it is. It's okay to be hurt about things that have happened to you, and it's just as okay to leave them behind and create your own beautiful life somewhere else. I promise that doesn't make you a bad daughter or a bad person."

"I'm worried about being out in the world on my own. I'm worried about the guilt eating me alive if I cut her off completely."

"Paige, you've been on your own your whole life. I think the real world should be afraid of you." I chuckle as a few tears fall. I've never had anyone validate my feelings this much. "And I think that it's okay to cut off people who aren't good for your life—including family. A lot of people in the world like to use the excuse of being family with people to justify bad behavior. But no matter who someone is to you, that doesn't give them the right to treat you like you don't matter."

She wipes a few tears from my eyes and I notice hers are all glassy, too. I wasn't expecting this conversation to get so teary, but everything she's saying makes sense.

"Okay, I think when I go home for Christmas I'm going to tell my mom I'm leaving. I've been looking for jobs in Virginia after graduation anyway. I like it here. When I came here for college it felt like a fresh start, and then I met you about a week into the semester. It felt like a sign from the universe, you coming up to me at the library. I never told you how much that meant to me."

"Just a conversation about a book you were reading meant that much?"

I nod. "I always thought everyone saw right through me. I felt like a ghost floating around each day, trying my best not to be a bother. You were the first person who saw me, wanted to make a connection, and did it. It felt good just simply talking about a book we both read that day in the library."

"Well, you know I'd do anything to talk about that amazing series. I remember us reading the epilogue novel and being in tears the entire time. It was a defining moment for our friendship and I wouldn't trade any of it for the world," Ella says, a few tears falling from her eyes.

"Me neither." I smile at her. "Thank you, Ells. This helped a lot."

"Anytime, Paige. I'm always down to give some kickass advice." She winks at me.

"If you ever need to talk, you know I'm always here for you too, right?" I ask because she told me some things I didn't know about before today. I hope she knows that even if she's the one who always takes care of others, that doesn't mean she doesn't need someone to ask her how she's doing, too.

"I know. Now, can I ask you a question?"

"Uh, sure?" *I'm scared.*

"What's going on with you and Oliver?"

"Well, we were trying to solve a murder together, and that's not happening anymore, so nothing?" I try to deflect but I can tell by her posture, arms folded in front of her, and a mischievous look on her face that she knows.

"Cut the shit. There's something going on with you two. It's actually so obvious I don't know how anyone else hasn't called you out on it yet."

"I didn't think we were that transparent! Ugh! At this rate, everyone is going to know but Hads and that is not what we wanted to happen!" Now, I'm off of the couch and pacing around her living room. Hads is never going to forgive me and Oliver for lying so long. This is going to be a mess to try and navigate.

"Who else knows about you two?"

"Oliver, obviously."

"I would hope so."

"You, Amelia, Henry—"

"Henry knew before me? He just got here!"

"I know! I'm sorry! He was with Amelia when Oliver kissed my forehead and accidentally outed us to them. I think Grant knows too. He keeps winking at me and Oliver when stuff happens. I don't know for sure, though."

"So, everyone but Hads? Paige, you're so fucked. You have to tell her before this blows up in your face."

"I know! We're planning on telling her soon, but it's all become so complicated!" I slump down on her couch and she leans over to me.

"Okay, how about next time you both see her, you just tell her? You need to consider how much this is going to hurt her, and I know that's the last thing you want."

It *is* the last thing I want. I never want any of my friends to hurt because of something I said or did. I couldn't live with myself if that ever happened.

"Well, thank you for the advice, Ells, but can we mention the elephant in the room?" I ask as she raises her eyebrow at me. "I was getting vibes from you and Leo when I walked in. Care to explain that?"

"Paige Yarrow, I swear if you say that again I'm going to cut your tongue out!" Ella's now the one pacing around her living room.

"Sorry, but I could cut the tension in the room earlier with Oliver's pocket knife! It got me wondering—"

"If you mention the word relationship in the same sentence as his name, I'm kicking you out of my apartment."

"Okay, well, in that case, I must be going!" I say as I rise from the couch.

"Are you serious?" Ella yells at me and I'm laughing all the way to her front door.

"This was a great chat! I swear I'll get you to tell me your history with Zimmerman one day!" I whip open her front door and throw her a wave. "Bye! I love you!"

"Text me when you get home, and don't even think about making a profile on him!" she yells after me. I close the door to her apartment and calmly walk down the hallway, smiling to myself.

I'm so going to figure those two out.

Maybe I should enlist Alissa's help. Or maybe I could get both of them drunk and make them spill their guts to me.

Both are decent ideas, but I table them for now.

Oliver: Movie night tonight? I was thinking we could watch *Midsommar*. It's been a while since I've seen it.

Paige: You know the way to a girl's heart, Ol.

Oliver: How did the conversation with Ella go?

Paige: It was good. She always knows the right thing to say.

Oliver: I'm glad.

Oliver: Oh by the way, you mentioned wanting to talk about the investigation tonight, but I'm officially banning that. Just tell me what you were going to ask me.

Paige: I think the two slit throat cases are connected.

Oliver: Well, yeah. But how do we prove that?

Paige: Well… we could try blackmailing the acting dean or something.

Oliver: Blackmail? With what and why?

Paige: Because he might be in on this with the receptionist!

Oliver: Are we talking like email blackmail, or some weird shady magazine cutout note?

Paige: Either one works for me, but we can discuss that another time. Movie night sounds fun!

Oliver: I'll see you soon, sunshine.

Paige: See you soon, Ol.

38

Monday, November 28th

I HAVE BETTER THINGS to do, but my sister has dragged me to the library to study with her. I couldn't exactly say no because then she would ask why. Then I'd have to lie to her again about what I was going to do instead.

I was going to ask Paige if she wanted to get together and talk about the blackmail note she mentioned, but if I tell my sister that she'll smack me with her ruler.

So, I'm in the library with my sister as she drinks her third coffee of the day and grumbles at her computer.

"Is something wrong? You sound like me?"

"My computer keeps freezing!" She slams her laptop closed and takes out her iPad and her Bluetooth keyboard.

"Why do you even need a fucking laptop if you have a keyboard for that thing?"

"Oliver, you just don't get it," she tells me.

"I know, that's why I'm asking you!" I say a bit loudly, and I get shushed by a few people.

"I never thought that would happen to you, of all people." She smirks at me and I roll my eyes.

"Well, look who we have here, the prettiest girl on campus and Oliver." Grant slides next to my sister and I feel someone sit next to me. When I look over it's Jacks, Grant's roommate and best friend.

"Hey dude," I say to him.

"Oliver, always nice to see you and Hads out and about." He smiles at me. Jacks has blond hair and he sort of reminds me of Tyler Durden from Fight Club. "Hads, how are you on this lovely day?"

"It would be wonderful if my computer stopped freezing! Can you ask Claire to look at it for me? She has magic hands when it comes to technology."

"Hand it over, and I'll see what she can do." My sister hands her laptop to Jacks and Grant leans over to kiss her on the cheek.

"Adorable." I roll my eyes at them.

"Oliver, when you fall in love, I'm going to make fun of you every chance I get." Grant leans over and touches my hand. "When you're older you'll understand."

He only gets a glare from me. "Hush it, pretty boy."

"I would pay millions to see my brother all googly-eyed over someone," my sister says. *Fucking hell.*

"Please tell me that nickname Oliver used is transferable? Permission to start using it, Hads?" Jacks asks her.

"Granted." Hads side eyes her boyfriend. "What? I think it's funny."

"Of course you do, you're the one that came up with it. It doesn't matter anyway, I take it as a compliment." Grant smiles at us.

Jacks sighs at him, clearly used to Grant being how he is.

"Well, I prefer the nickname Hades. It flows nicely."

"You only named me that because I was mean to you at first," Hads tells him.

"Yeah, and why were you? He literally knocked you over and then offered you his hand. You made it sound like he was trying to kill you or something," I joke with her, remembering all the times Paige would text me about my sister and Grant last year.

"Honestly, it was funny watching it go down in real-time." Jacks laughs. I like this kid. Why isn't he around more often?

"Jacks, you told me Grant was nice and that I was going to love him," Hads tells him.

"Well, you do now!" Jacks exclaims. "I didn't even understand why you didn't like him in the first place. Grant was head over heels for you the moment he saw your face."

My sister blushes at that.

"I know Kyle left a bad taste in your mouth, but did you think this golden retriever idiot was going to hurt you as bad as he did?"

"I'm going to get my ruler out if you all don't shut up," Hads sighs and types more aggressively.

"I've been good! It's those two you have to worry about." Grant points at Jacks and me.

"I'm just saying that keeping up with you two last semester was a whirlwind. Grant went to war on pink after Hads wore a fucking pink sweater one time," Jacks tells them.

"As I've said a million times before, it was unrelated!" A few people around the library shush Grant when he says that.

"I barely knew you then!" Hads smacks his arm. "It wasn't even my sweater! It was Amelia's!"

His eyes widen. "Well, I like the color pink now. Again, unrelated."

"Try hearing about all this from Paige secondhand. She was calling it from the beginning." I turn to Grant. "You were all my sister would talk about every Saturday when we went for our walks, so it's safe to say she was also obsessed with you from the start."

"Hey!" She reaches across the table to slap me but I pull back before she can.

"Oh, a big topic of conversation I was?" Grant smiles over at my sister.

"No. Goodbye," Hads tells them. "You interrupted our study session."

"I wasn't doing anything important," I say as my sister's phone buzzes on the table. She looks at it for a few seconds and then gets up to leave. "Where are you going?"

"Paige has to go to the store, which leaves Amelia by herself, so I'm going to go study with her. I'm sure she'll be better company than you three."

Amelia's better company than me? Yeah, right. She'll probably cast a spell on Hads or some freaky voodoo shit.

"I'll see you later, boyfriend?" Hads quickly pecks Grant on the lips.

"Sure, baby. Do you want me to walk you over?"

"No. I'm sure you three want to continue whatever conversation this has turned into," and then she turns and walks out of the library. After a few minutes of awkward silence and stares, I get up and head out of the library as well. But as I walk away, I feel the two of them saddle up next to me.

"So, Oliver, how is everything?" Grant asks me as I walk back to our apartments.

"Why are you being so weird?"

"It's just a question!"

"So, you and Paige huh?" Jacks asks me. *How the fuck does he know?*

"I couldn't tell Hads! Jacks was in the room and I needed to tell someone! You can't expect me to keep it a secret much longer. Are you going to tell her soon?" Grant asks me. "If the answer is no, then you're an idiot."

"Yes." I actually don't know. Paige and I haven't talked about that yet. I think the two of us are more secure in this relationship, especially after we had our first official date. We laid a lot of our fears out that night, and I think talking it out together helped a lot.

I think it would be good for us to be out in the open. I also want to hold my girlfriend's fucking hand when we walk to class without being afraid that my sister will see.

"Good. I'm sick of hiding your secrets so you and Paige can sneak around all forbidden and shit. Plus, Hads is going to kill you both if you keep hiding this from her," Grant points out.

"We didn't just keep it a secret because of my sister. There are many other reasons why we did it this way that you don't need to know about.

"You two are so different it makes my head hurt." Grant puts his fingers to his temples. "I will say that I love the whole opposites attract trope you two have going on. It's adorable."

"Whatever, pretty boy," I say as I swipe us into our apartment building. "Just keep your mouth shut, okay?"

"I'll do my best," he says before they head off to their place.

Why do I have a feeling this is going to blow up in our faces?

Part of me doesn't care because Paige deserves the world, and I'm going to try my best to give it to her even if we have a few speed bumps along the way.

Grant: Henry, please tell Oliver he should tell Hads about his relationship before it blows up in his face.

Henry: What relationship?

Oliver: Henry, he knows. You can drop the act.

Henry: Oh thank God. I felt bad keeping it from him this whole time.

Grant: The whole time?! How long have you known?

Henry: The morning it happened, according to Amelia.

Oliver: It was an accident.

Grant: I'm a little hurt by this discovery.

Henry: Back to the matter at hand, yes, you should tell her.

Oliver: To be fair, this is the reason why we kept it quiet. All of you like to meddle and it's annoying.

Grant: It's called having friends, Oliver. You should be glad we tolerate your stares.

Henry: What's the worst that could happen by telling people?

Grant: Hads is going to kill him, for one.

Oliver: I can handle my sister.

Henry: Was that a joke?

Grant: Good one, Oliver.

Oliver: You know what...

39

????

Tomorrow night, it all ends.

Revenge is finally mine, I can taste it on the tip of my tongue. This is the final countdown. He's not going to know what hit him. It's going to be slow and painful. Just like what he did.

A coward dying as one should. Slowly and alone. With nobody around to hear him scream.

40

Friday, December 2nd

3:30 PM

I'm sitting at the library with Oliver when Hads and Grant appear across from us.

"Hey, you two." Grant winks. "Are you guys still doing that project?"

"Uh, yeah," Oliver tells him as he shoves some papers into his bag.

"Well, it's better than an investigation. I was starting to get worried about you guys," Hads says as she takes her iPad out.

"Well, that's over, so you can stop worrying about us," I say nervously.

"So, does anyone have any scoop on Amelia and Henry? And should we change our group chat name? Oliver, what do you think?" Grant asks, and Oliver glares. He was never a fan of gossiping or small talk, but he's warming up to it the longer he spends around me.

"I'm going to go grab a coffee," Hads says to the table. "Does anyone want anything?"

"I think we're good, baby."

When she gets far enough away, Grant leans over to us.

"You two are going to get killed," he whispers to us. "Why haven't you told her yet?"

"What?"

"I've had to keep this a secret from Hads for two weeks! It's putting a strain on me, so when are you idiots going to tell her?" He pauses. "How long has it officially been?"

I look over at Oliver and he's rolling his eyes. "Since the night of the break-in," I whisper to Grant, and his eyes go wide.

"That was like a month ago!"

"Yup," Oliver says as he smiles at Grant. *Is he enjoying this?*

"You can't tell Hads! We've been trying to figure out how to bring it up but nothing seems right," I whisper to him. "Everyone knows but her!"

"Ella doesn't know," Oliver says.

"Of course she does! She figured it out the same night Grant did!"

"So, my girl is the only one in the dark? This is going to be fucking horrible," Grant whispers as Hads comes back.

"What's going to be horrible?"

"Paige and Oliver failing this project, of course!" Grant awkwardly laughs.

"Nice one pretty boy," Oliver tells him as he gets up.

"Where are you going?" I ask him.

"Back to my apartment. I left a worksheet there. I'll be right back." He goes to leave when two police officers walk up to him, the acting dean of students trailing behind them. "What's going on?"

"Oliver Baker and Paige Yarrow?" The officer looks at me.

"Yes? What's going on?" I ask them, my stomach dropping through my feet.

"Is something wrong?" Hads asks while looking between the two of us.

"We need you both to come with us," the officer says.

"Why?"

"Don't make this harder than it needs to be. Get your stuff and follow us," one of them says.

"It would've been easier if you two were at home. I tried not to do this in public, I swear," the acting dean of students tells us.

"Can someone explain what's happening, please?" I ask, my breathing is getting heavier. I'm scared. Something doesn't feel right.

"You both are under arrest for one count of tampering with evidence and one count of tampering with a crime scene," the officer tells us, and my heart stops working. "We need you both to come with us."

"Under arrest? They didn't do anything!" Grant tells them.

"Oliver, what's going on?" Hads asks.

"Let's go. Right now." The officer grabs Oliver by the arm and tugs him forward. The other guy reaches for my arm and I trip as he jostles me toward the exit.

"Hey!" Oliver tells the officer who grabbed me. "Don't fucking touch her."

"Let's go," one of them says. Students are looking over to see what's happening as I feel tears start to fall from my eyes.

"Oliver! Don't say a word!" Grant shouts to him, and I see Hads typing aggressively on her phone, probably calling their parents.

"Paige had nothing to do with it. I forced her. It was all me. I swear. I threatened her," Oliver lies to the officer. "Let her go. She didn't do anything."

"What are you doing?" I ask, tears streaming down my face. *This can't be happening.*

"Don't say a word," he bites at me, and I know he's trying to protect me by lying to these officers, but I can't get the words out. "It was all me. You got your confession. Let her go." He looks to the officer and signals for the one holding me to let me go.

"Did he threaten you?"

I can't form words, and when I look over at Oliver, I can tell he's silently telling me to say yes, but I can't. The thought of telling someone he threatened me to do something hurts. Oliver would never do that, but for right now, I can tell he doesn't want me coming with him. He nods his head slightly, coaxing me to say it. *Fuck.* "Y-Yes. He did."

"Oliver, what's going on?" Hads yells and I turn around to face her while the officers pull Oliver away. "Paige, why are they taking my brother?"

"I—" What am I supposed to say to her right now? She scoffs and I turn back around. "Oliver, what are you doing?" I yell as I watch him get further away from me.

I'm frozen to the floor as I lock eyes with him, and he doesn't break our stare until he's forced out of sight. Somehow, my feet move, and when I get out the doors and see Oliver being shoved into a police car, his hands behind his back, I fall to the ground.

"Oh my God, what did I do? What did I do?" I say as I feel someone lift me off the ground.

"Paige, you're okay. He's going to be okay." Grant picks me off of the ground. "Hads is calling her parents right now."

"This is all my fault," I say as more tears fall. Oliver just took the blame for all of it. He didn't think twice, and it's my fault he's in this position. First, Amelia gets hurt because of me, and now Oliver will have a criminal record because I dragged him into this.

"Paige, were you guys still investigating? Why did this happen?" Grant asks me and I nod.

"What did I do, Grant? This is all my fault," I say as Hads comes over and hugs me.

"Paige, can you tell me what you know? I need to tell my parents something but I have no idea what's going on." She wraps me in her arms, and I cry. I want to cry until I wake up from whatever fucked up nightmare this is.

"I did this, Hads. It's all my fault."

"What are you talking about?"

"Guys, we should go," Grant says, just as I notice a crowd of people has formed around us.

"I can't. Just leave me here. I can't do this." I deserve it. I'm the reason Oliver is in this mess.

"No can do, Paigey. Come here." Grant picks me up fully and throws one of my arms around him so I can lean on him for support. We walk back to my apartment, and they might be talking but I can't hear a word they're saying. All I'm thinking about is Oliver in that fucking police car staring back at me like he just lost me forever.

Maybe he did. Maybe we both lost each other today.
I don't know how I'm going to fix this. Grant opens the door to my apartment and I see Henry and Amelia sitting on the couch.

"What the hell is going on?" Amelia asks. "The dean or whoever the fuck that guy is showed up looking for you Paige—with two police officers."

"Oliver was arrested. Paige almost went with him. Nobody has no clue what's going on," Grant tells them.

"I sent a text. Ella should be here soon," Hads says and I look over and she's crying, too.

"I'm sorry. I'm so sorry," I say to anyone and everyone.

"Paige, stop apologizing. You almost went with him," Grant reminds me. I feel Amelia come over to me and start rubbing circles on my back.

"I thought you two stopped investigating?" Henry asks.

That question makes the room tense. I can feel everyone staring at me because I'm the only one who has the answers, but I can't speak. For some reason, no words will come out.

"Paige, care to explain why my brother took the blame and got you off the hook?" Hads snaps.

"Babe, give her a minute," Grant tells her. "This is a stressful situation for everyone."

"My brother is sitting in a jail cell, so someone needs to explain what the fuck is going on and the only one that can is Paige! So, say something, please." Her voice cracks at the end of her sentence and I feel my body break in half.

I fucked up. I kept secrets and I went about this all wrong and now I have to face the consequences.

"I'm sorry," I say to her, and she looks at me while waiting for an explanation. I don't know how I'm supposed to get words out other than those two. I can't get Oliver's face out of my head. All I see is him being shoved into the back of that police car.

"Paige, if you apologize one more time instead of explaining, I'm going to punch you." She should hit me. She should punch me. I deserve it.

"Go for it, Hads," I say to her.

"Woah! Can we all just take a second—"

"Grant, stop!" Hads snaps at him. "Paige, explain!"

Before it all comes tumbling out, Ella walks in. "What the fuck is going on? Oliver was arrested?" Ella looks at me and her eyes soften. I don't deserve that. I don't deserve anyone feeling bad for me right now.

"That's the word on the street," Henry says.

"Hads and Paige, how are you both?" Ella asks us.

"I'd be better if Paige started speaking," she trips on her words a bit. "And why are you asking her if she's okay? She wasn't arrested!" Hads yells, rightfully so.

Everything she's saying about me is true. I watch Grant go over and try to calm her down, but she swats him away, too.

"Hads, I know you're worried, but he'll be okay," I tell her and she starts to walk toward me but Ella intervenes.

"Take five," she says to Hads.

"No! Paige, tell me!"

I can't stop it from tumbling out. No more hiding. No more lies.

"Oliver and I kept investigating even after we told you all we stopped. Something caught our eye and we agreed to look into it on the down low. Whoever killed the dean has possibly killed two other people, and now we're wrapped up in all this shit and we still don't know for sure who did it. All we know is that it's all connected! The reason that our apartment was trashed was because of me. Amelia got hurt because the person who broke in was trying to scare me away from investigating. It worked, for a few weeks, but then we just kept going, and I'm sorry Hads, I didn't know that this was going to happen. I didn't mean for this to happen. I swear." Tears are still streaming from my eyes and I feel Amelia wiping them off as I sit down on the floor, feeling like my legs have turned to jelly.

"So, if you two had stopped for good after Amelia got hurt, none of this would have happened!" Hads yells at me.

"Hads—" Ella tries to grab her but she walks over to where I am.

"I'm glad you aren't sitting with Oliver right now, but you two were being reckless! Now I have to explain to my parents why all this shit is happening."

"It's all my fault. I'm sorry, Hads. I'm sorry," I tell her. "Tell your parents it's all my fault if you need to."

"Why do you care so much about this anyway? You two were just investigating together! He's my brother Paige. My big brother..." She pauses and looks at me. "My big brother is going to jail because of what you talked him into doing."

"Hads—" Grant shakes his head at her.

"I think we all need to take a second and get our heads together," Ella says to the room.

"Great idea!" Henry says awkwardly.

"I love my brother, but why did he take the blame for you? Huh? Tell me, Paige. Why would he do that?"

"Hads, back up a bit," Amelia tells her and I cry more because this room feels tense. I no longer feel like I deserve these people around me. Maybe my whole purpose in life was to be alone. Everyone would be better off without me.

"I love him, too," I whisper.

"What did you say?" she asks me.

"I love him, Hads," I say, my voice still low.

"W-What? You guys barely..." She looks around the room, but nobody else is saying a word. "None of you are surprised by this? Why am I the only one that's—"

She stops herself when she realizes what their silence means. I've done it. I've ruined everything.

"Oliver and I have been dating since the morning after the break-in," I tell her. "And I–I love him. More than I love myself most days," I say while she stares at me. I can feel my heart sink through my body for the second time today.

"You're lying," Hads says. "And all of you—" She points to the room, her eyes glassy before she lands on Grant. "You knew? And you didn't tell me?"

"Hads, I only figured it out two weeks ago, and it wasn't confirmed until—"

"Oh, only two weeks!" Hads yells at him. "You're all lying. There's no way that my best friends and my own brother kept this from me." She's shaking her head and nobody's saying a word. The only thing I hear is the sounds of Hads and I sniffling.

"I'm sorry," I say to her again, knowing she doesn't care. "I roped everyone into this and I didn't mean for this to happen."

"You didn't mean to keep this from me? It sure seems like it since you could've told me a million times, but chose not to!" she yells back at me. "You had my own boyfriend keeping secrets from me!"

"I'm sorry," I say again, not sure of what else to tell her. "It wasn't just hidden because of you, Oliver and I are terrible at relationships and neither of us wanted to mess it up."

"Well, you failed because you messed up by keeping this hidden. Your apology means nothing to me and I can't look at any of you, right now." She shakes her head and heads for the door.

"I'm going to fix this. I promise," I say, and she stops in her tracks before turning around.

"Paige, I think you've done enough. Just stay out of it. Nothing good can come from you intervening in something you're not supposed to again." She turns back and slams the door to my apartment. Nobody says a word as I collapse into myself on the floor.

"Paige, she just needs to cool off. Give her some time, but I have to go after her," Grant says as he too heads for the front door.

"Go. We'll be okay," Ella tells him and I hear my door open and shut again.

"You guys should leave too," I tell the rest of them. "I deserve to be alone right now."

Amelia leans down. "Why don't we go sit on the couch and settle for a second? Ella, can you get her some water?"

"Just leave me alone. Please. I deserve it," I say as I slump my head into my knees.

"Like I told you freshman year, you're stuck with me." Amelia holds her hand out for me and I take it. "Come on."

"I'm sorry I kept investigating. I'm sorry I put you in danger. I'm sorry you got hurt because of me, and I'm—"

"Paige, I'm not mad at you. Stop apologizing and come sit with me." She grabs my hand and leads me to our couch. Ella brings my water bottle over and hands it to me.

"Why are you guys being so nice to me after what I did?" I ask because I genuinely don't get what's going on here. I fucked up. I deserve to be sitting here alone.

"Because we love you, you're our family and you need us right now," Ella tells me with a smile. "Paige, we're not going to leave you alone because of what happened."

"But I deserve it," I say, feeling more tears fall.

"No, you don't," Henry says to me. I forgot he was here for a second. "You made a mistake, that's all. Hads will forgive you. If I know you girls, I know she'll come around. She just needs a second to wrap her head around it. It's been a hard day for her, too."

"If she doesn't forgive me, I don't blame her. I not only kept a huge secret from her, but I roped you all into it too, and I—"

"Let's not focus on what happened and let's focus on what we're going to do going forward. What's the plan?" Amelia asks me.

"I don't have one," I say to her.

"Come on, Paige. One thing I know about you is that you always have a plan," Henry tells me and I smile for the first time in hours.

"I think I need to clear my head," I tell them. "I'm going to go for a walk."

"Are you sure that's the best course of action right now?" Ella asks me.

"I just need to think, and I can't do it here," I sniffle.

"Okay, but text us where you are so we don't get worried," Amelia tells me.

"I will. I'll be back soon." I get off the couch and grab my tote bag from the floor. I turn around before I leave. "Thank you."

"For what?" Ella asks me.

"For being here for me, even when I don't deserve it."

And then, I walk out of my apartment and head for my favorite spot on campus, hoping to erase the past few hours from my memory.

41

Friday, December 2nd

9:05 PM

"I ALREADY TOLD YOU I'm not saying anything without a lawyer," I say to the two cops in front of me. They're sitting across the table, looking at me like I killed someone. I've been in this interview room for hours, and I'm exhausted. Seeing my sister's face earlier when I was dragged away was horrible, and seeing Paige collapse in tears was the worst thing I've ever seen.

I'll never forget seeing the look on both their faces as I got taken away. I hope Paige is doing alright and my sister is with her. Those two need each other now more than ever, and I hope they can put their heads together and get me out of here.

"Son, you said that you threatened Paige to go along with this. Is that true?" one of them asks me.

"Anything I said to you before you read me my Miranda Rights is inadmissible. Lawyer. Now." I'm still handcuffed to the table, and my wrists are starting to hurt. "And I want my phone call."

"We're aware, son. Just hold tight," they say as they leave the room. I'm starting to think they're holding me in here because they assume I'll confess to killing the dean, but that's not going to happen. Not only did I not kill him, but they didn't arrest me for that.

Fuck this. I need to get out of here, but apparently, they have security footage of the two of us breaking into the offices. We just assumed they weren't watching, and we were reckless.

I didn't plan on taking the blame for this, but I couldn't imagine Paige here. I'm better equipped for this, and one of us needs to figure this out, and between the two of us, she would be the one to solve this. She's always been better at this than I've been.

I close my eyes for a few seconds, feeling the weight of the past few hours on me, but all I see is Paige's face from earlier, and my eyes shoot open.

Fuck.

I should've told her how I felt about her on our first official date. I should've said something. Granted, I didn't know this was going to happen, but I wish she knew. I wish she knew if I had to do it all over again, I would do the exact same thing.

And I wish we were braver and could have loved each other out in the open from the beginning.

I wish.

I can't change any of this now, but I hope I'll get released because the minute I do, I'm telling Paige I love her. I can't wait a second longer without her knowing. It's ripping me in half that I'm not with her right now, and I can't fix any of this. I can't fix it, and it's killing me.

"There's no service here," one of the officers tells me. "You can use that phone to call someone in the hallway," he tells me.

The cuffs leave my wrists and relief hits me. I rub my wrists as I get out of the chair they had me in. I grab the phone he threw on the desk and exit the room. I go down the hallway away from them and punch a number into the phone.

When she picks up, she sniffles. "Hello?"

"Are you okay?"

"Ol?" She sounds shocked. "W-What? H-How?"

"I get one phone call, you know that. Where are you? Is my sister with you?" I ask, hoping that she is.

"No. I'm by myself on the roof. Hads..." She trails off and I can tell something must've happened just by her voice.

"What happened?"

"I ruined everything, Oliver. I fucked up." I can hear her start to cry harder. "I don't know what to do."

"Paige, please don't cry when I'm not there to wipe your tears. It's killing me to hear you like this." I take a deep breath before I speak again. "Please tell me what happened, love."

"Hads was angry at me after I told her we kept investigating and then...I told her." She sniffles again. "I told her about us. She was yelling about how much she loves you and how I didn't deserve to be breaking down how I was, and it slipped out."

Fuck. This is not how either of us wanted her to find out.

"She yelled at everyone for keeping it from her and then left. Grant went after her, but I haven't seen her since. I came up to the roof to think."

"I'm sorry, Paige. I'm so sorry I wasn't there when you told her and I'm sorry you have to deal with this alone. Is there anything I can do?"

"Not much you can do from a holding cell, Ol. It's okay. She probably won't forgive me, and I wouldn't forgive me either." She sniffles and I can hear her breathing quicken across the line.

"P, you need to slow your breathing for me, baby."

"I'm trying, but it's hard when this is all of my fault."

"It's not your fault. We did this together. Hads just needs time to come to terms with it." We should've just told her. Why the fuck didn't we tell her?

"You didn't see the look on her face, Ol. You didn't hear what she said to me. It was all true. No matter how horrible it felt to hear it, she was right. I don't deserve her friendship. Maybe I should just be alone."

"Please don't retreat from me or the girls. You know how much they love you, and you know how much I—" I stop myself because I can't say that over the phone. Not now. No matter how much I want to scream it out loud.

I love you, Paige. I love you more every second, and I can't imagine my life without you.

"I know, Ol," she whispers into the phone.

"Five minutes, Baker!" one of the officers shouts at me.

"Good. So, what are you thinking about?"

"I'm thinking about you," she says like I should have known that. "And what to do about all this. Where to go from here. We failed, Oliver. Why did we think we could do this?"

"I think we have all the pieces. They're just scrambled," I tell her. "I have a gut feeling about this. Look over all the pictures we took, and check the profiles we have on suspects. The answer is in there somewhere. I think our top two suspects could be behind this. Why else would he have us arrested other than to get us out of the way?"

"What if it's not them? What if I can't get you out?" She sniffles more. "I can't do this without you, Ol. We're partners in crime."

"Paige, no matter what happens, I know you can do this. I need you to know that I'm still here, and I'll always be by your side. I'm not going to leave you after this ends, okay?"

"Okay," is all she says.

"Love, you're a lot braver than you think, and I'm proud of you. I'm *so* proud of you, no matter what." I swipe my hand down my face. "I have to go, though. I'll see you soon."

"Oliver, I l—"

"Don't. Not now, please." My voice breaks and I feel my emotions start to take over, but I steady myself. "I'll see you soon."

She almost said it too. And knowing she feels the same way I do about her makes all this shitty stuff worth it.

"Be safe, and don't you dare say a word to the police."

"Understood," I whisper to her. "Don't do anything I wouldn't do. And be careful in whatever plan that beautiful brain of yours conjures up. Tell Hads and my parents that I'm okay."

"Okay. I'll be safe, I promise. See you later, Oliver."

See you later. It's not goodbye. Not forever, at least.

I hang up the phone and walk back to the interview room, knowing I'm not going to say another word.

42

Friday, December 2nd

9:45 PM

I DROP MY PHONE from my hand and feel the tears come even harder. I feel like I lost him. He didn't say goodbye, though, which might be a good sign. I don't know why I thought I could do this. What would Oliver and I have done anyway? Would we have given all of our information to the police? They would ask us how we found all of it out, and the outcome would've been the same.

The only thing that hasn't changed is this being my fault.

Oliver told me we probably have all the pieces to figure this out, but the only thing I want to do is give up.

When is it my turn for life to get easy? When does that happen? Haven't I given enough? When does everything stop hurting all the time? When does the guilt go away? I have all these questions I can't answer because I'm in the same place I always am.

Alone. Sitting on a roof.

The one thing I learned these past few years is that you can't outrun the memories that chase you. You can't change what happened to you. I wish I could—I tried. But I also learned that if everything constantly crumbles around you, it might be time to look in the mirror. Maybe everything was my fault. Maybe things would be okay if I hadn't existed in the first place.

Oliver and the girls deserve better than me, but the least I could do for them is figure this out and get Oliver out of jail—one final thing to make all this right.

I grab my phone and start to scroll through the album that I made with all the pictures I've taken throughout our investigation. The one thing that has stuck with me is that we found a gun in the office safe. I never understood why he would need that, let alone keep it so close to where he sat all day. None of it makes sense.

I switch tabs and type my mom's number in. It rings for a few moments and when I think she's going to pick up, I get her voicemail again.

"Hey, Mom. I don't know why I called. I figured you were too busy to answer but..." I pause, unsure of what to say. "I just feel so lost right now, and for the first time, I don't know where to go. I wanted to call you to see if you had some advice, but I should've known better. I don't know what to do." I stop and take a deep breath.

"I wish you cared about me, and I wish you'd pick up once and apologize for forgetting about me. I think you're my ghost, Mom. Did you ever want me? I guess it doesn't matter anymore." I drop the phone down from my ear and take a breath. "I think I'm going to stop calling for a while. I love you, even though you never watched me grow up, even though you—" The call drops on me.

I needed her to know that, even if it's the last thing she gets from me. In my mind, I'll always feel like that young girl afraid of her shadow, having to pick herself back up when she falls.

Where did she go? If she saw me right now, would she be proud of me? I don't think so.

Do the past versions of ourselves live inside us or do they watch from a distance, silently cheering you on?

Paige, no matter what happens, I know you can do this.

Oliver said that to me earlier and I don't believe him. I know he said he would never leave me, but part of me knows it might happen. He might be forced to choose between his sister and me. If I were him, I'd choose Hads. If I had a sibling, I'd do the same thing.

But Oliver feels like home to me. He feels like warmth and love, and he's one of the only people who truly understands me. Can you feel homesick for a home you barely had? Can home be a person?

But if he thinks I can do this, then I can.

I take another breath and flip through my photos again, and as my eyes start to become fuzzy, one of them catches my eye. I swipe back to it and zoom in. It was from the night we searched the office for the second time.

It's a picture hanging up on the wall behind his desk. I never looked too closely at it before because it was just him on some fishing trip with three of his friends.

But three of those four people are now dead.

My mouth drops open when I realize the connection. All the deaths that Oliver and I were looking into are connected, and this proves it. They all knew each other. They were all friends.

But why does someone want them all dead?

I recognize the only one alive as the current District Attorney—the one Oliver and I worked under for our internships last year. Fuck, is he next?

I wipe my tears away with my sweatshirt before I grab my tote bag and practically sprint down the stairs and to my car. As soon as I get in, I punch in the directions for his office, and start driving.

I need to warn him he's in danger, or his death will be on me, too.

But why would he listen to me? And what if he's not in danger? *What if I'm wrong?*

I hope I'm right because if I'm not, I don't know how else I can fix this. With all of the shit I messed up lately, I hope I can finally do some good for someone.

10:15 PM

I SLIDE INTO A parking spot outside the office, and my phone buzzes before I can jump out of my car.

Amelia: Paige, where are you? Are you okay?

Ella: We're worried about you. It's been a few hours and you haven't come back.

Paige: *Location Sharing On*

Paige: Following a hunch. I'll be back soon.

Ella: What?

Amelia: Maybe you should come back. It's been a long day.

Paige: I have to do this. I have to make this right. It's all on me. I should be back in an hour, this won't take long.

Ella: Paige, this isn't all on you. Just come back.

Amelia: Be careful. Please.

Ella: Paige Yarrow... this is definitely danger-ous. Come back, please.

I put my phone on mute and shove it into my bag.

As I hurry across the street, I notice the receptionist I used to talk to every day is packing up to leave. I yank open the door and calmly walk up to her. I shouldn't be trying to cause a panic right now, so I try to even my breathing out before I speak.

"Hello, Barbara. Do you remember me? I interned here about a year ago. I used to bring you coffee sometimes." I smile. "I have an emergent situation I need to speak to the District Attorney about. Is he still here?"

"Paige, right? I don't think I could ever forget someone with such a sunny disposition! Yes, he's still in his office. Do you want me to tell him you'll be coming up?" She picks up the phone and I hold my hand out to her.

"No, no. That's alright. It will just be a quick chat. Thank you!" I say as I head for the elevators. I didn't think it would be that easy, but the simple act of being nice to people can go a long way. It's good that she has a better memory than I do, or I might've had to start crying to get her to let me up.

The last time I was in an elevator, I was with Oliver. We were just friends at that point, and it feels like a lifetime ago. All the things we've been through together in the span of such a short time is hard for me to wrap my head around.

I hope he's okay. I hope he knows I'm going to make this right.

I hope I get to tell him that I love him. Even if he already knows, I need him to hear me say it.

The elevator dings and I spot him immediately, sitting at his desk with piles of folders all around him. His office is bigger than I remembered, but I was only up here a few times during my internship.

"Mr. Khan? I need to speak with you. It's urgent," I say as he looks up at me, confused. I can spot when the recognition hits his mind, and I'm scared he's going to just throw me out of his office.

"Miss Yarrow, how did you get up here? It's after hours. I'm calling security." He reaches for his phone.

"Barbara let me up, but please, I need to talk to you. All I need is five minutes."

He thinks about it for far too long, and as soon as I think he's going to say no, he agrees. "Fine. Have a seat."

"I'm good standing, but thank you." I'm afraid if I sit down, I'll never get back up. I just need to start talking. "I think you're in danger."

He scoffs at me. "I'm a District Attorney. If I'm not being threatened, I'm not doing my job right."

"I know, but this time, you're in actual danger. Three of your friends have been killed in the last three months, and I think you're the last one on the list. Look," I say to him as I pull my phone out and swipe to the picture from the dean's office. "This picture is hanging up in your old friend Erik's office. Notice anything?"

He furrows his brows, not understanding what I'm saying.

"You're the only one alive still. I think someone has a grudge against you four, though I'm not sure why, but I was hoping you could tell me."

He's looking at my phone before he shakes his head. "Sweetheart, two of my friends died in a similar manner, that is true, but the other committed suicide. I think you're looking too much into this. Go home." He shoos me away with his hand and I don't move.

"Sir, don't you think it's odd that they all died within such a short time? That's not a coincidence. I need you to listen to me when I say that I'm fairly certain you could be next."

"I'm not going to turn this office upside down based on one person's assumption..."

"Can you please just—"

He cuts me off. "Miss Yarrow, you seem like a bright girl, but I'm perfectly capable of handling myself."

"I understand that, sir, but this evidence is credible! Do you have any idea who would have it out for you all? I know I sound crazy right now, but I promise that you should at least let the police know about this."

"I'm sorry, Paige. I am, but your five minutes are up. I'm going to have to ask you to leave my office."

"Sir, I think you should reconsider—" I see his face twist, and then I feel something cold against the back of my head.

"You should've listened to her when you had the chance, Khan." I hear the safety of a gun being clicked off. "The girl is a lot smarter than I gave her credit for."

I'm frozen where I stand. I feel the cold end of a gun against my head. I don't know who's holding it, but knowing it could go off at any moment is freezing me in place.

Leave it to me to figure this out the same night the killer planned to be here. Just my fucking luck.

The person behind me pushes the gun into my head, and I know for sure I'm probably going to die tonight.

I'm never going to see the girls again. I'm never going to tell Oliver I love him and I'm never going to know if Hads will forgive me. My mom isn't going to see me ever again, and my father will never know that he outlived me.

Of all the ways I thought I'd die, old age, at my father's hand, or my own, I never thought it would be like this. I never thought I would be filled with regret.

I feel a searing pain in my head. The last thing I hear before I fade into darkness is a gunshot.

43

Friday, December 2nd

11:15 PM

I'm sitting in the holding cell at Grand Mountain's police station when I hear a radio go off about shots fired at the District Attorney's office. A bunch of officers get up from their desks, and the one stationed to watch me gets up, too. *What the fuck is going on?*

"Don't move," he says as he walks away. "Someone get a rookie up here to watch Baker!" he yells to someone else.

As if I could leave. That's hilarious. I slump back down on the floor and do my best not to think about what's happening or where I am.

44

Friday, December 2nd

10:40 PM

I feel cold.

My vision slowly starts to come back as I orient myself. *Where am I? What's that smell?*

I see a figure moving before me, and everything returns to my mind. Did I get shot?

I look down and I don't see any blood coming from my body. I don't feel injured besides the pounding in my head. I recognize all the signs of a concussion since I've had a few before. I take a few breaths to steady myself before I feel what I'm assuming is blood trickle down my neck.

I look around and try to get up when I'm forced back down, feeling something around my hands. I look behind me and realize that I'm tied to one of the chairs with what feels like the tie the district attorney was wearing. When his name pops into my head, I look around and see him slumped against the chair he was sitting in, blood pouring out of his shoulder.

That solves the mystery of the gunshot.

"Is he alive?" I ask the room, unsure if the other person is still in here with us.

"For now. I can't say the same will be true for you after tonight, Paige."

I know that voice. Why do I know that voice? The person comes into my field of view and sits on top of the desk.

"Penelope?" *I freaking knew it!*

"I told you to stay away, Paige. Do you ever listen?" she asks, waving her gun around as if it's not a lethal weapon.

"I knew it." I shake my head. "I knew you had something to do with this."

"You and Oliver were one variable I didn't see coming. I thought you two finding the body would leave you away from all this. I guess it had the opposite effect, and now you're in the middle of all this."

"You knew what I was walking into that day? Why did you—" She points the gun at me and I freeze.

"Now, Paige. You're asking the wrong person these questions. See, I'm not the bad guy here." She turns around and points the gun at him again. "He is."

"What did they do to you? Why are you doing this?" I scream at her. I can feel the adrenaline pumping through my body. I'm on the verge of a panic attack.

"Let me tell you a story, Paige," she says as she comes over to where I'm tied up. "As a parent, you send your child off to school and you expect the adults in charge to take care of them. To protect them. I'm sure your parents expect the ones at Grand Mountain to keep you safe while you live here, right?"

I don't answer her rhetorical question and she continues speaking.

"The last time I saw my son alive was Valentine's Day in 2018. He was dressed in his pink shirt, all excited to go to school and exchange valentines with his friends. He was in fifth grade. Brightest smile you could ever see on a kid. I hugged him goodbye, watched him get on his bus, and off he went. A few hours later, I got a notification from the district saying an active shooter was opening fire on their school. They directed us to a hospital where some of the kids were being taken, so I dropped everything and rushed there." She takes a deep breath. "Only to get there and find out he was one of the victims. My son was dead."

She gets up and has to brace herself against the desk—her gun still in her right hand.

"I can't imagine going through that." Tears are clouding my eyes because it's horrible that this is a reality for people. Nobody should ever be afraid to send their kids to school. No kids should be afraid of not coming back home when they go to school.

"I had a hard time dealing with my grief the first year. Then came the news that school officials were the first ones out of the building and didn't do anything to stop what was going on. The principal hid in a closet until it was over, and some of the cops didn't enter the building when they were told to, and it all got covered up. Their negligence was sealed from everything. By him." She points her gun at the DA. "Until one cop came forward about it a year and a half later."

A cop? "The one that committed suicide a few months ago?" The pieces are falling into place, little by little.

"Not a suicide, technically. I forced him to do it, telling him that this would be better than his family finding him with his throat cut open from ear to ear."

I flinch at the words she's saying. I need to tread very carefully with what I say going forward.

"The former dean was the principal of my son's school. The one who hid like a coward while someone rained bullets all over the school. The police commissioner was the one to hold the cops back until they were sure the shots were over. If they had gone in immediately like they were supposed to, my son would still be here. He was in one of the last classrooms the shooter entered."

"Why kill that cop if he was the one who came forward and told the truth?" I ask, tears falling from my eyes, but I don't know who I'm crying for.

"He was still negligent. He held onto that information for too long." She pushes her shoulders back, trying to stand tall. "I did what needed to be done."

"None of this needed to happen. Nothing you've done will change anything." In one quick movement, her gun is now underneath my chin.

"I could permanently shut you up right now, but I'd rather tell you my story before I do." I know she would pull the trigger. I can tell just from her eyes. She's still in so much pain, and I can't even begin to imagine what her pain feels like. I can't imagine how hard it's been for her to carry it all these years.

"Since they couldn't prosecute the shooter—he had killed himself before the cops could—they all moved on. Unfortunately for him, I didn't forget," she says, nudging him with her gun. He stirs awake and I exhale a breath of relief, knowing that he's still alive. This whole situation is fucked up and I find myself feeling bad for her, even though she went about this all wrong.

"None of this will—"

She cuts me off as she cocks the gun against his head. "You did this."

"I'm sorry," I hear him choke out. "I had to."

"Not good enough. You covered up all this shit, and while all of you got promotions, the families of the victims were left with nothing!" she yells and I flinch. "We had to grieve and all you had to do to stop that was your job! You should have reprimanded them, not promoted them. Did you think nobody would find out about what you did? I had to get a job at the college the dean got transferred to. I had to find out where the four of you went. I hope you used this extra time, because the clock is ticking. My son's redemption is almost here," she tells him, and then she shifts her head over to me. "I'm sorry, Paige. I never meant for you or your roommate to be collateral damage. I just needed you to get off my back. You're a smart girl."

"You were the one who broke into my apartment? You didn't have to hurt Amelia. You could have just trashed it and left!" I yell at her. She can hurt me all she wants, but I draw the line at hurting my friends.

"I needed to make a statement. I needed you and Oliver to back off. It worked, didn't it?" She smiles at me again and a chill runs through my body.

I have no idea how I'm going to get out of this alive.

"It worked for a short time, but doing this is not going to bring back your son. This was not the way," I say to her while more tears fall. "You don't solve violence and pain with more violence. It doesn't work that way. Pain does not erase pain. I promise you that."

"You don't know what I went through! You don't know what they did to my family!" she yells and I see her move toward me in one swift motion and then darkness consumes me again.

11:00 PM

I WAKE UP COLD again. I don't know how long I was out this time, but now I definitely have a concussion. I know that for sure because Penelope has doubled.

"I'm sorry. I'm sorry, you're right. I don't know but please don't hurt me again." When my eyes return to focus, I notice a different gun pointed in my face.

"Oh, Paige. I'm sorry, but I can't promise we won't hurt you," a voice says.

We?

"W-What?" I breathe out, and the second face comes into focus.

Penelope didn't duplicate. There are two *separate* people in front of me.

Because the other face staring back at me is Professor Craig.

"No. It can't be you."

"Sorry to disappoint you, but we're doing what we have to, Paige." Gone is the professor who used to chaperone the criminal justice club with such sweetness. In her place is someone I don't recognize.

"She's just a kid, but she knows who we are now. We're going to have to take care of this," Penelope says to my old professor.

"If you kill me, Oliver will never stop trying to put you where you belong. Prison—for the rest of your lives."

"Oh, honey. We took care of that already." Penelope smiles at me.

"You what?"

"How do you think the acting dean found out about your little side project? An anonymous source must've slid some security footage to him or something..." Penelope laughs as she swings her gun around the room. "I just figured getting you both out of our way would be easiest, but apparently Oliver chose to go down for you. How noble of him."

We got ambushed. They knew we were investigating again, and they tried to get us out of the picture because they thought we would hinder their plan.

Turns out it was just me who was stupid enough to get caught in a hostage situation. I'm glad Oliver isn't here, though. I couldn't handle seeing him hurt or tied to a chair.

"So, how do you know each other?" I say while my head pounds. I hope I don't pass out again. I'm trying my best to stay awake, but it's difficult.

"We met at a support group for parents who lost their children to school shootings. We got to talking and realized we wanted the same things. So together, the two of us created this plan, and now here we are four years later. It's almost complete." Professor Craig smiles at her partner.

"One thing I don't understand is why you kept switching how you killed them? Was it to throw the police off so they didn't connect all of them? Or did you both have different methods?"

"I knew I taught you well, Paige." My old professor smiles at me. *Is she proud of me?*

"We each traded off. I killed the dean because I was right outside his office all day, it was almost too easy. The police commissioner was me too. I was proud of that one." Penelope smiles proudly at herself.

"Who did you lose?" I look to my old professor.

"My two daughters. They were in third grade."

"Both of them?" I ask and she nods. I feel my gut lurch, and one of them brings over a trash can for me to throw up in.

These two care so much about their children that they would go to extremes to get even with the people who caused them pain. Meanwhile, my own mother doesn't even notice me when I'm standing right in front of her. *What a strange dichotomy I've found myself in.*

"So many lives were lost that day because of careless actions by the people who were supposed to protect our children. So now, a life for a life." Penelope cocks her gun and points it at West, and I summon all my strength to speak. " It's the only way."

"Don't!" I pant. "This isn't the way. You can stop. You can leave right now, and nobody will know. Don't let what they did four years ago ruin the rest of your lives. Please just let us go, and leave. I won't say anything, I swear! I know you've felt enough pain. You deserve to heal from this and not let it take up your entire life. I can't imagine losing someone the way you both have but—" I pause for a moment. "I know what it's like to want revenge on someone who hurt you. I get it—the feeling of wanting them to hurt as much as they hurt you. But that's not how the world works. You have to be better than them. You have to—"

Penelope cocks her gun at the District Attorney while my old professor cocks hers at me.

"I'm sorry it had to end this way, Paige. I don't want to do this, but it has to be done."

This is it for me. This is the end of my story. It doesn't end with a happy ever after, and why should it? My whole life has been unfinished.

At this moment, I realize I'll never feel Oliver's embrace again. I'll never look into those eyes and feel like I can take on the world with him.

I feel my necklace against my skin and remember my girls. I'll never sit on the floor in my apartment with Amelia and debrief our days again. I'll never have deep talks with Ella about life. I'll never annotate books with Hads. I'll never go to book club again.

All these things that make me who I am will vanish when I leave this earth. I'll never tell any of them that I love them. Grant will never call me my nickname again. I'll never see my mom or my dad again. I'll never tell them how much I love them even though they treated me how they did. They'll never know that the only person that's half of each of them is gone. Tears are streaming down my face as I stare down the barrel of this gun.

Why couldn't I have just let this go?

I tried to be brave, and it's going to get me killed. It's this moment when I finally know who I am.

I'm Paige Yarrow—the girl who always tries but never succeeds. Soon, I won't even be Paige. I'll just be a memory to the people that loved me the most. Soon, all I'll be is a story. Soon, my life will become a period, indicating the end of the short sentence that my life has been. I close my eyes and take a deep breath while I wait for the shot to go off, thinking about all my favorite memories with my friends.

I hear a bang, but I don't feel anything.

"Grand Mountain Police! Don't move!" I open my eyes and as I do, two shots go off and I flinch where I sit. I feel some blood splatter on my face as I hear two bodies slump to the floor. In front of me, my old professor and mentor is on the floor with a hole through her head, blood leaking out of it. She's all I can see. I sit with my mouth wide open and my body shivering as light comes in front of my face.

"Are you okay?"

No.

"What's your name?"

Paige. My name is still Paige.

"Any injuries?" Two separate voices are speaking to me, but they both sound far away. I keep my eyes on the body in front of me, unable to look away. Tears are still leaking from my eyes as I feel one of them wrap me in a blanket as they untie me.

"Is he alive?" I whisper to one of them.

"He's in critical condition, but he should be alright. He's going to the hospital, same as you." They help me off the floor, and suddenly, I'm in the elevator going down to where I assume an ambulance is. I don't know how I get anywhere because all I can see is the hole on my old professor's face.

I'm assuming Penelope was shot too, since I heard two shots fired. I can't help but feel for them. They just wanted their kids to be safe and protected, and they were failed by the people around them. I hope wherever they are, they've reunited with their kids again. I hope they're okay.

But another part of me wants to scream. Because they might've thought they were doing the right thing, but I'll never forget what I saw tonight. By taking matters into their own hands, they changed my life forever.

I'm guided out of the building and toward an ambulance, seeing nothing but red and blue lights flashing around me. It makes my head hurt, and the questions they keep asking me aren't helping my headache either.

A few minutes later, I think I'm hallucinating or something because I hear someone shouting my name, so I stand up and look around, unsure of where it's coming from.

"Honey, I'm going to need you to sit back down. We have to go," she tells me, but I don't listen as I follow the shouts to the edge of the police line that's up.

A few people are standing around, curious about what's going on, and lots of cop cars are here. I scan the crowd until my eyes land on a familiar set of heads. I see Ella yelling at an officer to let her through.

"We were the ones who called you all here! So technically, you're here because of me! The least you can do is let us find our friend!" She's pointing her finger in his face, and I laugh. It's such an Ella thing to do. "Can I speak to whoever's in charge? I need to tell them about your incompetence!"

I laugh at that, my head still pounding before Amelia's eyes meet mine. She pokes Ella and she whips her head around to face Amelia.

"Why are you poking me with your bony elbow?" Amelia's pointing at me and I smile wide when I see Ella lock eyes with me. Hads and Grant turn in my direction, and I even see Henry poke out from behind, dropping his phone from his ear. I feel more tears fall from my eyes because they're here. They came to find me. I force my legs to move, and soon enough, I'm jogging in their direction and when I reach them they pull me into a hug.

My girls.

"What are you guys doing here?" I ask them, not letting go.

"We got worried when you texted us your location and saw that you were here. We figured you wouldn't come here this late if it weren't for a good reason," Ella tells me. "Plus, your texts were shady as hell, girl."

"We called the police after half an hour because we were worried something happened. I know you said an hour, but we were too nervous. I know from the documentaries you made us watch that it's better to call them sooner rather than later," Amelia says, and I pull back to look at her.

"I *knew* those would come in handy!" I pull them all in for a hug again. "I'm so glad you guys are here."

"Including me?" Hads asks me, and I pull away from Amelia and Ella and hug her tighter.

"Especially you." Tears fall from my face again. "I'm so sorry, Hads. For everything."

"I'm still mad at you, but I'm tabling my anger for now. I'm just glad you're okay, P," she tells me, her voice breaking at the end.

"Paigey! Thank God you're alright my little investigator!" Grant yanks me into a hug.

"I missed you too, G." I smile into his shirt, and when I pull away, Amelia grabs me again.

"Don't you ever do any of this again, Paige. I thought you were— I was scared that you—" I feel her tremble in my arms, which makes me start to cry again.

"I'm okay, Ames. Except for the bumps on my head from where I got knocked out."

"You were knocked out?" Ella yells at me, and I wince. "Sorry, head injury, my bad. Who did this, and where can I find them?"

"They're dead," I say, trying not to think about what I saw in that room.

"They?" Henry asks me.

"Professor Craig and the dean's old receptionist. It was them. They did all this."

"I didn't see that coming," Grant tells me.

"Me neither," I sigh. "I'm sorry that I worried you guys, but I'm so glad you're here because I never thought I would see your beautiful faces again. I love you." I pull them in for another hug.

"Paige, if I hear you apologize one more time, I might slap you," Ella tells me, and I laugh, feeling a bit off balance as I do.

"Are you okay, P?" someone asks me.

"Yeah, no, I'm fine. I think the adrenaline is wearing off." But the world around me is getting fuzzy, and my vision blurs. Next thing I know, I'm falling to the ground, and I hear my friends yelling for help as the world turns to darkness.

45

Saturday, December 3rd

6:00 AM

"WE'RE GOING TO HAVE to take care of this," Penelope says.

"I never hurt you. I'm taking care of you! Why are you so ungrateful?" my father says.

"I'm sorry. I'm sorry. I'm sorry," I plead to the figures in front of me.

"I'm sorry it had to end this way," my old professor says.

I don't want to die, please. I don't want to die. I have people I need to see again, people I need to love. The gun cocks and she pulls the trigger and—

I wake up in an unfamiliar place. It's dark and I feel like my lungs will give out at any moment. As I try to catch my breath, I see someone in front of me.

"Take this, honey. It's a nasal cannula. It'll help you breathe better." A nurse. She's wearing scrubs. I must be in the hospital. *How did I get here?* "You collapsed from exhaustion and your head injury at the scene. No internal injuries, just the head wound. We're observing you for now, just to make sure you're alright, so sit back and relax."

She hooks the tubes over my ears and under my chin. A few minutes later, I can feel my breathing return to normal. My head hurts a bit less than before, and I lift my hand and feel a few stitches.

"Where are my friends?" I ask. I'm all alone in this hospital room, and I don't know how I'm going to pay for this. I have some money saved up, but I know it's not enough.

"We called your emergency contact, but I'm afraid we didn't get an answer. Some people were arguing with the nurses in the waiting room. They were asking for you, but only family's allowed back here, and none of them had proper identification."

My emergency contact—my mom. Of course she didn't answer. Her daughter's in the hospital, and she couldn't even pick up the phone. I feel a few tears fall from my eyes, and all I want are my friends. And Oliver. But he's probably still sitting in a holding cell. "They're family in every way that matters. Can you send them back here, please?"

"I'll see what I can do." She smiles before leaving. When I'm alone, I take a deep breath and try to center myself.

I could've died. I almost died.

I'm definitely still in shock. It hasn't hit me yet how big the situation was. I feel my chest ache with pain as I pull my feet up, curl into a ball, and cry.

I'm so tired. I'm *so* tired.

I told my mom I wasn't going to contact her for a while, but knowing the situation I was in, I figured she would drive all night to get to me. Or hop on a flight.

But I overestimated her like I always do. In a way, it feels peaceful knowing someone doesn't care about you. I know it'll be tough going forward, but I'd rather know this now than keep getting disappointed in the future.

Sometimes, people who become parents aren't meant to be parents. I've always forgiven them for acting how they did, but I can't keep making excuses for their behavior. I remember as a kid crying like this most nights—alone and quietly. I'm just so fucking tired of feeling like a burden.

"Paige?" Amelia's voice is the one I hear first.

"Oh, babe," Ella says.

I feel my bed sink down with the weight of my favorite people as I untangle myself from my position. Amelia, Hads, and Ella are all sitting on my bed with me, while Grant stands at the foot of it.

"I'm sorry, I'm just getting it all out, I think." Amelia wipes some tears from my face like she always does. "How long have you all been here?"

"The girls tried to ride in the ambulance with you. They couldn't, so we followed it here. It's been a few hours," Grant tells me with a yawn.

"We would've been in here when you woke up, but the fucking nurses wouldn't let us back here!" Ella says, and I feel Amelia lying down next to me. She wraps one arm around me and I lean into her embrace.

"You guys waited here all night for me?" I ask them.

"Of course we did," Hads says.

"Except Henry. He left fifteen minutes ago after he took a phone call," Grant tells me and I look at Amelia.

"Nothing to worry about, I promise."

"I didn't mean for you guys to see me like this." My wrists are bruised from how tight they tied me to the chair, and my head is all stitched up.

I look at my clothes on the end of my bed and they have blood all over them. Some of it probably isn't even mine.

"Like what, Paige? Strong? Fearless? Resilient? Because that's all I see." Ella grabs my hand and squeezes it.

"Does anyone know if the District Attorney is okay?" The room gets quiet all of a sudden, and my stomach drops.

"I think he's alive. People have been shuffling in and out all night, but last we heard, he was okay. The only thing that matters to us is that you're awake now," Ella tells me. "Are you okay? Do you need any food or water? Grant go get her some chips or something."

"I'm on it," he says, jumping into action.

As Grant leaves, I feel the tension start to sit on my chest of all the unspoken things between Hads and me. "Hads, I—"

"Paige, stop. None of that matters right now." She smiles at me as a few of her tears fall. "I'm just glad you're okay. "

"If you guys don't stop crying, then I'm going to cry again," Ella says, clearly already crying. I look up at Amelia's face and see a few tears fall down her face.

"Paige, we were so scared when we got to the scene and we heard someone say two people were shot. We thought—" Hads tells me.

"We all thought you were—" Amelia pauses. Nobody's able to finish that sentence.

"I thought so too," I whisper. "I thought last night was it for me."

"Paige, all of us are so glad you're okay. But you are not allowed to do that ever again. None of us could survive without you here." Ella tries to sound stern, but through her tears, it sounds like blabbering.

"No more investigating active murder cases. Got it." I laugh and cry at the same time, and my statement causes all the girls to laugh. All four of us lean in and group hug. We're all still crying and I'm grateful to be living this moment, wrapped in the arms of my best friends.

My family. The people who always show up for me, no matter what. They may not be related to me by blood, but our bond has nothing on that.

I used to think that family was just who you were related to, but now I know it's the ones who show up, see you at your worst, and love you for it anyway. The ones who sit in a waiting room all night and wait for you to wake up.

"I love you guys so much," I whisper to them.

"Am I interrupting?" Grant asks as he comes back in.

"No, it's okay." I laugh as he throws a bag of chips at me. "Thanks."

"The least I could do for you, Paigey." He ruffles my hair a bit and I wince.

"Grant, she has a head injury!" Hads smacks him and I laugh.

"I'm okay. It just hurts a little."

"Fuck, I'm sorry. It's been a weird few days." Grant wipes a hand down his face.

I open the bag and for the next fifteen minutes, we talk about normal and mundane things. It helps me get my mind off of everything, but I make a mental note to call my therapist in a few days. I have lots to discuss with her, and I want to start moving forward, not backward.

"Does anyone know if Oliver's okay?" I ask the room and everyone shakes their heads. It's the first question I had, but I was nervous about saying anything in front of Hads. I know she's still mad at me, but I need to know.

I don't know if they'll drop the charges because we tampered with a crime scene. I just thought if I was able to fix this, it would magically solve everything, but nothing is ever that simple.

The sneaking around was fun while it lasted, but I should never have been afraid to love Oliver out in the open. I should've never lied to Hads about it.

"Knock, knock," I hear Henry's voice say and just as I look up, a familiar figure comes racing into the room. I see those same brown eyes that I've memorized looking back at me. "Can we come in?" Henry asks, but all I see is Oliver.

He's here.

He's real.

He's okay.

"Yeah, sure, come on—" Grant speaks but stops when Oliver enters the room. He comes right toward me and pulls me into his arms when he reaches my bed. I wrap my arms around him.

"You're okay," he whispers to me. "Oh my God, you're okay."

"I'm okay," I say as tears cloud my vision.

"I'm going to go ask the nurses a question," Ella says while leaving the room.

"Us too!" Grant says. "Come on, Hades. Give them a minute."

"I'm glad you're okay, Ol," says Hads. Oliver throws a nod in her direction.

"Hen and I are going to get some snacks," Amelia says, and I can hear her grab his hand and rush out of the room.

Neither of us moves for a few minutes. We just sit and exist.

"You're here," I whisper.

"I'm here, love. I'm here."

Oliver

5:30 AM

I'M HALF ASLEEP IN my cell when an officer bangs on the rods and wakes me up. "What?"

"You're free to go," he tells me while opening the door.

What? "Why?"

"All charges against you have been dropped, per the District Attorney's office." He hands me my phone. "Call someone to come pick you up."

I'm not going to say no to that, but part of me is confused how the District Attorney was able to drop the charges since I heard there were shots fired at his office a few hours ago.

I click Paige's contact, and the line rings and rings until I get her voicemail. Who the fuck else can I call?

Hads? Nope, pissed at me.

Grant? No, he might be mad at me by proxy.

Amelia? Nope, I'm too pissed off for jokes.

Henry? Oh, that's not a bad idea.

I have this weird feeling in the pit of my stomach as if something bad has happened. I need someone to tell me that everything is fine, or I might punch a wall.

"Hello?" I hear Henry say.

"Thank God, where are you? Can you come pick me up? I'm at the station."

"Hold on," he says, and I hear him whisper to someone, and a few seconds later, he speaks. "They let you go?"

"Yeah, all charges were dropped. Can you get me? Don't make me ask your fucking girlfriend, or I'll never hear the end of it."

"I'm at the hospital," he tells me.

"What? Why?" I ask him, my heartbeat suddenly picking up. Did something happen to Paige? I shove the sinking feeling down in my stomach. "Hayes, you better start fucking talking or I swear to God I'll do something to get me charged this time."

"I'm on my way. Sit tight." *Is this guy fucking serious?*

"Henry, just tell me what the fuck is going—" He hung up on me. He fucking hung up on me. I clench my phone in my hands, and my heart starts racing even more. Not only am I worried about whatever the fuck is going on, but I haven't gone into a hospital since Mia.

Is Paige okay?

Is my sister alright?

Is Paige alive?

She could be dead right now. What if she was at the DA's office? She could be dead on the scene right now. Was she shot? Is that what I heard on the radio?

Am I going to get to the hospital and find out that everything was taken from me again? I can't lose anyone else like this. I can't.

Fuck. My thoughts are racing. Why couldn't he tell me over the phone? I fucking hate this. I hate everything about this situation. I get out of the station and sit on one of the benches outside the building. It feels like hours until I see Henry's white car pull up.

"Please tell me Paige is okay because you hung up on me before explaining, and I'm a few seconds away from stealing your car and leaving you here."

"Hello to you, too. It must have been a long night. Do you want me to change the music, or is it okay?"

"Henry, I swear to—"

"She's okay, I think. They wouldn't let us see her since we aren't family. I don't even know if she's awake. When I left, Ella was yelling at a few nurses."

"Start fucking driving," I tell him, and he does. "What happened?"

"I don't know, exactly. Ella, Mills, and I were at the apartment, and Paige sent her location to the girls. She was at an office downtown. She said she had to do something and if she didn't respond in an hour to call the police." He pauses. "They only waited half an hour because they were nervous. Thankfully they did because the cops got there in time. I saw Paige before she collapsed. She said she got knocked out—"

"She collapsed? Where? Is she okay? Was she bleeding? Fuck, can you drive any faster?"

"I'm going fifteen over already, so, no. She collapsed and was taken to the hospital in an ambulance. The nurses said something about keeping her on concussion watch, and I think she got a few stitches, but I don't know for sure." Henry looks over at me while he drives. "She's alive, Oliver. Don't worry."

"I'm always going to worry about her."

"I know," he tells me.

"Is my sister there?" I ask him and he nods. I have to have some tough conversations with her at some point, but I hope for Paige's sake she's with her.

I promised my sister I'd be more open and honest with her, and then I lied to her for an entire month. She didn't even hear about it from me. She had to hear it after she saw me get arrested. The past day has been a complete shitshow, but first on my list is telling my girl that I love her.

My breathing starts to pick up, and I try to shove all the emotions I'm feeling down. The anxiety of returning to a hospital for the first time in five years, the guilt of lying to my sister, and the worry that Paige isn't awake or breathing when I finally get to her.

I can't do this again. I can't lose her. I won't survive losing someone like this again.

A few minutes later, Henry pulls into a parking spot and parks his car. I whip open the door and run to the entrance. I freeze when I reach the double doors.

"Fuck." I feel him stand next to me.

"Are you okay?"

I nod. "I just need a second."

"Not a big fan of hospitals, I take it?"

"No," I tell him.

"Me neither. My dad got in a car accident a while back—the freakiest thing. A drunk driver hit him. It scared me to see my hero in that room, this person I loved so deeply, so fragile. It shaped me, I think, as a person from that point on." He pauses for a second, and I look over at him.

"My last girlfriend was killed in a drunk driving accident. The last time I was at a hospital was when I found out," I tell him, and I don't know why I'm sharing this right now, but it feels good to open up to somebody who understands.

"I'm sorry. That sounds awful."

"It was." I take a breath. "I'm sorry about your dad."

"It's alright. He's okay now. I don't want to negate anything you're feeling, but the girl you're in love with is up there right now." He pats my shoulder. "I know you can do this, Oliver. Not even to prove to yourself that you can, but to prove it to her. That girl upstairs believes in you, and what would she tell you to do?"

I smile at him. "She would tell me to climb."

"So, climb then. I'm right behind you, buddy." He smiles at me when he says that. I like this kid. I really do.

That's all it takes for me to start running into the building. I feel Henry on my tail as we climb the stairs, but I don't see any of our friends when I get to the waiting room.

"Paige Yarrow's room, please." Henry smiles at the desk.

"Are you family?" the nurse asks us.

"No, but our friends are with her right now." Henry pauses. "They just texted me they were in her room and to come straight away."

She looks at us, skeptically, and I'm going to be so pissed if she doesn't let us through. "353, down the hall, should be straight ahead."

I don't hear anything besides the number, but I feel Henry stop me before I go in. "Take a breath, dude. I'll go in first."

"Go." He turns around and knocks on the door.

"Knock, knock," he says, and I walk in behind him, immediately locking eyes with Paige. She's wearing a hospital gown, and I can tell from her eyes that she's in pain but trying to hide it. Someone says something, but I don't know what because all I can focus on is that she's right in front of me. I walk over to her and immediately wrap her in my arms as if nobody else is around.

"You're okay," I whisper to her. "Oh my God, you're okay."

"I'm okay," she whispers back to me, her voice strained. She probably has tears in her eyes, and I feel a few fall from my eyes too. I've never felt so relieved in my life.

Our friends mumble some excuses to leave, but I tune them out because I only want to focus on this girl in my arms.

"You're here," she whispers to me.

"I'm here, love. I'm here." I pull back from her, not fully letting go yet. "Are you okay?" I run my hands all over her face and search her features for discomfort or pain. Externally she looks alright, but internally could be a different story.

"I'm okay. I just can't believe you're really here, and I have so much to tell you about the past day. You're not going to believe it. It feels like a dream at this point—" I cut her off with a kiss, and she sighs into my mouth as if she thought she'd never touch me again. As if she didn't believe I was here. I pull away from her and begin to speak, saying every word I've wanted to say for the past few weeks.

46

Saturday, December 3rd

6:15 AM

"Paige, I love you." I'm looking right at her, and as soon as I say that, her eyes start to water. "I fucking love you so much. I never thought I was going to be able to love someone as much as I do you. The past few months, albeit some of the craziest of my life, have also been some of the best, and that's because of you. Hell, the past four years have been better because you came into my life. Paige, every time I'm with you I can feel the clouds over my head go away," I kiss her forehead before continuing.

"When I realized my feelings for you, I think part of me knew I was never going to be able to let you go. I fucking love you. I love you, and I should've said it a million times before, but I was always too scared. But with you, nothing feels scary. Loving you was the best thing to happen to me, Paige, and I don't mind being the sun for you when you feel like you can't find the light. Because you were that light for me, and I love you."

"I love you too, Ol. I always thought love was this sacred thing that only certain people got to have, and I never thought I was one of them. I thought I was put on this earth to give more love than I'd receive." My heart breaks when she says that to me. I'm never going to let her forget how much I love her. I silently promise myself that right now. "Until you. I love you, and you feel like home to me." She smiles, and I lean in and kiss her again because this girl loves me, and I love her. I feel like I won the fucking lottery with this girl. She's everything to me. *Everything*.

"I love you," I tell her again, smiling so hard that my cheeks hurt.

"I know. But did you know that I love you?" she asks me, slightly giggling. Fuck, if that isn't the best sound I've ever heard. I have no doubt that this girl saved my fucking life, literally and figuratively.

"I missed your smile. I missed *you*."

"I missed you too, love. Now, tell me what the fuck happened tonight," I say to her as I climb into the small hospital bed and get under the covers. I lift my arm up, and she crawls into me, leaning her head on my chest.

"Okay, so I was on the roof, looking at the pictures we took," she pauses to yawn, and I know where this is going already.

"If you want to rest for a bit, I can stay with you."

"The doctor told me I was supposed to stay awake because of my concussion."

"It's been a long night. I'll make sure you're okay while you sleep."

"Promise?" She looks up at me with those big green eyes, and I want to memorize every curve of her face looking at me right now.

"I promise, Paige." That's the first of many promises I don't plan on breaking.

I wake up to someone smacking me, and like I figured it would be, it's my sister.

"She's not supposed to be sleeping," she says while sitting down on the foot of the bed. "But it's been a long night, and she's been through a lot, so I won't wake her up."

"Where's everyone else?"

"The waiting room." We're both quiet for a few seconds.

"I'm sorry, Hads," I say to her because where do I even begin?

"For what?"

"Everything. All the secrets, and not being more open. I know I broke your trust, but believe me when I tell you this is not how we wanted you to find out." I look at her, and her glare is starting to rival mine.

"I bet it wasn't, but it happened. I'm fucking pissed at you two, but we'll talk another time when Paige is feeling better." She turns her gaze to the sleeping beauty beside me, and I look down at her. "You really love her."

"So fucking much, Hads. More than anything on this planet."

She simply nods at me before walking back to the waiting room. I don't know if that's necessarily a good or a bad thing, but for now, we're okay. I feel Paige starts to stir next to me, and I think she's having a nightmare.

"I'm here," I whisper to her, and I hear footsteps shuffling into the room. It's Amelia. She looks at me and immediately walks to the other side of the bed.

"Paige, you're okay." She joins me as we try to soothe her out of her nightmare.

I look at Amelia, and a moment of realization flicks between us. We have a mutual understanding at this moment. Paige's eyes flutter awake, and she grabs onto me as her breathing slows.

"How long was I out?" Paige asks as soon as her breathing calms down.

"About an hour. This one fell asleep about five minutes after you did. Just a warning, he snores," Amelia tells her.

"I don't fucking snore," I say to her.

"You do a little bit. But it's cute!" Paige smiles at me, and Amelia starts laughing.

"You know, Amelia, I was starting to like you for a second," I say to her.

"I must not be doing my job correctly." She smiles at me.

"Can you guys just get along for one minute without arguing?" Paige asks us.

"No," Amelia and I say at the same time.

"Well, that's a start, I guess." Paige leans into me as Amelia leaves.

"Are you okay?"

"I am now." She smiles up at me.

"Good." I lean down and kiss her when I hear a knock at the door. "Amelia, I swear, I've had enough of your—" A nurse walks into the room. "I'm sorry, I thought you were someone else. Let me get out of your way."

I start to climb out of Paige's bed, and she latches onto my arm. "Don't go too far."

"I'll be right outside." I press a kiss on her forehead and walk toward the door.

"Paige, I just have a few things to talk to you about, and then you should be okay to go. Does that sound good?" the nurse asks her.

"Yup! The sooner I'm out of here, the better." She chuckles. "Oliver?"

I poke my head back into the room before I close the door.

"Can you send Ella in here?"

"Of course." I leave the room and lock eyes with Ella where she sits. "Paige needs you."

She gets up immediately and goes toward her room. "I'm on it."

I take a seat next to Henry. Grant is still asleep when I look over at him, and my sister isn't too far off from sleep either.

"No time to change your clothes?" Amelia asks me, smiling. Can she really not go more than five minutes before pushing my goddamn buttons?

"Mills, leave him alone," Henry tells her, grabbing her hand.

"Mills? Like a windmill?" I ask them.

"No, like my name is Amelia and it's a nickname. Get your head out of your ass."

"Can you guys just get along for once?" Henry asks us.

"Paige asked us the same thing earlier," I tell him.

"No kidding." He rolls his eyes and turns back to Amelia.

"You know, Oliver—" Grant pauses to yawn as he wakes up. "You and Paige should start some sort of murder podcast. Some of those blow up, and maybe that will negate any chance of you two doing this again in the future."

"Grant, don't encourage them," my sister tells him.

"Just an idea! How's Paigey doing?" he asks us.

"No clue. Ella is in with her and the doctor. I'm hoping we can just take her home and keep an eye on her."

"Oh, home? Is that because you *love* her?" Grant smiles widely at me. I'm back to being annoyed at him again.

"Stop being gross," Hads says.

"The only gross ones here are those two." I point to Amelia and Henry.

"Says you, *love*," Amelia mocks me.

"That's a top-tier nickname, Oliver. It doesn't beat Hades, though." Grant kisses my sister on her head. I can't wait to get out of here. My knee is bouncing and I feel panicked sitting in this waiting room. Henry knocks his leg into mine, stopping my movements.

"You're okay, buddy. We're all here, don't worry."

"Yeah, thanks."

"No problem. Just take some deep breaths." He smiles at me and then Paige's door opens. Out comes the doctor and then Ella who waves us over to the room. We all get up and hurry over, I enter first and go right to Paige.

"You okay?" I ask her, and she smiles back at me.

"I'll be okay, eventually."

"The doctor said she's good to go. I have a prescription for pain medication to pick up from the pharmacy, but the stitches must come out in a week, so she'll have to come back then." Ella tells us, and I lean down and kiss Paige's head. "She's also not allowed to sleep tonight, just in case."

Ella's grabbing all of Paige's stuff and throwing it into a bag when she stops on the clothes she wore before getting here. I feel Paige freeze up as she looks at them.

"Here." Henry hands her a bag. "Amelia made me stop to grab you more clothes before I picked Oliver up."

"Thanks," Paige tells them. "I'll be out in a minute."

I squeeze Paige's hand. "I'll tell the nurses to give your clothes to the cops in case they need to test them or anything."

"Hen, can you pull the car up?" Amelia asks him.

"Hen and Mills, how adorable of you two," I say to them.

"Oliver, if you're going to sleep over at our place, I suggest you shut up," Amelia snaps at me.

"Are you two going to be okay while I get the car?" Henry asks. I think he's being genuine too.

"Yes. I can be nice, unlike Severus Snape over here. I thought Paige would make you nicer, but that's not the case."

I stifle a snarky comment and Henry looks between us before leaving. The rest of us stand in silence for a few minutes, just waiting for Paige to return.

"Ella, how did she seem in there?"

"She seemed far away. I can tell she's trying to hide how she feels for the sake of all of us. She feels guilty, too. Paige kept apologizing to the doctor when she was looking at her head as if it was her fault she got whacked."

"Christ," Grant says while shaking his head. I hear my sister sigh heavily. She feels just as bad, I bet. But I know all that anger she feels will bite me in the ass in a few days. I just hope she doesn't do anything rash when she finally wants to talk to us about everything.

We hear Paige's door open, and she walks out, timidly. I grab her hand, noticing the bruises still on her wrists. Fucking hell. What happened to her in that office? I hold back the emotions crawling up my throat at what she's been through and how I wasn't there to protect her. She must notice what I'm thinking because she squeezes my hand and kisses my arm.

"I'll be okay, Ol," she whispers to me. "It'll take time, but I'll be okay."

"You're one of the strongest people I've ever met," I tell her. "I'm here with you every step of the way. Got it?"

She nods and smiles at me. "I wouldn't have it any other way."

"Are you guys ready to go?" Ella asks us.

"I certainly am. If I never see another waiting room, it'll be too soon," Grant says as he grabs my sister's hand and heads for the elevator. Ella, Amelia, Paige, and I follow closely behind them. When the elevator opens, we all climb inside and silently wait for the doors to close. When they do, Paige whispers something to us.

"I love you guys. Thank you for being my version of a family when my biological one didn't show up." Nobody says a word, but we all feel the weight of what she said.

Family. We kind of are, aren't we? None of us are related by blood, except Hads and I, but we've all kind of molded into one. I've slowly welcomed them all into my life over the past few months, and it feels good. I never let myself have any of this before because I was afraid that one wrong move would rip it all away from me again.

I'm not afraid anymore. This girl standing next to me makes me brave—braver than I ever thought I was capable of. It's funny how these four girls who bonded over their love of reading have morphed into so much more. Paige never had people who would stand by her and love her just as she was, not who she pretended to be. She's been alone for most of her life, and now she's not.

Now, she has six people who would do all that and more for her, and so do I.

Except for Amelia, maybe.

The elevator dings and Henry meets us outside the hospital doors. Grant and my sister head to their car, and Ella to hers.

"Paige, we're doing a sleepover tonight. I'm not letting you out of my sight. I'm going to grab some snacks and meet you at your apartment," Ella tells her.

"Ells, it's like seven in the morning," she says to her.

"I don't care. I'll see you in a few!" Ella gets into her car, and I hear a song start blasting from her speakers.

"Grant and I are staying over, too. We'll bring some blankets and another air mattress." Hads says as she climbs into Grant's car.

"Okay," Paige says. I don't even have to look to know that she's smiling.

"Are you guys ready to go home?" Henry asks us.

"I'm ready," Paige says.

I lean down to her ear. "I love you," I whisper.

"I love you too," she says as she kisses me. I never thought four words could hit me so hard in the chest as those did just now. "Will you stay over tonight?"

"I'll be by your side every night until you get sick of me."

"That could never happen. I'm keeping you forever, if that's okay?" she asks me.

"That sounds fucking perfect," I tell her as I open her door, and we both slide into the car.

I am home, I think to myself. I am home.

47

Wednesday, December 7th

I HAVEN'T SLEPT IN three days.

When I got back to the apartment from the hospital, Ella wasn't kidding when she said she wasn't letting me out of her sight. She wouldn't even let me go to the bathroom alone in case I passed out.

I didn't hate it, though. It felt nice to have people care.

Everyone stayed until Sunday, and we all sat around playing board games and watching movies. Oliver even did a puzzle with Amelia and me, and they only argued once.

I told everyone what had happened before they left—every detail. I didn't want there to be any more secrets, so I decided it was better to get it out now than hold it inside and keep dwelling on it.

It happened to me. It changed me. But it's not who I am.

I'm not going to let this dull my shine. I still believe the world can be beautiful.

Oliver had to kick everyone out so I could finally sleep. I didn't, of course. But he's stayed up every night with me since, watching the sunrise each day and making me breakfast in bed. I don't know what I did to deserve him. He's been so patient with me.

I still haven't talked to my mom since I left that voicemail. She never called to ask if I was okay, but she sent a text saying she was glad I was fine. Oliver assured me that she'd reach out soon enough and even if she didn't, it was for the best.

I'll be okay though. I keep reminding myself that my real family has been around me this whole time. My girls. My Oliver. My family.

Everyone's coming over to our place tonight because Oliver offered to cook us all dinner. It technically is book club night, but book club is slowly becoming our weekly hangout. We talk about books around twenty percent of the time, and the rest is other things. I don't mind what it's turned into. I just hope that when we all get older, it doesn't change.

Amelia knocks softly on my door and pokes her head in.

"What's up?"

"I just wanted to check in and see how you're doing." She comes into my room and sits on the floor with me. Oliver and I have resided here the past few nights, but I sent him back to his apartment to grab a few clothes to keep in my closet. I shoved him out the door half an hour ago, and these past few minutes were the first time I was truly alone since everything happened. I was waiting for myself to fall apart again, but I haven't yet.

"I'm okay." I smile at her.

She leans her head on my shoulder. "It's okay if you're not, you know."

"I know. Part of me wants to forget it all. It still seems so surreal."

"Have you talked to your therapist at all?"

"Yeah. I've called her every day. It's helped a little," I say.

"Well, just know I'm glad you're still here. And if you want, we can bond over our shared traumas of being knocked out." She laughs when she says that, and I join her. It's not really that funny, but laughing is better than crying.

"Amelia, that's terrible."

"I know, but it got you to laugh. I missed that sound around the apartment."

"Me too."

Amelia stands up and offers me her palm. "Need a hand?"

"Always." I smile at her, and she pulls me up to stand with her.

"Hads texted me and said that she was coming early, so I'd get dressed before she—"

Our front door opens suddenly, and I hear someone shout my name. "Paige! Get out here!"

"Okay, well, good luck!" Amelia tells me as she shuffles over to her room. As soon as I head out to the living room, I see Hads dragging Oliver into my apartment and shoving him down to the floor.

"Hads, what the fuck?" he yells.

"What's going on?" I ask them, seeing Amelia crack open her door so she can still see out here.

"Both of you, sit down." She points to my couch, and I grab Oliver off the floor, and we walk over to sit. The guilt about lying is creeping back into my mind, but Oliver's quick kiss on my cheek helped. "Do you know why I'm here?"

"Well, everyone is having dinner here in an hour." I smile at her, hoping that I can break some of the tension.

"Hads, you couldn't have waited a few more days?"

"No, my rage has reached its limit. We're doing this now." She takes a deep breath before she speaks. "Look, I love you both separately and in different ways. Oliver, you're my brother. Paige, you're one of my best friends. So, imagine my surprise when I found out about your relationship after everyone else already knew. Are you imagining it?"

We both nod wordlessly, and I want to cry, but I hold back.

"Good. Imagine that feeling times ten over because that was how hurt I felt when you blurted out that you loved my brother." I can't meet her eyes with mine. I feel guilty, but I love Oliver. I don't love the steps we took to get here, but having him is everything. "I just wish you guys had told me from the start."

"I'm sorry," I whisper to her.

"Hads, we wanted to. We did, I swear. Paige isn't good at relationships, and it's been a while since I've done this. We didn't want to fuck this up before it had a chance to get started. Also, you told me to stay away from her like seventy times, and I tried—"

"No, he didn't," I add.

"Okay, well, emphasis on the word try." He smirks at me.

"I just don't understand why you knowingly did this behind my back after our conversation about sharing our feelings and lives with one another."

"The bottom line is that you were worried you were going to lose Paige if this happened, and I can tell you for a fact that you won't, sis," Oliver says.

"You can't know that," she tells him.

"Yes, I can. I would never keep the two of you apart, especially since you've been friends for years. I tried to shove all those feelings down, but with this one over here, it's hard to."

"Hads, I'm so sorry that you found out how you did, and I've been kicking myself ever since, but I love Oliver. I love him more than I've ever loved anybody. I don't want to be loved by anyone but him for the rest of my life." I take a breath. "And no matter what, you're not getting rid of me. We're family. Our bond with Ella and Amelia is one for life, so I'm sorry to say that you're stuck with me indefinitely." I grab her hand from where it's resting on the loveseat.

"I promise you that even if Oliver and I break up," Oliver grunts when I say that, "which we won't, but if it did, I'll still be by your side forever."

She smiles at me. "Okay, but going forward, no more secrets."

"We promise." I grab Oliver's hand. "Right, Ol?"

"I swear, Hads." She's silent for a few moments, and I'm worried she's going to stab both of us or tell us we have to break up.

"Okay," she says quietly.

"Okay?" Oliver asks her. "Does that mean—"

"Yes. PDA all over the place or whatever you two do in your free time." She stands up and goes to my front door, opens it, and shoves Grant inside.

"Were you just standing outside the entire time?" Oliver asks him.

"Yeah, but I couldn't hear anything through the front door, so Amelia was texting me updates." He looks over at Amelia, who's coming out of her room. "I was waiting for Hads to bring out her ruler. I'm glad that didn't end up happening."

"Yeah, I was hoping for some sort of brother-sister fight or something. Unfortunately, they just talked." Amelia plops down on the couch next to me.

"I saw you eavesdropping. You're not slick," I tell her while shoving her shoulder.

"I wasn't trying to be. Plus, I almost had to throw up in one of my plants after what Oliver said. You two are disgustingly in love. It's gross." Amelia smiles at me.

"You and Henry practically communicate telepathically. It freaks me out!" I yell at her.

"Yeah, but Henry is cute. Oliver is Oliver." She glares at him.

"Paige, I know I said I would try to be nice tonight, so I'm going to take a deep breath and start cooking," Oliver tells me, and I find myself missing Henry. I hope he's on his way because I can't deal with these two alone.

"Ol, do you want help?" Grant asks him.

"Sure. Do you know how to slice carrots?" Oliver asks as he gets up and enters the kitchen.

"Do I know how to slice carrots? Do I know how to slice carrots?" Grant hypes himself up.

"Yeah, do you?" Oliver asks again, and I laugh a little bit.

"Oliver, yes. I used to help my mom cook. I'm a good assistant." Grant smiles at him.

"Technically, he's my sous chef! At least that's his contact name on my phone." Hads smiles at us, and I laugh, knowing she's called Oliver that nickname since they were kids. "Grant, be careful. Oliver might try to stab you!"

"Got it, babe!" Grant yells to her. "You're not going to stab me, are you?"

"If you call my sister babe one more time, I will," Oliver tells him.

"I brought wine!" Ella shouts as she enters the apartment. "And my karaoke machine!"

"Yay!" I say as I jump up. I love karaoke, especially with Ella. "Let me help you!" I get off the couch and grab the wine from her hand, placing it on the new kitchen table Amelia and I bought.

It seats eight people now. Our little group of four has almost doubled in size. Ella sets down the karaoke machine and pulls me in for a hug. "Paigey, how are you feeling?"

"I'm okay. I get my stitches out this weekend," I smile at her.

"Good! Do you want me to come with you?"

"Oliver offered to take me, but the more the merrier."

"Okay. Just let me know when and I'll be there!" She hugs me again and whispers into my ear. "Are you and Hads okay again?"

I nod my head into her shoulder. "All good."

"I'm glad. Now, boys! Should we trust you with dinner, or do you want me to help?" Ella asks, and they turn around.

"None of you girls are allowed to lift a finger tonight. Henry can help us when he gets here. Which is when Amelia? I miss my favorite almost author." Grant smiles at us.

"Any minute now," Amelia tells him without looking over. "Ells, can we pop open the wine?"

"Absolutely! Let me grab the bottle opener." She walks over to the drawer, and I head over to where Oliver stands at the counter and wrap my arms around his waist.

"Are you sure you don't want me to help?"

"No, love. Just go talk with the girls, laugh, drink, and leave it to us."

"Oh shoot, am I the last one here?" Henry asks as he walks in. "Sorry, I'm late. Amelia told me to change my shirt a couple of times after I told her what I was wearing."

I can hear Oliver start to laugh. "Do you really let her pick out your outfits for you? Man, you're a whipped son of a bitch."

"I think that's cute! Hads does the same thing to me." Grant smirks.

"True that!" Hads says, raising her glass.

"Oliver, I would not be talking about Henry being whipped when you three are all whipped for my girls. Paige was able to make you have a personality again," Ella tells him. Us four girls are sitting in the living room with our wine glasses, watching the boys cook. Henry flawlessly jumps in with the boys, scuffling around the kitchen.

"So, how does it feel being the only single one?" Hads asks Ella.

"Empowering," Ella says as she pours more wine into her glass. I can tell she's lying, but I don't want to press. I hope she knows we love her and she's worthy of being loved.

Maybe I should give Zimmerman a call...

We spend the next twenty minutes talking about the most random things we can think of, and it feels good just to unwind and not think about the past few days. I can hear things sizzling in the kitchen. Amelia puts on the playlist that she made for December, and a bunch of sad songs filter through the apartment. Oliver made Banh Mi—Vietnamese sandwiches—which we girls got way too excited about.

The seven of us sit around the kitchen table. Before we eat, Oliver clinks on his glass filled with water as he stands up. I look at him confused because he usually isn't one for words.

"I, uh, just wanted to say that I'm grateful we're all here tonight and thankful for this little bubble we've all created. I'm not one for long speeches, but I wanted to thank you all for everything." He pauses before abruptly sitting back down. I lean over and kiss him on the cheek.

"That was nice, Ol."

"I didn't know he had that in him." Grant chuckles at Oliver.

"Wow, Paige did a number on him." Hads nods her head. "I like it."

The next few hours are filled with one of the best meals I've ever had, and after, we migrate to the living room for karaoke. All of us girls are a little tipsy, but it helps that the guys are here, watching us exist and laugh together. I'm surrounded by the people who I love more than anything, and all of us are laughing and smiling like nothing else matters. Maybe nothing else does matter. Maybe this is the feeling that I've been chasing for years. I belong here with these people—I'm certain of it.

The night is filled with all of these beautiful things and moments that I never want to forget. When it all winds down and we're sprawled all over the living room, I look at Ella.

"Do you remember that day in the library when you came up to me for the first time?"

"Like it was yesterday." She smiles at me.

"I think you saved my life that day." I start to tear up. "I never thought that simple gesture could get us all here to this moment."

"This just proves my theory that books are magical." Amelia sounds like she's about to cry, too.

"Who knew twenty-six letters arranged on dead trees could make such a difference," Hads says.

"I love you guys." I smile at them.

Grant raises his wine glass. "To book club."

The rest of us raise ours with him. "To book club."

We all clink our glasses together and spend the rest of the night talking, laughing, and making memories that are going to last a lifetime.

I hope we never lose each other. I wonder where we're all going to end up next year. I think Oliver and I are going to stay in Virginia, but who knows where the future could take all of us?

I know one thing for sure: no matter where we all are, we'll never become strangers. All of us have strings connected to one another, and no matter how far we go, if one of us calls, we'll be there. No matter what.

That is what family really is.

And I have one—the best one, dare I say.

48

Saturday, December 10th

9:30 PM

"OLIVER, WHERE ARE WE going?" Paige asks me as I walk her up to the roof. It's been a long few days, and I wanted to get us out of her apartment. We've been too cooped up, and I came up here earlier to set up some snacks and a projector, courtesy of Ella.

"It's a secret." Paige giggles when I say that. Every time she laughs lately, I smile.

Life has been especially crazy lately. Paige has barely been sleeping, but I haven't left her side since the hospital, and I never want to. She's been struggling, though nobody has seen it. Hell, I've been struggling too. All my emotions and feelings about losing Paige made me realize it might be time to talk to someone again, and it's helped. I feel like I'm slowly cracking at the walls I put up all those years ago, and I can see light shining through them for the first time in a while.

Light in the form of a blonde girl who makes me feel like I matter. Who makes me feel things again. The future doesn't seem so scary anymore and I'm thankful for that.

I push open the door to the roof and walk her over to where I have a bunch of blankets, some pillows, and the projector all cued up.

"Okay, are you ready?"

"Yes." She smiles at me. I untie it from her head, and she looks around at the scene before her. "What's all this?"

"I thought we could watch *Peter Pan* and eat snacks for our second official date." I kiss the top of her head, lightly because she got her stitches out earlier. I can still see the scar on her head, but her hair should cover it eventually.

"This is perfect!"

Paige and I have spent a lot of time on this roof. I've wanted to take her out for a proper date, but she's been weary about going places, so I figured this was a good idea. Paige bundles up underneath the blankets as I get everything situated.

"I love you," she tells me, and I swear I'll never get tired of hearing that from her.

"I love you, too," I say as I wrap my arms around her, two of us getting situated in the blankets.

"Can I ask you something?"

"Always," I tell her.

"Do you ever think about Mia and what you could have had?"

That question startles me. "Not lately, no. Why do you ask?"

"Well, I remember you telling me that part of you will always love her. I just wanted to tell you that I don't mind if she takes up a small part of your heart. I know she always will, but I want the rest, if that's okay?"

"Paige, you have every single part of me. I'm not going anywhere. I'm with you till the end, got it?"

"Got it. But I think we should still go to a bar every year to remember her. If you don't want me to come, that's okay, but I want to honor her, too." She smiles at me, her eyes glassy.

"We can do that, Sherlock. I would love for you to come with me."

"Okay, good." She presses a kiss to my cheek. "Let's get to the movie! I'm so excited for you to finally watch this."

I nod as I take the remote and press play as the screen comes up. Right before the movie plays, I hear her whisper something under her breath.

"I wish they were still here to explain things better."

They. Penelope and our old professor.

I read an article that explained everything about why they decided to do what they did, and I also heard it firsthand from Paige. What they had been through was horrible.

But I'll never forgive them for putting Paige through what they did.

Apparently, they were able to get jobs at the school because they changed their names and used fake identities. Their backgrounds were clear, and they faked papers that allowed them to teach and assist the former dean how they did. They built a rapport at this school and with its members, secretly knowing they would break all that down one day.

The school's a mess now. A bunch of higher-ups got fired, and the college is being transformed with new staff.

They also canceled finals week. No tests are allowed to be administered, but I still have papers that are due. It's ridiculous, and it's all a mess. Paige was also granted an automatic passing average for the semester. When the District Attorney woke up from surgery, his aide called the school and immediately told them Paige saved his life by showing up when she did. He said she stalled the two shooters by pleading for her life and wanting to hear their stories. His office was also the one who dropped my charges after everything happened.

Hearing that Paige was pleading for her life made me feel like I got stabbed through the heart. But I keep reminding myself she's alive and okay.

He also came by Paige's apartment and personally thanked her. He told her that if she needs any help after college finding a job, he's more than willing to make any calls he needs to. Paige declined his offer, and when I asked her why, she said she didn't want someone like him helping her. I didn't understand that until she told me the full story.

Now I get it. I wouldn't want his help either, knowing that he helped people get promotions and jobs after what happened at that elementary school. I still don't know who to be mad at, but lately, I've been focusing on the fact that Paige and all our friends are okay.

Hads has been slowly warming up to us, especially after I told her this was how I felt when Grant and she started dating. It's a weird thing seeing my baby sister happy and in love, but it didn't take me long to realize that I was happy for her.

She's taking longer than I did, but with the circumstances, I get it.

"Oliver?" Paige's hand waves in front of my face. "Are you okay?"

"I'm all good, Paigey." She snuggles into me more. "I'm all good."

"Don't let Grant hear you call me that."

I roll my eyes at her. "I can handle the pretty boy."

"I know you love him and don't want to admit it. He could be your brother-in-law at some point in the future," she reminds me.

"By that logic, Hads could be your sister-in-law."

"That would be so much fun!"

"In the future, love. Let's just live in the moment for now, okay?"

"Okay, but you know I'm prone to overthinking about the future. This is your only warning that I might already be planning to live in the same neighborhood as the girls. We might be two doors down from your sister someday." She smiles at me as the movie starts, and I take in our conversation.

Living in the moment. All I've done my whole life is try to get through everything. Get through the day, the month, and the year with nothing to look forward to.

Now, I want to stay in each second and remember it all. But for once, I don't feel scared about the future Paige mentioned. I would love nothing more than to be surrounded by this group I'm now a part of for the rest of my life.

I trust them all. I *like* them all.

Except for Amelia most days, but she's been okay, even though she gags every time I call Paige by her nickname.

But for the first time in my life, I can clearly see what I want—a life with Paige full of sunshine, happiness, and all the beautiful things it offers.

No reconsidering necessary.

49

Friday, December 16th

I'm sitting on my bed surrounded by suitcases, when Amelia knocks on my door and walks into my room.

"Can I come in?"

"Always," I say, motioning her in. She walks over to my bed but doesn't sit down, even though there's space for her. We sit quietly like this for a few moments. I think both of us are taking in what this means.

School is officially done for the semester, and in a few months, the two of us will be going our separate ways. We won't be living together after next semester and who knows if we'll even end up in the same state?

It's going to be weird waking up and not seeing her face. It's been like that ever since freshman year and I hate that it's changing soon. Man, that feels like a lifetime ago after everything this semester put us through.

"I'm going to miss you over the next month," she whispers to me.

I look over at her and smile. "You'll see me in January, Ames. I've already started a countdown."

"I know, but it's not the same."

"I know." I reach over and grab her hand. "I used to hate the idea of growing up. It always felt so scary to me. Now as our senior year comes to a close, I want life to slow down. It's going too fast for my liking."

"I agree." She pauses for a moment. "How are you feeling?"

"I'm okay. Nervous, mostly." I'm packing to go home and tell my mom that I want to go no contact for the next chapter of my life. It's not going to be forever, but for now, it's what's best for me.

"You're strong, Paigey. You can do this, and if you need a last-minute pep talk, feel free to call us all. I'm sure we'll help however we can." She smiles at me. "I'm proud of you for doing this. You deserve the happiest life possible."

"Thanks, Ames. I'm proud of myself too." My eyes start to tear, and she shakes her head at me.

"None of that today, please. I don't feel like crying anymore than I have already." She pats my hand before she leaves my room. "Do you need any help packing?"

"No. Ella is coming over to help load up my car," I tell her.

"Oh, right. When is she coming?"

"She should be here any minute. I just can't bring myself to pack anything." I slouch back on my pillows.

"Have you talked to Hads at all? I know things are still a bit off between you two."

Ames is unfortunately right. Hads said she forgave us, but I can't help but feel like it might take a little longer than one conversation. We still talk, obviously, but it's more strained than normal. I just hope that as time passes, it'll get easier. It's only been a few weeks since everything happened, and time will heal it. I know it will. I have to trust that it will.

"On and off over the past few days. I don't want to force it."

"She'll come around. Once she sees Oliver smile as much as he does when he's with you, she'll realize you two are good together."

"Did you just compliment Oliver? I never thought I'd see the day." I smirk at her.

"No, I complimented Oliver when he's with you. It's very different." She raises her chin at me. "Now, let's go watch a comfort movie while we wait for Ells to come and pack for you."

"I can do it, Ames."

"Yeah, but you know she's going to repack anything you do anyway. She's better at this than we are, you know that."

I chuckle, knowing she's right, and we get forty-five minutes in when Ella shows up locked, loaded, and ready to pack up all my stuff.

"Paige, did you lay out all the outfits you're bringing home?" Ella asks me as she sets her bag down on our kitchen table.

"I did! Thanks for your help, by the way."

"Anything for you. You know that." Ella saunters off to my room, and I get off the couch to follow her. My phone starts buzzing, and I grab it from my bed and pick it up, not looking at who it is.

"Hello?"

"Hey, love. Are you at your apartment right now?"

"Yeah, is that wind I'm hearing? Are you on a run right now?" I ask him.

"Something like that," Oliver says over my phone, and then a few seconds later, I hear a few knocks at my door.

"Come in!" Amelia shouts, not knowing who it is, and Oliver enters. "Get out!"

"Amelia, always nice to see you out of your cave," he says to her as I lean against my door. Watching those two interact never gets old, but I wish they would stop bickering all the time. Though, they do it out of love. Love that comes from deep down.

"Oliver, it's always nice to see you out of jail!" Amelia smiles at him.

"I've told you a thousand times that I was not in jail. I was in a holding cell."

"Well, that sounds like jail to me!"

"Amelia," I say to her in my best stern voice.

"Too soon? My apologies. I'm waving my white flag." She puts her hands up in defeat.

"You guys have to get along at some point," I tell them.

"No." They both say before I shake my head and return to my room, where Ella is almost finished packing.

"Who was at the door?" Ella asks. "Was it Hads? She texted me something about stopping by here today."

"It was Oliver. I didn't know Hads was thinking about doing that."

"She wanted to say goodbye to everyone before she left for California."

Right. She and Oliver are going back later tonight on a flight. It's going to be weird being separated from him for so long. He's basically been sleeping in my bed every night for the past few weeks.

Oliver walks into my room, my water bottle in his hand, and he places it on my side table before giving me a quick kiss, his smile beaming on his face.

"What are you so happy about?" I ask him as he wraps his arms around me. "You know we'll both be on opposite sides of the country?"

"Nope. Because we're not going to be," he tells me.

"What are you talking about?"

"Well, I told you that Hads booked two tickets back to California, but I never said I was using the other one. Grant is." He smiles at me. "I want to come back to New York with you."

"You do? You realize I wasn't planning on staying at my house, right? That's part of the reason I'm going back. To grab what little I have in my room at home and spend the rest of the break at Sadie's."

"Well, can I offer another option?" he asks me.

"Sure..." I'm skeptical because this seems like it's been planned for a few days, and I knew nothing about it.

"We road trip to New York and pack up your room. You can talk to your mom while Sadie and I load up your car, and then we go back to California."

Is he serious right now? "What about your parents? They don't even know me! Are you sure they're okay with it?"

"Hads and I talked to them. They're excited to meet the girl who makes me happy. With me graduating next year, they know a big move is coming anyway."

"You want to drive with me from New York to California? Isn't that like a two-day drive?"

"I figured we could make some stops along the way. See a few new states..." He trails off, and I can feel my face light up.

"I would love that!" I jump into his arms. "I've never been anywhere but New York and Virginia!"

"I know, love. I thought it could be a fun first trip for us. Plus, it ends at my house in California, and Hads is already planning different things for us all to do at home. She's excited to have you over break, rather than just me and Grant like last time."

"Hads is excited to hang out with me for the month?"

"I am," I hear her voice come from behind Oliver, and I look and find her standing in my apartment. Grant is on the couch chatting with Amelia. When did they get in here, and why didn't I hear them? "It was my idea, actually."

"Really?"

"Yup. Grant is staying in California until Christmas Eve, and then he's returning to Vermont for Christmas Day, and I'm joining him there for New Years." She smiles over at him. "But before then, I'm going to force you to the beach, and all my favorite photography spots, if that's okay with you?"

"That sounds perfect, Hads." I smile at her and turn to Oliver. "I assume we're leaving today?" My cheeks hurt from smiling so much. I've never gone on a trip like this before. I *was* planning on working over break, but I have enough money saved that I should be okay. I've worked two to three jobs at once since I was old enough to work. I deserve some fun, especially after all that's happened.

"I have to say, seeing Oliver this happy is kind of freaking me out," Ella tells us as Grant knocks on my door.

"I assume you told her? Also, Oliver might try to teach you how to surf but don't listen to anything he says because he's terrible at it. I can teach you in no time." Grant smiles at me.

"Pretty boy, you grew up in Vermont. Stick to ice skating." Oliver smirks at him.

"Fine, but don't come crying to me when I catch more waves than you!" Grant walks out of my room, and I hear Ella zipping my suitcase up.

"Done! I'll bring this to your car. Is it unlocked?" she asks.

"Don't worry about it." Oliver grabs it from her. "I got it." He walks out the door, and Grant follows him with another one of the duffle bags that I left by the front door.

Now, just us girls are left standing in my apartment and not wanting to say a word.

"So, we all know Paige and Hads' plans for the break, but how about you Amelia? Any plans with Henry?" Ella asks her.

"No plans. This will be the most time we'll have spent apart since we met. It's making me feel weird," she tells us.

"How about you, Ells? Just working like normal?" Hads asks her.

"Yup. The new job has been great so far, and I'm excited to see where it takes me." She smiles when she says that. I'm happy she's found her dream job. She deserves it after all the hard work she put in. "I think my dad and my sister are going to visit soon. They're coming up for Christmas since Alissa is returning to England with her brother."

"That sounds nice," Amelia tells her, and the four of us are back to silence.

It's like we don't know what to say to each other. I feel like we're all being dramatic because we still have another semester on campus, and we'll be back here in a month. But it feels different. This last semester was one of the craziest that we've experienced.

I discovered a dead body and inserted myself into an active murder investigation.

Amelia and I almost died.

Ella got her dream job after years of hard work.

Oliver and I fell in love.

Oliver spent a night in holding and almost went to jail.

Our little group grew by two more people. We're now seven strong—seven members of our little family.

Books may have brought us together, but the bond we created over them will last us our lifetime. I never knew words could be that powerful. I never knew they could bring me my favorite people on this planet.

We all soak this moment in, knowing that in a few months, we may all be gone and scattered across the state or the country.

I used to be afraid of change and all that came with it. It made me feel unstable growing up. But now, I'm welcoming it because I know that no matter what the future brings us, we'll always be Grand Mountain girls at our core.

"Are you guys ready?" Oliver asks us.

"I didn't even hear you guys come back in." Hads is the first to stand up and walk over to where Grant is. He's holding his arms wide open for her, and she walks right into them.

"Ames, is your car packed?" Ella asks her.

"Yeah, I'm all set. Henry is meeting me soon to say goodbye." She gets up and heads outside. I remain sitting on the couch, fully capturing this moment for my memories.

"Are you okay?"

I take a breath. "I'm perfect."

"Are you ready for our next adventure?" He smiles down at me.

"I'm ready for every single one as long as they're with you." I stand up, and the two of us walk together, hand in hand, ready to take on anything else the world wants to throw at us. I close the door to my apartment and head to the parking lot where everyone else is waiting. We exchange hugs, and Amelia is the last person I hug before I leave. She pulls me tight to her and whispers in my ear.

"If you ever get lonely or sick of the statue, call me and I'll book you a flight back here."

"I will. I'm going to miss you. Are we still on for morning debriefs?" I ask her.

"Always. Just let me know your time zone, and we'll make it work." As we pull back from each other, a few tears fall down our faces. I see Henry walking up behind her, and he puts his hands over her eyes when he reaches us.

"Guess who?"

"Hm, is this Henry or my other boyfriend?" she asks, and I hear Oliver scoff behind me as he wraps his arms around my center.

"Very funny, Mills." He uncovers her eyes, and she spins and looks at him. I've never seen Ames this happy. I love it. I love seeing my friends bursting with happiness.

"We should get going, love. We have a long drive ahead of us," Oliver says to me.

"Are you going to let me drive?"

"No, but maybe we can switch out every once in a while." He grabs me by the waist and hauls me over to the passenger side of my car, placing me firmly on the pavement. He opens my door for me, and I look back at my favorite people.

"I'll see you guys soon?" I ask them.

"Not if we see you first," Grant says back to me, and I laugh, forcing myself not to cry because for some reason I want to.

"Drive safe!" Ella tells us.

"She'll be okay with Oliver driving. He taught me how to drive, and I'm amazing at it," Hads tells them.

"Oliver, make sure to play me back in Scrabble!" Henry tells him.

"You guys play together, too?" Grant looks between the two of them, a look of betrayal on his face, and I start laughing again.

"I love you guys." I pause. "So much." I climb into my car, and Oliver walks over and gets into the driver's seat. He turns my car on, and I can't help but think that this moment is when everything changes. Where do we go from here? What's next for us?

Toward the future, I think to myself. That's where we'll go. To a future full of new opportunities, experiences, and love.

I can't wait to experience all of these new things with Oliver and the rest of the people I now call home.

Let's do this.

Epilogue

Sunday, June 30th, 2024

"Oliver, that was the best dinner I've ever had in my entire life."

"Love, you say that every time I cook." He smiles at me. "I made this extra special for my favorite person's birthday."

Today is my twenty-third birthday, and Oliver and I are sitting in our apartment having a quiet night in. When he asked me what I wanted to do to celebrate, I said I wanted to relax, eat dessert, and watch a scary movie.

His only addition to my list was to cook me dinner, and I'd never say no to that. He cooks all the time in the apartment we moved into after graduation. I think us girls are getting together next weekend to go to a karaoke bar, and I can't wait to get us all together again.

Oliver works as a youth correctional officer in a juvenile facility about half an hour from where we live. He likes his job, but it's not what he wants to do forever. This is just a good starting point for him. Eventually, he wants to go private sector and make a bit more money, but he's content with this for now.

I work with a small local police department as an intelligence analyst. I'm one of two people the department hired to work alongside detectives to surveil social media and help them with other things. It's basically a lot of chart-making, connecting people, and surveillance. I *love* it.

"I can clean up if you want to go find a movie to watch," Oliver tells me.

"I don't mind helping with the dishes." Doing the dishes with Oliver is one of my favorite things to do. Basically, anything we do around our apartment is my favorite thing. I love experiencing the little joys in life with him. It never gets old.

"P, just go relax. I got this, okay?" He leans over and presses a kiss on my forehead. "It's your birthday. You're legally obligated not to lift a finger today."

"Is that why you carried me up the stairs earlier?"

"Yes. Now go pick a good movie for us all to watch." He smiles at me.

"Us all? Who else is—" A bunch of erratic knocks at the door makes me stop what I'm saying.

"You should probably answer that," he tells me while putting our plates away. I run over to our front door, and as I'm about to open it, I hear a voice yell at me.

"Paige, I swear if you don't open this door—" I swing it open, and Amelia's face is staring back at me. I feel my eyes instantly start to water. "Don't you dare start crying. Hads and Grant are right behind me."

I pull her into a hug so hard that both of us fall onto the floor of my entryway, all tangled up.

"I missed you so much, Ames! Phone calls are not good enough when you're thousands of miles across the pond!"

Amelia moved to London after graduation. It was such a sudden thing that I never had time to process that I wouldn't be twenty feet from her anymore. Not having her so close has been hard, especially with everything that blew up before she left.

"I missed you so fucking much, but can we get off the hardwood? My face hurts," Amelia says to me.

"I should've known you two would have ended up on the floor at some point. I just thought you'd be a little drunk before it happened," Hads' voice floats into the room, and I look up and see her and Grant standing in the doorway with a bottle of wine.

"Hi, guys! What are you doing here?" I ask them as Oliver comes over and pulls me off the floor.

"Oliver invited us to watch scary movies all night for your birthday. Did you think we would miss this, Paige?" Hads pulls me into her arms, and I smile into her shoulder.

"Happy birthday, sunshine!" Grant holds his fist out, and I bump it as I pull away from Hads' embrace.

"Thanks, Grant." I turn to look at Oliver. "You didn't tell me they were coming over!"

"Well, that's the thing about surprises. You're not supposed to know about them." He smiles at me as Hads walks over to him, and they hug.

Grant and Hads just graduated a month ago, and we all celebrated then, but too much time has passed since we've all been together. I miss the old days when we were on the same campus and could walk a few minutes between our places. Now it takes a drive to get to where Hads and Grant live, but Amelia is a plane ride away. Ella lives in Richmond with Alissa, about an hour away.

"Is Ella on her way?"

"She should be. I think she got stuck dealing with something at work because when I called her, she sounded pissed," Hads tells me.

"Did you pick a movie yet? I brought popcorn that I bought at the airport when I got in," Amelia sets it on our table.

"Wait, why do you have a suitcase? Are you staying for a few days?" I ask, hoping the answer is yes.

"I took a few days off to hang out with you guys. I missed you guys so much." She smiles at me.

"I can put that in the guest room for you, Amelia." Oliver reaches out to grab her suitcase, but she pulls away from him.

"I can do it myself. First door on the left?"

"Yup!" I smile at her.

"I should've known better than to offer to do something nice for the she-devil," Oliver mumbles.

"No fighting is allowed between you two on my birthday!" I remind them.

"Sorry, P."

"Sorry, love."

"Thank you. Now, tonight's triple feature is all of *The Conjuring* movies!" I smile at them as I walk over to our couch and sit down. Hads grumbles a bit, an avid hater of scary movies. "I'm so glad you're here, Hads."

"Me too, Paige. Happy birthday," she says as she hands me a small box.

"What's this?"

"Open it," she tells me, and I do. It's a small gold ring with a tiny pearl in the center of it. "It's your birthstone, and now we all have rings with our birthstones. All of us girls are matching." She holds her hand out, and a gold band with a small garnet sits on her right ring finger. I slip mine onto my hand, and it fits perfectly.

"Thank you. This is so beautiful," I say to her.

"Wait, did you give it to her already? Dammit! I wanted to see the look on her face." Amelia plops down next to me on the couch.

"Where's yours, Ames?" I ask her, and she holds up her right hand with all her rings, but a new silver one with a small sapphire sits on her ring finger.

"First matching necklaces, and now rings. You girls are cute." Oliver sits on the floor in front of where I am on the couch, and I hold my hand out to him.

"Isn't it pretty?"

"It looks beautiful, just like the girl who wears it. I'm guessing Ella's is a diamond?" he asks his sister.

"Yup. Ells and I picked them all out," Hads tells him.

"You guys did a wonderful job," Oliver says to us as I stare at my new ring.

"Hey, Ol, do you have wine glasses?" I hear Grant ask him from the kitchen.

"Yeah, they should be in the top cabinet next to the fridge," he yells to him. "I see you had time to get wine but not play me back in Scrabble!"

"Listen, I have a bunch of games going. I'll get to yours." Grant smiles at him. "I know how much you like losing to me."

"I remember beating you last time, so I don't know what you mean, but I can play multiple at once, so you should get better at that if you want to win more." Oliver is very competitive when it comes to online games like Scrabble. He and Grant—and maybe even Henry—play Scrabble and this other game where you have to build a town and fight each other. I woke up one night to Oliver celebrating that he had taken down Grant's village.

The girls and I don't ask questions anymore. As long as they're not blowing each other up, it's a win.

"One for you, baby." Grant hands Hads a glass of wine. "One for you, birthday girl."

"Thank you, kind sir." I smile at him.

"And Amelia, I brought you your favorite bottle Paige keeps stashed for you when you come home." He hands Amelia her favorite prosecco.

"Thank you for no glass. I'm surprised you remembered I prefer it this way."

"I must remind you that my memory is phenomenal." Grant bows to Amelia, and then sits next to Oliver on the floor in front of Hads.

"I don't know why I doubted you, pretty boy." Amelia smiles at him as our phones buzz.

Ella: Someone better have a bottle of wine for me when I get to your place because I'm gonna need it.

Hads: A whole bottle?

Amelia: I have mine ready, but I'll tell Oliver to get one for you.

Oliver: Amelia, I'm in this group chat, and I can read.

Amelia: Oh, I thought this was the book club one.

Grant: Nope. Although, I'm technically in that one too!

Ella: Just have it ready for me please, or I might kill one of you.

Paige: Is everything okay?

"No, everything is not okay!" Ella shouts as she whips my apartment door open, and Oliver quickly stands and goes to our wine rack to get her a bottle. Ella drops her purse on my floor, stalks over to the loveseat, and slumps down. "I have to quit my job."

"What?" Hads questions her.

"Wait, why?" Amelia asks.

"But you love your job!" I say, hoping to lighten the mood.

"What do you do again?" Grant asks, and Oliver simply says nothing as he hands her a bottle of red wine.

"Thank you." Ella takes a long sip from the bottle, and when she's done, she starts telling us what happened at work today. "Everything was fine until I got called into my boss's office at the end of the day. I'll admit, I was nervous because I thought she was going to fire me or something."

"Did she have a reason to fire you?" Hads asks her.

"No, but you never know in this economy. Anyways, she calls me in, and when I get to her office, a guy is sitting in the chair across from her desk. She tells me he was just hired, and that I was picked for him to shadow me for thirty days while he learns the ropes. I was fine with that because I had trained other people before this. But then, he turned around." She stops to take a long sip of her wine again.

"That was a terrible cutoff point for the story," I say to her. "Just tell us who it was!"

"I'm on the edge of my seat," Oliver says in the most monotone voice ever. I smack him on the head. "Ow, what the fuck? I was being serious!"

"Shh! Let her tell it!" Amelia snaps at Oliver.

"It was fucking Leo—pain in my ass—Zimmerman. He's going to be working with me, at my dream job, the one place I love. He's going to ruin *everything!*"

"Oh my God." Hads reaches out and grabs her hand. I can hear Amelia laughing, and Grant turns his head to lock eyes with me, both of us probably thinking the same thing. Both Grant and I want the best for our friends, and we've had multiple conversations about how Leo and Ella are going to end up together. We haven't told anybody, and Ella may claim she hates him, but it's so obvious—at least to us two.

Grant and I are everyone's biggest love cheerleaders. We just want happiness for the people we care about. I'm glad someone's on the same page as me because when I tell Oliver this stuff, I have to remind him who everyone is.

"Is Leo the British guy? Alissa's brother?" Oliver asks her.

"Yes. Seeing him around my apartment when he comes over to visit Alissa is bad enough, but now I'm going to have to interact with him five days a week! This is my worst nightmare."

"But wait, why were you working on a Sunday?" Grant asks her.

"Our company has a major deadline soon, so a few of us worked overtime to get shit done. But now, I have to quit!" She sips her wine again and makes a weird face. "Do you guys have anything stronger than this? Wine is not going to cut it right now."

"Tequila, I'm guessing?" Oliver asks her while getting up.

"I knew I liked you." She hands him the wine back, and a few seconds later, Oliver gives her an entire bottle of tequila.

"Ells, you don't have to quit, just avoid him or fuck him, whichever works best to make him less annoying," Grant tells her, and she glares at him.

"I'm only going to say this once, but I'm never going to get naked with that man," she tells us. "I'm avoiding him at all costs."

"Don't you have to train him?" Amelia asks.

She slumps back into the loveseat. "Fuck!"

"Ells, just look on the bright side. You two have to be professional at work, so how annoying can he be?" I smile at her, hoping that she won't just up and quit her dream job that she worked so hard to get.

She sighs heavily. "I'm not actually going to quit, but I hate this so much. Since I worked today, I took tomorrow off. Are you good if I crash on your couch tonight? I need to get insanely hammered to try and forget that I'll be working with Leo for an unprecedented amount of time."

"Ells, you can crash in the spare room with me. They have a pullout couch, but I don't mind sharing the bed. It'll be like old times." Amelia smiles at her.

"I can blow up the air mattress if you two want to stay over too!" I look over at Hads and Grant, and Hads just smiles at me.

"I'm only agreeing to that if you sleep on it with me, P."

"Of course I can! A birthday sleepover! This is the best day of my life!" I beam, and Oliver tilts his head back at me. I smile at him and lean over to kiss him.

"Does this mean I'm rooming with Oliver tonight? What's a little light cuddling between two almost-brothers?" Grant looks over and smiles at him.

"You're on the couch tonight, pretty boy. Don't worry. It's memory foam, so your back will be fine." Oliver slaps him on the shoulder.

"Okay, now that sleeping arrangements are all set for tonight, can we get to the movies? I want to get them over with as soon as possible," Hads asks.

"I'm pressing play, Hads," Oliver tells his sister.

"Not fast enough, Oliver!" she quips at him while sipping her wine glass.

Amelia raises her bottle. "To the best year ahead for all of us, and to Paige. Happy birthday, my girl." She smiles at me, and I raise my glass while Hads and Ella raise theirs too.

"To Paige," Hads says.

"Happy birthday, P!" Ella says, already a little drunk. We clink our glasses together as Oliver turns all the lights off, and before he sits back down, he presses another kiss to my lips.

"Happy birthday, love."

"Thank you for doing this. I love you so much," I whisper back to him.

"I love you, too."

"Down in front!" Amelia softly kicks Oliver, and he crouches back down next to Grant as the movie starts to play.

A few hours and three scary movies later, we girls are camped out in my guest bedroom, gossiping and catching up about our lives. I *missed* this. I missed us all being close to one another. Of course, we're all still attached at the hip, but it's been too long since we got drunk and ended up sleeping in the same room together.

Oliver made this happen because he knew I would love seeing my girls again. I make a mental note to thank him profusely for this tomorrow. He always seems to surprise me in the best ways, and I'll always be grateful that our paths crossed at Grand Mountain.

They usually say nothing lasts forever, but these three around me right now? We're going to defy those odds. Because no matter how many miles apart we are, we'll always be those four girls from that tiny classroom on campus. We'll always be our little book club.

And nothing on this planet can ever change that.

Extended Epilogue

Thursday, October 24th, 2024

5:28 AM

"Paige, we have to go or we're going to miss the sunrise." I'm trying to get my beautiful girlfriend out of bed but she swats my hand away.

"But sleep," she whines at me. I'm practically shaking over here because of how nervous I am.

"Love, please. As soon as you get up and see the sunrise, you'll feel better. I promise." We decided to make it a tradition that every year on October 24th, we watch the sunrise together on the beach. I drink my coffee, Paige has her emotional support water bottle, and we watch the sun come up. We only do it once a year because we live far from any beach, but the date holds significance.

October 24th was the day that Paige and I first admitted our feelings for each other and began our relationship.

We've done this only once before, and little does she know, today is different from last time.

Last time we sat in our car, listened to Paige's favorite playlist and talked quietly while the sun came up.

This time I'm asking her to marry me.

We've talked about marriage before and agreed that we wanted to start our lives pretty quickly. Life is short, and the sooner I can call Paige my wife, the better. It's been two years since we started dating officially, and I can't think of a better date than today to take that next step.

My phone buzzes on my side table, and I look at it.

Grant: Have you left yet?

Grant: I'm just saying that I planned Hads' proposal perfectly. I expect nothing less from you.

Oliver: Calm down. She just got out of bed. We still have time. It's only 5:30. The sunrise isn't until 7:15.

Grant: Aw, you know the exact time. How cute.

> **Oliver: Shut it. We'll be there. Does Hads have her camera?**

> **Grant: Yup. Both of them. One will be set to video, and she's going to take pictures with the other.**

> **Oliver: And they're both charged?**

> **Grant: Why are you even asking me that? Of course they are, it's Hads.**

> **Oliver: Thanks for doing this, by the way. I appreciate it.**

> **Grant: Anything for you two.**

"Who are you texting this early in the morning? Is your boss asking you to come in? You need to tell him to stop doing that. I've been looking forward to this for days." Paige stumbles out of the bathroom, still in her pajamas, and I can't believe I'll wake up to this every morning for the rest of my life.

Hopefully. She could say no. But she won't say no.

But what if she does? Fuck, why am I so nervous?

"It's just Grant playing me back in chess." I smile at her, and she gives me a puzzled look.

"You guys play chess, too? I swear I'm going to lose track of all the shit you two play." She scrunches her nose at me, grabs some clothes, and lays them out on our bed. Her hair is still in the messy bun she slept in, all her hair scrambled all over the place.

I never thought I'd feel like this—completely and wholly in love with this girl.

Paige pulls on a loose sundress and grabs her sandals. She always wears some sort of flowy dress when we go to the beach. She told me it's for the aesthetic—whatever that means. But most of the ones she wears are ones she stole from Amelia's closet and never gave back. She misses her a lot, especially after what happened after graduation.

Paige lets her long hair flow loosely when she takes it out of the bun and doesn't bother to brush it, but it still looks great. Her hair is naturally wavy, so it falls into place pretty evenly after she runs her fingers through it. I opted for brown dress pants and a white button-down. My pants match Paige's dress, and I silently high-five myself for that.

Paige used paid time off for today, and I luckily had a day off from training at Quantico. Paige still works at the same job as an intelligence analyst, which she loves a lot. I, however, am four weeks into a sixteen-week training program to become a DEA agent. Once the training is done, I'll officially be an entry-level Special Agent. The commute to Quantico sucks, but I'm glad I got out of my old job at the youth correctional facility. It was a great start to my professional career, but this is much better for my future.

"I'm going to start your coffee." She gives me a quick kiss before leaving our bedroom. I walk over to our closet and sift through my sock drawer, looking for the fucking box I keep losing. It only takes a few seconds of panic before I finally find it. As I leave the closet, I grab a jacket for Paige, and one of our blankets in case she gets cold. My phone buzzes a few more times before I leave our bedroom.

Grant: You are the worst at this. Have you guys left yet?

Oliver: I have time, Grant!

> **Grant: Yes, but you want to do it at sunrise, you dumbass. Hurry up!**

> **Oliver: I'm going to block your number.**

> **Grant: We're fifteen minutes away from the beach. Get a move on, brother!**

I don't respond back to the three texts he sends me after that as I make my way out to our kitchen. Paige is pouring coffee into my favorite coffee tumbler, and I grab her water bottle to fill it up for her.

We do this little dance every morning and it's one of my favorite parts of every day.

"Here you go." She hands me my coffee, and I hold her water bottle for her. She grabs her tote bag and throws the car keys into it.

"Can I drive?" she asks me, and I look down at the gold watch Paige bought me for my birthday last year.

5:50 a.m.

That gives me eighty-five minutes to get to the beach, which is an hour from us.

"Not this time, Yarrow."

6:53 AM

I PARK THE CAR at our usual spot, and I'm looking all over for my sister and Grant, but I can't fucking find them. I guess that's a good thing, or it would be insanely obvious what I'm about to do. I just have to trust that they'll get good pictures.

"Oliver, are you okay?" Paige asks me, probably noticing how tense I am. Nothing gets by this girl.

"I'm perfect." I pause for a second to make it more believable. "Actually, can we grab the blanket out of the trunk and sit on the sand? It's a better view."

"Okay, but I forgot my—" She stops when I hand her the jacket that I grabbed for her. "You know me so well." She smiles at me, and my stomach drops.

Fuck, I'm so nervous. I climb out of my car and swing around to let Paige out. She hasn't been allowed to touch her car door in two years. After I do, I open the trunk and grab our beach blanket. I throw it over my arm and my front left pocket, so Paige doesn't notice the giant box sticking out of it. She grabs my hand as we walk down the path and onto the sand. I check my watch, 6:58 a.m., and I still have time.

Just relax. It's going to be fine.

I lay the blanket down for us, and we both sit and take in our surroundings. There are a few people down the beach, but other than that, it's pretty empty. A few surfers are out on the water, and Paige and I watch as we sit and wait for the sunrise. My legs are straight out in front of me, my left foot is shaking, and Paige is crisscrossed with her water bottle on the sand beside her. I take a few sips of my coffee and am about to say something, but Paige beats me to it.

"I don't know if you need more coffee right now, Ol. Your foot has been shaking the entire time we've been here."

I smirk at her. "You're probably right, P. I'll hold off for now." Maybe coffee wasn't the best choice this morning, but if I changed our routine, she would know something was up.

For the next few minutes, we sit quietly. We take in all of our surroundings as we watch the sun peak over the horizon. I look down at my watch as Paige lets her arms out of my jacket, letting it rest on her shoulders.

7:05 a.m.

"Are you excited for game night this week?" she asks me.

"Always. You know how much I love beating Grant at everything."

"Ol, I love you, but we both know he always wins and you sulk about it for days after." She's right, of course.

Hads and Grant come over once a week for game night. It's been hard for everyone to get together, so it's usually just the four of us. We see Ella a bunch—Paige goes on night drives with her and my sister a lot. Leo's driving her crazy.

"I know, but this time, we're doing an unsolved cold case, and if we don't win, I'd be surprised." My sister thought of that idea for this week. Grant agreed to it because he thought it would be funny since nobody would go to jail or get hurt.

Paige and I weren't laughing, but everyone always likes to shit on us for our college investigation. It's gotten very old.

"We'll be fine. I have faith in us." She grabs my hand and squeezes it, her smile punches me in the chest. I look down at my watch again.

7:09 a.m.

I take a deep breath before I grab Paige's arm, hoisting her up to her feet. I walk us a few steps away from our stuff.

"Oliver, what are you doing?" I take another deep breath, still feeling nervous as fuck, but when I look over at Paige's face, all of that fades. She's all I see right now, and she's all I want to see forever.

"Do you see that?" I ask her as I point to the sun rising and hear her laugh at me.

"Yes, Oliver. I can see the sun rising. Why?"

"Well, I know this is your favorite time of day, but my favorite time of day is also the sunrise. Except the sun rising for me is when I open my eyes every morning and look at your beautiful face. You are my sun, Paige." I take both of her hands in mine. Tears have already clouded her eyes, and I'm not even done yet. I feel my throat start to clog up with emotions, but I shove those down so I can say the rest. "You are the reason I want to wake up every day and be better than I was yesterday. You are the fucking light of my life, and I can't imagine not having you by my side as we navigate the future."

I take another deep breath. I never thought this would feel so terrifying. "I know we orbited each other for so long, but when we finally reached each other, I knew I never wanted to drift apart. I've known for a while that it would be you and me, but..." I drop to one knee, and Paige has tears falling from her eyes as she bows her head in front of her. "I wanted to make it official. So, Paige Yarrow." I grab the box from my pocket and open it while I grab one of her hands with my free one. "Will you marry me?" I ask, and she falls to her knees in front of me, still holding onto my hand. I'm nervous until her face looks up to mine, and she's shining brighter than I've ever seen her. She launches herself into my arms, and I almost fall over, but I feel her nod into my shoulder as I steady us on the beach.

"Yes," she whispers into my ear. And I pull away from her, studying her face.

"Yes?" I ask again, unsure that I heard her correctly.

She nods, and I lean forward and kiss her. *She said yes.* I'm going to marry this beautiful fucking girl. I'm going to spend the rest of my life hearing her laugh and waking up with her every morning.

I've never felt so happy before. This girl walked into my life in freshman year, and little did I know that we'd end up here.

"I love you so much, Oliver. I can't imagine not taking on the future with you." She smiles at me, and I stand us up. I slide the ring onto her finger, a gold band with a simple circle-cut diamond. All the girls gave me their approval on the ring last week, and I love seeing it on her finger. I pick her up and spin her around in my arms. When I set her down on the sand again, I make my first promise to her as we embark on this new chapter.

"I'll love you forever, Paige. I promise."

Paige has had a lot of empty promises from people who have been in her life, promises that were broken over and over again by the ones who were supposed to love her the most. But I can say with one hundred percent certainty that I'll spend the rest of my life proving to her she's worthy of being loved how she deserves.

Wholly, completely, and unconditionally.

Acknowledgements

First and foremost, I would like to thank my Mom. Thank you for answering every single call and text that I send you, and for being at every sports game regardless of if you had to work. You never missed a single one. You always showed up for me, so thank you. I know it may have seemed like I didn't notice that, but I did. I feel grateful to be your daughter every single day. You're the best parent I could've ever asked for.

Lexi & Hannah—my team. My partners. You two have helped me in so many ways and there are not enough words I can say that will prove how much I love you. I cannot believe books brought us to writing and creating our own little universe together. I truly wouldn't have it any other way. Hannah, your cover designs continue to amaze me. I love everything you create, and I'm eternally grateful that life has brought us together. You're one of the most talented people I know. Lexi, you're like the big sister I never had but always wanted. The way you just understand me and my crazy will be something I'm always grateful for. Thank you for always checking in on me. Thank you for being you. Grand Mountain girls for life.

My beta readers—Amy, Maine, and Sof. This book would not be what it is today without you guys. I trust all of your opinions so highly, so being able to share this book with you and get your feedback was everything to me. Amy, thank you for everything. I couldn't have done any of this without you. This book would not be what it is today without your feedback. Maine, I love how excited you get over the little things. Sof, you're my favorite mystery loving girl. I was so excited that you agreed to read this for me, and I was even more excited when you were updating me with all your guesses.

Cassidy Hudspeth—You always make my stories shine. I absolutely adore working with you. Thank you for being the freaking best editor of my first to book babies. I'll never stop shouting about you!

Josh—my favorite person to laugh with. Thank you for boosting me up every time I feel down on myself. Thank you for being so patient with me throughout this process, especially on the days where I was in a writing hole and not answering your messages (whoops!). You're my favorite person to do life with, and I love you *so* much.

Alyssa—my real life Sadie. How have we known each other so long? And how did we get so old? I'm eternally grateful for you. You understand me like nobody else in this world, and I'm thankful every single day that you exist. Thank you for being my biggest cheerleader when I told you I wanted to start writing books. I love you SO MUCH, and I'm so proud of you always. I can't wait to see where life takes us.

Shannon and Tony—for "and then he died." I'll always laugh anytime anyone says those four words together.

To you—the reader. Thank you for taking a chance on me and my words. I'll never stop thanking you guys for the support and love. You guys made this happen for me, and I'll always be grateful for every single one of you. Grand Mountain forever and ever.

Also by Emily Tudor

The Grand Mountain Series
Replaying the Game
Redefining the Rules
Reconsidering the Facts

The Hart Sisters
The Road Not Taken
The Road Less Traveled By

About the Author

Emily Tudor creates characters and stories about platonic and romantic love for anyone and everyone. She lives in the state of New York and loves listening to music and creating stories. She loves Marvel movies, the song *mirrorball* by Taylor Swift, and buying too many books when she already has many to be read at home.

You can find her on Instagram at:
@authoremilytudor
@emil.yslibrary